BY THE LIGHT OF A MEMORY

A Novel By
Jake Keeling

©2025, Jake Keeling
All Rights Reserved.

ISBN: 979-8-9866009-4-9

Cover Image: Hallie Gage and Glenda Harris

Author Photo: Sarah Dowden Mault

First Edition: September 20, 2025

Published By
Jumbo Exchange and Communications
8515 State Hwy. 315
Long Branch, TX 75669
903.658.0128
jumboexchangeandcommunications@gmail.com
or visit our Facebook page

Dedication

In loving remembrance of
Aunt Myrtle Simmons Acker, Aunt Ada Poovey Collins, and
Aunt Louise Keeling Tillison

Contents

The Fictional Pate Family and Their Connections

<u>Missy Kimbel Pate</u>: 1904-1972 This gifted horsewoman and twentieth-century southern belle impacts numerous lives despite the onset of a permanent handicap.

Big Jim Pate: Missy's deeply flawed but fiercely protective husband

Alma Pate Evans: Missy's much younger sister-in-law, raised like a daughter

Nadine Pate Webber: another of Missy's young sisters-in-law, also like a daughter

Jimbo Pate: Missy's son (born in 1928) lives his life as an East Texas horseman, cattleman, and Baptist deacon.

Papa Kimbel: Missy's father and the owner/operator of Red Bog General Store

Cleve Pate: Missy's adult brother-in-law and Red Bog neighbor

Eva and Annette: Missy's adult sisters-in-law and occasional detractors

Tobe and Gert Washington: Missy's friends across racial and sharecropping lines

<u>Laura Beth Pate Chandler</u>: Missy's great-granddaughter is 33 years old when the story opens in 2007. She has single-handedly established a thriving urban business, but undue stress forces her to search for relief by the light of a memory.

Bradley Chandler: Laura Beth's rootless but deeply smitten ex-husband

Kimmy Chandler: Laura Beth's 13-year-old daughter

George Kelly: avid hound dog man who befriends Laura Beth through Bradley

Vesper Denton: longtime associate of Laura Beth's Uncle James Allen Pate

Belinda Radcliff and Vida Gomez: friends who work in Laura Beth's business

Bill and Margaret Pate: Laura Beth's kindhearted parents

Braxton and Elaine Chandler: Laura Beth's supportive ex-in-laws

Chapter One

~October 2007~

Laura Elizabeth Chandler coordinated events the way she lived her life, with old-fashioned charm and modern efficiency all wrapped up in a pretty little package. Ever so gradually, long hours and chronic stress outpaced her metabolism. The tummy (a neatly camouflaged but stubborn new reality) felt out of place on her naturally slender frame, and a last-minute dash between wedding venues elevated her heartrate to match the rapid click-clack of stylish pumps on the sidewalk.

Distracted by a chime from her ever-present Blackberry, Laura Beth checked the screen but found only a trivial news item on the latest fad diet. Algorithms and 2:00 a.m. searches aside, she gasped at this small betrayal, raised her eyes briefly to the traffic signal, and stepped off the curb directly into the path of an oncoming vehicle.

Calls and text messages erupted like some kind of chain reaction. Word filtered through professional and social networks in Houston. Naturally, then, it spread here and there across prosperous suburbs. Elizabeth Chandler, affectionately called Laura Beth by all who knew her, had been struck by a car downtown. Bill Pate, a hardworking tax consultant, took the call at his desk. Reeling inwardly, he maintained an outward calm so as to get the details straight. He phoned his wife and then Braxton Chandler. One of the last independent oilmen, Braxton was also Laura Beth's ex-father-in-law and still very much interested in her welfare.

Bill trusted the Chandlers to collect their granddaughter from school and break the news as gently as possible. At least one more call lay before him. Three resilient senior citizens, anchors of the family, still lived and worked on the old Pate homeplace in the tiny East Texas community of Red Bog, but that conversation would have to wait until he reached the hospital and his daughter's bedside. Old Jimbo Pate and the aunts would expect nothing less than first-hand information.

~ ~

Eighty-eight-year-old Alma Pate Evans leaned ever so slightly against the weathered planking and surveyed the scene before her.

"I declare, Jimbo… The place is overrun with horses and dogs. Some boys grow out of it, or so I'm told."

This sounded like a mild scolding, but laughter bubbled just beneath her unhurried drawl.

"Big Jim and Missy's boy, grow out of it?" Nadine Webber guffawed across the fence. Her voice echoed familiar East Texas tones, but the younger Pate sister spoke more definitely even when her thoughts took the form of a question.

The sisters were Jimbo's aunts, but at seventy-nine, he was only a decade or so behind them. In fact, the three interacted more or less as siblings, having grown up together during the Great Depression.

"They're running on good grass," Alma ventured, gesturing toward the horses and a lone white mule. "How come you feeding so early in the fall? I've heard you muttering time and again that horses today are either grossly overfed or dry lotted and half starved. Besides… The money, what little there is to be made, is in our cattle."

Short-coupled and wiry, the old cowboy tossed her a grin over his shoulder.

"True enough. I just sprinkle a little meal and salt along the bottom of the troughs. Keep 'em looking for a handout, and they'll come to call. Used to feed our mules and horses straight corn, but they worked harder for their livin' back then."

"We all did," Nadine remembered wryly.

Alma watched silently until the other two came back through the gate to stand beside her.

"Big Jim and Missy," she mused, returning to an earlier thought. "Gone all these years… Yet, not a day goes by that we don't think of them and call their names in conversation."

"Only natural, I guess, with all three of us back together on the homeplace," Jimbo observed.

"Missy and Big Jim made a dandy pair," Nadine recalled with her signature half smile.

That said, she took her sister's cane and hung it over her free arm. She and Jimbo fell into step on each side of Alma, providing a little extra support as they moved off toward the house.

"They weren't perfect," Alma said in a fond tone, "but they got us raised."

"Our brother Jim never got within spittin' distance of perfect," Nadine snorted. "But I'm still undecided 'bout Missy."

"For shame, Nadine. She taught you more Bible than that. Ain't but one perfect human bein' ever walked this earth."

Jimbo adjusted his grip on Alma's elbow as they started up the back porch steps and, simultaneously, smiled over his memories. This sort of constant back and forth between the aunts was as natural and familiar as the springtime call of a whippoorwill, but a ringing phone broke into his thoughts. The black wall-mounted unit in one corner of the kitchen was not quite as old as telephone service in Red Bog, only because it had replaced a hand-cranked model from his childhood.

~ ~

Hours after Jimbo answered that call in the Pate kitchen, Quint Parsons wrapped up a similar conversation on his satellite phone. Shrugging into a fleece-lined jacket, he pushed aside his tent flap and found the outdoor photographer, a guest of sorts, splitting stove wood while the hired help leaned against a tree with arms crossed.

"Don't strain yourself, George," he warned laconically.

"I didn't put him up to it, Quint. Bradley took the chore on himself."

"Right neighborly of you not to fight him over it. Now, I've got to tell the boy his wife's been run over by a car."

George Kelly let out a long, low whistle.

"Durn, I thought it was rough losin' hounds to the highway."

"She's not dead, you old reprobate. Just bunged up, they think."

"That's some better… 'Least he wasn't driving the car. I've taken a liking to young Bradley."

"Well, in that case—"

"Don't look at me. You've got the guide license, Quint, and you're running this camp. Best be about tellin' him."

Slightly taller than average, Bradley Chandler was not at all awkward or oversized. His dark hair needed a trim, and the lean face sported some stubble. Quick-thinking, capable, and artistic, he had captured Laura Beth's imagination first and then her heart.

Nights turned cool way up in the mountains, as fall swept along toward winter, but physical effort generated more than enough heat. Though he still thought of Laura Beth more often than he liked to admit, she usually limited their conversations to friendly updates on Kimmy. Both loved their daughter dearly, but the arrival of a baby early in their marriage had forced a reassessment of priorities.

Even now, careful of the axe head and its keen edge, he frowned at the memory of Laura Beth abandoning her writing. This cherished creative outlet fell by the wayside as she set out to achieve some financial stability for herself and the baby. She wished Bradley well in the pursuit of his own dreams but obviously preferred the comfortable insulation of cheering him on from a distance. The thought deepened his frown, and he finally caught sight of the two men watching him. Bradley shook his head to clear it, sank the axe into the makeshift chopping block, and strolled over to join them.

"I'm just as sorry as I can be, Chandler. It seems your wife got hit by a car sometime around noon. Happened down in Texas. Houston, as near as I could make out over that confounded wilderness phone. Now, she's not bad off, or at least they don't seem to think so. But I… Well, somebody thought you ought to know."

"Me and Laura Beth divorced years ago. But we have a daughter together, and they've been on my mind ever— all day." If Bradley sounded somewhat numb, the next words removed any doubt as to his concern. "Been a fine hunt, y'all, and I hope to do it again sometime."

"What do you mean do it again?" George interjected. "You can't get off this mountain alone and in the dark, not without a good chance of…"

"Well, I've got it to do. Down off the mountain by first light, and I ought to make Houston by tomorrow evening."

Seeing the younger man's resolve, Quint sized him up and then grunted in resignation.

"Take my Ruby mule. Best saddle animal I ever owned. If anything can carry you out tonight, she will."

Just then, George startled the other two with a snort of laughter.

"I'll trail along, boy. Got three ex-wives myself. Can't live with none of 'em, but there ain't a one I wouldn't break my neck for in a tight. Besides, I've got the last can of snuff in camp."

"I'll just bet you don't," Quint contradicted.

"Yes siree! Come right out of your saddlebag."

The lanky outdoorsman helped himself to a dip and then passed the can to its rightful owner.

"You'd leave me up here with fourteen hounds, six head of mules, a paying hunter, and the cook? Bradley here's making a pretty fair start for a flatland photographer, but with him gone, you and me are the only sure-enough mountain hands in camp."

"Tell you what," George offered by way of a solution. "The fiddler ought to have laid out his fifteen days in jail by now. If we make it into town, I'll send him back with your mules and a couple rolls of snuff."

"Wait just a minute. You're not really gonna catch a flight to Texas with this camera crazy friend of ours?"

"You know me, always itching to see what's around the next bend. Just keep my dogs in with yours unless I send for 'em, will you?"

"Alright," Quint agreed reluctantly, "but you tell the fiddler I want him sober."

"He can ride, drunk or not. Old Ruby'll pack him back up to camp. The other mule's likely to follow, and a dose of mountain air ought to straighten the fiddler out before long."

~ ~

Dark-blond ringlets fanned out against the institutional white of the pillowcase, highlighting Laura Beth's soft feminine features. Despite an outward appearance of serenity, her mind whirled in a panic. She was no longer the up-and-coming event coordinator with clients to please and appointments to keep. She thought of herself only as a single mother with a daughter who needed her healthy and strong. Kimmy might be testing a bit of independence at thirteen, but Laura Beth had always been the rock in her daughter's life. Now, she fought her way upward through the brain fog and confusion.

"Kimmy?"

The scream that tore at her throat emerged as a faint murmur. Kimbel Grace Chandler cried openly and, with their roles suddenly reversed, covered her mother's cheeks and forehead with fluttery little kisses.

"You're okay, Mama. I'm right here, and everything's fine."

Laura Beth managed a smile and then lay there, content to hold her daughter's hand for a long while. Without bothering to raise her head off the pillow, she knew who would be there with them: her own mother and father and, quite possibly, her wealthy ex-in-laws.

"Thirsty," she finally murmured. Someone offered a small cup of ice water, but Laura Beth turned her head away and gazed imploringly up at her daughter. "I'm thirsty."

"She wants her Dr Pepper," Kimmy realized in a sudden flash and issued succinct instructions to the room at large. "In a can… And cold… Find one!"

Minutes later, that wonderful fizz hit the back of her throat. Laura Beth felt a particular set of nerves in her brain, essential to organization and efficiency, wake up and stretch. Time to figure out what had gone so terribly wrong, deal with it, and get on with her life.

Nearly as upset as Kimmy, Margaret Pate struggled to control the tremor in her voice and hands. She assured Laura Beth of her love and brushed the hair gently from her daughter's face. Elaine Chandler, the ex-mother-in-law and much more than that, proved coolheaded.

"You're bruised from head to toe, sweet girl. That is to say, you will be. There's a slight concussion, too, but they can't find anything broken. Your phone… Your Blackberry… Well, a man gave us some pieces in a plastic baggie."

"Oh, no," Laura Beth replied sickly. "Still, I should be counting my blessings. I'm alive and well. Calendars and customer info can be accessed through the laptop, I hope."

Finally, Bill stepped up to the bedside. He explained the accident as best he could and tried to cradle his daughter's hand without squeezing.

"Your granddaddy wants to hear from you just as soon as you're up to it," he added almost apologetically, but Laura Beth's smile lit the room.

"Sure, give me a phone."

"I've always been pretty well in awe of Daddy, and the older we get the less we find in common. You two, though, no doubt of a special bond there."

Before she could place the call, a young man in a department-store suit tapped lightly on the doorframe and edged his way into the room. They all turned expectantly, hoping for a doctor's report.

Some people, inclined to overestimate their own intelligence, found it easy to dismiss Laura Beth due to her impeccable manners and unhurried drawl. Behind these endearing traits, though, her mind functioned with the precision of a razorblade. Even in her dazed and battered condition, she was the first to see through the visitor's spiel. Unfailingly pleasant, her voice took on a note of incredulity.

"Beg pardon, sir, but I don't want to sue anybody. I stepped out in front of a car."

"The driver of said car tried to beat the light," he explained almost gleefully. "Witnesses on the scene said the crosswalk signal was in your favor."

"I truly do hate to rain on your parade… But I'm willing to bet those same witnesses saw me look from my phone to the light and back to my phone before stepping briskly out into the street. Now, if you don't mind, I'd like to rest."

The young lawyer opened his mouth to argue, and Braxton Chandler suddenly found an outlet for his pent-up nerves and boundless energy.

"Son, I've got a litigation team that can eat you for lunch any day of the week and twice on Tuesday. The lady told you to clear out in the sweetest words she could find, but I don't labor under any such constraints. Now, git!"

Laura Beth smiled gratefully at the sound of her father-in-law's authoritative voice, and the hurried clatter of retreating footfalls along the hallway brought a shuddering sigh of relief.

"Thank you, kind sir. Bradley always did say you were good in a tight spot."

A jaw muscle twitched at the mention of his son, but the startling blue eyes softened as they fell on Laura Beth's face.

"No telling where that boy's off to this time. Anyhow, Laura Beth, I… Well, I… No fast-talking lawyer is going to push himself on you while I'm around."

She gazed up into his face for several long seconds and then answered softly.

"I love you, too, Pop."

"Well, then, that's alright." After a breath or two, he managed a more businesslike tone. "Try to rest, Laura Beth. There's a landline in the room, but I'm leaving a plain old company phone, too, until you can replace that gadget of yours. Kimmy took the number down, and I laid the mobile here on your nightstand."

"Don't be mad with me, Pop, but I'll need a copy of the bill."

"Now, let's not get into… Everybody knows you don't take charity, Laura Beth, but family is a different ballgame altogether." Tears welled up as she slowly shook her head, and he melted at once. "Softhearted beauty with a backbone like steel, and my idiot son just… Mad at you? I can't even put up a decent argument, not looking into those great big eyes."

Her parents headed for the door shortly after Mr. and Mrs. Chandler, promising to eat supper, pack an overnight bag, and come right back. Bill planned to spend the night in a hospital chair while Elaine took their granddaughter home for some rest.

"Kimmy will probably want to stay until the last possible minute,"

Laura Beth reasoned, "and I'll be just fine through the night. You've seen the nurses popping in and out of here. Why don't y'all go out to eat? You can come back, visit a little more, and take Kimmy home together."

"That works," her daughter seconded. "Bring us a pizza or something."

"Yes, please. Get some cash out of my…"

Most days, Laura Beth fueled her body on caffeine until solid food became an absolute necessity. Some people practically wasted away under stress, but she enjoyed no such luxury. Given a moment to catch her breath, Laura Beth sought comfort in sweet treats and simple starches. If being hit by a car wouldn't kill her appetite, she reflected, dieting might be an uncertain proposition at best.

"Your purse is here," her mom offered reassuringly.

"Blackberry hit the pavement," Kimmy blurted, ready to have a little fun with her mama, "but they found the handbag clutched to your chest."

She added air quotes around the word handbag to good effect, and Laura Beth smiled tolerantly.

"There are things a lady won't be parted from. Besides, it matches my shoes."

"Don't remind me," Kimmy groaned.

"We took Laura Beth out of Red Bog fairly early, but we'll never get Red Bog out of… Leave her purse alone," Bill finished with a chuckle. "I'll buy the pizza."

Laura Beth closed her eyes briefly, soaking up the silence, but then rallied and asked Kimmy for the phone. She pulled out the antenna, flipped up the outer cover, and dialed a number from memory. Jimbo Pate answered on the second ring.

"Granddaddy," she said in recognition, and a heavy, contented sigh escaped on the same breath. "Started to call your house, but I figured you'd sit up with Aunt Alma and Aunt Nadine waiting for news."

"You found me alright, doodlebug. What's the news?"

"I can surely thank God for His loving care. The Good Shepherd must have a soft spot for foolish sheep amongst His flock. They tell me I'm fine. Probably have some real aches and pains for the next few days, but nothing I don't deserve."

"Hush, now. Place like Houston, with so many folks jammed up together, anything's liable to happen. Listen, don't get your feathers ruffled, but I took it on myself to track down that runaway husband of yours. Never actually got him on the phone. A hunter or guide or… Anyhow, somebody in that high-mountain camp was supposed to give him the word. I never heard back. So, you can pretty well bet he saddled up and rode out of there. That boy has shown plenty of faults, but gutlessness ain't one of 'em."

"Oh, Granddaddy," and her voice sounded smaller somehow. "I could never be mad at you for taking care of me however you think best, but an ex-husband just doesn't have the same duties as… Besides, it won't do for me to be around Bradley right now."

"How do you figure?"

"I'm tired. Always so tired… I'll naturally want to lean on him, and that's the one chance I can't afford to take."

"Husband and wife ought to lean on one another, but I'll not argue. He's comin' to Houston, or I've misjudged him a plenty. Why not let him spend some time with Kimmy while you get back on your feet. If you'd rather keep him at a distance… Well, you're more than welcome here."

"I miss Red Bog something awful, and I know I've neglected y'all. The business is really taking off, though, and I just can't—"

"Neglected," he echoed, and the tone conveyed gentle sarcasm. "Me and Alma and Nadine? We ain't exactly a bunch of houseplants."

"No, sir," she said, laughing a little at the very idea. "I'm sorry. Truly, I am."

"Now, doodlebug… Don't you fret. I'll see after the homeplace while Alma and Nadine see after me. You know where to find us if need be. Long as you're taking good care of yourself, I'm more than satisfied." The conversation trailed off for a moment, and in that brief time, Jimbo reached a new conclusion. "But, now, walkin' out in front of cars don't quite measure up. I'll get a hold of Billy Boy and tell him to fetch you on home just as soon as you're able to travel. Red Bog's about due for a little taste of sunshine, anyhow."

Laura Beth seldom allowed anyone to make decisions for her, but Granddaddy was a special case. Overwhelmed by daily cares, to say nothing of this accident, she gladly deferred to his judgment. Besides… A trip to Red Bog might be just what the doctor ordered. Bone-weary, she said goodbye to Granddaddy and laughed softly at the timely arrival of an on-duty physician.

The doctor, a young woman with Asian features but no trace of an accent, read details from Laura Beth's chart under her breath before opening a conversation.

"Laura Elizabeth Chandler, thirty-three-year-old white female… Didn't make it across the street, huh? Not how you planned your day, I'm sure. Still… You're very fortunate, bruising and a few minor lacerations, but nothing serious. We can probably get you out of here sometime tomorrow morning."

"Most people call me Laura Beth, and I'm pleased to meet you. Not here by choice, obviously, but I do feel very blessed. Things could've easily gone worse."

"True," the young hospitalist admitted tersely, once again distracted by the chart. "Your sleeping pill is listed here. And I see you take something, as needed, for anxiety. Any chance you're also being treated for hypertension?"

"High blood pressure? In my thirties?"

"Regardless of age, your numbers seem to be edging toward the high side."

Kimmy stirred a little, sitting up straighter in her chair. Meanwhile, Laura Beth reached deep down for the strength to smile.

"Well, now, being run over by a car is quite stressful. Pain could also raise my blood pressure, couldn't it? And there's no telling what all they've given me today."

"Even so, I believe … While it's safe to assume that your weight falls consistently within the expected range, changes in body composition can occur without a drastic fluctuation on the scale."

"Beg pardon?"

"Noticed any recent accumulation of fat? Perhaps on or around your midsection?"

Laura Beth lay there very still and quiet for a time but finally spoke two words.

"I've decided."

"Decided what?" the doctor asked with genuine curiosity.

"After carefully considering each alternative," her patient responded in a light tone of voice, "I'd rather lay here and die than answer that question."

The conscientious medical professional actually cracked a smile.

"Sorry... I'm interested in the human body from a purely scientific standpoint. My people skills are definitely a work in progress. Just be careful, okay? Maybe monitor your numbers over the next few days. Sodas are not your friend, all those empty calories."

Laura Beth felt instantly parched, as if she had a mouthful of cotton, but the telltale can at her bedside was oh-so-sadly empty.

"I can certainly appreciate your scientific knowledge. But, in all honesty, it's my turn to apologize. Giving up Dr Pepper just isn't going to happen right now. Are there other things I should do?"

These quiet, drawling words hung in the air between them for several long moments before an answer came.

"Well, environmental factors can be at least as impactful as nutritional choices. Take a short break from your worries. Is that a possibility?"

"Sounds lovely, and I do appreciate the advice. A little trip to visit my grandfather and his aunts might be just the thing."

"His aunts? Perhaps their longevity will work in your favor."

"Well," Laura Beth answered with a chuckle, "the generations sort of ran together in our family. If I say great grandaunt out loud, it sounds quite distant. But nobody who spent any time with Alma and Nadine could ever describe them as distant relations!"

"That's nice. Sounds like a bit of family time might provide just the kind of relief you need."

"Mmm," Laura Beth agreed readily. "I'm definitely considering it. Anyhow, you take care."

The young doctor smiled, gave a slight shake of her head, and set off down the hallway. She had heard about southern belles, abstractly, ever since moving to Texas, but this was her first real-life encounter. Though not a particularly tractable patient, Laura Beth Chandler brought genuine warmth into what most would have considered an impersonal interaction. Some of this warmth spilled over as the physician motioned Kimmy out into the hallway.

"Your mother should recover nicely. Go ahead and buy her a cold soda. I'm in no mood to fight that kind of losing battle this evening."

"How do you do that?" Kimmy inquired brightly as she reentered the room.

"Do what?"

"Get people like that doctor to eat out of your hand," she answered, dangling the Dr Pepper can above the bed like a coveted prize.

"It's nothing intentional, baby, not like some kind of plot or strategy. I just treat folks the way I'd like to be treated and maybe try to make them smile. Most will come around to that kind of gentle courtesy. A few are bound and determined to run over you, but when they find out you're willing to stand your ground…"

"How's Granddaddy Pate?"

"Just fine," Laura Beth answered after the first long swallow of her soda. "Maybe a little worried about me, to tell the truth, but I tried to reassure him. You know, hearing his voice always takes me right back to Red Bog."

Catching a glimpse of her mother's wistful expression, Kimmy ventured a comment.

"I never could see anything so special about Red Bog. I mean, there's nothing wrong with it for a place in the very middle of nowhere… Tell me, Mama. Tell me why you love it so much."

"That's a tall order," she answered with a sigh. "It's mainly the people, I guess. The people and my childhood memories, but the place itself is special and kind of hard to describe. It was farmland once, but not now. Not in today's world of gigantic fields and multi-row equipment. A mix of pine and hardwood timber with rolling pastures cleared off here and there… It'll run cattle, but it's not exactly ranch country on the scale of the wide-open west. I guess you could describe Granddaddy's place as a stock farm, but I just always called it home."

Having traveled to Red Bog a handful of times with her mother, Kimmy found little if any new information in the carefully constructed word picture. She frowned slightly and let the subject drop. Laura Beth wanted to continue but trailed off for lack of energy.

Bill and Margaret returned with the pizza, and after a late supper, finally hustled Kimmy out the door. Laura Beth drifted off to sleep, dreaming of the East Texas landscape she had tried so hard to describe.

Chapter Two

~April 1920~

After three years of hard fighting in Europe and a bout with Spanish influenza, Jim Pate looked more like a dried-up corn shuck, cast aside after harvest, than the handsome young rascal he had been before the war. A more-or-less permanent scowl replaced his easy grin, but nobody blamed the well-liked local boy. Folks knew the story; he had come home just in time to bury his parents and take on the responsibility of two young sisters, one scarcely big enough to toddle along and the other a babe in arms.

Mighty few things lifted his spirits these days, but a sure and gentle touch with driving horses brought enjoyment as well as pocket money. Then, too, the sound of hound dogs throwing their voices to the wind as they trailed up a fox and jumped it to run always fetched a shadow of his old smile. The Pate farm was plenty big enough, supporting five tenant families along with Jim and the two young sisters, but general store owner, Crawford Kimbel, held title on various tracts of land in and around Red Bog.

On this particular spring evening, Jim and his brother Cleve made it to the hill overlooking a stretch of Kimbel's uncultivated bottomland well before dark. Never one to waste time, Jim turned loose his favorite strike dog and spoke soothingly to the rest of the pack as they strained against cotton lead lines, eager to join her.

"Just wait, now. Wait 'til Maude gets one started."

Sure enough, Maude struck a hot track before Cleve even managed to kindle a bit of fire for their coffeepot. Leaving his task, he scrambled to help Jim untie the other dogs. Just about dusk, the fox circled, causing an increase in the volume of hound music as it boiled back up the long bottom toward the two appreciative listeners.

"That's my Trumpet dog right up there pushing old Maude. Younger and stouter… He'll get the best of her directly."

The banter brought a rare smile, but Jim answered dryly.

"I wouldn't count on that, brother. No, sir, I just wouldn't count on it." Suddenly, a rapid pounding of hooves joined the noise of the chase. Jim's smile faltered as he leaned forward in curiosity. "Who in the Sam Hill?"

The fox crossed their line of sight first with maybe a minute's lead on the pursuing hounds. Moments later, the brothers spied a graceful rider sitting sidesaddle atop her long-legged sorrel mount. The horse's white markings showed plainly as he galloped along through the fast-falling dusk, and Cleve recognized the rider.

"Missy Kimbel," he grunted on a wave of laughter, "couldn't be nobody else. What does she think this is, Virginia or maybe Old England?"

Jim answered with a rousing whoop and sprang to his feet beside the little fire.

"Don't know what she thinks," he enthused as the girl plunged out of sight, "but I never saw the day I could ride hard enough to stay up on them hounds. You ain't neither."

"She's a nice girl and pretty as they come, but she'll cripple a good horse or break her own neck one of these days. That sorrel is the fastest thing in the county, and Missy's plumb crazy once she lines him out after something."

Jim saw the horse's white markings just as well as his younger brother but also glimpsed a tailored riding habit of robin's egg blue and honey-colored locks whipping out behind.

"Cleve, I'm gonna marry that girl!"

"Do what? You're crazier than she is!"

"I'm dead serious," Jim answered, "and I'd like for you to name me one good reason against it. You're married, the older girls are married, and I'm left with them two little bitty ones at home."

"If you wasn't so hardheaded about keepin' Alma and Nadine together—"

"Now, Cleve… You've got a young'un of your own on the way, and I wouldn't ask either brother-in-law to raise so much as a hound pup for me. Them girls will do fine right there on the homeplace."

"Life with Missy ought never be dull, providin' old man Kimbel lets you live to court her. She's probably the mothering kind when she ain't tearing across the country a'horseback. But Alma and Nadine have already buried one mama, and that hard-runnin' sorrel's apt to leave Missy piled up somewhere one of these days."

"Quit your jawing, Cleve. I gotta talk to that girl, and there ain't no catchin' up to her. Where can I cut her track, do you think?"

"Dark's coming on… If that fox makes another circle before he goes to ground, Missy's likely to turn and ride for home."

"Well, then, that's where I'm bound. Try to stay in hearin' of the dogs, and don't worry none about me. I'll pick you up directly."

Without the ravages of war and prolonged illness that marked his older brother, Cleve found little in life to hold back the broad Pate grin.

"Missy favors her sidesaddle over a buggy, but that road-eatin' trotter of yours will take her eye quicker than any tin-can automobile. Luck to you, Jim!"

Blessed with vibrant good looks to match the warmth of a joy-filled nature, Elizabeth "Missy" Kimbel might have commanded a double handful of suitors, but their absence seldom troubled her. Most of the boys she knew fancied themselves outdoorsmen, and if they couldn't ride well enough to keep up… Such polite indifference toward eligible young men kept jealousy to a minimum and won her plenty of friends amongst other girls.

Missy often yelled like a Comanche while urging her horse along dirt roads and across pastures. In other settings, though, she radiated a soft-spoken, genteel courtesy. Older folks found it easy to excuse a lively thirst for adventure and held her up as an example of grace and charm.

Any man who thought to court Crawford Kimbel's daughter and only child faced the added problem of his undisputed status as the big fish in Red Bog's small pond. Respect for the merchant's years of work and careful management seemed only right, but after a trip to France with Uncle Sam's army, nobody intimidated Jim Pate. The quick-stepping gray trotter made good time along the road, and Jim chose his destination wisely.

The Kimbel house, boasting fresh paint and every modern convenience known to Red Bog, nestled in the shadow of the larger store building. Jim ignored it and drove straight to a well-kept shed situated between and to the rear of both buildings. He stepped down from the buggy just as Missy's outline emerged against the inky blackness of the doorway.

"Figured you'd stable your own horse," he said and flashed a quick grin by way of greeting. "Never saw anybody could ride up with my hounds, and I just had to get a closer look."

"Good evening, Mr. Pate. You've got me tallied up just about right. Always see after Laddie myself. I wouldn't trust him to anyone else.

I've rubbed him down already, but there might be just enough light out here to see by. I'll go back and get him if you want that closer look."

"No'm, it ain't the horse I came to see. And 'less you want to be called Miss Elizabeth Kimbel every other breath, I'd swap that Mr. Pate business off for just plain Jim."

With that, he stepped smoothly down from the buggy and took her by the elbow. Six years her senior and stocky of build, he was just tall enough that a petite young lady could look up to meet his gaze. Faintly troubled eyes only accentuated his rugged good looks. From brief interactions around her father's store, she knew a little about the care he took with those poor orphaned sisters. Her heart, which beat steadily along in spite of the swiftest gallop over the roughest ground, gave a strange little flutter.

"Jim'll do, I reckon, and you just call me Missy. Walk me up to the house?"

Not one of the carefree boys her own age could have walked Missy Kimbel home that way and hoped to make it past the front door, but Jim Pate was man-grown and well respected in the community. These factors, along with Missy's determined sponsorship, carried him through the door and all the way to the supper table.

Crawford Kimbel acted a bit flustered at first but soon fell into easy conversation with his young neighbor. In addition to the store and his real estate holdings, Crawford owned a controlling interest in Red Bog's only cotton gin. The two men discussed preparation for spring planting and speculated about what kind of market to expect in the fall.

"Pa loved to turn his fields over and plant. Waited for the ground to warm up like a kid waits for Christmastime. Every year's cotton was just bound to be the best crop we ever made. I wish he was here to make one more."

"You've done a good job with the place, and he'd be proud. A war like you boys fought, and then to come home to…"

Crawford trailed off uncertainly, but Jim lived with the sudden loss of his parents every day. Mentioning it in conversation did little good or harm, either, at this point. Wanting to brighten things up a little, Missy offered coffee and dessert.

"Supper's not my doing," she told him sweetly, "but I made the pie myself. How are your little sisters? Pert and sassy, I suppose?"

"Don't know as I'd go that far with it," Jim answered, accepting his slice of pie with a chuckle, "but Alma and Nadine keep each other pretty well occupied most of the time. They're at home with Gert tonight. Safe in bed, I expect, but I left Cleve by a little campfire out yonder to keep track of our hounds."

"Gertie Washington? Why doesn't one of your grown sisters—"

"Eva and Annette are full of their own notions," he drawled with a fleeting smile, "but I told Mama I'd keep the little ones at home. Gert's around when I need her and knows when to make herself scarce. I don't aim to see them girls separated or taken off the homeplace until they're grown."

"I can understand that," she decided after a moment's thought.

Jim made short work of the chocolate pie before him and then glanced up at her.

"You may be the only one in the county who sees any sense to it, but that's how it's gotta be."

Missy's serene gaze, the eyes a greenish hazel in color, never missed much. She saw him reach up unconsciously to fiddle with the pack of Chesterfields in his breast pocket and suddenly decided to try and prolong their evening.

"I've never heard many hound races, Papa, but the one I caught on my ride home was a real treat. Those hounds raise a clamor that somehow pulls your heart right up there to run with 'em."

"I had no notion girl children ever felt that little tug. A young lady probably shouldn't admit to it, anyhow."

Crawford spoke his challenge in good humor, arching an eyebrow at Jim as if to invite support of the assessment.

"Oh, I don't know," the young man drawled casually. "Ladies, real sure-enough ladies, generally have a sight more spirit and backbone than they get credit for. She is your daughter, and I hear tell you kept some pretty hard-running hounds until you gathered up too many business interests to leave unattended."

"I still like a good race, time to time," the storekeeper admitted in a speculative tone.

"I've got Gray Boy hooked to a light buggy that ain't scarcely big enough for two, but if we can take your automobile, them dogs'll probably scare up another race or two for you and Missy to listen at."

Before Papa could object to her inclusion, Missy neatly handled the issue of using his prized Hutmobile.

"Night's too pretty to mess up with the clatter of a car engine. We've still got a surrey out in the barn if you don't think it'll hinder your horse's road gait too much."

In full sympathy with Missy's plan, Jim acted quickly before any objections could be raised.

"Won't take a minute to drop my buggy and re-hitch him. You throw together some coffee, quilts, a lantern, and whatever else you'll need to make the outing more comfortable."

"How'd you get in on this deal?" Crawford inquired, pushing up from the table to follow his daughter as she bustled out of the room.

"I'm not a little girl to be left at home, Papa," she quipped, scarcely bothering to look over her shoulder. "Besides, with me along, you can enjoy the hounds and not worry about getting right on back."

"Why, Missy, you're a joy! Always thinking about your old Papa…"

That got her attention, and she whirled around to kiss him affectionately on the cheek. When she spoke, her tone was light and teasing, but the words conveyed a truth.

"If you leave me here, I'll throw my saddle right back on Laddie and follow."

"To be such a joy," he grumbled, "you're almighty full of the mischief, too."

Minutes later, the young lady clasped Jim's hand warmly as she stepped up into the surrey. Settling onto the rear seat amid a pile of quilts, she left him to share the front seat with her father. Gray Boy snatched them effortlessly along the road until she caught a bit of sound on the cool night air and reached to lay a hand atop Jim's shoulder.

"The hounds," she said briefly, and every syllable vibrated with excitement.

Jim slowed his horse to a walk and then a full stop, listening just long enough to adjust their direction.

"That's a mighty fine ear," he complimented her. "Won't take you no time a-tall to learn each dog's voice and call it by name."

Having relocated twice and built himself another fire, Cleve Pate saved up plenty of conversation before Jim drove onto the scene.

"You work fast, brother," he commented under his breath, nodding politely to Missy and her father.

All jokes aside, Cleve handled his part nicely. He entertained Crawford with a running commentary on each race, leaving Jim to sit undisturbed and hold Missy's hand.

High-strung and sensitive as any yearling filly, she thrilled to the moonlight, the hound music, and the heady breath of spring. Jim's gaze, usually distant and shadowed by grief, found rest as it settled on her face. Shying away from long declarations that might draw unwanted attention to their side of the fire, he simply enjoyed her nearness. This silence allowed Missy the fanciful notion that Jim had somehow arranged the beauty around them especially for her enjoyment.

~October 2007~

The day after her accident Laura Beth overruled concerned loved ones and spent a few hours in her small, tidy office. She reassured clients and doublechecked suppliers, tying up loose ends as best she could, but the majority of her time went into pacing and fretting over what would become of the business in her absence. Having built *Finishing Touches by Elizabeth Chandler* from the ground up, she depended on its continued success to earn a living for Kimmy and herself.

Yesterday's pumps clattered back and forth across the office floor with a faint catch in their rhythm as Laura Beth limped ever so slightly. She bit her knuckle almost unconsciously and wracked her brain for a solution. Biting nails proved totally incompatible with the price of a manicure. If careful not to overdo it, though, a stressed-out business owner could allow herself a bit of knuckle chewing. Nearly oblivious to all this frantic activity, Kimmy lolled behind the desk and doodled on her ever-present sketchpad. It might take another Dr Pepper or a slightly tooth marked knuckle, but Mama would find a solution. She always did.

Laura Beth paced and gnawed, but no solution came.

"I'll figure it out tomorrow," she finally blurted. "I've done all I can do here, and we need to get home before your—"

She bit back the word "dad" to avoid disappointing Kimmy, just in case Granddaddy missed his bet.

"I'm with you," Kimmy responded, failing to notice the slip. "Let's go home."

Laura Beth gave an involuntary groan as she settled behind the wheel and resolved to thank her parents yet again for moving the car to her office. Traffic always presented a problem, but outbound lanes were not completely snarled at this hour of the afternoon. Laura Beth liked their neat little house in the suburbs. She and the bank. a turn of phrase picked up from the farmers around Red Bog, owned this chunk of brick and mortar. She valued the stability it symbolized for Kimmy, but walking through the door never offered the sense of refuge she craved. This was her house, alright, and its upkeep depended totally on her. *Home* lay deep in the piney woods.

She and Kimmy ate out a good deal, but with an overarching interest in hospitality and her rural background, Laura Beth was far from helpless in the kitchen. She showered and changed, promising herself a long soak in the tub later. For the time being, cooking a simple supper and carefully arranging her table bathed tattered nerves in the comfort of routine.

When Mama cooked, they often enjoyed leftovers for several days. So, had Kimmy looked up from her latest drawing, she would have found little reason to question the size of this meal. Laura Beth fried several cutlets, fixed a large bowl of potatoes, opened some frozen broccoli, and drizzled a spicy white queso over it. She kept rearranging cutlets on the platter and stirring at her broccoli on the back of the stove until Kimmy ventured into the kitchen and pulled her into a careful sidelong hug.

"Are we going to eat this food, or are you going to poke and prod it to death? The world won't end if you stop and sit down, Mama."

"Just a few more minutes," Laura Beth stalled, fighting down the note of tentative anticipation in her voice, but the doorbell rang even as she spoke.

"Oh, Mama! Only you would invite company on the day after…"

"Never mind; go answer the door. I'll put this on the table."

Kimmy rolled her eyes but started obediently into the front hall.

"They told me at the hospital that she'd been dismissed, but when I didn't see any extra cars here…"

Laura Beth caught her breath at the faint edge of panic in the familiar male voice from the doorway, but Kimmy's squeal of delight drowned it out completely.

"Dad!"

The girl sometimes tried for a bit of teenage indifference, but it deserted her in a matter of seconds. Bradley hoisted her into the air as he had done for years.

"Hey, kiddo… Where's she at?"

"Dad! We had no idea you were coming."

"Aw, now, I don't buy that for a minute. Maybe she wanted to surprise you, and naturally she's got other things on her mind. But I know Jimbo Pate. He didn't send out that kind of summons expecting me to ignore it, and he ain't about to let me catch his doodlebug off guard. She knew. Like I keep telling you, Kimmy girl, your mama knows a lot of things."

"No joke," Kimmy responded, but she laughed and kissed his cheek as she said it. "She's in the kitchen, Dad, or maybe the dining room by now."

Three or four long strides, and his blue eyes drank her in just like a desert traveler takes his water. Slow and careful, but with deep appreciation. Once satisfied as to her wellbeing, Bradley noted a slight weight gain, not much in light of the intervening years. Just enough, he thought, to soften her curves. Laura Beth nearly always resisted change, but she stood before him more beautiful than ever.

"Mr. Pate never was the connivin' kind," he finally said aloud, "and I doubt the old gentleman's gone senile. So, I'm reasonably certain you were hit by a car yesterday. Explain all of this, please."

The sweep of his arm took in the freshly arranged hair, the casual perfection of her outfit, and the heavily laden table.

"Oh, you know me," she answered lightly. "I'll go until I just crash."

"You did crash, right into somebody's car, and now you should be resting. Surely there was another way for you and Kimmy to get supper tonight?"

"It really is good to see you, Bradley."

"She's been pacing like a cat since we left the hospital this morning," their daughter supplied helpfully. "Now, it's starting to make sense."

"That's about enough out of you, young lady," Laura Beth decided, and her tone hovered somewhere between laughter and a warning. "Y'all sit down so we can eat."

"The imperturbable Laura Beth Pate would never fret all that much on my account," Bradley joked, moving gallantly around the table to seat her, "but she might have been plotting her revenge on that poor unfortunate driver."

Caught briefly off guard by this special treatment, she settled herself at the table and then glanced up to meet his gaze.

"My fault," she answered shortly. "Walked right out into the street and never looked up until I landed in the hospital. Now, sit down and let Kimmy bless our food."

Kimmy offered a prayer as expected, chattered through most of the meal, and then left her parents suddenly and completely alone.

"Hey, don't go anywhere. I'll be back in just a minute with three of Mama's famous hot fudge sundaes. Well, these won't be Mama's, but you know what I mean. Don't go anywhere!"

Watching their daughter dash happily out of the room, Laura Beth smiled tolerantly and tried not to think of the mess Kimmy would leave in her kitchen. She accepted Bradley's compliments on the meal, more or less as her due, and then decided to clear the air.

"As our daughter so artlessly revealed… I have, in fact, been pacing like a cat all day. You're still the only man who can give me butterflies, Bradley, but it takes more than butterflies to make a home and family. This time, the fretting's got more to do with my business."

"Why fret over the business? You're a gold-plated success, Laura Beth. I always knew you would be."

"Successful, maybe. But what I built is a one-horse wagon, and somebody's got to pull it. Granddaddy says I'm due for a little time in Red Bog. He's right, but I just don't…"

They sat there in silence while the minutes ticked by. Bradley snagged another small piece of meat off the platter and picked at it for something to do. All at once, though, he looked up from his plate with a broad smile.

"What about that old warhorse you worked under when I first met you? Belinda E. Scrooge… Sold her firm to some kind of big conglomerate years ago, didn't she? The old girl has surely enjoyed enough retirement by now. I bet she's sick to death of her own company. Couldn't you hitch her to the wagon?"

"Belinda G. Radcliff, and please don't call her names. Still, I can't argue much with your personality assessment. Belinda is a terrific organizer, but she scares people. These folks hired *me*, for pity's sake. One go-round with Belinda, and they'll head for the hills."

"Might be an issue," he admitted. "You catch flies with honey, my dear, and Belinda has always snatched hers right out of the air." He toyed with that last piece of meat on his plate while his mind toyed with the problem.

"How on earth do you make it sound so sinister? My clients adore me, and I care a great deal about them, too."

"Oh, don't misunderstand me. It's real, genuine Red Bog honey. No sugar water for your handpicked flies." Sight of his daughter emerging from the kitchen with a couple of sundaes in hand brought a flash of inspiration. "That's it! I'll be with Kimmy, of course, and she's in school during the week. I could never juggle everything you do, Laura Beth, but if you'll sweet talk Belinda into pulling the wagon, I'll make sure she doesn't wreck it."

"I never took it for granted, Bradley, that you'd stay in Houston with our daughter while I recuperate at home. She's safe enough with my parents or yours. It's a nice thought, and your offer to help run the business is beyond generous, but we both know you won't last. Why, the minute these skyscrapers start crowding in on your horizon, you'll be off and running. I'd rather not make an impromptu trip through the desert southwest or explore the uttermost reaches of the Grand Canyon to retrieve my little girl."

Kimmy plopped a small glass of ice cream and hot fudge down before each parent and inserted herself, briefly, into the conversation.

"Desert? Grand Canyon? Sounds exciting! I'll grab my sundae and be right back. Don't go anywhere, not without me."

As she hurried from the room, Kimmy saw Dad leave his chair and step over to take Mama by the hand. Laura Beth yearned to stand, rest her head on his shoulder, and feel his arms encircling her. Oddly enough, she experienced a contrasting urge to squirm and pull her hand out of his tender grasp. In the end, she sat still but averted her eyes as a means of self-preservation.

"You're a wonderful mother, and we all know it. Now, you need to take care of yourself for a little while. Why not let me spend this time with Kimmy? If all the concrete gets to me, I promise I'll bring her straight to Red Bog. I could never take her off rambling, Laura

Beth, and leave you behind to worry. In terms of overseeing the business… Well, I seem to recall my people skills as being good enough to turn your head."

Chapter Three

"You have no idea…" She breathed the words out softly, somewhere between a sigh and a groan, and then gently freed her hand from his grip. "Now, get over there and eat your sundae before it melts."

With her ex-husband seated once more across the table, Laura Beth felt herself breathe again. The first spoonful of ice cream slid down, cool and delightful, almost as sweet as the approaching solution to her problem.

"Thought for a minute we might get our very own fairytale ending," Kimmy quipped. "I've seen both versions of *The Parent Trap* more than once, you know."

"Oh, Kimmy," Laura Beth whispered gently, and the instinctive desire to comfort pushed her halfway to her feet.

"I'm alright, Mama, really."

"She's just fine," Bradley observed, "and it's all thanks to you."

"Congratulations… You have raised a well-adjusted miniature human," Kimmy added with a goofy grin. "Are you going to let Dad help with the business, or not?"

"I'll pay you, Bradley, if you're willing to try."

He had no intention of taking her money and started, automatically, to shake his head. Fortunately, though, he caught himself in time. If this turned into an argument, Laura Beth would set her jaw, dig in her heels, and never give an inch.

"Whatever you decide will be fair, I'm sure."

They fell silent then, and Laura Beth allowed herself a smile. All they needed to do now was address the details, and details were her specialty. Bradley neglected his own ice cream and devoted most of his attention to her. He enjoyed the tiny shifts in her expression, from careful thought to uncomplicated bliss and back again with each dainty bite.

"This is really good, Kimmy," she observed sweetly. "Best part of the meal, if you ask me."

"The perfect finale, anyway," Bradley agreed.

"Oh, well… I get that from Mama. *Finishing Touches by Elizabeth Chandler*, remember?"

All three shared a laugh, and then Bradley started a conversational end run around his ex-wife's preoccupation with complete and total independence.

"Say, Laura Beth… Kimmy and I could always stay with the folks. But you tolerate my nonsense much better than Pop, and I never even divorced him. Then, too, I'm traveling with George Kelly, and he ain't house broke enough to suit Mom.

"Who's George Kelly?"

"A lion hunter and old-time rounder. He led me down off the mountain when we got the call about your accident. As much as told me how I wouldn't do you a bit of good piled up in the bottom of a canyon somewhere. He's out at the Super 8, now, but I can't leave him stashed there forever."

"Lion hunter?" Kimmy repeated, envisioning some kind of safari.

"Mountain lion or cougar or whatever you want to call them… I was photographing a hunt when Mr. Pate tracked me down." Then, turning his attention back to Laura Beth, "George is a hound dog man in more ways than one, but he's country as cornbread and a friend through and through. I didn't dare bring him with me tonight. 'At old silver fox would steal your heart before I could turn around good."

"Mercy me; I'll just have to meet George Kelly one of these days." Then, in a more serious tone, "Why don't y'all stay in the house with Kimmy. She won't need to pack, and with me gone to Red Bog, there ought to be plenty of room for you and your friend."

"Well, if you don't mind… Are you taking your car up to the homeplace this time?"

"No, Mother and Daddy probably don't want me driving that far anytime soon."

"Good deal; I can return my rental and drive yours." She hesitated briefly and then nodded. Bradley recognized that nod for what it was, and like any good fisherman, set his hook. "But wait… If you pay me to do a little PR work for your business, I'll have to pay you rent, with George figured in, and a little something extra for using the car."

"I see where this is going, and I'm not about to let you work for nothing."

"Wait, just wait. I'll get to visit with our daughter, and old George will have a whole town full of Texas beauties to sweettalk. Why not call it a trade?" She opened her mouth to object, but his next point sealed the deal. "Me and George can cook, but it would just about work poor Kimmy to death cleaning up after us. Why don't you pay for somebody to come in once a week and keep the house up to your standard? Let Belinda handle it through the business."

"Alright," and her smile spilled over into laughter. "I'll only be gone a couple of weeks. From the sound of it, though, my trip may turn into a nice little vacation for you."

"You're the one who won't take help, so don't go bellyaching about the terms of our trade."

"As long as Belinda's agreeable…"

"Belinda's never agreeable, but she likes to work."

"Yes, I expect she'll take a percentage. If money won't do, I may have to swap her the clothes right off my back. That's about all I've got left after negotiating with you." This brought fresh laughter until another more pressing thought changed her demeanor entirely. "Just one more thing, Bradley. I'm assuming you trust this George Kelly around our daughter?"

"George is good people. He's never even seen Kimmy, apart from photographs, but he'd kill to protect her without a second thought."

Some might have taken this as needless exaggeration, but Laura Beth simply nodded.

"I'll fix up a plate of supper, and you can take it back to him at the hotel."

Over the next few minutes, George Kelly's plate multiplied into several dishes. Still, Bradley managed to balance them along one arm without looking at all flustered. He paused in the doorway for one more glance at his wife and daughter.

"Help your mama pack, Kimmy. She leaves for Red Bog first thing in the morning."

Without stopping to think, Laura Beth played up her reaction just a tad. What came out fell somewhere between a gasp and a huff.

"It's not very flattering, Bradley, that you'd be so anxious to get rid of me. Why, I don't even know who's taking me up there. Mother or Daddy or both will need time to make arrangements at work."

"I know you, Laura Beth. Your eyes light up at the mention of Red Bog, but if we put this off, you'll decide a day or so in bed would do just as well. Thing is, if Jimbo Pate said come home, you'd better strike out in a long trot. Bill and Margaret don't need to take a vacation day. Old George will be tickled to drive you."

"Aren't you afraid he'll turn my head?"

"George is edging into his sixties, but if he handles your Red Bog stubbornness any better than me, I wish the two of you nothing but happiness."

Bradley's offhand response to the little joke stung more than it should have, but she managed a haughty smile and then swept from the room.

Laura Beth awoke the next morning with a groan. Her body ached all over, redoubling the previous day's soreness, but it hurt her even more to admit that Bradley had been right. Her first instinct was to cancel the trip home and try not to even roll over in bed for at least twenty-four hours. However, she found it hard to escape the role Grandmother and the aunts had played in her upbringing. Laura Beth was a lady all the way to her bones, and she wasn't about to meet this friend of Bradley's looking as if she'd been run over by a car. She rose, unsteadily, and set about making herself presentable.

"No cooking this morning," and Kimmy literally planted herself in the kitchen door. "Dad says he's taking me out for breakfast and that you and George can get something on the road."

"If Bradley Chandler thinks he can just waltz in here and start telling me—"

Too accustomed to her mother for any sense of awe, the girl greeted this outburst with a roll of her eyes.

"Sit down, please, before you fall down."

"I can't sit down, Kimmy. I'll never get up again. But if you'll move out of the doorway, I think I can lean against the kitchen counter until they get here."

"Oh, Mama, I didn't know it was that bad!"

The instant worry on her daughter's face twisted Laura Beth's heartstrings.

"I'm alright, baby, just really sore. I need a Dr Pepper and maybe some Aleve. That'll go a long way toward…"

Kimmy reached out to help but then drew back, afraid to touch Mama and add to her pain. Instead, she darted to the refrigerator and then to the medicine cabinet. Dressed in her most comfortable slacks and a loose-fitting blouse, Laura Beth propped herself in an upright position and nursed the Dr Pepper until it came time to leave. At first sight of her, George Kelly swept off his battered felt hat in a courtly gesture from another time and place.

"I'm already in your debt, Mr. Kelly, for guiding Bradley down off the mountain. And then there's this trip to Red Bog. Now, to welcome you into my house without so much as a cup of hot coffee… Well, can you forgive me?

George flirted with all women, especially the pretty ones, but Laura Beth's genuine warmth and that soft southern drawl did strange things to the old mountain goat. His habitual flattery dried up and was instantly replaced with something approaching reverence.

"Nothing to forgive, little lady, and I'm glad to be of service just any way I can. Hope you don't mind making this trip with a stranger?"

"Don't worry about that, George," Bradley interjected with a grin. "You two will be thicker than thieves before you ever get out of Houston. Now, grab a suitcase."

Long and tall without an ounce of spare flesh, George scooped up some luggage in each hand. Even as he did, though, a grin broke over his face.

"You're almighty free with the orders this morning. I'm here to help Mrs.— Miss... Well, anyway, I ain't workin' for you."

"Laura Beth," she supplied with a smile. "Please call me Laura Beth. Bradley's always been too bossy for his own good. You and I will get along just fine."

"You think I'm the bossy one?"

"If you'll call me George, ma'am, I'll try for Laura Beth. Don't you pay Bradley boy no never mind. Anytime you want him tuned up a little, you just say so."

"I'm afraid it's too late for that, George, but I can already tell we're going to have a mighty pleasant trip to Red Bog."

"Excuse me, princess," Bradley quipped, "but if we can get your royal consent, George is going to drive you home in my rental. I've got the mileage to spare, and it will save wear and tear on your car. I'll pick George up at the designated return point this evening. Let him tarry long in Red Bog, and he might not leave 'til mid-summer. Oh, I put a case of Dr Pepper in the back seat."

"That's very thoughtful, Bradley, and I really do appreciate everything."

"Watch it, ma'am... You don't want to give him the big head."

Laura Beth hugged her daughter tightly despite the painful bruising.

"Enjoy the time with your dad, and remember, baby, I'm only a phone call away."

She spared Bradley a final glance and tried to hide a wince as she sank down into the rental car.

Laura Beth chattered brightly as they made their way over to Highway 59 and settled in for the trip north, but the effort cost her considerably. Her whole body ached, and she wanted nothing more than a long nap.

"Bradley tried to tell me you were special," George volunteered rather suddenly. "Come to find out, the boy never said half of it. Nothing against the general run of women, you understand. I can surely appreciate the average human female. But you… You're a lady. The difference is hard to pin down, but it's there."

"Well… You're very kind, but we'll just keep it between us so as not to offend the *general run of women*."

"Yes'm, that might work out for the best on my end."

A certain cadence in his voice marked George as a natural storyteller. Laura Beth enjoyed listening to such folks and, accordingly, steered him onto a subject that would require very little input from her.

"My granddaddy keeps black mouth cur dogs on the homeplace and uses them to gather cattle. Bradley tells me you run hounds. Do you favor certain bloodlines? I'll just bet you've got some good hunting stories, too."

That topic carried them all the way to East Texas with her drifting in and out of the conversation. Laura Beth dreaded the prospect of hauling her aching body up out of the rental car but felt a surge of contentment as familiar scenery slid sedately by her window.

"Pretty country," George observed from behind the wheel. "Kinda close and hemmed in for a mountain-raised fella, but pretty just the same."

"Thank you; we like it. Granddaddy grew up here, raising cotton, and then spent his adult life as a cattleman. When you operate that way, open ground is productive ground. He never minded a little bit of timber, something for the cattle to shade up in or use as shelter during bad weather. But he fought pine trees like the plague."

"Sure enough?"

"Mmm," she answered with a nod. "They'll take over if you let 'em. Of course… My Uncle James Allen, Granddaddy's oldest boy, claims timberland can pay better than farming or cows ever did."

"Sounds reasonable, over a good stretch of time, but the old man couldn't work no dogs in the log woods or spend his days horseback, either."

"You sized that up just about right," she admitted with a chuckle. "Yes, sir… I think you and Granddaddy are going to enjoy one another."

"I'll bet your uncle's got more in common with him than either one of them realizes. He could be working a company job somewhere, but he's out in the woods doing his own thing."

"Funny you should say that. Granddaddy is a horseman all the way to the bone, and Uncle James Allen prefers to run equipment. They've got a good relationship. Either one will pitch in to help the other when it's needed, but mostly they each stick to what they know."

"Pretty good way to do it. Only, it ain't every father who'll turn loose that-a-way. My old daddy was a bricklayer. Just about disowned me when I gave up the trade to follow hounds."

"Well," she ventured, "the life you chose is not exactly settled or predictable."

"No, ma'am," he answered with a grin. "But if I was settin' home with a lap full of grandbabies, I'd never have made it to Red Bog or got to meet you. Red Bog is one thing, little lady, but not knowing you would have been quite the loss."

She smiled warmly at the compliment and then indicated a turn up ahead.

"Here we are, just about home! Watch out going up the driveway; it's apt to be rutted if they've had any rain to speak of." Then, a tilt of her head directed his attention to a boxy frame structure across the road. "That's Granddaddy's home over yonder, where my dad and Uncle James Allen spent their childhood. I have good memories there, too, but it's kind of a bachelor camp since Grandmother passed away. He'll expect me to stay up at the house with Aunt Alma and Aunt Nadine."

Several of her relatives spelled "the house" in capital letters or, at least, managed to give that impression. After years of accommodating only family reunions and occasional guests, the old place stood ready when Alma and Nadine finally circled back.

"Well, now," George mused at first sight of the house. "That's worth comin' home to. Set up off the ground with a big front porch, just right for a passel of hounds to shade up under!"

"Careful what you wish for," she said with a fond chuckle as a barking mass of dogs rushed forward to meet the strange vehicle.

Jimbo met his granddaughter at the car and lifted her out by the hand. His work-roughened fingers showed some arthritis, but their grip remained strong. The special greeting reminded Laura Beth of being scooped from her parents' backseat as a child. Today, for the first time, she actually needed the extra help. Despite the residual soreness, Granddaddy brought her effortlessly to her feet and right into the comfort of his arms.

"How's my pretty little doodlebug?" the old man inquired when he finally stepped back for a look. "Tired, I see, but not too much the worse for wear."

"Aww, Granddaddy. You're the only one who could tell me I look like nine miles of washed-out road and not even make me feel bad about it. They say the car got dented up worse than me," she added with gentle laughter in her tone. "Meet a new friend of mine… George Kelly followed my ex-husband all the way down from Wyoming, but don't you go and hold Bradley against him."

The two men exchanged greetings and then assisted Laura Beth up on to the porch where Alma and Nadine took charge of her.

"There'll be plenty of time to visit with your granddaddy later, child," Nadine declared. "Right now, you need three things. Something simple and nourishing to fill you up, a long soak in warm water and Epsom salt, and a soft bed. The only thing you get to decide is which comes first."

"Thank y'all for letting me stay. The thing is, I don't intend to be a burden around here."

"Burden?" Nadine snorted, but Alma took over in a gentler tone.

"You're at home now, Laura Beth, and no burden a-tall."

"Thanks again, George, for everything," she said, with a smile and a helpless little shrug. "Enjoy your time with Granddaddy. It seems I've got orders to follow."

Laura Beth wondered in passing if George would cut his visit short in time to return the rental car but dismissed this concern as she settled down to rest. In fact, the pleasant murmur of male voices swapping tales on the front porch acted as her lullaby. The first dose of sleep aid kicked in, and from that point on, Laura Beth found very little need for medication.

The next few days passed in a blur. Concern for her daughter motivated short but earnest attempts at prayer. Even as she rested, guilt stirred at the edges of conscious thought. Guilt for leaving Kimmy and guilt for falling asleep midway through her prayers, but a strange sense of peace soothed her troubled heart. Her Heavenly Father understood this overpowering weariness, and more to the point, He was perfectly capable of watching over Kimmy's teenage life without her constant hovering.

Granddaddy and Aunt Nadine checked on her between daily tasks. More often, though, she felt Alma's motherly presence, adjusting the covers or smoothing stray hair away from her face. She awoke several times, determined to get out of bed and make herself useful. To her surprise and chagrin, these good intentions usually surfaced in the middle of the afternoon. With most of the day gone, Aunt Alma as the willing caregiver, and a clear need for rest, her urge to do something soon faded.

Alma and Nadine generally kept fresh milk. The same hand-dug well that might run low on wash day provided good, sweet drinking water from the kitchen faucet by way of an ancient electric pump. Bradley's parting gift ensured an adequate supply of Dr Pepper, but for the first few days, Laura Beth found it easier to simply take whatever was offered. She mustered enough energy for a bath or two, and each long soak in the tub sent her drifting back to bed.

One morning after breakfast, Jimbo stepped quietly into her room and sat down on the edge of the bed. The mingled earthy smells of horses, leather, and woodsmoke reached Laura Beth even before she felt a gentle hand on her shoulder. She awoke willingly enough, though none too quickly, and he waited until the hazel green eyes opened to gaze softly up into his own.

"Morning, doodlebug."

"Good morning, Granddaddy. I'm glad you woke me. Feels like I could just about snooze my life away, but a normal sleep schedule is probably best in the long run."

"That's how I figured it," he agreed. "What about taking a little walk with me?"

"Yes, sir, I'd like that."

"Alright, then. Get some clothes on, try to eat a bite, and we'll go."

Aunt Alma questioned the idea of taking a walk after three days and four nights in bed. Watching Laura Beth put away a small bowl of oatmeal and a cold glass of milk, though, she felt a little better.

"This is the best milk I've ever tasted," the girl commented brightly.

"No call for a whole lot of butter 'less I'm on a baking spree," Alma said with a smile, "so we get kinda lazy with the churning. That's Jersey milk, and the biggest part of it is cream. Goes down easy and gives plenty of nourishment."

Laura Beth stared blankly until Nadine offered an explanation.

"Ever since me and Alma moved home, Jimbo's kept a couple or three milk cows. By the time one dries up, another's coming fresh. It's a holdover from our childhood and a kind of hobby, I reckon."

A few minutes later, Laura Beth followed her grandfather down the back steps. The old man's chuckle made her think of leaves rustling in a gentle breeze. It came softly, but when the sound finally registered, she shot him a smile and arched one eyebrow.

"Taken as a group," he ventured by way of explanation, "horsemen and cow people don't do much walking. I was raised a farm boy, though, tromping through the fields and woods. Aunt Alma wanted me to wrap you up in a quilt and take you out on the wagon, but I figured a walk to build your strength might serve better."

"Quilt? The air's just cool enough to be pleasant."

"Yeah, and it'll warm up by dinnertime. Still, Alma's got definite notions on takin' care of sick folks."

"I'm not sick, Granddaddy."

"Maybe not, but it looks to me like you were worn to a frazzle, even before you took it in your head to stop traffic."

"I guess so," she admitted reluctantly and then changed the subject. "Wagons, milk cows, and handmade quilts… Y'all fixing to open a living history exhibit?"

"Naw… The wagon belongs to James Allen, and you ought to see that little rig. Got modern axles and rubber tires under it with springs and hydraulic brakes all the way around."

"That won't hardly do for a museum piece," she said, smiling as she slipped naturally into his way of speaking. "What's Uncle James Allen want with a wagon, even the cutting-edge variety?"

"I doubt if he ever really stopped to look at it. That boy keeps plenty of irons in the fire. His business partner, Vesper Denton, saw this wagon at an auction sale somewhere and called on the mobile phone.

Said it was just what I needed for taking the edge off salty horses without gettin' busted up. James Allen told him to buy the thing and drop it off here. With a steady mule in the team and all four wheels locked up, runaways don't last long."

"Uncle James Allen works all the time, don't he?"

"Pretty nearly, but that's the way I raised him. On a farm, you work as long as there's something to be done."

"And there is always something…"

"Sunday's the Lord's Day," he put in matter-of-factly, "but Saturday don't mean much. Ain't no harm in honest labor, doodlebug. James Allen gets plenty of fresh air out in the log woods, and he can swing by here for a hot meal whenever he thinks about it."

"Dad's got the same hard-driving attitude, only cooped up in an office."

"Mmm," he responded with a nod.

They moved along in silence for some time, and his dogs ranged ahead into a little patch of bottomland timber. Laura Beth dropped back to travel single file when necessary. As the old cow trail widened out again, she moved up beside him and voiced a troubling thought.

"How come they just keep going, but I feel so overwhelmed? Don't lay it off on fresh air and homecooked meals, either. Dad's work isn't that much different from mine. If anything, I move around more and interact with a wider variety of people. Those things are supposed to be healthy."

Jimbo kicked some good kindling loose from a knotty-pine stump and then gathered it in the crook of his arm. He could have argued, rightly enough, that neither of his sons faced the cares of life alone. They each drew strength from a loving, Godly marriage. For whatever reason, though, the old man's mind drifted farther back.

 "Scratching a living out of the ground ain't easy, doodlebug. I come up raisin' cotton through the depression. We worked hard 'cause that's what it took, but there's a difference between working hard and tryin' to do it all by yourself."

Laura Beth walked on ahead for several paces but finally turned to look back at him. A little sigh of frustration escaped, and she plopped herself down on a fallen log.

"I know that tone… You're trying awful hard to give me a little piece of wisdom, but somehow, it's going right over my head."

"The 'Elizabeth' part of your name comes from my mother. I reckon you know that?"

"Yes, sir. Elizabeth has a pretty sound. Why doesn't somebody actually use it? They called her 'Missy', from cradle to grave, and I guess 'Laura Beth' will follow me just about as long."

"Can't say one way or another 'bout use of the name, but Missy was crippled all the time I knew her. Paralyzed, I guess you'd call it."

Chapter Four

Great-grandmother Missy's disability wasn't exactly news to Laura Beth, but it tended to slip to the back of her mind.

"All those stories… Your mother comes across as quite active."

"She kept busy, wheelchair and all, but Alma and Nadine knew her before… They remember Missy as the prettiest young lady in the county. Decked out in long skirt and sidesaddle, and yet, a regular daredevil a'horseback."

"That's really something," Laura Beth murmured, eyes dancing as her imagination kicked into overdrive.

"Riding days lay behind her, time I come along, but Daddy sure had the touch with fine driving horses. He always kept her a good, fast trotter. She couldn't work cattle anymore, but we burned up the roads."

"Gave her some freedom and you a great childhood, huh?"

"The best," he agreed, "but that ain't exactly what I set out to tell you. Missy held the family together through good times and bad. Her poise and determination kept us all going. She was tenderhearted when it came to others, but I never saw her shed a tear in self-pity."

"That's wonderful, Granddaddy. But I don't need another unachievable standard to measure my failures."

"Can't you see, doodlebug? Skill and beauty and even old-fashioned grit, they'll never be enough. Missy couldn't get along all by herself. She counted on Daddy, Alma, Nadine, and me just the same as we looked to her. Big Jim Pate was kinda rough. Not tender or sentimental except with her, but he would've laid right down and died for his Missy. Any of us would, I reckon. She didn't get crippled alone, and she didn't have to live it alone."

Stories of this long-gone relative seemed a strange response to current difficulties. Even so, her grandfather's memories offered a means of escape. Laura Beth yearned for the challenge of a blank Word document and the suspended energy of fingers hovering just over her laptop keyboard. These family tales needed recording, and Missy Pate struck her as the type of strong female character who might drive an entire novel.

"Call the dogs, Granddaddy. Let's go home."

"We are home, doodlebug. I'm at home anywhere on this place. All over Red Bog, really."

"Yes, sir, but I'd better head for the house. Way I've laid around the last few days, Aunt Alma and Aunt Nadine must think I'm bone idle, unsociable, or both."

"They know better," he offered reassuringly but whooped for the dogs anyway.

"You were always a lot of fun, Granddaddy, and I developed a pretty good case of hero worship. But I don't remember you having much time for walks through the woods."

The words held an obvious question, and he offered a slow, deliberate answer as they strolled along.

"Even as a boy, I could see time running out on the East Texas cotton farmer. Missy saw it, too. She encouraged my cowboy ways in a time and place when anybody else's mother would've hung her head in shame.

"You were very close to her, huh?"

"Folks said I picked up calling her 'Missy' from Alma and Nadine," he answered, piecing together his thoughts. "But it might've been because I shared her with all of Red Bog. She was everybody's mama or daughter or sister. Only Daddy had any kind of special claim on her."

"She sounds warmhearted and lovely, but that must've been a lot for her only child to process at the time."

"Well, she was as much my Missy as anybody's. That was always good enough. Anyhow, the cow deal just seemed to fit. I courted Melba, and we settled down on the homeplace. Job market around here picked up some after World War II. Could've hired on at LeTourneau or Eastman or somewhere, but I didn't. I caught cattle for the public, played veterinary about half the time, and built up a herd of our own. Sweet Melba not only put up with it all but pitched right in to lend a hand."

"Everybody says you did what you loved, and I always admired that."

"Love it, I reckon so… More to the point, I did what I knew. Lots of days, it wasn't no picnic. Some thought I played at life like a game. Horses, cur dogs, and good times! But I never quit work at the end of a five-day week, nor an eight-hour day, either."

"And cur dogs are a breed all their own, right?"

"Why, sure. I don't mean 'cur' the way folks say mongrel or mutt but a particular type of stock dog. Had some good ones over the years, too."

"Yes, sir. But you were saying?"

"Me and Melba pushed hard just to get our boys raised. Time you grandkids come along, we could've slacked up some. Only, I didn't know how. Still had pastures scattered over the county, cows to catch for other folks, and our own hay to bale. Then, Melba died, and it shook me."

"Shook all of us," Laura Beth admitted with a poignant smile, recalling her grandmother's gentle nature and underlying strength.

"When Alma and Nadine moved back home… I cut my cows way down, turned a bunch of leases back, and quit hiring out to catch the wild ones."

Laura Beth's musical laughter stopped the old man in his tracks, and she reached out automatically for a sidelong hug.

"Oh, Granddaddy… You're a pistol! Nobody else could hear what you're saying, but I've solved the mystery. Nearly two hundred head of beef cattle, several acres of garden every summer, one or two milkers the year round, and a revolving string of outside horses to train is your idea of easy living."

"Found time for our little walk, didn't I?"

"Yes, sir! That's why I'm laughing. Only you could pull off that kind of crazy stab at retirement."

"James Allen's been after me to sell the cows, but I ain't plumb helpless yet. We buy hay these days, rather than cuttin' our own. Far as numbers go, I never did overgraze this place. Some of the trail riders, people I school horses for, have kids who like to work out here for a while. I'm on the third generation, now, and it's become a kind of tradition for some of them folks."

"They probably learn a lot from you."

"With that little bit of outside help and Aunt Alma to keep house, me and Nadine get by alright. Anymore, we're doing just about as

we please. If I was young again and scrapping out my livin' today…
I'd part ways with them Jersey cows and a good many of the horses,
too. Unroll my winter hay and feed it more like square bales so as to
make it stretch. Keep the weeds sprayed out and raise as many black
bald-faced yearlings as our grass would stand."

"A roadmap to the future?"

"Not hardly… That's just my notion of how to make this old place
pay out a little better, right here and now. Can't never tell about the
future, but anybody with intentions of stayin' on the land has got to
adapt to what works. Horse sense, backbone, and an extra helpin' of
God's grace is just about what it takes. You've got the makings,
doodlebug," he finished with a dry chuckle, "but it ain't likely you'd
ever want to take over here."

"No, sir," and her words came out on a soft sigh. "Just the same,
Granddaddy, I'll remember what you've said.

From that point on, busy days and restful nights fell into their natural
alignment. Laura Beth gathered eggs each morning, helped around
the house, and rode the pastures horseback. Vigorous activity offset
the home cooking and ever-present baked goods just a bit, giving
her newfound bursts of energy at the same time. Normal blood
pressure readings, jotted down on a notepad, proved she must be
doing something right.

Unaccustomed separation from her daughter left a nagging void, and
regular phone conversations never quite satisfied the anxious
longing of her heart. On the other hand, she enjoyed a family bond
and a kind of shared purpose that had long been missing from her
life. Jimbo Pate and his aunts worked together seamlessly. They
laughed, joked, and even squabbled, in patterns as old and well
established as the changing seasons. Laura Beth slipped naturally

into the rhythm of their daily lives with a comfortable sense of belonging.

~ ~

Bradley and the old backcountry lion hunter moved along on either side of Kimmy as she strolled happily toward her first carriage tour and other downtown attractions. George Kelly occasionally dropped back a pace or two to accommodate other pedestrians, but his long stride closed the gap effortlessly. With her dad on hand and George's refusal to spend even one whole day cooped up in the house, Kimmy's perpetual boredom had all but disappeared. Even in October, she judged the Saturday morning pleasant enough for blue jean shorts but not too warm for a nice walk.

"Mama likes seeing the horses and always points them out to me, but we've never actually taken a buggy ride."

"I don't much care if we take that drive today," old George admitted. "I just need to smell a horse, maybe lay my hand up against him for a minute, and remind myself that the world's still real. How folks live shoulder to shoulder like this is beyond me."

Bradley heard this little exchange with only half an ear. Despite an honest effort to enjoy the outing, his mind replayed snippets of conversation from the previous evening.

While George stayed in, watching John Wayne movies on television, he and Kimmy had attended a charity banquet. *Finishing Touches by Elizabeth Chandler* sponsored a table, and Belinda insisted they go. Bradley enjoyed the time with his daughter, but several young executive types called Kimmy by name and asked after Laura Beth with what seemed like more than polite concern. These up-and-coming businessmen were her contemporaries, potential customers even. Women and plenty of older folks inquired, too, but their questions triggered considerably less emotional confusion. Asking Kimmy about her mama's romantic involvements would be uncomfortable at best and seemed out of place at the moment.

"Laura Beth and I actually took a carriage ride on our very first date," Bradley volunteered, putting his inner thoughts aside to join the conversation. "She raised an eyebrow at the price of our tickets but was too sweet to call me an idiot. A horse-drawn tour of downtown Houston doesn't offer much excitement for a Red Bog girl, but I'm sure her horse savvy conversation impressed the driver."

"The driver?" Kimmy snorted. "I hope she didn't ignore you altogether?"

"Oh, I could hardly string two words together that night. You know your mama, the way she can light up and glow. I just sat on that seat beside her, soaking up the warmth.'"

"Aww…"

An intriguing question occurred to Kimmy, but they reached the carriage stop before she could ask it.

"Take your daughter for a drive," George advised quietly. "I'll stay behind and see if I can't stir up something for us to do when y'all get back."

"You do know they won't let us squirrel hunt? Not even by chunkin' rocks."

"Just get over there and buy the tickets. Leave the rest of it to me."

"Pretty horse," Kimmy enthused as she and George walked up to the animal.

"Big sucker," he grunted in return. "Percheron cross, I'd say." True to his word, George laid a gentle hand on the iron gray hide and breathed in deeply. As they pulled away in the carriage, he offered a parting piece of advice. "Tell 'em you'll pass on the tour-guide spiel, and just listen to that clip-clop."

In spite of the city noises around them, steady hoofbeats provided a measure of relaxation. Eventually, Kimmy asked her question.

"How did you and Mama meet, anyway?"

"Laura Beth wasn't exactly on board when her parents left Red Bog, but a teenager doesn't get much say in those matters. Writing helped her cope with city life, and like any aspiring young novelist, she dreamed of publishing her work. Meanwhile, she finished two years of college and hired on as an assistant to Belinda Radcliff. Belinda planned all of Mom's dinner parties back then, and I swear, Pop was the only living soul in Houston who wasn't scared to death of her."

"Belinda and Pop? I can't even picture them in the same room."

"Ever seen a trainwreck?"

"Sparks, huh? Nothing romantic, but maybe some flying debris for good measure…"

Bradley nodded, waited for her giggles to subside, and then continued his tale.

"Belinda brought in this new foreign chef that had the whole town buffaloed. He and a couple of helpers were supposed to come into your kitchen and—"

"Gran's kitchen is just about commercial size anyway."

"Yep… I don't know what went wrong, but a few hours before the party, Belinda's hot new chef lost his accent and started cussing in good, plain English. He's ranting and raving, throwing pots and pans when this petite and soft-spoken blond steps in to handle things. I don't know where Belinda had gone, but Laura Beth decided he wasn't about to come into somebody's home and act like that on her watch. Pop and I caught the very tail end of it. I suspect we both fell in love right then."

"You and Mama?"

"No, Laura Beth didn't know I was in the world. Had both hands full at the moment. I'm talking about me and Pop. She captured our hearts in different ways, of course, but it's one of the few things we agree on to this day. Mister chef kept screaming obscenities and said if she fired him, he'd never work for Belinda again. Then, the threats got personal. As I found out later, your sweet mama only knows one curse word. It's a barnyard description of manure, and by the time she's upset enough to use it, that little bitty word comes out in at least three syllables."

"I've heard it," Kimmy admitted, snorting her amusement, "but I can count the times on one hand."

"All those threats amounted to just exactly what she called them, too. Laura Beth picked up a big cast-iron pan and mister chef cut a trail. Me and Pop intended to take up for her, but he shot past before we got through laughing. His kitchen help followed at a slower pace, and Laura Beth turned bone white at the prospect of having ruined her first major event. Told Pop over and over that she'd make everything right and the evening would go off without a hitch. But he could hardly let her get the words out for making apologies of his own."

"Apologies?"

"I'd never seen such gentle concern from him and for a stranger, too.

He vowed and declared that nobody would ever talk to her that way in his presence again. Made it hard for me to get a word in edgewise, but I must've said something right."

"Well, I'm guessing she saved Gran's dinner party?"

"Not much guesswork there. That chef had several ducks on hand. Now, most duck is just barely edible, but he had done something right with those birds. Your mama mixed up a staggering amount of cornbread dressing, cooked his high-toned vegetables into actual tenderness, put in a little bacon grease for good measure, and baked buttermilk pies to serve in place of the chocolate soufflé. Mom and Belinda exchanged several pointed looks over the course of the evening, but the guests… Laura Beth's culinary style was old-fashioned enough to be brand new in certain circles, and nobody ever forgot that party."

"Great story!" Then, in a more reflective tone, "Wish y'all could've found a happy ending for it."

"We did, kiddo. You're the happy ending."

"Thanks, Dad. But that's not the same, and you know it."

By the time they returned to the drop-off point, George had secured a verbal all-access pass to the carriage company's stables. It meant a drive to the outskirts of town, but Kimmy chattered happily as they brushed and admired off-duty horses. Bradley snapped countless photos, and for no reason in particular, George explained the various parts of a driving harness. The old rascal tried to hide his delight at finding a nondescript dog hanging around the barn, but Bradley brought it up as they drove away.

"Between you and Kimmy, I had visions of us bringing that scroungy-looking mutt into Laura Beth's house this evening."

"Pshaw, he's got a good home there with horses to look out for and all them lady drivers willin' to give him most of their lunch. Still… No kid, boy or girl, ought to grow up without a dog."

"You tell him, George," Kimmy teased.

"If your mama wants a dog," Bradley countered smoothly, "she'll bring a pup back from Red Bog."

"She never has before."

"Well, there's your answer. I know you've accompanied her home plenty of times, but if you want to understand Laura Beth, you need to spend some time in Red Bog with your eyes open."

"What do you mean?"

"Late in the evening, after a day's work… She might sit for hours with some old cur dog, stroking ever so gently while its head rests in her lap. But Laura Beth Pate won't keep a dog around to feed if she don't have a job for him to do."

Back at the house, all three settled in the living room while Vida Gomez, the young woman Belinda sent over once a week, finished her work upstairs.

"Nice day," George intoned, stretching booted feet out before him. "If y'all are agreeable, I'll fix us up a good old camp breakfast in the morning."

"Sure," Kimmy decided, looking up from her sketchpad. "Just try not to start banging around in the kitchen too early."

Bradley chuckled along with them, but his nagging questions had resurfaced. Glancing around, reluctant to broach the subject, he considered a more private conversation. In the end, though, he realized that he and Kimmy had become so accustomed to George's presence that the discussion might seem less awkward with their friend in the room.

"Say, kiddo, does your mama date much?"

"Mama? She'll go out with a man sometimes. Hardly ever more than once, unless maybe it's business."

"What about the guys from last night, all those white-collar Casanovas who asked about her?"

"You mean Trevor Quinlan and Cory Stinson and Phil Mitchell?"

Before he could answer, a fit of giggles overtook her.

"What's so funny? I'm no expert on the kind of looks that attract a woman, but those boys weren't exactly mud ugly."

Vida, a Hispanic beauty in her late twenties, picked that moment to plop down on the arm of Kimmy's chair and join in the fun. Only George realized that she had heard the entire conversation from the foot of the stairs. As their laughter subsided, Vida draped an arm around Kimmy's shoulders.

"Missing her, huh?"

What sounded to Bradley like a personal taunt was in fact an innocent comment on his daughter's latest drawing. As realization dawned, he opted to make light of his momentary discomfort.

"I can take being laughed at," he announced with a grin, "but I'd sure like to be let in on the joke."

"I'm sorry, Mr. Chandler. Truly, I am."

As she spoke, Vida lifted the sketchpad gently from Kimmy's lap and turned it outward for him to see. A rocking chair on its wide verandah and much of the lady's long skirt had yet to be finished, but even from across the room, her facial features proved unmistakable.

"Bradley," he suggested, absently correcting Vida's form of address before speaking to his daughter. "That's amazing, Kimmy. Your mama will love— Oh, she'd like anything you might draw, but I—"

"Yeah," Kimmy answered softly, "I thought you might like it."

"There's no inside joke, Mist— Bradley. Your daughter probably can't give a reason for her laughter. We women just know things. But if you'll forgive the intrusion, I can try to explain."

"No intrusion… If you can explain, please do."

"You see, I know Laura Beth. I've worked with her and for her. Belinda didn't just pick somebody off the street to clean this house."

"Well, now, the average person would cross the street just to stay out of Belinda's way."

Vida snorted, even while nodding her agreement, and then continued the original conversation.

"Laura Beth is a very feminine woman, and I don't mean silly or helpless. There's an indefinable quality about her that either brings out every last bit of masculine virtue in a man or highlights his lack of the same."

"Gosh, Vida, you should be a psychologist or something."

Kimmy's words came out in an awestruck tone, but her mama's young friend responded with a gentle chuckle.

"Oh, yeah. Given enough time for observation, I can make a spot-on analysis of just about anything but my own mental tangle."

"Well, let's hear some more."

Bradley kept his request friendly but failed to mask a slight edge of challenge in his voice.

"More about… Laura Beth is warm and authentic and full of charm, but so much of what surrounds her at this point in life is artificial. She drives herself forward on sugar and caffeine and then takes pills to go to sleep at night. Mixed with all that career stress, her precious Dr Pepper creates a layer of survival fat right on the midsection. Hardly even qualifies as a belly… It is, however, one more source of worry."

"Sheesh," the teenager quipped, "if you ever feel the urge to analyze me, go ahead and skip it."

"Give me a break, Kimmy. Everybody knows your mama is a gorgeous little blond with a golden personality. Her warmth and affection are very real. But where is her dose of reality? Where's the comfort she craves?"

Bradley digested that for a few seconds and then raised his main objection.

"Look, Vida, I don't buy what you said about highlighting a man's lack of… Laura Beth is far too kind to emphasize anybody's faults without good reason."

"You misunderstand me. The obvious difference in behavior lies not with her, but in the man. Those men you met last night… Well, Kimmy's laughter said it all. If your ex-wife ever marries again, it'll take an hombre more like the Marlboro man than those junior executives. Real men are kind of scarce in her world." Having casually dismissed most of Laura Beth's dating prospects, the perceptive young woman tacked on a rather significant afterthought. "Present company excluded, that is."

~ ~

With her strength returning, Laura Beth enjoyed productive daylight hours in Red Bog, but the long evening visits took on a particular importance. They sometimes watched the sunset from rocking chairs on the porch, but the night air always sent them back to the front room. There, Jimbo, Alma, and Nadine shared childhood memories while Laura Beth typed busily on her laptop. Having heard the phrase "online" from grandchildren, Nadine teased her a little about airing family business over the worldwide web.

"Ain't no airborne internet dodgin' through the pine trees to Red Bog," Jimbo assured her, "more 'specially since we ain't paid for none."

The old man was right, of course, and Laura Beth explained her computer as an up-to-date typewriter. They might have clammed up if interviewed by a stranger, but questions from one of their own tapped a well of untold stories.

Various parts of a worn bridle lay scattered over the hearth near Aunt Nadine's chair. Giving careful attention to each task, she worked over the metallic bit with a clean rag and then applied a light coat of oil to the headstall and reins. Alma pieced yet another quilt top while Granddaddy made swift, sure passes across the whet rock with a bone-handled Case knife. Busy hands all around fostered a steady flow of conversation.

"I doubt if Missy and Big Jim said much of anything on that first evening hunt together," Nadine speculated, "not sitting around the fire with her papa and Cleve to hear. But whatever words passed between them must have been enough. They each found something in the other, and that was it."

"You were too little to know much difference," Alma reminded her sister, "but Missy came into our lives like sunshine breaking through the clouds."

Instead of resenting the interruption, Nadine leaned forward and nodded in ready agreement.

"Watch that oil," Jimbo admonished.

Pulled back into childhood by her sister's recollection, Nadine draped a bridle rein absently across the arm of her chair, and their nephew's observant gaze had caught the trailing stain.

"Jim kept us safe," Alma continued, "while Gertie Washington filled our bellies and mended our clothes. They done the best they knew how, but Missy taught us to laugh. A big sister to play with and a loving mama all rolled into one beautiful package… Topped off with fancy ribbons, just like the ones she pulled out of her own hair and then braided into ours."

"It's more of a feeling than anything based on memory, but a change came over Jim, too." Shifting her gaze to Laura Beth, Nadine smiled fondly as she continued. "Missy just seemed to brighten up the whole world, and we romped around together like four kids."

"They courted for a while and married in late summer. Jim planted his cotton then got it chopped and laid by before wedding time. Missy took a hand in everything, and the change for us girls happened overnight. She tied her horse out front just before sunup, probably the very next morning after chasing them hounds. Jim got a quick smile and a soft word or two as he headed out to the fields, but Missy descended on us like something out of a fairytale."

"And Gert was there with y'all?"

"Same as always…"

"What did she think about this fairytale princess waltzing through the door to take over?"

Despite being two years behind her sister in terms of actual memory, Nadine knew the people involved well enough to offer an explanation.

"Missy liked people. And black or white, rich or poor… They just naturally seemed to like her in return. She buttered Gert up, bragging on everything the old girl done for us. But her praise was real and genuine. So, Gert never resented the new lady of the house. No more than Tobias Washington or any of Jim's other tenants thought to question Missy's gentle oversight of their farming."

"I can see how Missy might've charmed her way past the usual resentment of a meddlesome outsider," Laura Beth ventured, speaking slowly as she formed her thoughts into a question. "Still, I would've thought Big Jim gave all the direction they needed?"

"Missy never failed to ask his opinion," Alma recalled. "It's hard to describe just exactly how the two of them worked together, but they did."

"Daddy loved the land," Jimbo asserted, taking up the explanation. "He was more comfortable outdoors than in, but I wouldn't exactly call him a born farmer. Not in the way he always described my grandfather… Daddy had rather fool with his hounds or a quick-steppin' driving horse. He bought and sold mules as a matter of course but fancy horses and fast hounds kept him pretty well occupied. Back when Missy was able to work alongside him, they even turned out some nice type riding horses."

Nadine's fingers moved deftly, reassembling the freshly oiled bridle as she offered her thoughts.

"Before Big Jim and Missy ever locked eyes, that spring night in 1920, automobiles had become a fact of life. They weren't a common sight, nor yet a novelty, but somewhere in the middle. By '25 or so, there was practically no market for fine driving horses in East Texas. Farmin' stock, mules or horses, was a different matter because pickup trucks and tractors lagged behind the family car."

"Henry Ford eventually whittled the light driving horse market down to a little bit of nothing, but Missy kinda shielded Big Jim. Shielded…" Alma paused briefly, questioning the choice of words. "No, that's not exactly right. He was too sharp not to see the facts. She just made 'em easy to ignore. Cotton and mules made our living, but a good bit of his time went into top-notch buggy horses that nobody wanted."

"I never saw anybody to equal my daddy with a young driving horse," Jimbo drawled as his mind traveled back over the years. "He wasn't no rider unless it came down to a matter of have-to, but Big Jim telegraphed something through the driving lines and his voice."

"I'm here to tell you," Nadine seconded, "he could just about teach 'em to read and write."

"Missy loved the saddle as much as Daddy liked a buggy," Jimbo continued, "but she figured out right quick what kept us going. She could judge a cotton crop as close as anybody I ever saw. Developed a kind of instinct for when and where to plant, how many extra hands we'd need to get it all picked, and so on."

"Big Jim was just too good with the horses for her to let him quit," Laura Beth surmised.

"That's right," Nadine answered softly, "and once she lost the use of her legs, a good road horse put to a light buggy offered more freedom than just about anything else."

The room went silent, and Laura Beth typed busily at her notes, but a sudden realization stopped her. She needed to address an obvious gap in her knowledge.

"What exactly happened to Missy? I assume some kind of accident paralyzed her, but…"

Chapter Five

Laura Beth's question faltered and died as the three older folks exchanged looks, communicating with their eyes. Oak logs shifted and crackled faintly in the stillness, a ribbon of sparks wafted up the chimney, and Aunt Alma finally nodded.

Despite his age and a lifetime of hard work, Jimbo rose from his chair in one fluid motion. Snapping the blade closed against his britches leg, he returned the pocketknife to its accustomed place.

"Hand me that bridle, Nadine. Might as well take it back down to the barn."

She passed him the bridle, wadded up the rags used to clean it, and got to her feet.

"I'll just go along with you."

A moment later the screen door slapped behind them, and Laura Beth crossed the room to sit on the arm of Aunt Alma's chair.

"Did I say something wrong?" she inquired softly.

"No, child… We took a little vote just now, and I lost."

"You three are pretty good at those silent consultations," Laura Beth observed with the faintest hint of a smile. "If you'd rather not talk about Missy's accident…"

"I don't mind telling you. As the oldest, I guess maybe they figure it's my place. Then, too, this is a woman-to-woman kind of talk."

Without another word, Alma rocked to her feet and led the way to a little-used space at the rear of the house. The room contained an iron daybed, an ornate writing desk, and an old but serviceable cabinet-type safe. Despite the clutter, Laura Beth took in certain details. A quilt on the little bed reminded her of Aunt Alma's work but showed considerably more wear than others in the house, almost threadbare in spots. Two coal-oil lamps sat within easy reach atop the safe. Filled with kerosene, she noted, as if ready for use. Something behind the desk caught her attention. Was it a half-forgotten antique or, perhaps, a stage prop?

"Looks like some kind of cross between a rocking chair and a bicycle," she ventured wryly.

"Folks called 'em invalid chairs," Alma explained, rounding the desk to trail her hand over the curved chairback. "Invalid, the very last word anybody would've chosen to describe Missy Pate, but she used this chair here in the house and another up at the store."

"Y'all describe her as such an active person. When? How? I mean…"

"February 4th, 1928, and cold as all get-out," Alma began in a far-off tone. "I'll never forget that night as long as I live."

"Granddaddy's birthday," Laura Beth murmured, and her mind groped for the missing details as she began piecing things together.

"Jim and Missy waited almost eight years for a child. Well, I say they waited. Me and Nadine never thought of our little family as anything but complete. They loved us like their own. Still, looking back on it, I imagine they liked the idea of a Pate boy. Jimbo finally came, a great blessing in all our lives, but his birth… It cost Missy, and it cost her dearly."

As she spoke, Alma moved over to the bed and patted the quilt in unspoken invitation.

"How sad," Laura Beth murmured as she settled into place, "but surely Granddaddy doesn't blame himself?"

"No, we raised him better than that. Thing is, Missy in the chair is all he ever knew. Nobody talked about what happened, and like you, Jimbo naturally figured she got into some kind of mishap with a horse."

"Oh, no."

"He knows the truth, now, and he wants you to know. Just left the telling to me."

"Like I said, Aunt Alma, if you don't want to rake over painful memories…"

"Life ain't always pretty, and I've known too many blessings to shy away from the rough parts at this late date."

"Yes, ma'am. I'm listening."

"Missy suffered a good deal with female trouble, but we never saw it slow her down much."

"Menstrual problems?"

"Of course, child. That kind of thing was pretty well closed off as a topic of conversation. Maybe a few days out of each month, she favored a buggy over her sidesaddle or might even stay indoors. Whatever the trouble was, eight years passed before me and Nadine ever heard her mention a baby. When the announcement finally came, we had gotten up big enough to be excited about it. I don't remember feeling even a little bit of jealousy."

"Jealousy hardly seems out of the question, but Big Jim and Missy probably reassured y'all."

"Oh, yes. For a couple of orphan girls, we grew up with plenty of love and security. We all worked hard, but Big Jim and Missy played alongside us just like a couple of kids. She softened his rough edges some and knew how to read our big brother's moods. He was a father figure, alright, and just crazy enough that we felt mighty well protected."

"Protected?"

"Red Bog was, and is, a fine community made up of good people. What few rough customers we had knew Jim Pate, and they walked mighty soft around his little sisters. As you come to understand those early years, you'll see how the prospect of a baby only added to our joy."

"Y'all looked forward to his arrival, I suppose."

"Pregnancy just wasn't talked about in those days, 'specially not outside the family, but me and Nadine could hardly contain ourselves. We didn't care anything about Santy Claus in '27, too anxious to hold our baby! Being the oldest, I caught a few whispers and worried glances between Eva and Annette, but Missy always shut 'em down right quick. Like I said, that February night was bitter cold. Young Dr. Brown rushed out here, Eva and Annette too. Cleve and Papa Kimbel rode herd on Jim while he paced like a caged wildcat."

"Sounds just about right for a new father."

"You never knew Big Jim. He and Missy were quick-thinking, quick-moving people right from the start. The war left its mark on him, too. Folks said he favored ready-rolled cigarettes and the occasional cigar mainly because he never stopped smokin' long enough to fool with loose tobacco and papers. Eva and Annette left their little ones with Cleve's wife, but Missy wouldn't let 'em send us over there."

"I imagine Gert was on hand?"

"Yes, Missy wanted it that way. Don't get the wrong idea about Eva and Annette. They were our sisters, and devoted enough. They loved Missy, too, but tended to give her a hard time. Full of advice, you know… Once Missy made a decision, Gert just said yes'm and got right to it. Little girls grew up sheltered, even on the farm. Still, I knew that was a-way too much blood. I wasn't supposed to see, anyhow. But that first glimpse scared the voice right out of me, and I went unnoticed there in the doorway."

"Oh, Aunt Alma, you must have been petrified."

Dismissing the childhood terror with a quick shake of her head, Alma went on with the story.

"I can't imagine how Missy must've hurt, and yet she came right back to herself. Weak as a ragdoll, but five or ten minutes after Jimbo arrived, she took the situation in hand. Dr. Brown gave her the bad news, and she quizzed him pretty good. Aside from the obvious, he said the baby was healthy and strong and Missy herself must be too hardheaded to die. She nodded and even mustered up a little smile for him. 'I know you did all you could, Doctor, but my Jim ain't likely to take this news sittin' still. You best head on home, and let me do the telling. Don't come back, either, until I send for you.'"

"The obvious? He told her she would never walk again, and she processed all that without shedding a single tear?"

"Spent herself bringing Jimbo into this world, I reckon. At that point, she had neither time nor energy for tears. She caught sight of me in the doorway about that time and motioned me over for a look at the baby. All my excitement had gone, somehow, and I couldn't even take a peek. Just buried my face against her neck and sobbed out something about all that blood."

"With everything else to take in, I guess physical traces of her recent ordeal had yet to register."

"Maybe so, but my fearful questions brought her around right sharply. 'Run get some fresh bedsheets, Gert. Slip these out the backdoor and burn 'em. Then go ask Tobe to ring the dinner bell a good crack so as to welcome young Mister Pate.'"

"Some kind of tradition?"

"Just Missy's notion… She told us to sponge her clean and set the room in order. Sent after a glass of Papa Kimbel's peach brandy, too, only time I ever saw her take a drink. Then, she goaded Eva into slappin' her across the face."

"I've heard of slapping the baby's bottom, but why slap Missy? Especially after all she'd been through…"

"To bring back some color, I reckon. Eva hemmed and hawed, but I'll never forget Missy's smiling little jab. 'You've wanted to do it for months; better not miss a chance like this.' Eva drawed back and whacked the daylights out of her coming and a-going but then fell down there beside me crying harder than I was. Poor Missy, half dead, and she had to comfort us."

~February 1928~

Tendrils of smoke from a hastily extinguished Chesterfield followed Jim Pate as he strode into the room. Kneeling at the bedside, he gazed almost reverently on his wife and baby.

"Just look at him, Missy girl. Times, I wanted to cut my own throat for puttin' you at risk, But he's near about perfect. A fine baby boy!"

"Another Jim Pate, my love. Why, no other name would do for our baby. Pull up that rockin' chair, and I'll hand him to you."

"Hold him? Me hold that perfect little baby? After you done all the work…"

"You're his daddy, ain't you?" she asked with a rather exhausted but loving chuckle. "You'd think my part in this was some kind of magic trick."

She no sooner got him settled with the baby in his arms than he tried to jump up again.

"I'd best call your Papa in here before he busts a gusset."

"Sit still, now. Still and quiet so you don't upset little Jimbo."

"Jimbo Pate; I like the sound of that. Hand me them driving lines, Jimbo. Hop down, Jimbo, and get the gate."

"Yes, well, that'll have to wait a few years." She grinned at his eager anticipation of working alongside their son, but the smile finally flickered and died. "Right now… I need to give you a piece of news, and you've got to set there and take it. Something didn't go just right. Vincent says— Well, he's doubtful I'll ever walk again."

Jim remained perfectly still, and his mind refused to take in the words.

"You don't walk now," he finally snorted. "I bring your horse to the front door, or send somebody around with him. Up into the saddle and off you go."

"Careful; don't squeeze the baby so tight." She spoke as if trying to gentle a wild-eyed colt with her voice. "If he's right, and I reckon he is… There'll be no more strolling out to my horse. No more sweeping gracefully into a room. I can't leave this bed on my own. Can't so much as stand."

"Vincent Brown had better set his house in order," he spat in response. "What's he supposed to be, a doctor or a butcher?"

"Steady down; no call to rile the baby. The good Lord moves in mysterious ways, my love. You know as well as I do He's got a reason. Bad as this looks, He could be keeping me from something worse. Cleve always did say I'd break my own neck someday. Then again, maybe the Lord's setting me up as a stronger witness. Raking poor Dr. Brown over the coals won't do a bit of good. Our baby's gonna need you, Jim, and so am I."

He leapt to his feet and thrust the baby at her. Missy reacted with a sudden intake of breath, but Jim gathered them both into his arms.

"Oh, my girl," he sobbed brokenly. "My poor brave darling. Young Dr. Brown didn't do this to you, I did."

"Hush, now. I won't hear it! You go blaming yourself, and next thing, you'll up and blame our baby or even God Almighty. I'm not going anywhere, Jim Pate. We've got a son to raise. There'll be days I might cry for my horse and for the wind in my face, but I'll not live my life in bed or be any more of a burden to you than I can help."

"I'm a fool, Missy, but not fool enough to blame God for what's happened or to ever count you as a burden. Your poor little body tried to tell us. We knew the risks but turned a blind eye. Ain't nobody to blame but me."

"Now, Jim… When did I ever draw rein on Laddie just because the ground got rough? When did you ever pull back from a task just because somebody said it couldn't be done? It ain't in our nature; that's all. Run show everybody the baby, and send them home. Papa, too. I'll tell him tomorrow. You send them all home and come lay down here beside me. Hold me close, love, and I can face anything."

Jimbo stopped short. Rather than enter his mother's long-neglected office, he rested a hand on the doorjamb and surveyed the scene before him. Ordinary enough in appearance, the wiry little horseman always seemed to fill up a room.

"Thought I might find y'all holed up in here." His gaze lingered briefly on the old wheelchair and then shifted to his granddaughter's face. "Didn't mean to run off, doodlebug, but I reckon Aunt Alma got you up to speed."

"Yes, sir… We covered a lot of ground while you and Aunt Nadine hung up that bridle."

"Checked things around the barn, too," he insisted with a touch of humor in his voice. "I left Nadine shakin' some popcorn over the stove. Let's drift into the kitchen and help her eat it."

"I figured this talk was coming," Alma observed as she closed the rarely used door. "Even dusted Missy's little office yesterday."

Aunt Nadine gave Laura Beth a smile, offering unspoken reassurance, and allowed Jimbo to take up Alma's story as they settled around the kitchen table.

"Time I got big enough to know anything, life at Red Bog had slipped into well-established patterns. Work the ground and put in a crop. Thin the plants to a good stand and plow the grass out. Pick cotton, settle accounts, and start again. With Missy overseeing it all like some kind of attending angel…"

"Easy enough to keep busy," Laura Beth ventured with a raised eyebrow.

"He ain't told the half of it," Nadine snorted. "Just living day to day meant cutting and splitting wood, hauling water, cooking meals on a wood stove, and keeping us kids in clothes. Big Jim bought and sold mules all the time and trained his horses, too. Missy kept Papa Kimbel's books as well as ours, helped in the store, and generally looked after the old gentleman. Of course, he looked after us, too. Me and Alma got us a grandfather by way of our Missy."

"Despite all that," Alma remembered, "most everybody found plenty of time for church. Sunday School and preaching, revival meetings, singing schools, and cemetery cleanings with dinner on the ground…"

"Don't forget about the hands, either," Jimbo added, smiling faintly at the recollection of all his parents might confront in a single day. "Six families, give or take. If anybody got sick or hurt or worried… From jail, they sent for Mister Big Jim, but any other time they wanted Missy."

As Laura Beth considered the never-ending round of unmechanized farm life, she developed a deeper understanding of Alma, Nadine, and Jimbo. No wonder they still found time and energy for whatever tasks came to hand and then went looking for others, witness the homemade butter on her popcorn. But before she could voice these thoughts, Granddaddy spoke again.

"Something in Missy's personality, a kind of spark, set her apart. Over the years, the chair somehow blended into that. This was Missy Pate… Why would anybody expect her to get around just like other folks?"

"She was a born manager," Nadine remembered. "Eva and Annette found her a little bossy. Maybe a few others did, too, but Missy was sweet and loving and so much fun! Most everybody just naturally wanted to please her. Take me, for example. I hate housework, always have, but doing something for Missy made it worthwhile.

She taught me enough to be a decent homemaker but also gave me the special privilege of riding Laddie. Taking her horse out because she couldn't anymore."

They fell silent then, content to enjoy their memories and watch the wheels turn in Laura Beth's mind. Alma offered one last comment as they finally left the kitchen.

"Missy taught both of us girls everything a young lady was supposed to know in that day and time, but she knew which one took to housework. She trusted Nadine with Laddie and Laddie with a ten-year-old child because both of 'em needed those rides."

The next morning found Laura Beth lingering over breakfast. She toyed absently with a final piece of bacon, but the first Dr Pepper of the day took priority. Her full tummy triggered a fuzzyheaded sense of contentment, and Laura Beth sat quietly while the caffeine worked its magic. Predawn drowsiness, pleasant though it was, vanished when Granddaddy took an unexpected phone call. The rotary dial phone broadcasted Uncle James Allen's voice as plainly as if he stood in the kitchen alongside them.

"That Vesper Denton's gonna help me right into the poorhouse! If something's too cheap, Daddy, he just can't pass it up."

"Steady, now, son. What's he done this time?"

"Went down around Martinsville to look at a Beagle pup and bought eighty-some-odd head of long-eared, crossbred cattle instead. Wild as deer, and he bought 'em with my money. Half mine, anyhow."

Jimbo stood listening with one shoulder propped against the wall and the receiver held firmly to his other ear. All at once, he quit messing with the telephone cord and pushed off the wall to stand upright.

"Why, sure he did, son. That-a-way, he knew we'd catch 'em."

Laura Beth took in both sides of the conversation and felt a definite change come over the room. Not quite excitement… Gathering cattle had once been an everyday occurrence for her grandfather at certain times of the year, and it remained a fairly common chore. She finally chalked this new energy up to shared purpose and maybe the jolt of a sudden change in plans.

"Too wet to get much done in the log woods today," James Allen admitted reluctantly. "Can you meet us down there? I'll need a horse to ride. Ask Aunt Nadine if she'll come, too."

"Say," the old man observed with a chuckle, "Vesper's cow deal's got you stirred up sure enough if you're aiming to ride after them yourself."

"Nadine's eighty-six years old, Daddy, and you ain't so very far behind her. How would it look for me to send y'all out after… Just bring that extra mount."

"I'll bring you a good horse, son. There won't be any leaving Nadine at the house, but I just might talk Laura Beth into coming, too."

"What a crew! Still, you and them dogs never did need much help. Y'all come on down. Meet me somewhere 'round the post office, and we'll see what can be done."

In short order, Laura Beth found herself perched on the bench seat between Granddaddy and Aunt Nadine. Four horses shared space in a gooseneck trailer, and an indeterminate number of dogs crowded the truck bed.

They drove south to the tiny town of Martinsville, Texas, and Laura Beth stepped out of the truck to hug Uncle James Allen. She judged the business partner to be a good deal older than her uncle and younger, although considerably less agile, than Granddaddy. Broad in the shoulders but running mostly to belly, he spoke with all the easy assurance of a longtime friend.

"I'll swan, Jimbo… Anybody calling hisself a cowman ought to invest in a longer trailer."

Laura Beth pegged Vesper Denton as what the older folks called a character, mainly because Granddaddy met his half-jesting complaint with tolerant good humor.

"When I had this thing built, Vesper, the next step up was a stock car on the railroad. Nowadays, it's all the trailer I need. I quit hiring out a long time ago."

Vesper's distinctive high-pitched drawl carried enough country twang to make even Jimbo sound as generic as someone on the evening news, and his eyes twinkled with mischief.

"Yessir, I know that. But the check that bought this bunch had James Allen's name printed right under mine."

"Well, then, I reckon we'd best go get 'em."

"That Vesper's something else," Laura Beth remarked as they caravanned down a narrow blacktop road.

Despite his little jab about the sixteen-foot trailer, Vesper and James Allen each pulled a longer rig to make up the difference.

"He is that," Jimbo admitted, "but likeable just the same. Vesper brings his Beagles out to the house and runs 'em. Cur dogs were a part of my work for years and years. I just can't seem to give 'em up, but I've got enough of Big Jim Pate in me to enjoy a good hound race."

"Vesper brags on Alma's cooking and mine, too," Nadine chimed in. "Times, I think he'll eat us out of house and home. But he's just about the only one who takes time to stop by anymore. Aside from our young pastor and his sweet little wife…"

"A new pastor?"

"That's right, sweetheart. Brother and Mrs. Hays moved up to Arkansas. Settled near their daughter and her family… We get a letter from 'em now and again."

"How come I haven't been to church?"

Nadine's eyes lit with a familiar twinkle right before she pounced.

"Well, now, I reckon that's between you and the good Lord."

"I go to church! Occasionally… Come on, now. You know what I mean. Why haven't I gone with y'all?"

"You slept through a chance or two when you first got here, but tomorrow's Wednesday night prayer meeting. If you're rested enough to ride out after cattle, I reckon you're plenty able to hold down a pew."

"You're right as usual, Aunt Nadine. You and that sneaky sense of humor…"

They followed the other vehicles into an overgrown pasture, and Laura Beth stepped out to close the gate. As she hopped back into the cab, Jimbo brought their conversation full circle.

"Folks don't hardly visit around the way they used to, but ain't nobody told Vesper."

Father and son worked together, arranging the portable panels which nearly always hung along the sides of Jimbo's trailer. While that went on, Vesper found it convenient to pass the time of day with

Nadine and introduce himself to Laura Beth.

"So, you're Billy Boy's daughter! And every bit as pretty as I heard tell."

Laura Beth knew for a fact that Vesper Denton couldn't have met her father any more than ten times in as many years, but the family nickname rolled easily off his tongue.

"How nice of you to say so," she offered vaguely.

Vesper acknowledged this with a nod, and his conversation ambled on, slow but unstoppable, like syrup from a leaky jar.

"Why, I've heard Miss Alma and Miss Nadine say it a many a time. Your granddaddy, too. They claim you're a livin' image of the old lady."

"Old lady?"

"Missy, they called her. Missy Pate… The way I take it, you're built something like her, got the same hair, same green eyes, and a lot of the same features to your face. Something else, too, but nobody's quite put their finger on it. Might be a good dose of the old lady's spunk."

Pleased but caught off guard, Laura Beth stood there speechless. Before she had time to really take in these remarks, Granddaddy called for her attention.

"Tighten your cinch and step aboard, doodlebug. Let's go to work."

Laura Beth never broke her horse out of a walk. Even the more experienced riders seldom needed anything faster, but her pulse quickened as she watched Jimbo Pate ply his trade. He might be seventy-nine years old with stiff, achy joints. But he was a cowboy and very much at home in his element.

Young and able bodied with enough riding experience to stay on her horse, Laura Beth set her mind to be a help and not a hindrance. Even as she focused on the new and exciting task of gathering cattle, thoughts of Missy remained. Did she really look like her great-grandmother? As far as she could recall, no one had ever mentioned a resemblance, but Vesper Denton, even though a comparative stranger, seemed absolutely positive.

The joy of watching Granddaddy work brought with it a new understanding of Missy's great loss. Having raised a son hardheaded and tough enough to be at ease in the saddle as he approached his eighth decade, Missy Pate surely valued her independence. Without a doubt, the sudden restriction of movement turned her body into a prison.

Laura Beth blinked away tears and stroked the horse's neck. She saw Missy's spark in Granddaddy. Had seen it all her life, really. And Vesper claimed she had inherited this unidentifiable quality, a certain something that drew others in with a contagious love of life. How could there be any truth in that? Hardly even a week ago… She had struggled to get out of bed every morning, be a mother to her little girl, and run her business to its full potential.

Chapter Six

Shaking off the fog of self-doubt, Laura Beth shifted her weight in the stirrups. She counted herself blessed to inherit even a little of Missy's grace and beauty. As for grit and determination, only time would tell. For now, she chuckled and hid a grin as Granddaddy scolded his dogs for the least little infraction.

"You better get outta that" or "Get around there".

A certain gruffness did little to disguise his obvious pride, and he surely knew how to use those dogs. Rather than wearing out horses and riders, Jimbo held everyone back and gave his pack of curs time to do their work. They bayed the Brahman-cross cattle into a fairly compact knot. Jimbo sat his horse, observing patiently as first one high-headed old cow and then another broke ranks. These bunch quitters generally came back with a dog swinging from each ear and shoved their way to safety at the center of the herd. Finally, the old man shook himself and seemed to straighten in the saddle.

"Fan out, now, and take 'em in easy. If Vesper ain't standing in the gate, this just might go our way."

Far from blocking the gate, Vesper Denton hovered safely on the other side of his truck until the last cow funneled into the makeshift pens. He knew when to make his move and did so faster than Laura Beth would have imagined him able. Rounding the truck, he hurried over and drug the last panel into place. Still wheezing from his unaccustomed sprint, he plucked a cigarette from behind one ear, rested the other hand on a knee, and grinned up from this stooped posture.

"Money in the bank!"

"I don't trust no bank made of forty-year-old panels and balin' wire," James Allen shot back. "Not when our money's got legs and a shaky disposition. Better let Daddy ride in there. He's the only one might can sort off a trailer load at a time without spillin' the whole mess."

"Aw, quit your bellyaching, James Allen. I figured me and you could load cattle a'foot without stirrin' things up too much." The younger business partner drew a sharp breath for his retort, but Vesper opened the gate once more, talking all the while. "If the boss man's willing, though, it'll sure save my wind."

"Doodlebug," Jimbo called over his shoulder, "you and Aunt Nadine take them dogs to water and then let 'em lay up somewhere."

The old horseman worked smoothly and quietly, not sorting cattle by age, sex, or quality but instead cutting out a load at a time to send up the chute.

"Well, Jimbo… You're plenty old enough to be losing a step or two, but I can't tell it. That little trailer loadin' exhibition took you nine minutes."

Jimbo acknowledged Vesper with a quick grin before his attention turned elsewhere.

"Op'n the gate and let me out, son. Two trips with them long trailers ought to get it, and mine ain't big enough to do you much good. Me and the girls can just wait here so as to pen 'em again if they tear out before y'all get back."

"He's awful quick to volunteer you, Aunt Nadine, but you're welcome to come along with me and get off that horse for a while."

Nadine exchanged a quick glance with Jimbo before she stepped down and handed over her bridle reins.

"Sounds like a good idea. I'm right behind you."

"Say, Vesper," Jimbo called just before the diesel motors roared to life, "bring us a bucket of chicken."

"Ain't nobody works cheap these days," the likeable scoundrel grumbled by way of an answer, "but I reckon we can manage that."

Jimbo and Laura Beth dismounted in a pleasant, sheltered spot at some distance from the pens.

"I've enjoyed the day, Granddaddy," she began hesitantly, "but if I can do all of this, I should probably be getting back to work."

"You're a grownup lady, now. I can't hold you here, but I've got to ask."

"Ask me what?"

"Not to make the same mistakes over again just because you're feeling a little better. You'll go back down there, get caught up in the daily rush, and forget all about taking care of yourself."

"I never said I wanted to leave, Granddaddy. I said I probably should. Don't misunderstand, my heart's yearning to get back to Kimmy. As for the rest of it… Well, I can't be a responsible parent without earning a decent living for us. I enjoy my career well enough, but sometimes it feels like I'm running up hill and never getting anywhere. Listen to me whine over these so-called problems," she moaned, turning away from him to bow her head against the horse's shoulder. "How did Missy ever do it?"

"How did Missy do what, doodlebug?"

Holding on to the gelding's mane as if for an anchor, she turned just enough to speak to him.

"From the little I know, Granddaddy, it seems awfully sudden. She's tearing across the country horseback. Then, all at once, she can't even stand and needs help with every little task. Can't so much as clean herself or dress herself or make love to her husb—" Heat rushed into Laura Beth's face, and she stammered for a moment before plunging ahead. "Missy couldn't even walk alongside you for your first steps. How did she take all that and stay in her right mind? Much less go on being the lovely, vibrant southern belle and everybody's favorite!"

Jimbo raked up some loose dirt with the toe of his boot and then slowly walked around the horse to lock eyes with his granddaughter across the saddle.

"Let's talk about you, doodlebug, and then we'll get back to Missy. You like your line of work, and if you don't necessarily love it, there's lots of folks in that boat. Your problem ain't so much what you're doing as what all you're taking on by yourself."

"I know, Granddaddy. I know, but if you're telling me to go out and chase another wedding ring, it'll never happen. I loved one man. Guess maybe I still do… What happens if a young lady falls in love, orchestrates her fairytale wedding, has a precious child, and then realizes her husband's not interested in happily ever after?"

"Now, Laura Beth. I'm not telling you to jump up and remarry. What I meant was to have good people around you and let them tote a part of the load. Kinfolks, church family, friends and neighbors, or even some good hired help. That last might be kinda scarce because you naturally expect folks to work as hard as you. Most of 'em just ain't gonna do it. And on the marrying subject… Don't close your heart and mind to whatever the Lord may have for you."

"It's almost funny… I do expect people to work hard, to give everything a hundred and ten percent. Nobody in my adult life ever met those expectations, and then I came home to find that you and the aunts can still work circles around me."

"We work hard," he admitted, "but none of us ever got frazzled enough to step out in front of a car."

"Oh, Granddaddy…"

"Old age ain't easy. To quote my daddy, 'Time'll teach you to do what you can and let the low side drag'. There's not a lazy bone amongst us, but we back off a little more with every year that passes. We depend on each other more, and most of all we depend on the Lord."

"I'm not sure how to achieve a permanent solution," she admitted, "how to develop the support system I obviously need. In the short term, though, I think I'll just hang around a little while longer. Finding new people is hard work, so why not stay in Red Bog where my people are. And now that you've got what you wanted all along… Can we please talk about Missy?"

Jimbo gave her saddle a quick slap by way of invitation and then turned to his own horse. He gathered the reins, stuck a foot in the stirrup, and swung his leg over the cantle. Not knowing what else to do, Laura Beth followed suit.

"My mother was one of a kind," he began after they had ridden a good little piece toward the back of the pasture, "but she'd settled into the chair and all before I got big enough to know much."

"Still, Granddaddy, you knew her better than anyone living," Laura Beth challenged, urging her horse up alongside for easier conversation. "You and Alma and Nadine… Hard as it may be, I really need to hear this. How in the world did she do it?"

"Missy had her faith, and she had the kind of grit that's bred into most countryfolk. She just didn't know how to quit. I'm sure there were struggles that us kids never saw. Might be daddy knew the whole story… They depended on each other absolutely, even before her trouble. She could let him see the hurt and still be Missy."

"Let him see the hurt," Laura Beth murmured. "Was she in physical pain on top of the emotional struggle?"

"Hard to say, doodlebug. I ain't no doctor, but Missy's paralysis wasn't the kind you'd get from a busted backbone. Anyhow, she wasn't a full-fledged para…"

"Paraplegic?"

"That's right. She got these shooting pains up through her lower back from time to time. You could tell when they hit her, but even that never stopped our Missy for long. She'd just take a breath, smile, and go on. The good side of it was, she had some feeling in her feet and legs. Not all the feeling, you understand, but enough so she didn't want her toe stomped."

"I see," Laura Beth answered with an unwilling giggle.

Sometimes a girl laughs just to keep from crying, and the twinkle in Granddaddy's eyes gave her permission. In the next breath, though, the seriousness of their discussion resurfaced.

"According to what they think now… Missy's trouble came from torn muscles, detached ligaments, and some sort of blockage restricting blood flow. People who ought to know say modern medicine could fix her right up."

"Advanced imaging and surgery?"

"Yeah; I expect so. Missy felt her body quit answerin' to her will and then heard a doctor say she'd never walk again. She set her mind to face things as they were and wasted no time trying to undo irreparable damage."

"That's understandable. Still, the need for daily care must have come as quite an adjustment for her."

"Missy was a little bitty thing, like you, but fairly strong in her upper body and arms. Gertie Washington helped out some. Aunt Alma and Aunt Nadine, too. Daddy nearly always bathed her himself. He might let somebody else fetch water and heat it on the stove, but no more. Her bath became a very tender, private time."

"So sweet… Good for both of them, I'm sure."

They rode along in an easy walk until Jimbo swung his horse around in front of hers, causing a sudden stop.

"They say young folks'll talk about anything. Well… I didn't come up that-a-way, but I'll lay it out straight. Big Jim Pate, my daddy, was a good man. Even so, his wartime service and high-strung nature made a mighty poor combination. Everybody knew he had that reckless streak."

"I don't quite—"

"Don't like tellin' off on nobody, doodlebug, much less my own daddy. But I need you to understand Big Jim as a wild, rough individual. Had an occasional fondness for whiskey, and he was unpredictable enough cold sober. Never quite let it get the best of him like some men, but I've seen times we all wondered."

"Yes, sir?"

"Tightknit community like ours, sooner or later, everything gets back to the family. One thing I never heard tell of was him so much as lookin' at another woman. Don't you worry none about Big Jim and Missy as man and wife. I reckon they got by alright."

Jimbo's cues to his horse, developed and refined over a lifetime, were all but invisible. Their sudden spin and departure, on the other hand, made a definite impression. He checked the forward rush after just a few strides, allowing Laura Beth to trot up to him.

"I know that discussion wasn't easy… Thank you, Granddaddy."

The two retraced their path in silence, but before they neared the pens, Jimbo shook out a small loop at the end of his catch rope. Nylon sang as he arced it up and back down again in a whip-like motion.

"Come in here. Come in here," he repeated in a low, guttural command. "Hold steady… Now, then." Sure enough, his little pack of dogs quit ranging out around the riders and gathered in a knot behind his horse. "That'll keep 'em from meddling them trapped cattle."

"You never told me I looked like her," Laura Beth ventured quietly.

"Way Alma and Nadine carried on over it, I thought you knew. 'Bout the cutest little girl I ever did see. As you grew up, though, a deeper kind of beauty rose to the surface."

"How much resemblance can you actually see?"

"My boyhood memories are of Missy in her thirties, and you're there now. Same pretty face, same hair, same sparkling eyes… You could've passed for her sister."

"Really?"

"The Missy I knew had already softened some with age. Got a little thicker through the waist, too, just like you've done."

"Yeah, well, at least she had an excuse," Laura Beth answered on a halfhearted snort of laughter.

"I didn't mean anything by it, doodlebug. You're a-way too hard on yourself, and even that's like her."

"She couldn't possibly get much exercise."

"Naw… Daddy, or some of the rest of us, carried her in our arms. Up and down the porch steps or out to her buggy or anywhere them invalid chairs wouldn't go, but Missy pretty well kept herself on a diet before most folks around Red Bog ever thought of such."

"A perpetual diet on top of everything else," she sighed. "I'd say Missy had the patience of Job and a stubborn streak fit for one of her mules."

~May 1934~

Missy Pate handled the sleek black gelding with a light but positive touch, and six-year-old Jimbo perched happily on the buggy seat beside her. A skittish sorrel mule ranged out in front, far enough to avoid pressure from behind but near enough to chance an occasional kick at the trailing farm collie.

They made good progress until a Model A Ford rounded a curve in the dirt road, inadvertently turning their mule back. Missy swung her buggy whip in vain as the mule passed and wished yet again for the long-gone rush of an agile horse beneath her.

Big Jim Pate harbored a kind of unspoken resentment against motorcars for cutting into his once lucrative driving horse trade, and Missy simply dismissed the loud contraptions. Foot feeds and stiff clutch pedals proved more or less inaccessible while a nice trotter offered partnership and some level of independence. Automobiles were seldom discussed at home, but even little Jimbo recognized

By the Light of a Memory 98

this one. Uncle Cleve's flashy green roadster, three or four years old now, stood out among the more common black cars.

"Beg pardon, Missy," and a familiar face grinned up at her from behind the wheel.

"Never you mind; Shep won't let her get far."

"How come you tryin' to push loose stock ahead of that buggy, anyhow?"

"Oh, I intended to lead the mule along behind. Fella never could hem her up close enough to catch, so I finally told him to turn her out in the road."

"I know that mule… All you've got to show for a bad debt? Ain't no wonder a certain somebody couldn't catch her. Jimbo's not quite big enough to get in there and do it, so the rascal figured to have you over a barrel. Found out different, I see."

"Don't go jumpin' to conclusions 'bout that mule," she hedged. "Undersized and half wild to boot… He kept the better one and sold this'n to buy seed."

"I'm just gambler enough to've furnished the seed myself. Passin' good farmer if he ever puts his mind to it."

"Now, Cleve, you'd best not meddle in my business."

Missy favored her brother-in-law with a sunny smile, but he caught the warning behind her gentle humor.

"One thing, Missy… I ain't near as scared of Big Jim as some folks 'round here."

"Is that a fact?" Without waiting for his answer, she arched an eyebrow and spoke again. "What about me?"

"Well, now," he answered with a chuckle, "Could be I didn't think 'at plumb through. I'll just go and see about your mule."

"Quit blocking the road," Missy teased," throwing a glance over her shoulder. "Shep's a-coming with her now."

"Hop down, Jimbo, and give me a hand. We'll just catch her as they come by and tie her on behind."

Reacting quickly, Missy reached under the seat for a halter and lead. She passed them to Cleve with a smile and watched in satisfaction as the boy and dog hazed their quarry into a steep roadside bank for him to catch.

"That'll do, Shep," and the dog wagged his tail as she spoke. "You done good, son. Much obliged to your Uncle Cleve, too."

"Take note of our rankin' order, Jimbo," Cleve shot back with that familiar twinkle in his eye. "Old Shep topped us both. Say," he continued before Missy could protest, "I've got a juicy little piece of news if anybody's interested."

"Family news?"

"Don't know about you, Missy, but I ain't claimin' no kin to Bonnie and Clyde."

Jimbo gazed up at his uncle, interested, but his mother cleared her throat as if to brush away this slight annoyance.

"I don't care if I ever hear another word about Bonnie and Clyde. That kind of mischief is exactly what your infernal gasoline buggies are good for. If Clyde Barrow had to stand and fight, I reckon he'd think twice before taking what other folks have worked for."

"Now, Missy… There's been robbin' and killin' plumb back to the dawn of creation. Don't you go blaming the automobile."

"Yesterday's badmen ran loose for a time… By and by, somebody'd fall in behind 'em with a faster horse."

Missy went silent then, glancing pointedly at her young son, and Cleve got the message. He turned to rummage in his car for a moment, produced a collapsible tin cup, and flipped it open.

"Ain't no shade along this little stretch of road," he told Jimbo in an easy, lighthearted tone. "I've kept your mama out in this heat a-listening to me jaw. Cut across yonder, down to the spring, and fetch her a cool drink of water."

As much as the boy longed to hear more about famous outlaws, he knew better than to question the adults in his life.

"Yes, sir."

"Faster horse or not," he continued as his nephew ducked under the bottom wire and into the roadside field, "they got Bonnie and Clyde this morning. Over around Gibsland, Louisiana."

Missy's chin lost its usual upward tilt, and her eyes closed ever so briefly. In that moment, she shifted from lighthearted banter with her husband's little brother to a hushed and prayerful tone.

"Both of 'em killed?"

"Graveyard dead," he answered. Then, suddenly aware of her changed demeanor, he stepped closer to the buggy and took off his hat. "Missy? I never meant to… You didn't exactly hold back on your opinion of Clyde Barrow just a minute ago. Now, all of a sudden, you're lookin' kinda pale."

"Oh, Cleve… Those two done more harm than a couple of mad dogs turned loose on the country. It had to happen, but whatever her faults, Bonnie Parker's a woman. Farm girl, they tell me. It just ain't the way things are done around here, and those poor lawmen'll have to live with it."

"No way to split her off from Clyde, I reckon. He would've cut and run at the first sign of a trap."

"A string of poor choices on her part, but like I said, whoever pulled the trigger's got to live with it."

"Anyhow, I never meant to upset you." He paused for a second, half ashamed, and then changed the subject. "How come you out buyin' another devilish mule when there's a cotton crop to be planted?"

"Got ours in the ground," she declared on a contented sigh, "every last bit of it."

"Looks like I'm runnin' behind. Soon as the boy brings my cup back, I'll get along down the road."

"That cup may hold water, Cleve, but you never could. You'll give Jimbo the whole overblown story first time I'm out of earshot. Reckon that's what uncles do… But, please, see there ain't too much blood in the tellin' of it."

"Now, Missy, a little excitement never hurt a growing boy."

Still radiant, even as she approached middle age, Missy smiled down at him and shook her head.

"I declare, Cleve Pate, you gossip worse than any woman I ever knew."

Jimbo returned with his mother's drinking water, and they eventually set out for home. Tobias Washington stood over a workbench mending several sets of harness but looked up to greet their arrival. Though bareheaded beneath a shading overhang of the main barn, Tobe touched a finger to his brow as if tipping a hat.

"Evenin' to you, Missy." Without waiting for a response, Tobe moved on to a more pressing matter. "Gert wants you up to the house and out of this hot sun."

Twice Missy's age, and still a good plow hand, Tobe knew things. He knew his wife took a personal and highly opinionated interest in the young lady's wellbeing. He understood Missy's gratitude for this concern, but he also knew she did pretty much as she pleased with little or no attention paid to the constant fussing and fuming.

"We're bound for the store to help Papa with any late trade before closing time. Turn this mule out for me, and I'll tell Gert you tried."

"Yes'm," he answered with a grin and then slipped Jimbo a wink. "If this place grew cotton like it grows hardheaded womenfolk, I reckon we'd all be livin' easy."

Jimbo returned the old man's grin but waited for his mother to speak.

"Watch that mule, Tobe. I believe she'd bite."

"She might slip one good bite in on me. After then, I'll just take up a good stout club and set in to change her mind."

"Takes that sometimes."

They heard the kicks and squeals of a brief scuffle as the new mule found her place in the bunch. In just a second, though, the old man returned to hand Missy her halter and lead.

"Why don't I trail along and carry you up them steps into the store?"

"Thank you, Tobe, but there'll be somebody around. You could stand on the boot and hold to the back of the seat. But, then, there's the walk home and no need of it."

"I got two good legs. Besides which… You know I think the world and all of your papa, but he's gettin' along in years now. Mister Big Jim don't want just anybody totin' you around. Better let me come and do it."

"I'll swan," Missy declared with a musical laugh. "Sometimes I think you and Gert know us better than we know ourselves. Jump on behind and take you a good hold."

Having embraced modern transportation over a decade earlier, Crawford Kimbel sold two grades of gasoline from pumps in the side yard of his store. Missy tallied the fuel receipts just like any other income. But marriage to a longtime horse and mule dealer, along with her own inclinations, ruled out further interaction with automobiles.

Missy liked her personal driving horses flashy, quick-footed over the road, and dependable. This worked out as a kind of advertisement for the type of stock Big Jim wanted to buy and sell. Midnight was a recent favorite and as good as anything she had ever held the lines on.

"That big rascal is a road-eatin' wonder," Tobe observed, smiling broadly as he stepped down in front of the store. "My extra weight on the back of this buggy ain't meant nothin' to him."

Missy returned his smile, but hers gave way to a sigh as she surveyed Red Bog's dusty main street.

"Midnight's as good as they come," she admitted, "but there's precious little left for comparison."

"Ma'am?"

"This is Monday afternoon. Plantin' time, too. Ain't enough people in town to go seining for bait… And, yet, I count four automobiles. Reckon the driving horse is gonna fade plumb out on us, Tobe?"

"Lordy, Missy, how come you asking me? I know of folks don't even have no land that's got 'em a car. Truth is… Them things scare me, but you ain't scared of a grizzly bear. Why not get in that Hutmobile of your papa's and see what it's all about?"

"The pedals, Tobe. I can't move my— Anyhow, there's no feelin' to an automobile. No heart… A horse'll work for you until he drops. A mule will generally scheme to get out of work, but he'll take care of himself and you in the bargain. No matter how bad things get, I can call whoa to whatever I'm drivin', and they just might stop. A car blunders right on until it slams into something almighty solid."

"Yes'm; that's the way I see it."

"What's more dangerous than a cotton gin or a saw mill?"

"Can't say as I know, not right off hand."

"Well, an automobile is just about the same proposition. Only, they've put it on wheels."

"I like to sit on Papa Kimbel's knee and steer the Hutmobile," Jimbo blurted innocently enough. "Nadine can run it all by herself!"

Missy opened her mouth to remind him to say "*Aunt* Nadine", but the new piece of information pushed this half-hearted battle right out of her mind.

"Do tell? How long has Nadine been runnin' a car?"

The boy faltered just a little at divulging this secret, but the light note of humor in her voice kept him going.

"Good while now… She drove me and Aunt Alma clear up to Henderson one time."

"Henderson? What's Alma want up there?"

"Bud Evans, I reckon. They got a picture show and a jimdandy ice cream shop, too."

"Evans," she repeated quietly, and her pretty brow furrowed just a little.

Mistaking the moment of concentration for displeasure, Jimbo tried to provide some comfort.

"That's alright, Missy. We'll always need horses. A car can take you farther and get you there faster, but it ain't near as much fun. I'd rather drive old Midnight than steer the Hutmobile any day!"

"Now, that can be arranged," and she smiled brightly, leaning over to tap the end of his freckled nose ever so lightly. "That can be arranged on our way home. As for this Bud Evans, I'll just have to… Well, never you mind."

~October 2007~

As I'm sure most of you have discovered, Finishing Touches by Elizabeth Chandler rests in capable hands during my absence. Each and every client is a valued friend. After all, I have watched your families celebrate many precious milestones. I am recuperating from a rather overblown accident and also visiting my own family. This time of reflection has allowed me to examine the origins of the Elizabeth Chandler commitment to excellence. Our East Texas home is not known for five-course meals or elaborate entertainments. It is, however, a place where each passerby has his or her favorite dish remembered and trotted out regularly. It's a place where conversations matter. Everyone is made to feel at ease, and everyone is welcome. Those are the Finishing Touches… They will remain the Elizabeth Chandler way!

Laura Beth glanced at her wristwatch before rereading the blog post a third time, linking it to her website, and logging off of the public computer. The library, once a three-story dry goods emporium, fostered serenity with its hushed atmosphere and precise organization. She browsed the shelves in search of just the right book but finally decided that recent attempts at writing filled most of her downtime. Smiling her thanks to the kind ladies up front, she strolled out to Granddaddy's old pickup.

"Now," she thought, "I'll grab a few things from the store and still make it home in plenty of time for prayer meeting."

Chapter Seven

Though memories of the homeplace consisted mainly of working together outdoors, Laura Beth also recalled the emphasis her grandparents placed on church attendance. Sunday morning, Sunday evening, and Wednesday night services brought a kind of rhythm to their lives, marking the passage of time and dividing one task from the next. Weeklong revival meetings stood out among the highlights of each summer, and special meals for the visiting preacher occasioned some of her earliest training in hospitality. She had gone to church with her mom and dad even after their move, but it always seemed more essential on her visits to the country.

Walking back into Red Bog Missionary Baptist after so many years, Laura Beth expected several new faces and minor updates to the building. A deep sense of homecoming, though, caught her by surprise. Like many a concerned mother, she had tried to instill the importance of worship, but Kimmy's friend group usually influenced their attendance. As a result, Laura Beth followed her daughter all over Houston without finding a true church home.

"I felt good all day yesterday and even better today," she confided as they settled onto a pew. "Need to get back to Kimmy and back to work, too, but a visit home wouldn't be complete unless I made it to church."

"I know that time's coming, doodlebug, but we'll sure hate to see you go."

"Does Aunt Alma still play the piano?"

"Naw... When you start crowdin' in on ninety, they'll let you retire." Turning in his seat, Jimbo glanced back at the wall clock and revised his statement. "Way it looks, though, she may have to play tonight."

"Oh, I hope so!"

As if in answer to this wish, Alma rose to her feet and stepped back out into the aisle. Nadine smiled, then, and leaned in for a bit of softspoken conversation.

"Missy was real strong on Sacred Harp singin'. You know, shape note or fa-so-la music… Went with the territory, I guess. From a little girl right on up through middle age, she catered to older folks. Had a lot of respect for their ways. They petted and fussed over her, too."

"Who didn't?" Laura Beth shot back with a teasing note in her voice.

"Even so, she bought a piano and paid for our lessons. 'Course Big Jim didn't take much convincing. He liked just about any kind of music."

"I never knew you played."

"My lessons only lasted three weeks. 'No sense throwin' good money away, child. Run catch a horse and make some tracks!' Missy knew I couldn't sit still, you see, and that sweet smile of hers took the blame right out of it."

Their conversation ended just a minute or two before services began, and Laura Beth spent that time trying to decide who all she was supposed to know in the little congregation. Several retired couples who had come home from Dallas or Houston paired well-known family names with unfamiliar faces, and a flurry of recent introductions left her thoroughly confused. The young pastor's name escaped her. His wife, quiet in a poised and charming way, offered a genuine welcome.

"Sus…, Chery… No, Cindy, that's her name!" and Laura Beth smiled at this minor triumph.

Alma still enjoyed playing, and her good old convention-style accompaniment called Laura Beth right back to her childhood. *Tell Me the Story of Jesus, Power in the Blood,* and *When We All Get to Heaven*! Laura Beth felt a bit self-conscious at first, but her voice mingled pleasantly with those around her. The old songs, so deeply rooted in Scripture, took her back not only to childhood but also to the busy days of mothering a toddler and establishing a thriving business. Verities she learned as a child, the faith that Granddaddy and others lived by, had never failed to comfort and sustain her. When the song leader called for special music, the pastor's wife made her way down front and then paused uncertainly for a moment.

"Would you sing with me, Ms. Nadine? Since your niece is here and Ms. Alma's playing, I thought maybe…"

"I generally come when I'm called," Nadine quipped in response. "Just try to pick somethin' I know."

Cindy's slight hesitation vanished then amid warm laughter.

"I'd just about have to throw the songbook away and pull one out of the air to get something you didn't know!"

"Precious memories, unseen angels, sent from somewhere to my soul. How they linger ever near me and the sacred past unfold."

The rich, weathered quality of Nadine's voice blended surprisingly well with the clear and youthful soprano lead. They sang two verses, repeating the chorus each time, and then paused for Aunt Alma's turn around on the piano. While playing, Alma indicated that they should sing the often-neglected fourth verse.

"I remember Mother praying, Father too, on bended knee. The sun is sinking, shadows falling, but their prayers still follow me."

Laura Beth caught Aunt Nadine's wink, but the gesture hardly seemed necessary. Knowing what she did of the family's story, the girl could almost visualize their recollections. Not of Mother and Father but of Missy's head bowed in prayer and Big Jim, so often rough and careless, kneeling humbly before the Lord.

"That was wonderful," Laura Beth whispered, blinking away tears as her aunts returned to the pew.

"Beautiful, ladies. Just beautiful," the preacher echoed, stepping up to the pulpit. "As most of you know, we're studying relationships in the Christian life. We discussed previously how a right relationship with Christ impacts the wellbeing of every other facet in our lives. Turn with me, if you will, to First Corinthians. A short but powerful verse of Scripture, and we'll use it as our starting point. Look at the fourth chapter and the second verse."

Instead of glancing down at her grandfather's open Bible, Laura Beth watched his mouth shape the words as he read along.

"Moreover it is required in stewards that a man be found faithful."

"Discussion of Paul, Apollos, and Peter in the previous chapter leads us to equate the stewards mentioned here with ministers of the Gospel, and rightly so. But every saved individual is called to serve. We should all be good stewards or prudent managers of whatever time, assets, skills, and knowledge the Lord may entrust to us. God expects faithfulness from His people, but faithfulness is sadly lacking in our world today."

"Amen," signaled agreement from all corners of the church building.

"Commitment of any kind is too often shunned in modern society. But it takes commitment to please our Heavenly Father. Commitment to Him, commitment to the truths of His Word, and commitment to one another. As the old saying goes, I'm preaching to the choir. Most of you demonstrate commitment within this church family and beyond. Even so, we can always use a reminder. I'd like us to look particularly this evening at commitment in a Godly marriage."

Laura Beth felt her breath catch as a mental picture of Bradley Chandler slid into focus. Keen blue eyes, dark hair, and the ever-present suntan on his lean, untroubled face... Warmth and tenderness stirred, but these feelings soon collided with the keen edges of abandonment.

"Abandonment?" she jeered inwardly. "You ran him off! So independent... So smart... Go right ahead and chase your dreams, Bradley. I've got my life neatly bundled and under control."

Official records listed them as divorced, plain and simple. But had she been wrong, all those years ago, to buy into the notion of loving someone enough to let him go?

"More to the point," she thought, "just how much had Granddaddy and the aunts told this preacher?"

"In the fifth chapter of Ephesians, Paul writes that we husbands are to love our wives as Christ loved the church and gave Himself for it. That, brethren, is a pretty tall order. Nevertheless... Any man who likes to quote the God-given instructions on submission, and take them totally out of context to browbeat his wife, is probably unwilling to honor her as God commanded. Much less risk his own life for her sake."

"Amen," echoed around once more, and this chorus of agreement proved even stronger than the last.

"Every relationship goes two ways, and in his letter to Titus, Paul states that aged women should teach the younger to be sober or serious-minded in their love and devotion to their husbands and children. I know we don't have any ladies here who'd admit to being *aged women*… Ms. Alma and Ms. Nadine might, but then everybody else'd look bad because we just can't seem to keep up with them."

As laughter rippled through the congregation, Alma and Nadine showed their regard for the pastor with warm smiles.

"Nevertheless," he said, refocusing their collective attention, "wives are directed to be virtuous and dutiful so as not to dishonor the Word of God."

As the Wednesday night study drew to a close, Laura Beth dismissed any notion of Granddaddy and the aunts tipping off their pastor beforehand. Being somewhat removed from her short years of married life down in Houston, they had offered nothing but love and support when Bradley left. Even now, the memory of a certain conversation with her dad brought a melancholy smile.

"I know you're upset, Laura Beth, and exhausted, too. But call your granddaddy or write him a letter. If I try to tell him what's happened before he hears from you, he'll go huntin' Bradley. None of us want that, but you know Jimbo Pate. If I keep quiet too long, he's apt to come huntin' me."

No, this preacher didn't know her situation. He didn't need to. The Holy Spirit had a way of… But what did it matter now? Her marriage was gone. Long gone, some might say.

"Maybe the message wasn't for me, after all," she rationalized, "at least, not in the way I first took it."

Though she chatted politely during the round of after-church visiting, butterflies in her stomach and a certain tightness in her chest proved hard to ignore.

"I know you've heard it several times tonight, Laura Beth, but we really are glad to have you," the pastor's wife confided, placing a hand gently on her arm. "Brother Jimbo and his aunts are very important to this church family, and your visit has thrilled them beyond words."

"Thanks; it's been good for me, too."

"Yes, I imagine so. The Pate property has a kind of serene beauty. I come out there occasionally for a walk. Ms. Alma and Ms. Nadine seem to enjoy spending a little time with the kids, and Brother Jimbo makes a point to tell me where it's safe to venture on any given day."

"Safe?"

"I'm out there for exercise, but a footrace with the cows feels more like running for dear life. Like I said, though, he's good about keeping me out of trouble."

"Granddaddy must like you a lot," Laura Beth rejoined teasingly. "Being the preacher's wife probably doesn't hurt, either. But he and Aunt Nadine have been known to watch that kind of race for entertainment."

"They're mischievous, alright, but too kindhearted for actual meanness. Anyway… I bet you've enjoyed walking through the woods and over the pastureland. It's much better than my little fifteen-minute circle at home. With so much to see, I don't mind walking a bit longer."

"Granddaddy's outside all the time, but he's generally horseback or running the tractor. Took me on a little stroll, once I felt up to it, just to chat. Beyond that, though, I guess walking never really occurred to me."

"Oh, this fall weather is just about perfect! It's wonderful exercise, too. Like Brother Jimbo says… 'This rolling country will fool you, but there ain't hardly a level spot in East Texas.' I'm walking up hill or down nearly all the time."

She liked this softspoken girl and appreciated her genuine enthusiasm for the beauty of the homeplace. Mothering two small children, while Laura Beth found herself raising a teenager, put Cindy at a different stage of life. Still, they couldn't be too far apart in age. Laura Beth treated everyone kindly but seldom took the time to cultivate deep, personal friendships. Though she hadn't come home looking for a walking buddy, she could certainly relate to Cindy's desire for the company of another young woman.

"I've written a temporary cellphone number on the back of this card," Laura Beth volunteered, rummaging briefly in her purse. "Give me a call the next time you're headed out our way. Maybe I'll tag along for a walk."

"Oh, good! I'll be over just as soon as it's convenient for Ms. Alma and Ms. Nadine to babysit."

"Cindy's about as sweet as they come," Nadine confided on the drive home. "You'd enjoy getting to know her, and we'll take those young'uns just any time. The daughter's about to turn six. Jimbo sometimes entertains her outside while me and Alma try to keep up with baby brother."

"I can't stay in Red Bog forever, Aunt Nadine, but a walk and some girl talk probably wouldn't hurt me. Especially the walk…"

Recollections flowed freely almost every evening and sometimes during the day. One story seemed to lead naturally into another, and Laura Beth typed steadily to take down as much as possible. Big Jim, Papa Kimbel, Gertie Washington, and others came up time and again, but her favorite tales hinged on the central character. She began to ponder the notion of continuing this project from a distance. Recording Missy's legacy might bring a bit of much-needed downtime to her life.

Having made plans for Friday, Laura Beth waited expectantly to catch a mid-morning knock on the kitchen door. She answered it, ran her gaze over Cindy, and felt her mouth drop open.

"Aunt Alma thought you'd dress comfortably, so I just bounced out of bed and covered up the jiggly parts. But look at you! Guess maybe Aunt Alma never heard of comfort in perfection …"

Laura Beth stood there in a long sleeve pullover and old pajama bottoms with worn elastic straining ever so slightly at the waist. Her tennis shoes had seen better days, and rich, golden hair dangled haphazardly in a ponytail.

Cindy, on the other hand, sported a white jogging suit with navy stripes on the sleeve and pantleg. The color scheme contrasted nicely with her dark hair in its fancy updo. Running shoes and a light application of makeup completed the picture.

"Don't be silly, Laura Beth. You look just fine."

"'Just fine', says the track and field star… If we're going to be all energetic this morning, I need another Dr Pepper. Come on in, and we can get the kiddos settled."

As the new walking partners visited briefly with Alma and Nadine, all four smiled at the happy chatter of Cindy's daughter and the contented jabbering of her young son. Laura Beth downed her caffeine fix in record time but also managed to pass along Granddaddy's advice on the day's route.

The two young women walked side by side, and their leisurely pace belied Cindy's rather athletic uniform. Still, navigating the constant ups and downs caused Laura Beth to breathe in shallow puffs and listen more than she talked.

"Thanks for coming with me, Laura Beth. Hope I didn't twist your arm too much. See… My connections in the community are limited, so far, to our church family. Wonderful people, like Alma and Nadine and your grandfather, but they're all— Older folks give great advice and lots of genuine warmth. I wouldn't trade those relationships for anything, but a friend my own age would be pretty special, too."

"I know what you mean…" Laura Beth waited a stride or two for her breathing to level and then continued. "I went from relying on my daughter for company to staying here with Aunt Alma and Aunt Nadine. Love them all, of course, but sometimes the transition feels like generational whiplash."

"Guess maybe I overdressed a little," Cindy admitted after a pause. "Call it a misguided attempt to put my best foot forward. You really are very pretty, Laura Beth. Even without makeup, your complexion is just lovely. They all say you look like…"

"Missy," she supplied in reluctant acceptance, "and you're far too kind."

After walking steadily for half an hour, Laura Beth produced two wadded grocery bags from her pajama pocket and suggested they stop in the old orchard, overlooking Caney Branch, to pick up a few pecans. Alma and Nadine would no doubt classify this as a useful activity. More importantly, it offered a pause in which to catch her breath. She instinctively liked Cindy, and the feeling grew stronger as they talked. Only three years younger, Cindy showed genuine admiration for the way Laura Beth had singlehandedly raised a daughter and established a thriving business.

"I hope you didn't feel targeted by that Wednesday night study on commitment," she ventured after Laura Beth shared some of her background. "Divorce isn't part of God's plan, but He can sure love you through it. Besides, there's no way Zack knew any of—"

"Brother Zack! I've been trying to think of your husband's name all morning. As for the Bible study, I learned a long time ago not to feel personally attacked whenever a message steps on my toes."

"Oh, good. We all enjoyed having you in the service and want you to come back. Like I said, our *easing-into-middle-age* group is sadly lacking."

"A better name might jumpstart things," Laura Beth teased, wrinkling her nose.

"I know it; that just kind of popped out."

"You can count on me for Sunday. After that, though… I love spending time with Granddaddy and the aunts, but Kimmy needs me. I've got to get back to her, and back to work for both our sakes."

Laura Beth turned away as she spoke, blinking away sudden tears. Every motherly instinct drew her back to Kimmy and all she had built for them. Her trip home felt more like a break from the inescapable duties and pressures of life than an alternative way of living. But, having nestled comfortably into her grandfather's world, it seemed almost unimaginable to simply waltz out again and resume the role of infrequent visitor. Despite her business acumen, highly developed people skills, and independent nature, Laura Beth felt like a confused little girl. From now on her days in Houston would carry the added weight of longing for Red Bog, and any stolen time in Red Bog would arouse guilt for the things left undone in Houston.

"They'd be embarrassed to hear it," Cindy observed quietly, "but those three old people are the heart and soul of Red Bog. I've watched them brighten up considerably since you came. Even those first few days when you just laid in bed gave them a renewed sense of purpose. They need you, too, Laura Beth."

"Thank goodness I didn't put on makeup," Laura Beth joked shakily. "Something in the air, I guess. My eyes have set in watering to beat the band."

"We just met and… Call me silly, but if you stick around very long, I'll probably come to depend on you myself. You seem to fit naturally into this community. I'm learning, but it's taken a lot of molding by Ms. Alma and Ms. Nadine."

Neither one was gathering many pecans at this point, and Laura Beth stepped over to lay a hand on the other girl's arm.

"We can enjoy our time together and then email or even talk on the phone. Just don't get used to having me nearby. Red Bog is a wonderful place to live, Cindy. But can you see anybody around here paying me to plan weddings, graduation festivities, or retirement parties? They've all got a Cousin Sadie who'll organize things out of kindness or, maybe, for the occasional thrill of telling everyone else what to do."

Shared laughter sealed a new bond of friendship. The girls gathered some more pecans, neither wanting Alma or Nadine to see a half-empty sack, and then headed back to the house. Coming up out of the creek bottom, they noted the approach of two horses. Laura Beth had long ago learned to recognize the way her grandfather sat his mount, and she could make a pretty good guess as to the happy little rider bouncing along behind him.

"Brother Jimbo's had her on that pony for a while now," Cindy volunteered, catching sight of her daughter. "Turned her loose sometime last month. If you want to know the truth, I'm scared of horses. But she's safe enough with him."

"Absolutely. Granddaddy wouldn't take her along if he didn't feel able to handle things." Laura Beth nodded at the finality of her own statement and then doubled back, letting a bit of amusement creep into her tone. "You're scared of horses?"

Cindy stopped walking and opened her mouth to challenge the teasing little jab. Before she could speak, though, Jimbo reined to a stop in front of them and drew one leg up to rest across the pommel. Loath to give up any riding time, Cindy's daughter trotted circles around them.

"Look, Mama! I barely have to touch the reins anymore. Bitsy can feel me move and know which way to go."

The pony was, in fact, fairly responsive. Especially for such a round, fluffy little creature…

"Y'all enjoying your stroll?" the old gentleman inquired.

"Yessir," Laura Beth responded. "Only… I didn't know I'd gotten so out of shape. Maybe I should have noticed all this panting on the long walk just prior to my accident. But, obviously, I was a little distracted."

"I give up smokin' years ago, doodlebug. That boosted my wind some, but it don't hardly apply in your case." He paused as if for a moment's consideration and then teased her just a bit more. "Next time, take a horse along. Ride up hill and walk down."

Both women dissolved into laughter, and the old horseman acknowledged their enjoyment with a wry smile.

"Oh, Brother Jimbo, you always make my day! But what Laura Beth really needs is a few more walks. Her stamina will increase naturally."

Rawhide tough, Jimbo Pate was the very definition of stamina, but Laura Beth never recalled hearing him use the word. They called it "bottom" in a horse. Bottom, or maybe "stayin' power". Taking two quick steps, she reached out to stop the dappled gray pony. If Cindy wanted to expound on the benefits of exercise, Granddaddy could listen while she chatted with this cute little girl.

"Tell me, young lady, is that pony any good?"

"Yes, ma'am! Bitsy's great! Brother Jimbo lets me ride her almost every time we come to visit."

Laura Beth returned the child's bright smile and paid no particular attention as Cindy chattered on behind them.

"I just love your granddaughter… Already! She's definitely got the Pate sense of humor, and spending time with Laura Beth is the most relaxing thing I've done in ages."

"You won't get any argument from me. Why, she… My doodlebug is like a good dose of medicine."

"It's too bad she seems determined to go back to Houston right away."

"Truth be told, I think Laura Beth would be a good deal safer and happier right here. As for her daughter, Kimmy's plenty young enough to adjust… Just like Laura Beth did when they plopped her down in the middle of all that craziness at Houston."

"Well, she's all set to go back, and I thought you ought to know."

"Yes'm, I appreciate that. Let's us talk to Aunt Alma and Nadine. If there's an answer to be had, we'll come up with it."

Jimbo caught his granddaughter's attention, then, to ask if she had noticed any fence down.

"Everything looks okay coming this-a-way from the house."

"Good," he said with a nod. "We'll ride on down Caney Branch while y'all finish your walk. Probably turn the cows back in here tomorrow."

As it turned out, Jimbo and his little riding partner got back just ahead of the two young ladies. Laura Beth helped care for the horses, and they all headed inside. The front room with its old-fashioned parlor furnishings saw lots of company and, lately, provided a setting for informal evening interviews. But everyone recognized Alma's kitchen as the heart of the old home. The little group laughed and chatted while Nadine bounced Cindy's young son on her knee.

"Y'all stay for dinner," Alma invited as a matter of course.

The pastor's family often enjoyed Sunday dinner here, but on walking days, Cindy politely declined the inevitable offer of food. In truth, she hesitated to undo her walk with Ms. Alma's cooking.

Today, though, Laura Beth seconded the invitation. Dr Pepper in hand, she started to sit down at the kitchen table, but a new thought stopped her short.

"Please stay? We've had a nice talk, but I barely got to meet the little ones. Aunt Alma and Aunt Nadine won't mind. I'll just run and change clothes. This homeless look works best in small doses."

"Change if you want to," Cindy said lightly, "but don't mind us. A little more time to visit would be a treat."

"Good; I'll be right back."

Alma lifted a fresh pan of cornbread from the oven to go with her chicken and dumplings. She also grabbed a jar of green beans from the storeroom, and Cindy stepped in to heat them over the stove. Working to set the table, Nadine moved around Jimbo a couple of times and then came to an abrupt halt.

"What's eatin' you, anyhow? You don't generally stand around gazing at nothing, like a blind calf without its mother."

Chapter Eight

"Ms. Cindy says my doodlebug's got her mind set to leave," he explained tersely.

"That's true enough," Alma said gently. "I've known it was coming, but there's precious little we can do about it. A mother's place is with her child, after all. You can't blame Laura Beth for missing her daughter."

"I love you like a brother, Jimbo Pate," Nadine chimed in a little more bluntly, "but you're a man and true to form."

"How's that?"

"Only see what you want to see… We all know Laura Beth's time here has done her some good, but she's been pining for Kimmy from the very first day."

"It don't have to be the rest of her life," he protested. "A little more time to recuperate might make a world of difference."

"Well, then," Alma suggested matter-of-factly, "send for Kimmy and get her up here."

"That might work! Only, the girl's with her daddy. He's likeable enough, but anybody who'd go off and leave Laura Beth…"

"I understand your feelings, Brother Jimbo." Cindy spoke softly, almost hesitantly, but the old man turned toward her with rapt attention. "The thing is I'm not sure your granddaughter shares that resentment."

"Beg pardon, Ms. Cindy, but I ain't gonna shake his hand and thank him for shirkin' his duties as a husband and father."

"No, sir. Nobody expects that, but Laura Beth seems pretty mixed up in her own heart and mind where Bradley Chandler is concerned. I'm an outsider and don't mean to push my opinions in where they're not wanted, but we talked quite a bit this morning and—"

"You're no outsider. We love you and Brother Zack like our own. Anything you've got to say… Well, I'm listening."

Despite an unsurpassed work ethic, Laura Beth never quite wrapped her head around the notion of exercise for its own sake. The little heart-to-heart with Cindy had provided a welcome break in routine. That evening, though, she returned eagerly to Red Bog's past and a world that seemed to be continually unfolding. Likewise, Jimbo and the aunts eased back into storytelling without revealing their concern at the notion of her departure.

"Midnight was as black as all get-out," Nadine recalled after a little coaxing, "and sleek, except for that jug head of his. Big-boned and stout enough for field work, but his road gait was just too pretty to waste."

"Not the kind of gait you'd want in a ridin' horse," Jimbo qualified. "But he could snatch a buggy along fast enough to bring tears to your eyes and not strain himself a bit gettin' it done."

"I can take horses or leave 'em," and Alma paused briefly as her admission hung in the air. "But floating along behind old Midnight put the smile on Missy's face, and that smile lit up our world!"

"A buggy horse is as useless today as an old wringer-type washing machine, but I'd still take half a dozen like Midnight."

"You'd wear out a pickup finding 'em, too," Nadine assured her nephew. "Midnight left us all with some good memories, but he was just one in the string of horses Missy drove over the years."

"Daddy fit her out with a dainty little red roan mare called Ginger one time," Jimbo remembered.

"Yes," Nadine seconded and then a hint of mischief crept into her smile. "Tell Laura Beth about Jeff, why don't you?"

"Missy's Jeff Davis was a bay gelding, undersized and not as flashy as some of her other horses. He could travel with a buggy, alright, but was smooth enough to make a good saddle horse, too. I rode him as far south as Redland one time before Daddy figured out what me and some of the hands had got up to."

"Racing," Nadine explained in response to the younger woman's blank expression. "Racin' and gambling…" And her tone hovered somewhere between a scandalized whisper and reluctant admiration. "He was beatin' full-grown riders at nine or ten years old!"

"Me and old Jeff beat 'em alright, but Daddy beat me, too, when he figured things out."

"Our hands cleaned up on side bets," Nadine recalled fondly. "They knew what Jimbo and that horse could do. You raced first at the old Reed's Settlement community back up there above Clayton. Learned to shoot dice in the bargain and then came home and taught me."

"Yeah, I had a good thing goin' for a while even after Daddy ended my horseracing. You done all my chores around here for a week or two. Right up 'til Aunt Alma told off on us."

Alma sat up straight, ready to vindicate her role as the eldest and most responsible of the trio, but Jimbo spoke first.

"Never did let Daddy hear us callin' for Teneha, Timpson, Bobo, and Blair… Missy put a stop to those dice games herself."

"Her methods were just as effective," Nadine ventured in a considering tone. "Maybe not quite as sudden, but we quit gambling all the same."

"She and daddy thought alike when it came to handling horses. Folks used to argue as to which one had the lightest hands, but only Missy applied that light touch to raisin' us kids. Still, to look into her eyes and know I'd disappointed her…"

"I loved y'all an awful lot and still do," Alma observed, taking in her younger sister and nephew with a glance, "but I kinda enjoyed those doses of disappointment. You two were riders and Missy's shadows to boot. Watching the pair of you rekindled just a bit of what she'd lost. But whenever she caught y'all in a jackpot and ran nearly to the end of her rope, she'd look over at me, give a satisfied little sigh, and nod approvingly. I was always the steady one."

~November 1938~

Big Jim placed his wife ever so gently in bed and dropped down on an elbow beside her. Tobacco smoke and a touch of aftershave mingled, as usual, with the smells of horses, mules, and good red dirt. Missy breathed in the familiar aromas and smiled up fondly.

"I knew that Jeff Davis horse of mine had been losin' a step or two. Even got Tobe to slip some loose tobacco in with his feed corn and worm him out good, but I never in my life…"

"Me, either," he answered with a chuckle. "I noticed some extra pocket money floating 'round amongst the hands, but you never can tell. Turns out they been raking it in right sharp bettin' on our boy and that horse of yours."

"How'd you find it out?" she wondered, not quite suppressing the snort that so often accompanied her laughter.

"Nothin' to it. Tully Havard ain't got sense enough to tell a good lie. Accordin' to Tully, our Jimbo rode Jeff over to Redland Saturday. Better than twenty miles, and he still cleaned up in the races! I thrashed him 'til he won't sit a horse right for a week, much less think about slippin' off with the hands."

"Any self-respecting mother oughta tuck Jimbo and the girls in of an evening. It's a little harder for me to manage, but still…"

"Hush, now. You hush, Missy."

Jim trailed a finger gently along her jawline and on down the elegant neck, murmuring his words of comfort directly into her ear. Missy shivered under his touch, and unwarranted guilt evaporated right along with the worry over her perceived deficiencies. When she smiled up at him a moment later, her soft voice betrayed just a hint of that pleasant tingle.

"Jim…"

"What is it, precious?"

"At least he won. They couldn't out ride our boy, none of 'em."

"And them grown, too," he marveled. "Lots of 'em I wouldn't call horsemen, exactly, but they can make one hold his gait and get over the ground. There's always a ringer or two hanging around the big doings. Race jockeys and professional gamblers, so to speak. He rode Jeff to a fare-thee-well and left every last one a-scratchin' their heads. I whaled the daylights out of him, just like I told you, but darn near bit my cigar in two trying to keep from laughing."

"What a boy! What a boy, and what a horse! They came nearly thirty miles back home, too."

"Jeff's grain fed and tough. Driving one the way you do is bound to keep him drawn down to hard muscle."

"Pshaw… Jimbo must've been riding smart to cover all that distance, win a race, and not do any real harm to my favorite buggy horse."

"Nothin' smart about a stunt like that. Plain old tomfoolery… Leastways, he had sense enough to take care of his mount."

"Knew he'd better make church, too. Some of the hands told Gert that Jimbo traveled those nighttime roads alone, hoping to get home before we suspected anything."

"Alone is right. None of the homefolks were well enough mounted to stay with him. Most of our hands made the trip by mule and wagon."

"Like as not, Tully and them were just getting started with their carousing when Jimbo pointed his horse home. Still… He might have waited, rode along with that wagon. Solitude can be a mighty fearful thing for a youngster. I'm sure he felt it, coming home in the dark over unfamiliar roads, but there ain't one bit of cowardice in him."

"I don't think he ever went to bed. No sleep to speak of, but still bright eyed and bushy tailed enough to convince both of us that you needed a Sunday drive behind the young sorrel mares I've been working. One look at your Jeff Davis horse and I knew enough to go sideling up to Tully. A little worse for wear, he was, but I got the whole story alright."

"Am I awfully wicked, Jim, to feel so proud?"

Over the next few days, cotton harvest busied every available pair of hands. Farmers all over East Texas neared the payoff to a year's work. Missy felt the urgency and excitement of shortening fall days as much as anyone, but her ability to judge a crop eliminated a good deal of guesswork.

"We'll come out alright," she murmured into the stillness of her kitchen. Nothing like '25… But enough to feed our people through the winter and let everybody put in another crop come spring."

Back in 1925 an exceptionally good crop had, for once, lined up with decent cotton prices. Nearly every family on the place cleared their debts with something left to spend. Missy liked to see the Pate hands do well. Besides… Any money she and Jim cleared that year went to feather the nest. They already had Alma and Nadine, and with a certainty born of faith, she anxiously awaited their own little bundle of joy.

Now, thirteen years later, Missy worked her way methodically through the family's breakfast dishes. Attuned to seasonal patterns with all the sensitivity of a wild creature, her every nerve strained to hurry. She wanted to sit behind a good driving horse, be near the crop and the hands, get outside where the work really counted. But Gertie Washington had gone to the field this morning right along with everybody else. The dishes had to be done, and Missy knew her body's limitations. The more she tried to hurry, the longer the job would take. Not to mention a shattered plate or two.

With the last of the flatware dried, Missy laid it on a porcelain-topped worktable and eyed the stack before her. Maneuvering her chair with one free hand and putting things away piece by piece was no light matter. Much easier to leave the chore for someone else who could do it in a fraction of the time, but Missy didn't know how to quit. The task was here in front of her and…

Before she could start, though, the rattle of trace chains caught her attention. She glanced out the window and confirmed it. The day's first wagonload of loose cotton headed to Red Bog and the gin… But sight of the driver, towheaded and slight, made her heart swell with loving pride. All of the morning's nervous energy broke forth in rapid motion. Propelling her chair across the room, she snatched a sunbonnet from its peg by the door, tied the strings under her chin, and hurried out onto the back porch.

Young Jimbo saw his mother roll out of the house and reluctantly signaled the team to stop.

"Whoa there, Kit. Whoa, Kate. Ready for me to fling out the dishwater, Missy? These mules'll be glad enough to stand for a minute."

"Sure, son. You can pour it around my roses. First, though, call Tobe or some of 'em up here."

"Want your buggy brought around? 'Fore long, I'll be able to lift you in and out myself." Then, a hint of mischief crept in. "Say, everybody on the place knows you can holler loud as I can, maybe a little louder."

"They may know it," she shot back, "but it ain't exactly ladylike to go around whooping at the top of my lungs. Not when I've got you right here to do it for me."

"Yes'm," and he threw his head back for a long, high-pitched yell.

As familiar as anyone with the informal system of calls flung across the fields and pastures, Missy recognized it as "come to me" without the urgent trill that might be added in an emergency.

Tobe Washington approached the house in long, swinging strides and raised his cheerful voice so as to be heard from a little distance.

"Gert told me it was 'bout time to fetch your buggy. Words just out of her mouth, and then we hear that holler. Bein' right all the time don't make that old woman no easier to live with. Little Mister can scat along to the gin quick as he gets them roses watered. I'll catch Jeff and hitch him up myself."

"As for Gert being right all the time, I'm 'fraid that's pretty much a fact of life. Jeff can stand in the barn lot a while longer. If you would, Tobe, just put me up on that spring seat yonder."

"The wagon… Behind 'at pair of mules? With your own good driving horse standin' ready?"

"Yes, on the wagon. The breakfast dishes are washed, if not put away, and I'm all set for a talk with Little Mister."

At a stage of life when most boys began to test their independence, young Jimbo Pate still felt the pull of Missy's magnetic personality. On this particular morning, though, their drive to the gin was apt to involve some motherly scolding. Tobe watched with a sympathetic half smile as his young friend trudged back inside to hang up the dishpan.

"No call explainin' yourself to me. It's just… Your buggy rides a sight easier than that old wagon."

"Does," she admitted, "but the wagon will have to do for now."

"Say, Little Mister," the old man called through his cupped hand.

Still in the kitchen, Jimbo forgot the near certainty of a good talking-to and answered cheerfully enough.

"Yeah, Tobe… You want a biscuit or something?"

"Naw… Fetch us a quilt out here, will you?"

"Sure thing."

By the time Jimbo reappeared, Tobe had lifted Missy from her chair.

"Fold that longways and lay it up yonder 'cross the seat," he requested, gesturing with his chin.

Jimbo situated the quilt and then clambered up to gather his driving lines. Moments later, Tobe swung Missy gently into place.

"Drive careful, now," and Tobe gave the boy's knee a friendly shake. "Your daddy's awful particular about his Missy."

"Him and everybody else," Jimbo acknowledged with a grin. "Step up, Kit. Get ahead, Kate." The boy could have hunched silently over his lines or tried some more conversation on the mules. Instead, he set out to distract Missy from any thought of his most recent escapade. "I wish I could pick cotton."

"Well… You can, son, just anytime you get ready."

"No'm, the thing is… I'd like to be good at it. Haulin' to the gin suits me fine, I reckon. But the idea that Nadine can pick circles around me just ain't real comfortable. Tobe and Gert's young'uns won't hardly tease me like Nadine, but they don't strain none keepin' up with her. Then there's Aunt Alma… Don't even like to be outside, and she's the best cotton picker in the whole family. It's aggravatin' to let them girls outdo me, but I can work twice as hard and still end up with half as much cotton."

"The girls are older, son. It ain't hardly a fair comparison."

"Aw, Missy, that don't hold water anymore. I'm plenty old enough."

Jimbo kept his mules up in their collars and pulling together. Missy admired his driving even as she winced with an occasional jolt from the rutted dirt road. The ride was bound to get rougher, coming home with an empty wagon, but she pushed that out of her mind and formed an answer.

"Big Jim's not much of a cotton picker, either. Why do you think he runs the scale all day?"

"Aw, Daddy's good at whatever he sets out to do. Tendin' the scales just kinda goes along with running things."

"Maybe so, but he's got the same trouble as you when it comes to pickin' cotton. Y'all plant it, plow it, and nurse it along… And then, naturally, want to get every last fiber out of every last boll. To pick any cotton, you've got to move across the field. The girls just reach down and snatch whatever comes away in their hand."

"How do you know? What the girls do, I mean."

"Because that's how every decent cotton picker does it. I favored the same method until…"

Missy went silent for a minute and could have bitten her tongue. She wanted, more than anything, to leave Jimbo's illusion of her "riding accident" intact. Thankfully, though, the conversation took a different turn.

"You picked cotton?"

"Sure, son. There ain't nobody above honest work, not with a job to be done. I didn't grow up going to the field. Papa's cotton… Well, you know, it's in patches scattered here and yonder around Red Bog. I helped out at home and in the store whenever they could keep me off my horse."

"I've heard all about you and old Laddie tearin' across the country," he ventured with a grin. "Papa Kimbel figures that's how come he went bald."

"Could be," she admitted breezily and then returned to the subject at hand. "I only saw Papa's tenants in the store or out in the community. All that changed when I married your daddy. Living close to the crop and among our hands, I just naturally took on my share of the work. You'll be running things one day, son, and it'll serve you well to remember… Me and your daddy have never asked anybody on the place to take on something we wouldn't do. If you'll work alongside somebody and hold up your end, he'll naturally do more for you."

Jimbo clucked to the mules a little and jiggled his lines over their backs to keep them in step. As the silence stretched longer, he worried that Missy might bring up his short-lived stint as a race jockey. With the keen powers of observation that only a bright and inquisitive child can muster, he opened his mouth and blurted the first thing that came to mind.

"The hands are right proud of Daddy. They know Mister Big Jim won't back up from nothin' or nobody. When he goes off somewhere cuttin' up, they generally get a chuckle or two out of it, but most of 'em hold you up like some kind of a storybook princess."

"Now, son… If the hands talk among themselves, that's their business. But don't you be listenin' to any wild tales about your daddy."

"Beg pardon, Missy. But those stories are mostly true, ain't they?"

Missy's jaw took on a rigid set and her gaze drifted aimlessly over the roadside fields. She allowed herself a long breath, but still couldn't lie to him.

"Be that as it may… I don't want you listening to such things, and I sure won't have you repeating them. Do you hear me?"

"Yes, ma'am."

Slowly but surely, Jimbo found himself drawn into the very discussion he had been working so hard to avoid.

"You need never duck your head on account of your daddy, Jimbo Pate. Why, if I'd seen half of what he saw over yonder in France and then come home to find both parents dying of the Spanish flu, not to mention two baby sisters sick and helpless…"

"Missy, I didn't mean—"

"Never found much use for liquor, myself. Then again, nothing ever haunted me like the war done him. I married Jim Pate for the privilege of standin' at his side, but I didn't take him to raise. Now, you, on the other hand…"

"Me?" the boy croaked.

"Don't you think you're settin' out on the path of sin and sorrow a little early?"

"I never meant no harm, Missy, and the hands got a big kick out of it just like they do when Daddy cuts up. 'Course he thrashed me for it, anyhow."

"Your daddy thrashed you," she explained in an unnaturally small voice, "to spare me the pain of takin' a buggy whip to you."

"He used a doubled plow line," Jimbo ventured with a tentative half smile. "Can't see where I come out much ahead."

"I said he did it to spare me, not you."

"Everybody knows Jeff Davis is the best single-footin' horse in these parts. All I did was show him off a little bit. What did it hurt if Tully and the boys raked in a little extra money on the deal?"

"Several of our hands are good, God-fearing people like Tobe and Gert. As for Tully Havard and the rest of that bunch… I didn't take them to raise, either. But you're my boy, mine and your daddy's. The folks on our place are naturally watching you. No sense leading 'em into temptation."

"No'm."

"More than that, son, you belong to the Lord. When you got saved last summer and then came forward for baptism, I hope there was more to it than a good soaking in the creek."

"Why, yes'm!"

"You identified yourself with Jesus Christ and with Red Bog Missionary Baptist Church. You know that poor choices can shame me and your daddy. Stretch that out to the rest of our kinfolk and the church, too. Above all else, your actions reflect on the Savior."

Sudden tears shimmered in Missy's eyes. Though beyond her control, they served her purpose just as well as if she had called them up intentionally.

"Don't cry, Missy, not on my account."

"The good Lord doesn't warn His people against certain things on a whim or to keep us from what looks like fun. He wants what's best for you, Jimbo. It's up to me and your daddy to hold you on the right path until you show us that you can make responsible choices." Missy went silent for a minute and then flashed him a watery smile. "You rode my Jeff just right! Ain't many grown folks could use a horse that hard without hurting him. I'm proud of your riding, son, but when it comes to your conduct, I expect better."

"Yes'm," he managed as his throat tightened. "Only... Quit that crying, won't you, please? I'd rather take another lickin' from Daddy."

Chapter Nine

~October 2007~

Laura Beth saved her latest notes on the laptop, leaned back in her chair, and blinked away tears of laughter.

"Oh, Granddaddy… Raising you would've been enough to keep any mother on her toes."

"On her knees, more like," Alma put in sagely.

The younger woman nodded in ready agreement but then continued her thought.

"How come I never heard that story before?"

"I don't know, doodlebug. Sneakin' off with the hands to race a horse ain't exactly the first thing that comes to mind when a fella starts sharing memories with his pretty little granddaughter."

"Well, thank goodness for Aunt Nadine. That tale is a jimdandy, and I sure would hate to miss it!"

"A body can always count on Nadine to stir the pot. Half the stuff I got into was because she put me up to it."

Nadine sat straighter in her chair, accepting his little jab as a badge of honor. Laura Beth joined the others in a fond chuckle, and her mind skirted the edges of Granddaddy's most recent story. She never consciously searched for follow-up questions, but her natural curiosity usually provided one or two.

"Was harvesting cotton each year really such a big deal in Red Bog? It's hard to imagine, now, with most of the land used for grazing or planted in pine trees. Maybe all the hustle and bustle just made it look important. From a child's point of view, I mean."

"Not a chance," Alma assured her gently. "Gathering the crop brought success or failure, and everybody in our little corner of the world felt it. Papa Kimbel kept store and never farmed for his main income. But everybody paid grocery bills, or paid on 'em, in the fall. Same goes for doctor bills and just about anything else you could name."

"Oh, I never thought of… Makes sense, though, now that you mention it."

"I never had this old red dirt running in my veins like Missy and her two little shadows. You've heard before how I favored housework. Come picking time, though, I went to the field and went gladly."

"I don't know how many times, along in late September, I've seen Missy look up and smile across the supper table at Big Jim," Nadine remembered. "Sometimes that smile was bright with unspoken promise and sometimes a little grim around the edges, offering solemn assurance of the good Lord's provision in a hard year. 'Better check your scales one more time,' she'd say. 'I called on the hands today, and they'll be ready come first light. Tobe's got a good stand of early cotton this year, so I figured you'd want to start there.'"

"If me and Nadine weren't too caught up in our own shenanigans, we saw Missy pay her little call on each family. Might even tag along, but Aunt Alma generally got her first clue at the supper table. I can't say for sure about Daddy. The mule business peaked when spring work started and then again when fresh money hit in the fall, but he trained and polished driving horses the year round."

"Jim was my big brother and the closest thing to a daddy I ever knew," Alma observed. "But he drank some, child. When they finally laid the cotton by in late summer, he'd like as not come up gone for a day or a week or…"

"Even when he made it home in time to gauge the crop," Nadine qualified, moving the conversation away from the painful uncertainty of those long-ago absences, "he'd let Missy give the word. Don't go thinking he was henpecked, not by a long shot. That's just how they operated. Big Jim had rather base his financial outlook for the year on that smile than whatever he might see in the field. Missy read the crop, and he read Missy."

"Every little community had a gin and most offered a cash prize for the first bale of cotton each year. When the old gin cranked at Red Bog, we could hear the clatter clear out here. That sound promised cooler weather, a few weeks' break from the new school term, and pocket money all around. I won't say it was more exciting than Christmas, just different, but I never looked forward to it any less."

Laura Beth looked up from typing and flashed her grandfather a smile.

"Lots of good memories tied up with the roar of the cotton gin, but it must have signaled hard work, too."

"Hard work's all we ever knew, doodlebug. But come fall, it paid. Then, too, there's something about everybody on the place pullin' together… Me and Nadine generally had about as much fun working as we did playing. Take that day Missy rode along with me. Once the serious talk lay behind us, bringing in that load of cotton felt more like a celebration than a chore. Missy was always good company, and the crowd around the gin was glad to see her. She held the team so I could go to the back of the wagon and run the suction pipe. Good place to lose a hat or a handkerchief… Mighty fine entertainment, though, for a shirttail boy. That pipe was nearly big around as I was. Come to think, it ran me more than I ran it."

"Suction pipe?"

"Why, sure. The gin ran off a big old diesel engine. Be an antique now, but Papa Kimbel had me cut it up for scrap iron. A pneumatic system sucked the cotton out of wagons, and later trucks, right up into the gin. That gin at Red Bog had four stands in it. Inside these stands, little saw teeth separated lint cotton from the seeds. Loose cotton went in, seed and all, but what came out were great big bales of marketable fiber."

"Hardly a trace of row-crop farming left in Red Bog. No cotton or anything else," Laura Beth mused.

"Still some old terraces sticking up here and there, but a cow will graze 'em the same as level ground. A lot of my boyhood went into fightin' grass outta the cotton crop," Jimbo added with a chuckle, "and I've spent all the years since praying for good grass in my pastures."

"You'll see pieces of old mule harness hung up as decoration and maybe the shell of an old gin standin' in for a haybarn," Nadine added.

"Missy Pate would've been a unique personality no matter when or where she lived, but the landscape has changed so drastically since her time that it lends a kind of mystique to the stories."

"Missy was quite a lady," Jimbo drawled in answer to his granddaughter. "As for the value of these stories, we'll just have to take your word."

"It's amazing to me that farming faded so completely from our East Texas landscape and yet continues to shape the people here."

"How do you mean?" Alma inquired gently.

"Work ethic, attachment to the land, and general hardiness… Of course, all that's fading fast. Just look at me, overwrought by the so-called strain of modern life to the point of wandering right into oncoming traffic. Still, that ingrained toughness has way outlasted the cotton fields."

"Don't go talking down on yourself, doodlebug. The strain you're under is real, and it comes of takin' the whole load on your own shoulders."

"Missy never brought in a crop alone," Nadine ventured, "not even before she got crippled. She'd have died tryin' before she quit, mind you, but it just can't be done."

"If I was young enough to start over," Jimbo mused, "I might just pick up and move to Houston so as to give you a hand. The notion of leaving here pretty well turns my stomach, but there ain't much I wouldn't do for you and Kimmy. Still, the fact is… None of us would be much good to you down there, nor much good to ourselves, either. Here in Red Bog, we can gather around you and shoulder a part of the load."

"Time will close in on us eventually," Nadine added. "All that's in the good Lord's hands as it should be. But no everyday kind of trouble could shake us loose from this place, not without a train load of dynamite. I'll tell you plain, child, what you need to do is hunker down in back of us and rest a while."

"I love Jimbo and Nadine," Alma declared, indicating and dismissing them with one economical flick of her wrist. "But they can be just a touch proud. A lifetime of hard work and independence made 'em that-a-way. By offerin' help, they're asking yours in return, Laura Beth. Why, just knowing that we're needed brings strength and purpose. You're like a breath of fresh air around here. Even the preacher's little wife said so."

"Nobody's trying to back you into a corner," Nadine stated with her usual bluntness, "or pushing for some snap decision to uproot your life. Just give this thing a little more time. Stand back and take a good look at where you're headed."

"Go to Houston and look things over," Jimbo advised. "Give the business a nudge or two in the right direction, put your mind at ease, and then get yourself back up here where you belong."

Suddenly full of nervous energy, Laura Beth sprang to her feet. She strode purposefully toward the solitude of the kitchen but then turned around to walk slowly back.

"Y'all aren't making this any easier," she blurted in a kind of plea for understanding. Her eyes conveyed all the intensity of a wounded animal, and even the familiar habit of knuckle biting let her down. Needing some measure of relief, Laura Beth slammed her small fist against the back of a vacant chair. The stormy gaze settled at last on her grandfather. "I don't want to go back; that's the whole trouble."

"Trouble? It's the best news I've heard since the drought broke in '57."

Walking over, she sank slowly to her knees beside his chair.

"Can't you see, Granddaddy? I'm supposed to… I have to… I absolutely dread leaving y'all, but I will do whatever it takes to make a life for my little girl."

The explanation seemed to exhaust Laura Beth, and her head dropped rather suddenly into his lap. Running his fingertips along her scalp, Jimbo hummed fragments of melody that could have been anything from *Red River Valley* to *Amazing Grace*. As one hand worked ever so gently through her hair, his keen old mind evaluated the limited options before them.

Further involvement with young Bradley Chandler, on any terms but those of superficial courtesy, put his granddaughter's tender heart at risk. And, naturally, he shied away from any such notion. To watch her struggle along, though, with deep roots pulling her in one direction and a mother's instincts in the other… At the very least, he decided, they needed to get Kimmy out to Red Bog and try the situation on for size.

Laura Beth slept surprisingly well that night, but all her worries returned the next day. In fact, nerves soured her stomach to the point of regretting the wonderful morning meal. By lunchtime, she could hardly stand the sight of food, and it took a fresh Dr Pepper to keep Aunt Nadine's biscuits and gravy safely in place.

Her anxiety centered on a phone call, the one she had made right after breakfast. Granddaddy's obvious approval provided some comfort, but he and Nadine soon headed off to their outdoor chores. Laura Beth prayed in fits and starts, held back the tears by force of will, and threw all her nervous energy into cleaning the church house alongside Cindy and Aunt Alma.

Still queasy, she leaned against the vacuum cleaner and sipped her tepid soft drink from force of habit. She watched Alma's nimble fingers construct a silk flower arrangement down front and, when her breath finally steadied, struck up a conversation.

"Kimmy hasn't had many chances to spend time out here. I should be excited. I am excited, but I never exactly meant to invite Bradley along on her visit. The conversation just got away from me somehow."

"Oh, child… It's that ingrained sense of hospitality. Nobody drops a lifetime of training and instinct overnight. Besides, I'm inclined to agree with you. It wouldn't do to call the man up and dismiss him out of hand because his help's no longer needed."

"If I knew for sure I didn't need him, that I'd offered the invitation from nothing more than kindness, then we could all live happily ever after. It's the needing that scares me. To need Granddaddy, you, and Nadine is one thing. We're blood kin, and over the course of a lifetime, y'all have given me every reason to trust. Bradley Chandler, on the other hand…"

"Jimbo would never have gone off this morning if he'd realized what a state that phone call left you in. Of course, he couldn't have done much except work himself into a state to match yours. He's got Missy's head for planning and his daddy's knack for action. Come down to waiting in between, though…"

"So, you let him go off to work horses and sent Aunt Nadine right along with him."

The old lady joined in Laura Beth's appreciative chuckle, and her next words brought on a good dose of real laughter.

"Pshaw, that sister of mine is worse than Jimbo. Waitin' will turn her downright unpleasant nearly every time."

Drawn by their laughter, Cindy left off dusting and made her way up to the front of the sanctuary.

"Surely you ladies wouldn't be gossiping in church, and without me?"

"No," Laura Beth answered, wiping her eyes as she sank down on the armrest of a pew. "No, but Aunt Alma don't miss much."

"I've learned a thing or two in eighty-odd years. Change is a funny thing. Positive or not, it scares us half to death. Why, when Missy found out I'd set my cap for Bud Evans… Jimbo told off on us and him too little to know the difference. Up to that point in life, Missy had guided me along with her usual light touch on the bridle reins.

The way she cleared her throat could change my plans for the day. When hints and suggestions didn't quell my interest in Bud, Missy just flat dug in her heels."

"What was so objectionable about Uncle Bud?" Laura Beth inquired lightheartedly. "I remember him as a very nice man who always kept a twinkle in his eye and a pocketful of hard candy."

"Land sakes, everybody loved Bud. Missy, too, but it took her a decade or so to admit it. She wasn't used to being wrong, you see. The thing about Missy, Bud hardly ever realized she'd been cool toward him until after she warmed up."

"Ingrained hospitality?"

"Something like that. If Bud had given her the least reason, she'd have set the dogs on him. Nearly did, once, but that's a story for another time."

"I never knew your husband," Cindy put in quietly, "but I've read the plaque on his service as a deacon. You never answered the original question. What did your— Well, Missy, what did she find to dislike?"

"It wasn't dislike, not exactly. Missy believed in treating everybody kindly. Rich or poor, black or white, it just didn't matter. Even so, the Pate name meant something in Red Bog. She was a Kimbel and valued that connection, too. Missy figured the man I married ought to see me as quite the catch, a kind of princess, don't you know. But I went and picked a town-raised boy. Bud grew up at Henderson, and by the time I met him, had his heart set on pharmacy school."

"Missy was afraid he'd go off to college and forget you?"

"Either that, or come back and not appreciate what he had. Our family ties didn't mean anything to Bud. He fell in love with me, not a share of the Pate land or Papa Kimbel's store."

"Surely that's a good thing?" Cindy ventured.

"Absolutely, but Missy entered her marriage on more or less equal footing. She and Big Jim understood and valued each other. I suppose she wanted the same for me. Then, too, you'd best consider my brother's personality."

"Granddaddy's told me as lovingly as possible that Big Jim was a long way from perfect," Laura Beth interjected gently.

"Jim had some glaring faults, alright, but his virtues stood out just as plain. Having chosen herself a man like that, larger than life and tougher than nails, Missy placed my Bud somewhere about the level of a house cat. Nice enough company but precious little help when the trials of life come at you hard and fast."

"House cat?" Laura Beth snorted.

"She never quite said that, but I knew her well enough to get the drift. Bud Evans was a kindhearted, reliable man. He loved me, and I loved him. Didn't figure the family could stand but one Big Jim Pate, anyhow."

Cindy suppressed a burst of hilarity and then blushed prettily at the thought of laughing at a long-dead pillar of the community like Jim Pate. Still, the old lady's turn of phrase…

"Go on; please go on," she begged, making a rolling motion with her right hand.

"I don't think Missy ever really understood my choice, but she developed quite a soft spot where Bud was concerned. If we had a little tiff, she'd come down on his side. After all, anybody who couldn't get along with Bud Evans…Well, they must be plumb contrary."

"And she raised you better than that," Laura Beth chided teasingly.

"Exactly," Alma responded with a chuckle. "Listen, child. Bud and I survived the early years and had a wonderful marriage, but that doesn't do much for you in the here and now. Why, I can hear Missy's voice in my ear. Quit filling the girl's head with tales, Alma, and give her some sound advice."

"I love your stories, Aunt Alma, but I'll take the advice, too."

"I know you're scared, Laura Beth, only a fool wouldn't be. But you need to make the most of Bradley's time here."

"It's supposed to be Kimmy's time; her fall break from school hit just right. I'm not even sure how Bradley—"

"Be that as it may, he's coming. Same way he turned up right after your accident. This time you can meet him on your home ground with the three of us and all of Red Bog standing squarely behind you. Either make things right, or put him out of your mind once and for all. That's my advice."

Laura Beth drew in a sharp breath and then answered slowly.

"Whether I like it or not, our marriage is in the past. It's too late to salvage anything now."

"Maybe so, but you wore that wedding ring until… Did they take it off in the hospital?" When Laura Beth glanced involuntarily at her left hand, Alma soldiered on to make the crucial point. "Twelve years is a long time to carry a torch, child. You're a-way too young to leave your heart buried in the past."

Though gently spoken, the words cut deep. Cindy scooted closer along the pew and slipped an arm around her friend's waist.

"Come on, honey. That old soda has got to be flat. Let's all go out to the kitchen and find you something else."

As they sat down together in the fellowship hall, Laura Beth shook off the last of her sniffles and spoke in a clear but somewhat lifeless tone.

"There's no way to blame Bradley for the divorce, not even if I wanted to. We needed different things in life, and at the time, I thought it best to let him— Oh, Cindy, I sent him away. I sent him away, and now he's being chased by every sporty little adventuress who'd like to see her picture in an outdoor magazine!"

Reaching across the table, Alma gave her niece's hand a gentle pat. Then, exchanging a look with Cindy, she rose stiffly, and stepped into a small but serviceable kitchen area.

"Oh, honey," Cindy sympathized and then paused briefly to consider her next words. "Just because the divorce was your idea doesn't make it your fault. Anybody can see that you don't take it lightly, so there must have been very real reasons."

"I never craved security or financial stability or whatever you want to call it for myself. Bradley and I were young and able bodied. A kind of fearless duo, you might say. But Kimmy came along, and my world changed overnight. Poor Bradley just never did make the leap."

"Ice water or grape soda?" Alma called, glancing back at them from the refrigerator. Laura Beth came halfway to her feet, complex problems temporarily upstaged by this new and more basic dilemma. "I found your Dr Pepper stuck in the icebox door, child. That question was for Cindy."

"Ice water, please," and the three ladies shared a brief smile.

"Bradley saw his dad's success as our safety net," Laura Beth continued almost reluctantly. "I'm not painting him as some kind of leech, you understand. He never thought we'd actually need the help. In his mind, though, Pop's money was good enough for an emergency reserve. Mr. and Mrs. Chandler are wonderful. Still… Emergency or not, nobody else is gonna support my daughter."

Alma brought their drinks and half a package of store-brand fudge cookies as she returned to her seat.

"Sounds reasonable," Cindy admitted, "reasonable and very admirable. There's a good dose of Pate family pride involved. But I'm not about to judge you for it, especially with your Aunt Alma sitting across the table."

"Pshaw," Alma breathed with a gentle sort of chuckle.

"The thing is, Laura Beth… Whether divorce was the right answer or not, that choice is already made. What you're facing at the moment is a question of what to do with Bradley in the here and now."

Instead of answering, Laura Beth frowned ruefully at the small cookie in her hand.

"I've hit rock bottom," she announced with a sigh. "These cookies have gone stale, but I'd settle for chocolate-covered cardboard at the moment and probably find it very comforting."

"That's alright, sweetie. Chocolate's got healing powers," Cindy spoke these words with a smile and then resumed their serious discussion. "You said Bradley never made the leap. Never understood your need to provide a certain amount of security for Kimmy. But does that statement still hold true?"

A blank look passed over Laura Beth's face and a rather sickly expression followed.

"I don't know, Cindy. Heaven help me, I don't know. Worked so hard to keep him at arm's length and avoid another heartbreak. Now, I've made him a stranger."

"Stranger or not," Alma observed sagely, "the look in your eyes when you talked about the sporty little gals who grace those outdoor magazines would've made Jimbo double his lariat rope and hunt somebody to thrash."

"Oh, Aunt Alma…"

"There's wisdom in Cindy's question, and I'd say it's high time you started lookin' for answers. You're not alone in this, child, and we'll be praying."

"Absolutely!" Cindy agreed.

After finishing up some light chores, the three ladies said goodbye. Cindy headed off to her mother-in-law's to pick up the kids, and Laura Beth drove Aunt Alma back home.

Once there, she watched her aunt navigate safely up the back steps and then drifted down to the barn lot where Jimbo and Nadine were unsaddling a couple of horses.

"Y'all done for the day?"

"Naw," Jimbo answered lightly, "it's early yet."

"I'm about rode out," and Nadine's spoke with a grin even though the admission galled her a little. "Matter of fact, I just spotted my replacement."

"Sounds lovely, but with Kimmy and her dad coming, I really ought to help straighten up and get things ready. Besides, I'm nervous as a cat today. Don't horses pick up on that kind of thing?"

"How come you— Well, never mind. You've done enough cleaning for one day, and they won't be here before noontime tomorrow. Kimmy will stay in the house with y'all, of course, while old George and that Chandler boy bunk down at my place."

"Old George is nearly twenty years younger than you, Granddaddy."

"Figure of speech," he quipped. "Now, what about it? Nadine's got the right idea, doodlebug. A nice little ride will settle you down quick enough. As for the horse pickin' up on your nerves, the first time he jumps at his own shadow, you'll get your mind on the business at hand."

"Sounds like a cure me or kill me kind of deal," she snorted.

"I'd like to have the company, sure enough, but nobody's crowdin' you into it."

"I can't recall ever saying no to you, Granddaddy, and I doubt I ever will."

"I have and probably will again," Nadine chimed in, "but it don't generally do much good."

"What have you got me riding today?" Laura Beth inquired a few minutes later as they rode out on matching buckskin geldings.

"That's Buzz," Jimbo called, throwing a glance back over his shoulder, "and I'm on Woody."

"Do you have any idea where those names originated?"

"Not right off hand. Folks are apt to name a horse anything these days. Kinda makes me think of skeeters and sweet gum bushes, though."

"That's about what I figured," Laura Beth teased lightly. "They're from a kids' movie."

"Makes sense," he decided. "The fella who owns these horses has a house full, all of them running in different directions. "Baseball and soccer and ballet don't leave much time for trail riding, but I doubt he'll ever give up on the notion."

"Expensive notion," she observed, "and not ideal for the horses, either."

"Fella works a good job, and it don't hurt his feelings none that I'm still charging the same rate I did thirty years ago."

"Thirty years ago?"

"Yes'm, tuned up a fancy little palomino as a graduation gift for the girl he went on to marry, and I've rode several for them since the wedding."

"Ever thought about going up on the price?"

"How come? I'd be a'horseback anyway, whether he paid me or not. They don't send anything rough, just trail horses in need of a few wet saddle blankets. I price the ridin' where they can afford it, and we're all happy."

Jimbo took off in a trot and then slowed his mount just a little, setting their pace at a measured but purposeful walk. Laura Beth felt somehow steadier. Breathing deeply, she soaked up each moment, as the rhythm of her horse's gait worked a slow magic. Her anxiety faded, and the pressures of life seemed quite distant. Nothing much could trouble her way back here in the woods. Granddaddy had accumulated a world of knowledge in his seven decades of life on the land, and together they could tackle just about anything.

Because they traveled public roads on this ride instead of surveying the homeplace, Granddaddy offered no running commentary on cattle, fences, grass, or water. Still, Laura Beth knew better than to ride like a passenger. She directed her horse's movements almost by instinct and took gradual notice, after a couple of turns, as familiar hoofbeats shifted from their sharp click-clack on blacktop to steadily crunching gravel and finally to a muffled clop-swish in sand.

"We going anywhere in particular?"

"I never was one to live in the past," Jimbo drawled by way of an answer, "but calling up stories for you has got the old days much on my mind. Old days and the old folks, too."

Chapter Ten

Leaving the county road, Jimbo pointed his horse back into a little clearing. A well-kept graveyard spread out before them, shedding some light on his earlier statement, but Laura Beth watched uncertainly as he swung down and looped his reins casually over the chain-link fence.

"Missy's not buried—"

"No, doodlebug. She's resting on the main highway a few miles south of Red Bog. My Melba lays there, too, right along with the rest of our folks. You've seen Missy's grave, and I'll take you again sometime. Not on horseback, though. Traffic runs along there 'bout like water through a millrace, don't slack up for nobody or nothing."

She acknowledged his comment with a wry smile and then dropped down to stand beside him.

"You're right about that highway, but who… Why are we here?"

"Elm Grove Cemetery," he explained, gesturing to a sign over the gate. "I knew half these folks. Big Jim and Missy knew 'em all, or pretty nearly. But I reckon we're here on account of Gert and Tobe. These horses ought to stand," he assured her and then turned to open the gate.

Hinges creaked just a little as he motioned his granddaughter through and dropped the latch carefully into place behind them. The cemetery covered a couple of acres with headstones arranged in curving, slightly irregular, rows. Though months and sometimes years stretched between his visits, Jimbo Pate strolled unerringly to a simple rough-cut stone.

A step or two behind, Laura Beth watched as her grandfather

removed his small but carefully shaped Stetson and trailed the fingers of his free hand across the top of the headstone.

"Washington," she read, lips moving silently. "Tobias, March 4, 1870-November 28, 1940. Gertie, June 12, 1873-December 5, 1965."

"Gert kept Alma and Nadine fed and scrubbed until Mister Big Jim married. Then after I came along… With Missy using the chair and all, she hovered and fussed like a mother hen. Missy was independent and strong willed. Wouldn't abide no outside nurse, but Gert was already in place."

"And then there's Tobe. I've heard his name several times these last couple of weeks."

"I learned an awful lot walkin' along behind that old man."

"Sure enough?" she murmured, prodding gently with one of his own phrases.

"Maybe he never quite had Daddy's touch on the driving lines. Better than average, though, and he had a sight more patience with this shirttail kid. Daddy hired plow hands, hoe hands, and so on, but only Tobe got to mess with our better class of horses."

"You know what impresses me about Mr. and Mrs. Washington? From the stories, I mean."

"What's that?"

"The way they accepted Missy after so many years of living and working alongside Big Jim's family. They must have wondered, at times, who was calling the shots."

"Aw, doodlebug… That kind of thing's hard to spell out, but most everybody on the homeplace knew how things stood. We all took a certain pride in Missy, so warm and sweet and lively with an inner beauty that showed clean through. She was the boss lady, our mascot, you might say, and she made most of the day-to-day decisions. But if circumstances looked fixed to get rough, or just a touch unpleasant, somebody went and fetched Daddy."

"You've told me some of Big Jim's shortcomings," she mused, "but it sounds like they really did work at life as a team."

Jimbo set the hat back on his head in a single practiced motion, cleared his throat, and then turned to face her.

"That's what marriage is, doodlebug. Not just for Big Jim and Missy… You could say the same of Gert and Tobe or me and your grandmother."

Finding no ready answer, Laura Beth simply followed her grandfather as he strolled through the cemetery. Every now and then they paused as one headstone or another jogged his memory. She wished at first for her pencil and notepad, or maybe a small digital recorder, but finally let the anecdotes wash over her. Aunt Alma, Aunt Nadine, or Granddaddy himself could nail down any elusive details later.

Laura Beth felt a growing connection to her great-grandmother, and it seemed particularly strong just now. She wondered suddenly if this quiet little cemetery nestled deep in the piney woods might not have been a more appropriate resting place for Missy Pate than six feet of manicured earth alongside a busy highway. The question gnawed at her briefly, and familiar echoes of anxiety disrupted her newfound calm.

Ultimately, Laura Beth gave her head a little shake and mustered up a smile. Missy was not listening to the rush of traffic. She was enjoying the splendors of Heaven and had been since 1975. All that remained on this earth was a memory. A memory, and the lives she had touched. If Missy's legacy could be anchored to a location at all, it was more closely tied to the homeplace than to any gravesite. Between these private thoughts, the familiar cadence of Granddaddy's voice, and a fresh crop of stories, Laura Beth failed to notice the arrival of a smallish late-model sedan. A random glance toward the gate revealed two women, one young and one old, their attention obviously focused on the waiting pair of buckskin horses.

"Look up yonder," she advised her grandfather quietly, smiling as she slipped yet again into his way of speaking.

Jimbo followed her gaze and then gave an involuntary little start.

"Tarnation," he muttered. "I used to be harder to slip up on," but the wry tone of voice told Laura Beth he was more concerned with declining perception than by the arrival of these ladies.

They started for the gate then and the older of the two African American women called out in greeting.

"When did you go and get old, Little Mister?"

Jimbo struggled briefly to place the long unheard voice and match it to the frail nonagenarian standing before him. His stride quickened, even before full recognition, and Laura Beth found herself all but jogging to keep pace.

"Well… Time's apt to slip up on all of us, I reckon. Essie Washington?"

"Johnson," she corrected with a chuckle, "but that came about after I quit this part of the country. Who's following you there? Looks for all the world like— But I ain't plumb senile yet."

"I reckon not," he answered with a smile in his voice. "This here's my granddaughter, Laura Beth Chandler."

"A Chandler in name, maybe, and born a Pate. But the Kimbels marked this one. She's Missy made over! This is Destiny Washington. She's a granddaughter to my brother Elbert."

"Essie is Gert and Tobe's youngest daughter," he observed, bringing both girls into the conversation. "Grew up right there on the homeplace with us."

"Watched you grow up is more like it," Essie remarked. "I got the jump on you in that department."

"Yeah, but you weren't all that far ahead of the girls. I bet you didn't know they'd moved back to the homeplace."

"Moved— You mean Ms. Alma and Ms. Nadine are still living! Both of them? Why, I've gotten so used to everybody dying off on me until I just take it for granted sometimes."

"They're alive," he assured her with a grin, "and right lively, too. We better let you get on with your business here and then meet you back at the house. They'll want to see you for sure."

"The house? You don't mean they're back at Missy's…"

"That's right. I've got a home on the place, too. But the old house is right where you left it, and the girls live there together."

"Well, how about that! I ought to find them easy enough."

"S'pect so. You want any help gettin' out to the grave?"

"Aunt Estelle manages fairly well," the younger woman answered stoutly. "But if you all are finished with old home week, I would like to know what these animals are doing on the cemetery grounds."

Jimbo's eyes widened in surprise, and he greeted this rebuke with a slight noise from the back of his throat. His gaze took on a question then as it shifted back to Essie.

"Destiny can get touchy about the cemetery," the older woman said by way of explanation. "Some of her uncles, Elbert's sons, do most of the upkeep."

"Well, now… I've run across Elbert's boys time to time. They keep the cemetery looking good, but I don't recall seeing Destiny out here." Turning his attention to the younger woman, he continued. "Horses won't do any harm outside the fence. Never occurred to me to leave 'em way up yonder by the road ditch, and I see you didn't park your car up there, either."

"I'm sure my uncles will be glad to know you approve their maintenance of our family cemetery, but my car doesn't drop—"

Essie cleared her throat rather sharply, and all eyes turned in her direction.

"Sight of them horses brought you to mind right off, Jimbo. The very next thing I thought was how tickled Daddy would be to know you rode by and visited his grave. Tobias Washington was a horse man from the word go."

"I suppose that does put a different light on it," Destiny admitted without softening her tone much.

"He took so much pride in all of Missy's fine driving horses that a body might've thought they were his own," Essie remembered with a chuckle.

"Big Jim handpicked our best horses for her to drive," Jimbo put in, "and they were as good as anything that ever wore harness. We all came around to admitting cars were more practical. But to see one of Missy's horses stepping along, head carried just so, with mane and tail rippling as that buggy glided over the road… Well, it made a body want to stand up and salute."

"Quite a sight, and you called it up for me just like painting a picture." A sigh escaped, and Essie reached out to lay a hand on the nearest buckskin shoulder. "These two look more like cowponies than Missy's quick-stepping road horses."

"They're out of stock-horse breeding, alright, but more yard pets than anything else."

"Missy chased cattle, and just about anything else that would line out in front of her, on that big red charger up until— But I recollect your first cowpony, too. Mister Big Jim used to grumble that you never was much good around the place after that. Always gone to the woods or the creek bottom huntin' for some old wild cow."

"Missy got that little dappled gray mare off her favorite cousin, Hoyt Kimbel, and Daddy figured they'd started me on the road to wrack and ruin."

"It's natural to reminisce when you're back home," Destiny interrupted, trying to keep the impatience out of her voice, "and for better or worse, many of your memories are intertwined with those of the Pate family. But, Aunt Estelle, we don't want to use up all your strength standing here at the gate. Let's visit a couple of gravesites. Then, if we must, I can make time to swing by that desolate old farm."

"Desolate?" Essie queried dryly.

"Yes, ma'am. Childhood perceptions aside, it's not now and never was the center of the world."

Every bit of hard-won relaxation evaporated, but Laura Beth's personal anxieties could not have been farther from her mind. Already aware that "the hands" may have experienced Red Bog life from a vastly different perspective in the 1920s and 30s, she viewed Destiny's thinly veiled resentment as living proof. A newfound enjoyment of family tales did not make her obtuse or narrowminded. Even so… She had very little patience for anyone, regardless of skin color, taking an abrupt and dismissive tone where her grandfather was concerned.

Stepping around Granddaddy and placing herself directly in Destiny's line of sight, Laura Beth felt hot words rise in her throat. Without missing a beat, he reached out and caught hold of her arm.

"Y'all come ahead when you get ready, Essie."

The invitation came out in an easy drawl, but he nodded curtly to Destiny. Steel strong and yet somehow gentle, Jimbo's weathered hand guided Laura Beth firmly toward her horse. They started home in silence and covered two or three miles before she found her voice.

"Won't question your judgement, Granddaddy, but I wish you had let me give that insufferable woman a piece of my mind."

"You'd have been whistling into the wind, doodlebug. No call to get yourself all worked up and maybe ruin Essie's time here. Besides, I reckon young Destiny's got a right to her opinions."

"Yes, of course, but—"

"We all come through some mighty hard times together," he recalled. "Big Jim and Missy were poor by today's standards, and them Washington kids grew up a sight poorer. Destiny won't never know how hard they worked. How hard we worked, either, for that matter. But whatever picture she's drawn from their memories is hers. You'll not change her mind by exchangin' hot words in the graveyard."

"No, sir."

"Just as surely, though, all our tales about Missy and the rest of the bunch are yours if you want 'em. Take the bad right along with the good, Laura Beth, but don't throw the baby out with the bath water."

"The stories I've heard are overwhelmingly positive, Granddaddy. It's difficult to imagine someone having unpleasant memories of the homeplace."

"Missy was sweet as they come. Still, it's only fair to say that she was pretty well set in her ways. She gave her orders politely, but a body could follow them or hunt up somewhere else to live. Same goes for Big Jim. Only, he wasn't always polite. I loved my daddy, doodlebug, but he could be heavy handed, even with me."

"Doesn't make him a bad man," Laura Beth mused, "but when you put all that against a backdrop of poverty and factor in his problems with alcohol, the picture turns kind of grim."

"I'll tell you this; Gert or Tobe or… Well, nobody who saw his tender way with Missy ever hated the man."

"It all goes back to Missy, doesn't it?"

"She had plenty of good sense and what you might call strength of character. It took her efforts and Daddy's mean streak, too, just to keep us all fed. And keeping us fed didn't stop at our family. Maybe the folks who farmed for us had to put up with quite a bit, doodlebug. But I'm here to tell you… Nobody from outside, off the place you understand, ever worked up the nerve to mess with any of 'em."

Laura Beth pondered outdated racial norms with their strange mixture of care and condescension. Then, too, she considered the almost universal complexity of human relations. It was difficult, riding along behind her grandfather, to cast any kind of harsh judgement on the way of life that had shaped him. After much consideration, she decided that just maybe… People like Gert and Tobe Washington, and even their daughter Essie, had found a way to balance their justifiable resentment of inequalities with a genuine affection for the people they had lived and worked alongside.

"Thank God," she breathed, too low for Jimbo to hear. "Thank God for such people."

Unmistakable Christian charity called for some kind of response, even all these years later. Accordingly, she would strive for some connection with Destiny or, at the very least, make every effort to keep Ms. Essie's visit enjoyable.

Several hours later, Alma and Nadine bid Jimbo goodnight. The old man watched his aunts head off to bed, tired but still smiling over their pleasant reunion with Essie Washington.

"Say, doodlebug," he ventured, turning to his granddaughter. "How about coming down after breakfast to help me with a little cleaning?"

"At your house?" she questioned, rising from her chair to kiss him on the cheek. "I'll be glad to. May not be up to Grandmother's standards, but we'll have everything sorted before Bradley and them get here."

As she spoke, Laura Beth realized that thoughts of the past, brought on this time by their unexpected visitor, had once again calmed her fears of the future. She actually looked forward to the familiar routine of light housework. After all, she couldn't change the situation with Bradley by worrying herself sick before he and Kimmy ever arrived in Red Bog.

"Alright, I'll leave you to get some rest. Don't stay up too late, now," he teased in parting.

With the house quiet, she settled back into her chair and opened the laptop. By the flickering light of a banked nighttime fire and the dim electronic glow of her computer screen, she drafted a chapter on some of the more complex aspects of Red Bog life. "What we lovingly call the homeplace was never exactly a shining beacon of rural perfection," she wrote in closing, "but the families who worked it made more than a living off the land. Together, they made a life."

"A chapter?" she murmured into the empty room. Never having explored the full potential of her little project, she found the question almost startling. A brief tingle of excitement shot through her as she contemplated the possibility of an actual book. "Oh, well," she finally decided, "chapter or section or article… Whatever it is, that's all for tonight."

Jimbo came up for breakfast the next morning and then accompanied Laura Beth back down to his house.

"I hate to sit by and watch you work, doodlebug. If you'll sorta point me in the right direction, we'll get this deal knocked out."

"Yes, sir. It shouldn't take long."

They took on separate projects at first, but Laura Beth liked having him on hand to chat and pass the time. Soon, he observed from the doorway of a spare bedroom while she dusted the dresser and consolidated a few odds and ends into a single drawer.

"What all did you and the Washington girl find to talk about yesterday?"

"Oh, I would have enjoyed listening to Ms. Essie's recollections. But I wanted Destiny to feel welcome. She finally warmed up, and we got into a friendly argument over traffic."

"Traffic?"

"Yep," Laura Beth answered with a chuckle. "She claimed Dallas traffic was worse than anything in Houston but conceded the point after hearing that I'd been run over."

"Well, I reckon so! Thought she lived in California?"

"No, sir. That's Ms. Essie, I think. Destiny lives near Arlington these days. Her last name's not Washington, now, but I'd have to check Facebook to tell you what it is. What all did y'all talk about? Did I miss any good stories?"

"Some," he admitted. "Essie and the girls are quite a little bit older than me, you know, and I like to hear their tales from back before my time. Essie got to tellin' about her Uncle Snap Havard."

"Snap Havard, huh? Sounds like a born rounder…"

"You better believe it! Snap was still young and livin' single in 1925, but he hit on that particular year to put in a crop of his own. Lucky rogue caught the last sure-enough good cotton market East Texas ever saw."

"Really?" she chuckled, eyes alight with interest.

"Snap took his share of the money and cleared out. Ended up trainin' in the kitchen of some fancy Dallas hotel and made a baker, of all things. He married one of the hotel maids. She kept right on working, too. I knew Snap in later years, and you can bet he enjoyed flashin' that money around while they had it. Times, he'd call long distance to Papa Kimbel's store. Wantin' his big sister, Gert, or even Missy to help him work out a recipe… Still, I reckon Snap learned a good many tricks of his own. Aunt Alma talks about a nine-layer coconut cake he made one Christmas when they visited in Red Bog. Cooked it in Missy's wood-fired oven because that's the best we had."

"With pocket money and coconut cake," she guessed, "I'd say he was downright popular among the homefolks."

"Sure enough," he drawled, stepping into the room to help her with a fitted sheet, "but Snap was mighty well liked even when I knew him as a broke farm hand."

"Lots of personality," she surmised with a smile.

"You can say that again, and generous to a fault. Aunt Alma was a dutiful little girl, but Nadine was more like me. Always underfoot or somewhere she wasn't supposed to be. That same Christmas of the coconut cake, Nadine saw Snap pass Big Jim a couple of bottles. Bonded whiskey at that. Nobody in Dallas held onto that kind of liquor just to sell it to a black man right in the middle of prohibition. I 'spect Snap took his life in his hand liftin' them bottles off a bootlegger or maybe some rich hotel guest. Then give 'em to Big Jim with no more fuss than you'd make over a brace of ripe peaches."

"How did Big Jim react to a gift like that?"

"Kinda set him back, I guess, but they didn't know Nadine was anywhere around. Daddy took a notion to share his good fortune. He called for Tully to run and turn out the foxhounds and sent Snap over to fetch Uncle Cleve. They all counted on Cleve bein' sober enough to catch the dogs come daylight, and the fox chase itself served to get the four of 'em clear of Missy and Gert for a while. Of course, Missy loved to hear them hounds run. Big Jim wasn't near as slick as he might've been. Apart from bad weather, everybody on the place knew what it meant if he didn't take her along. Still… She hated the drinkin' as much as he liked it, and he generally went out of his way to make sure she didn't have to look at him drunk."

Jimbo's smile carried just a hint of sadness around the edges, and

Laura Beth returned it understandingly.

"Did they get by with it? What about Nadine?"

"Yeah… They got by with it, more or less, but she got a fifty-cent piece off of Big Jim. Mischievous and business-minded to boot. Whatever Missy and Big Jim didn't teach me, Nadine did."

The pair got started laughing, then, and Laura Beth collapsed for a moment onto the newly made bed.

"Why did Snap ever come back to live on the homeplace?" she finally asked in a determined effort to regain her composure and hear the rest of the story.

"Well, the crash in '29 got his bakin' job and cut her pay down to less than what they could live on. Farm prospects was awful bleak along about then, but nearly everything else looked worse. Snap had him a secondhand Studebaker, so Missy and Big Jim scraped together a little money and sent it up there to buy the gasoline."

"How did he adjust, coming back to Red Bog after the big city life?"

"Can't say for sure; he'd had plenty of time to settle in 'fore I got big enough to take much notice. Besides, Snap was one of the happiest fellas you ever saw. His wife, though, never did get over thinkin' she was just a little bit better than some of the other hands. And that particular bunch of Havard kids, around my age and younger, was by gum scrubbed and starched to within an inch of their lives."

~ ~

"I've enjoyed just about all of this city life I can stand," George Kelly said as he stacked the last suitcase in the car. "Besides, any place that shaped Laura Beth is bound to be pretty special."

Struck by the statement, Bradley tossed the older man a sardonic grin over the top of the sedan.

"One car ride and you're wrapped around her little finger. It's nice to know you approve of my ex-wife, good buddy."

"I approve, alright, but a fella's got to question your thinkin' on that ex part."

"You're one to talk," Bradley shot back. "Been married three times and standin' here single as can be."

"Laugh if you want to, sonny boy, but I'd have moved heaven and earth to keep a woman like—" George cocked his head at the sound of approaching footsteps, and his voice dropped suddenly to an earnest whisper. "Let it go. I don't mind a little headbutting contest with you, but durned if I'll upset Kimmy. She might not understand our kind of joshin' back and forth."

Bradley smiled again, shaking his head at this mix of ingrained toughness and tender concern. Kimmy rushed onto the scene in a happy little whirlwind of pencils, sketchpad, and half-finished bottle of chocolate milk.

"Road trip!"

"Well," Bradley quipped as he settled behind the wheel, "somebody woke up in a sunny frame of mind."

She smiled without comment, and nobody spoke until they got well under way.

"Having you around is new and different, Dad. I've really enjoyed our time together. Guess maybe I sometimes let Mama drift into the background like a piece of the furniture. When she's not here, though..."

"Only a teenage daughter could compare someone as vibrant as Laura Beth to a comfortable chair," he observed with a chuckle. "Still, I know you're excited to see her."

"Reckon you'll take to farm life?" George inquired.

"The city's all I've ever known, but I'm not exactly in love with it. Besides, having Dad and Mama together in one spot… Whichever way things go, boredom will not be an issue. How about you? You're used to the country, right?"

"Well, yeah. A stock farm is a little on the tame side for me, but it'll be nice to have some dogs under foot and a saddle horse ready to hand."

"Mr. Pate's dogs are bred to work cattle," Bradley ventured. "I wouldn't count on running many races behind them."

"Foot… Them old curs are meat dogs. Shoot some game out a time or two, and they'll go to lookin' up. Run a squirrel or a bobcat or just about anything that'll climb a tree."

"George?"

"Yeah, pumpkin?"

"Are you speaking a foreign language all of a sudden?"

"Just hang on, Kimmy girl. Red Bog's apt to be a mighty educational experience for you."

"Oh, I don't know… I've had more recent exposure to Laura Elizabeth Chandler than anyone in this car. Mama's not one to go around shouting demands, but be it client or competitor or contentious neighbor, she eventually wins them over to her way of thinking. Dad may be the one who gets educated."

Chapter Eleven

~December 1938~

An irregular line formed before the doorway that opened from a side porch into Missy's office. Each man stepped into the little room, hat in hand, and closed the door behind him. A connecting door to the rest of the house stood open, but no one wanted the other hands listening in on his business while awaiting their turn. Each exchanged a few words with the boss lady and tucked some cash money into the bib of his overalls before leaving.

"Now, Tully," and she offered up the trace of a smile from behind her rolltop desk. "That bankroll is on the light side, but I squared your debt with Papa. There's his bill if you want it."

"Beg pardon, Missy. Did I hear right? You mean I'm paid off at the store?"

"Sure enough," she affirmed with a nod.

"Good credit and a little bit of pocket money! What with you and Mr. Roosevelt lookin' after me, this here depression don't hardly mean a thing."

Laughter danced in Missy's eyes as she struggled to maintain her composure.

"Me and Big Jim ain't exactly on a level with President Roosevelt, but our interest in you and yours is a sight more personal. The Lord's still on His throne, Tully, and there's always hope for better times next year."

"Yes'm…"

"Maybe we'll get a spell of hog killin' weather before too long. Anyhow, Mister Big Jim will have a little something for y'all at Christmastime."

"Thank you, ma'am. Anything comes up between now and hog killing, and I ain't ready to hand, old Tobe will know where to start looking."

"That brother-in-law of yours does have kind of a steadying influence on the family, don't he?"

"Well, ma'am," he answered with a grin, "don't know as I'd go that far with it."

"You be careful," she called as he turned to leave, "and Tully… Don't pull my Jimbo into any more horse races."

Tully let his hand fall from the doorknob and turned to face her once again.

"Why, no'm. Mister Big Jim told us you was mighty upset by all that, and I been meaning to 'poligize. But, Missy, that boy can get more out of a horse than anybody I've done seen! Leastways, since you was tearing 'round here on that big red Laddie…"

Her grin matched his own, and Tully left the office with a light step and a lighter heart. Tobias Washington, always fairly careful with his money, took the last turn. Plunking a healthier roll down on the desk, she smiled up once again.

"Well, Tobe, we made it through another year. You'll find a little something extra in there for you and Gert."

"Thank you, ma'am. You know, my Gertie says you do a right smart of worrying about all of us through the winter. There ain't no call for that, Missy. If you gave them brothers of hers their pay and mine, too, they'd be just as broke come springtime."

"I know that, Tobe. Still, I can't help but fret some. Kind of goes with the territory, I guess."

"Maybe so," he mused. "Gert worries 'bout you just like you worry 'bout everybody else. But we'll get by, always have."

"With God's grace…" The reverent words hung between them until her smile broke through again. "And a roll or two of balin' wire."

"Yes'm! Say, Missy, you might get your shawl and stand ready. Mister Big Jim's stirrin' around the barn lot."

"Something in the wind?" she inquired lightly.

"He don't scarcely tell nobody what he's thinking, but him and Little Mister are down there hookin' up a light driving team and two single horses. Your Jeff is one of 'em."

A couple of nervous mares danced and snorted in the hallway of the barn, but Big Jim Pate anchored them with his touch and a steady stream of almost inaudible conversation. Jimbo worked quietly, passing his father first one collar, then the other, and various pieces of harness until everything was in place. He stepped around behind Big Jim and watched in admiration as the high-strung animals moved willingly over to a light wagon and backed into their places on either side of the tongue.

"Right there," the man grunted as if to himself and then passed the driving lines to his son.

Jimbo held the team steady while his father hooked everything but the inside traces. If the horses tried to strike out with the wagon and no driver, their outside traces would pull against each other, thereby limiting movement. When his father stepped back, Jimbo draped the lines carefully over the dashboard.

"If you say so, Daddy, I'll drive Missy's buggy up to the house and then get some boys to help me unload this kindling before y'all take off."

"Naw," Big Jim muttered around a dangling cigarette. "I want the kindlin' on this spring wagon for weight. Besides, you're comin' along."

"Yes, sir," the boy answered with a grin. "Want me with Missy or with you?"

Once again, Jim shook his head.

"We know you can handle a team of mules between here and Papa Kimbel's gin. They tell me you can ride the daylights out of a single-footer, too. I reckon we'll see how you get along with a pair of light driving horses."

"A pair of— You mean Duchess and Dolly? But Daddy, it's only the third or fourth time they've worked together."

"Aw, you'll do just fine. Missy can set the pace for us. I'll drive Pharaoh and the road cart along behind."

The young stallion was a new favorite with Big Jim, and Jimbo realized in a flash that Missy would be driving the only reliable horse. Knowing better than to question this plan, he squared his shoulders and followed his father down towards Pharaoh's stall.

"Missy'll be pleased to get out for a little while," the boy ventured as they walked.

Big Jim never broke stride, but he tossed a genuine smile back over his shoulder.

"Won't she, though!" A few minutes later, he issued succinct instructions before leaving the barn. "That team's not going anywhere with 'em traces dropped. You stand here with Pharaoh. I'll collect Missy and be right back."

"Ain't no time for Missy to be out runnin' the road," Gert grumbled to her husband a few minutes later as they stood on the back porch at either side of the wheelchair. "That wind's got a nip to it."

Tobe only grunted in response, and Gert stooped slightly to adjust the black shawl over her friend's gray woolen dress.

"Don't fuss, Gert," Missy interposed gently. "Why, Jim doesn't really need me on these little training exercises. That Jeff horse is as broke as they come."

"Jeff, he's steady alright. But it won't amount to much if one of them fool colts runs broadside into your buggy."

"I declare," and the scolding words sounded almost playful. "You can think up more awful predicaments than anybody I ever saw. It's just a little outing with our boy. Besides, I'd like to be on hand if Jimbo gets into any kind of a jackpot."

"Only you could set in that buggy with practically no use of your legs and still figure on helping a near grown and right nimble young sprout out of whatever mischief he gets into."

Tobe shook his head in fond amusement, coughed his throat clear, and set in to give the boss lady some relief.

"Hush, woman! If Missy lacked for grit, she'd never have made it this far alongside Mister Big Jim. Besides, horse sense means a lot. You let Little Mister find some trouble, and she'll think of something whether or not her le—" Missy's lower extremities were no fit subject for menfolk, and slightly flustered by the near slip, he backed up for another run at it. "Anyhow, she don't need to walk to lend a hand."

Missy knotted the bonnet strings under her chin and smiled up at Gert, fully expecting a parting shot.

"What a body can do and what she ought to do is sometimes two different things." Missy's smile lost a fraction of its glow, and Gert immediately softened her tone. "I still say it's a fool's errand, but you'll look mighty pretty doin' it."

When Big Jim brought the buggy around and swept Missy up from her chair, Tobe leaned in close for a moment, speaking for their ears alone.

"If I live long enough, could be I'll learn to handle my wife the way your Missy does it."

"Watch it, now," Jim shot back in a mischievous whisper. "You talking 'bout her way with Gert or the way she handles me?"

"Beggin' your pardon, boss man," he answered at normal volume, "either one looks like an improvement."

Missy liked to drive, but there would be plenty of time for that over the road. On their way back to the barn, she simply nestled in close beside her husband.

"I gave Jimbo a drivin' job. If he'll keep the little mares tucked in and traveling along behind you, I'll put Pharaoh right up against the spring wagon. Ought to make us a nice jaunt. But if Duchess and Dolly give more trouble than he can smooth over, I'm left settin' on that light road cart to try and talk Pharaoh down. Jeff Davis is steady enough, so just get clear and watch the show. I don't want anything happenin' to you."

"Horsefeathers," she remonstrated with a gentle warmth in her tone. "Whatever happens to you and Jimbo happens to me. But I will say… our boy's makin' quite the little horse hand."

"Sure he is, Missy, and you know better than to fret over me. Just give us a few middling quick road miles and then swing into your Papa's upper meadow for some turns and stops. Let 'em stand a minute or two, make a couple of figure eights, and hit the road again."

"I'll do it," she answered cheerfully, "but why Papa's little hay meadow?"

Both husband and wife replaced the last syllable of meadow with a "der" sound and, just as automatically, distinguished such land from a "field" dedicated to row crops.

"Gives us 'bout the right distance for road work, and there's no call to jounce you and this nice little buggy over last year's cotton rows."

Missy smiled up at Big Jim, absolutely content in the moment. His reasons went without saying, really, just another example of the loving care he always offered. But she enjoyed having such things spelled out from time to time, even if it took a leading question or two on her part.

Waiting for his parents, Jimbo tried not to telegraph nervous tension to the handsome black colt. His usual task on these outings was to share the buggy seat with Missy, implementing her gentle pointers while he handled Jeff or another seasoned driving horse. Sitting behind a pair of young mares all on his own offered a thrilling challenge, but to do it with Big Jim watching… His father had predicted that Duchess and Dolly would stand hitched to the spring wagon without any problems. Still, Jimbo felt the weight of responsibility for them as well as the head-tossing Pharaoh.

"Whoa, boy," he crooned, speaking just above a whisper as he stroked the glossy shoulder. "Steady, now. Don't you go and wreck Daddy's little road cart right here in the aisle of the barn."

Strolling purposefully onto the scene, Big Jim took charge of his favorite young prospect with a firm hand and a few softspoken words.

"Hey, big fella… We'll give you a chance to work off them jitters directly." That said, he tossed the bare hint of a grin at Jimbo. "Can you hook the inside traces on that team without gettin' your head kicked off? I'd purely hate for them mares to pick up any bad habits."

"Yes, sir," and Jimbo returned the grin in full force. "If they're mine to drive, I'll hook 'em."

"Well… Do it, and fall in behind your mother. She'll set us a pace. I expect you to hold that pace without snatchin' at the bits, too."

Missy's advice, delivered from just outside the barn, carried a certain degree of comfort and reassurance.

"Those young mares ought to be a good deal lighter than a team of mules. Lighter, but with more energy to their travelin' gait. Keep just a whisper of tension on your lines, and don't be scared to talk to them. That-a-way, you won't have to jerk and saw at their mouths. I'll miss having you with me in the buggy. But we can work more horses this-a-way, and you'll get the fun of drivin' on your own."

Jimbo hooked his inside traces with plenty of attention to the task but took in his mother's words at the same time. Springing lightly up to the wagon seat, he answered her with what he hoped was the same careful mixture of teasing and respect that so many adults used where she was concerned.

"Aw, Missy, I know better. You like driving Jeff Davis too much to ever miss sharin' him with me." Her warm laughter sounded good, and Jimbo grinned in relief.

"If Alma wasn't off sparkin' and Nadine gone to town with her, you could at least have some company in the wagon."

"No, ma'am! No, thank you," and his quick answer stemmed from repeated observations as a sharp-eyed younger sibling. "Alma would be nervous and squealin' the whole time while Nadine looked for some way to spook my team and provoke even more squealin'."

No laugh this time, but Jimbo could hear the smile in her voice.

"Alright then. Let's roll 'em out."

Legs too short to brace a foot against the dashboard, Jimbo planted both feet squarely on the floor and leaned back in the seat. Duchess and Dolly felt as different from the mule teams he drove back and forth to the gin as a live catch feels from a chunk of driftwood hung on the other end of a fishing line. They surged forward in boundless enthusiasm, and Jimbo set his mind to regulate it without fighting against them.

Big Jim raised his voice to be heard over the hoofbeats and harness jangle, but a trace of humor and the lack of a reprimand told Jimbo he must be doing alright.

"They'll step," he called in reference to the sorrel mares. "What do you think, son? Good as a horse race?"

"Well, sir," Jimbo chanced over his shoulder. "I still like the saddle, but if I can skip the whippin' and get some of this, I'll sure take it."

~October 2007~

By the Light of a Memory 180

Nearly eight decades of life, countless miles in the saddle, and assorted cowboy wrecks left Jimbo Pate a little on the gimpy side but failed to sap his strength. In fact, the old man offered his granddaughter a steadying arm as they crossed the county road and climbed a gentle rise on their walk back to the main house. Having no real need of physical support, Laura Beth treasured the reassuring anchor of his presence.

"You okay, doodlebug? Good manners are fine up to a point. But if you're uneasy about any of this, just hustle Kimmy into the house quick as they get here. I'll send that Chandler boy on his way."

"I'm not exactly thrilled with the situation, Granddaddy, but Bradley hasn't done anything wrong."

"He ain't done much right, either, over the years."

"Be that as it may," she answered with a fond chuckle, "I haven't gotten very far by keeping him out of sight and out of mind. Maybe a little time together in Red Bog will let us move forward one way or another."

"Whatever you think best… Just know we'll stand by you."

"First," she decided with a nod, "I'm going to spend some time with my daughter. This visit was supposed to be about her. We've never been apart for so long, and besides, Kimmy's getting older. I know she has some early memories of you and Grandmother, but Aunt Alma and Aunt Nadine are just names that she might be able to connect with my old picture album."

"There's a sight more to Alma and Nadine than any photograph will capture," he snorted. "I toted Kimmy in front of me on the saddle a time or two, but she probably can't recall much of it. That little doll is one of us; she just don't know it yet. We can leave y'all plenty of mother-daughter time and still get her pretty well initiated to life on the homeplace.”

“Oh, I’m counting on it! Like I said, we’re not used to being apart. But give her a day or two, and I’ll be old news again. A little visit with you and Alma and Nadine is way overdue. Granddaddy,” she reflected with a brief pause, “try to give Kimmy a different nickname. She’s my daughter, and I guess I’d do anything for her, but I kind of like being your only doodlebug.”

Shared laughter carried them the last few steps up the hill and right through the kitchen door. Grabbing a Dr Pepper from the refrigerator, Laura Beth looked up in time to catch Nadine’s grin and pulled the older woman into a sidelong hug.

“Well, I see you got over your nerves ’bout the company comin’ today.”

“I don’t know about *got over*, but Granddaddy did a fine job of distracting me. Say, do you think Aunt Alma would mind if I fixed supper tonight?”

“Mind? I reckon not, but don’t go making a habit of it. Me and Jimbo get along right well with the present situation.”

“Oh, Aunt Nadine, you can cook. So can Granddaddy.”

“Yeah, but we don’t have to… Alma runs her kitchen, Missy’s kitchen, and everybody’s happy.”

“Duly noted,” Laura Beth quipped. “I guess the next question is how y’all feel about homemade pizza? Kimmy loves mine, but there’s nothing all that special about it.”

“Don’t be so modest,” Alma chided, stepping into the room to join them. “Anything you fixed would just about have to be good. I don’t know that Nadine and Jimbo ever looked a pizza in the face, but they're not what you'd call real particular. Besides, there's a plenty of buttermilk and leftover cornbread. You go right ahead and fix Kimmy her welcome-home supper. Just holler if I can be of any help."

"Thanks, Aunt Alma. I'll probably need to run to the store."

"Mmm, I expect so. We've got flour and everything for the crust. You can build your shopping list from there on up. Although… I could take out a little package of Jimbo's ground meat if you want it."

"Yes, please. City shoppers pay a premium for grassfed beef."

"What do you know. All these years, me and everybody else figured I was just too cheap to pour the grain to 'em." The old man flashed his granddaughter a grin, and continued in the next breath. "Speakin' of grain, you can swing by and pick up ten sacks of range cubes for me. We're one hard frost away from wintertime."

"Yes, sir. My weeklong visit stretched out some, didn't it?"

"You hear anybody complaining? I'll call ahead. Back right up to the dock, and them boys will load the feed. They'll charge it to my account, so you can just smile and wave and drive off. If you need some company, though, one of us will be glad to ride along."

"I'll be alright on my own, Granddaddy, but if anybody wants to go… Feed store still down by the railroad track?"

"Right where you left it," he assured her with a nod. "Trip through the grocery store may be just about what you need. You'll be just occupied enough to settle the nervous jitters but not too busy to gather your thoughts."

"Enjoy your quiet time," Alma put in, "and don't worry none about dessert. I'll have just time enough to mix us up an apricot cake, bake it, and clear out of the kitchen before you get back."

"Thank you, ma'am. Just don't say apricot in front of Kimmy until she's eaten a slice or two and bragged on it."

The little group shared a laugh before going their separate ways. Freshening up for the trip to town, Laura Beth glanced in passing at the two medications on her bedside table. She needed the sleep aid regularly in her suburban neighborhood but scarcely at all in Red Bog. The other, prescribed for occasional anxiety, seemed like a good idea today. Still, she hesitated. The family and homeplace had a calming effect on her anyhow. If she held off taking the nerve pill, it would leave something in reserve if the situation with Bradley proved too much.

The county seat supported only one major grocery store these days, and it lacked the selection Laura Beth had grown accustomed to in Houston. Even so, the store offered plenty to get by on and without the rushing mass of strangers. She selected the necessary ingredients from memory, exchanged several polite greetings along the way, and lost herself temporarily in the familiar routine of shopping.

"How do, Laura Beth?" and she knew that high nasal twang the moment she heard it.

Her uncle's business partner looked out of place pushing a shopping cart, but the man was unforgettable. Granddaddy's assessment echoed in the back of her mind even as a smile lit her features. "Vesper's so easygoin' as to be almost lazy," Jimbo had confided. "But he's smart enough to get by with it and likeable enough to where you don't mind so much."

"Hello there, Mr. Denton. I didn't expect to find you in the grocery store."

"Look here, I'm practically one of the family. If you keep on with that Mr. Denton stuff, I'm apt to start calling you doodlebug."

"Fair enough," she acknowledged with a laugh. "We'll just stick to Laura Beth and Vesper."

"Yeah," he drawled, returning to the subject of their chance meeting. "I take most of my meals in Sue Jean's café. Your Uncle James Allen calls it my office, but a fella gets a taste for a pot of homemade chili now and again. What about you, little miss? For a city girl and out-of-town company, I meet up with you in the strangest places. First, out pennin' cows with Jimbo and Nadine and now up here pushin' a buggy full of groceries amongst the natives."

"Well, my daughter's coming this evening to spend a few days at Red Bog. Nobody cooks like Aunt Alma. But Kimmy enjoys my homemade pizza, and I decided to make it for her."

"Hold it," he drawled, patting the air for emphasis even though she had finished speaking and waited, with a twinkle in her eye, to see what might come out of his mouth next. "Hold it right there… Jimbo still talks like you was his little princess, Alma and Nadine ain't much better, and I see what I see. There just ain't no way you've got a daughter old enough to be out travelin' on her own."

"No, sir," she answered, laughing warmly at his teasing tone. "Kimmy's dad will bring her."

"Well, then… Y'all enjoy your visit, and tell Jimbo me and the dogs will drift out that-a-way soon to run rabbits. I'd like to meet your husband and little Kimmy, too, if she's got any of her mama's charm. Red Bog's known around these parts for turnin' out ladies with that little bit of extra spark. Fact is, I've held it against James Allen all these years for not havin' an older sister on the place."

"Why, thank you," she answered simply, recognizing a genuine compliment behind his trademark banter.

"Ain't much use," he quipped, "thankin' me for the truth."

Laura Beth started to correct the casual assumption; she really did. Started to tell him that Bradley was her ex-husband, but it seemed easier somehow to just let things stand.

When Vesper left her alone with her thoughts once again, Laura Beth moved on through the store but turned much of her attention to silent prayer.

"I'm only nervous, Lord, because I care, but knowing that doesn't help much. I care about Bradley. And, yes, I care about my own happiness… But most of all, Lord, I care about Kimmy. I want the things You want for her. My little girl is such a blessing, a precious gift from You. She needs time on the homeplace, Lord, but I'm not sure she needs a front row seat while Bradley and I sort out whatever it is I've tried so hard to ignore for the past ten years or so. Still… You're in control, and I wouldn't have it any other way. Thank You," she prayed in closing and felt unexpected tears welling in her eyes. "Thank You for Granddaddy and his precious aunts. If I've really got to face this, Lord, I'm gonna need them."

Laura Beth powered right through lunch on Dr Pepper and nervous energy. She kept busy with supper, dragging her preparations out to minimize the anxious waiting.

"Are you gonna take a bath on your own," Nadine finally drawled from the doorway to the kitchen, "or do I have to fill the tub and dunk you myself?"

A good deal of understanding lay just behind the gruff tone. Smiling ruefully, Laura Beth headed off to bathe and change. Alma started to set the table from force of habit, but Nadine pulled her up short. Their girl would need that task to occupy her hands through the last interminable minutes of anticipation.

Chapter Twelve

Laura Beth greeted her daughter joyfully, smiled a welcome to George Kelly, and camouflaged any hint of awkwardness with Bradley by rushing everyone to the supper table.

"When I take the time to cook at home, it's usually something very similar to what Aunt Alma might fix. A little taste of Red Bog…"

"Nobody ever left hungry," Bradley remembered, "not even when they caught us low on groceries."

He smiled a little, admiring Laura Beth in her pretty green blouse and black slacks as she checked over everything one last time. This radiant beauty selected her clothes like a suit of armor but somehow remained oblivious to the fact that she looked every bit as good in a pair of faded jeans. At the moment, a small pendant necklace and matching silver wristwatch caught the light. Her hair, pulled back and tied with what looked to be a piece of green ribbon from Alma's sewing basket, shown just as brightly.

"Well, anyhow," she continued, slipping into her place at the table. "Kimmy ate lunch at a friend's house one day and could not stop raving. Listening to her describe the meal, I finally realized it was a frozen pizza." Laura Beth gave an involuntary little shudder and then smiled around the table, making light of her own reaction all these years later. "Couldn't exactly lecture an eight-year-old girl on culinary excellence. Instead, I decided to show her just what Mama could do. This has been a favorite with her ever since."

An appreciative chuckle spread around the table and then Kimmy punctuated her mother's story.

"Laura Elizabeth Chandler can be just a little *extra*," she teased, already helping herself to another slice of pizza, "but it's not necessarily a bad thing."

Bradley's chuckle broke into laughter and George stifled a grin. When everyone bragged on her supper, Laura Beth pointed out that Granddaddy had raised the beef and instructed them all to save room for Aunt Alma's special dessert.

Over coffee and the famous apricot cake, Bradley produced a sleeve of top-quality photos. None of the Pates, from Alma right on down to Laura Beth, found anything spectacular about brushing and pampering a string of off-duty carriage horses. Still, by capturing Kimmy's enjoyment in those moments, the pictures won unanimous approval.

"Seems like nobody wants to fool with real photographs nowadays. My kids and grandkids are forever trying to show me something on a screen."

"Looks like social media is here to stay, Ms. Nadine. As a matter of fact, I printed these especially for y'all."

He intended to pass the prints around for individual inspection, but the Red Bog contingent gathered to stand eagerly over his chair. Already familiar with the images on display, Kimmy and George divided their attention between Alma's cake and the happy chatter over each new set of prints spread across the table.

"Oh, Bradley, they're just…"

Laura Beth trailed off, somewhat embarrassed by the awestruck wonder in her tone. When Bradley turned his head toward the sound of her voice, their eyes locked, a scant few inches apart.

"Our daughter makes a beautiful subject, Laura Beth. So much like… Well, anyway, thank you for giving me the time with her. In Houston, and especially here. Inviting me and George out to stay on the homeplace couldn't have been easy."

"That's alright," she drawled, straightening up slowly and then lifting the hand that had settled unconsciously on his shoulder. "George won't be any trouble a-tall."

Recognizing a faint note of humor in the words, Bradley tracked Laura Beth with his gaze as she drifted over to stand behind her vacated chair. They smiled at one another, across the table, like a pair of old friends. Detecting a matching hint of sadness around the edges of each smile, Jimbo and the aunts could only wonder if the emotion stemmed from simple regret or a genuine longing for something more.

Drawn to Nadine's dry wit despite their limited time together, Kimmy rolled her eyes surreptitiously.

"Painful, huh?" she murmured. "It's like watching a rom-com that never ends. Everybody realizes but them."

"Eat your cake," Nadine retorted, softening it with a conspiratorial wink.

"You've still got an eye for the right shot," Laura Beth admitted, gesturing toward a particular photo. "We used to subscribe to a couple of magazines that carried your work, but when Kimmy didn't turn out to be the outdoorsy type, I finally canceled them."

"What she means," their daughter put in from across the room, "is that I got too old to sit in her lap while she flipped through the pages, describing your technique in great detail. Nobody knows if I'm outdoorsy or not."

"You're in Red Bog now, little bit," and Jimbo settled back into his chair as he spoke. "We'll soon find out."

"Thanks for showing her some of those magazine spreads," Bradley said almost confidentially, "and for explaining a little of what goes into them. I'd like to see some of your recent work, Laura Beth. Still got everything you ever let me keep, but typewritten pages don't hold up too well to my gypsy lifestyle."

"Funny," she answered pointedly, "I couldn't quite hold up, either." Then, relenting somewhat, "I haven't written anything in years, Bradley, nothing you'd care to read."

"Why, Laura Beth," Alma chided. "That's just not so. She's taken an interest in family history. Been writin' up a storm every evening and stealing a few minutes here and there during the day."

"Genealogy?"

"More like folklore," she tossed back with a smile.

"Ah, the good stuff!"

"Maybe so, but there's nothing wrong with genealogy. Leastways, not mine."

"Careful," he teased right back. "Can't go running down my ancestry if you want to stay in good with Pop."

"But, Bradley… You make it so very easy for me to be his favorite. No complaints about the Chandler line, though. After all, my beautiful daughter comes off the same tree. I just didn't particularly appreciate your tone of voice on *genealogy*."

"Pop wanted a son and got one, but what he needed was a daughter to soften him up some. Took a while, but I brought home the very best."

Laura Beth afforded him a genuine smile and let the subject drop. Better to enjoy this bit of harmless flattery from a distance than to examine his sweet words for some kind of hook or teasing little jab.

"Everything going well at *Finishing Touches*?" she inquired.

"Running like clockwork when I left. Say, that reminds me. I've got Vida Gomez taking some calls as a kind of stopgap measure while you and I are both out of town."

"I should've thought to… Good move on your part, though. How'd Belinda take it?"

"Like a champ. That old woman's mean as a snake, but she didn't dominate the competition for years by ignoring her main weakness. Belinda hired you, remember? She's got a knack for surrounding herself with the right people."

"Believe I'll show George the place tomorrow," Jimbo announced. "Just sorta mosey around and see what all we can get into. What do you and Kimmy aim to do, doodlebug?"

"Well, sir," she teased gently. "Seeing as how we're not invited on George's little tour, I expect there's somethin' else you'd like us to do."

"Can't slip nothin' by you," he observed with a grin. "Was she my daughter, I'd put her a'horseback. I'll stick old Gopher in the corral after breakfast, but y'all do whatever suits your fancy."

Laura Beth gathered eggs as usual the next morning, but George took on the milking. She hovered close by for the first minute or two, resting a hand gently on the fawn-colored flank to calm any reaction to an unfamiliar touch.

"Been years and years," George said lightly, "but it ain't something you forget."

"Kimmy needs a good taste of this," Bradley interjected from the doorway of the barn, "but she's still in bed."

"Her rest is important, too. Plenty of time yet to ease into a routine."

Glancing over his way, Laura Beth noticed the camera and stepped smoothly away from the cow. She wore jeans this morning, a denim jacket, and a pair of Nadine's old boots. The bit of green ribbon in her hair caught his eye, a kind of memento from yesterday, and Bradley instantly regretted missing his shot.

"Don't run off, teacher. Get back over there and smile down on George. He's doing an awful good job, and besides, that's the picture I wanted."

This little bit of foolishness prompted her spontaneous laughter, and Bradley brought his digital camera into action. Surprise cut the laughter short, but after a momentary pause, Laura Beth gave a slight shrug of her shoulders and stepped back into the original shot.

"Here," George instructed, handing over a bucket of milk, "tote this back up to the house for Laura Beth. Looks like Mr. Pate's callin' in his horses. I'll lend a hand and see y'all directly."

Something about the old-fashioned kitchen sparked Bradley's creative impulse, and he faded inconspicuously into a corner. Alma, Nadine, and Laura Beth worked together seamlessly. They strained milk, set it aside to cool, fried eggs, and lifted a pan of homemade biscuits from the oven, all without bumping into each other. Bradley absorbed the low hum of voices along with an occasional chuckle. This gentle murmur provided a kind of soundtrack, and the very best of his photos might allow someone else to hear it.

Jimbo and George entered the kitchen deep in conversation, and

Bradley continued his little project more or less unnoticed. When Kimmy appeared, still wearing pajamas, he captured her soft, sleepy-eyed reaction to the unfamiliar scene and then called it quits. Any good photographer can take a step back from direct interaction, but Bradley figured his daughter would pull him into conversation quicker than anyone else. Besides, the homecooked meal looked too good to miss.

The underlying tension from last night's supper, not all of it negative, had largely evaporated. Bradley still noticed occasional stiffness from Jimbo and a glimmer of something unreadable from Laura Beth, but such things drifted gradually from his mind as they explored a new but enjoyable kind of family time. Kimmy, an instant favorite with Alma and Nadine, helped wash the breakfast dishes. That done, Laura Beth caught her daughter's attention.

"Time to get you outside for a little fresh air," she said lightly. "Come along, and I'll help you find some clothes that'll do for riding."

"Right," the girl answered with a smile. "Almost forgot about my horseback ride!"

"Speaking of clothes, young lady, I may have been a little lax in your upbringing. That matching pajama set is cute enough, but it wouldn't have done a-tall for Missy Pate's breakfast table."

Kimmy recognized her mother's teasing tone, but the name Missy struck only a faint chord. Before she could ask any questions, though, Alma spoke.

"Now, Laura Beth, it won't hurt us none to unbend and modernize a little."

"No, ma'am," and Laura Beth flashed a contagious smile. "Not on my watch."

"Let that child alone," Nadine drawled mischievously, "her pajamas ain't near as threadbare as the ones you wore out joggin' with Cindy."

Though she strived for perfection, or something close to it, in so many areas of life, Laura Beth possessed an endearing ability to laugh at herself. No wiggling off the hook with Aunt Nadine. Besides, Bradley's irrepressible grin triggered a rush of fond memories. She laughed, right along with the rest of them, hard and long enough that tears ran down her cheeks.

"I don't jog," she finally managed by way of defense, "not now and not ever. Why on earth would I know how to dress for it?"

"You tell 'em, little lady," George answered warmly. "Don't never run unless maybe something's chasin' you."

"Even then," Bradley ventured, suddenly lost in thought, "she'll pick a spot to turn and stand her ground."

Laura Beth strode purposefully out of the room, mind on her daughter's wardrobe, but Bradley's comment produced a quiet little smile. In spite of their divorce and years apart… He automatically overlooked what she and others might consider a flaw, neglect of physical fitness, and highlighted her boldness in the face of a challenge.

"Coming along, Dad?"

A blue-jean-clad Kimmy tossed the question over her shoulder as she followed her mom back through the kitchen.

"Well, I'd like to. Maybe get some pictures of your first real horseback ride, but I don't want to get in the way."

"That's okay. Mom can tell you where to stand."

Laura Beth swallowed her grin and arched an eyebrow at Bradley behind their daughter's back.

"ATVs, snowmobiles, and the like seem to be takin' over, but anybody calling himself an outdoor photographer needs some basic survival skills around a horse. Your dad is more than capable of looking out for himself."

"Gee, thanks," Bradley quipped but then turned serious. "You two must be ready for some mother-daughter time. Take her out to the corral, and have a nice visit. I'll slip down there in a little while and try for some good shots. One thing, Laura Beth…"

"Mmm?"

"George is off with Mr. Pate. Your Aunt Alma is a sweetheart, but Nadine ain't gonna tolerate me hanging around underfoot. How about setting me up on your laptop so I can read a little? I know it's a lot to ask. But you've been looking at my work, and it's only fair to share some of yours."

"Those were pictures of our daughter, Bradley. It's a little different, don't you think?"

"These stories you've been recording, would you say they're part of our daughter's heritage?"

"Just be glad Kimmy slept in this morning," she relented with a smile, "and I don't have time to argue." Kimmy ran to fetch the laptop and Laura Beth opened it on the kitchen table. She pulled up three files for him and then straightened. "These are far from perfect, but they'll get you started. The other stories are completely unpolished, just notes really. You'll find Missy Pate, Kimmy's great-great-grandmother, is a kind of central figure for the whole project. I'm out of practice when it comes to writing and not sure of my endgame here. Don't judge too harshly, but I would like to have your opinion."

Minutes later, Laura Beth caught the little brown gelding and tied him in the hallway of the barn near her daughter.

"Meet Gopher," she quipped. "He's Aunt Nadine's mount and probably the steadiest horse on the place."

"Gopher? Does he dig in the dirt or something?"

"His color," Laura Beth suggested with a fleeting grin that wrinkled her nose. "I'd guess that's where the name comes from. When you and George brushed those carriage horses, it was for fun and relaxation, but brushing serves a more immediate purpose. Most old-time horsemen aren't real formal with it. Granddaddy might use a dried corncob or even the flat of his hand, but I expect Missy was a touch more fastidious."

"Corncob?" Kimmy shot back, accepting the proffered curry comb, "and tell me more about this Missy."

"Oh, honey child… Missy Kimbel Pate was Granddaddy's mother. Then, too, she raised Alma and Nadine as her own. Missy shaped those three, and they helped to shape me. I feel kind of silly for not mentioning her, especially after naming you Kimbel. Only, I didn't have a clear picture myself until recently. We'll get to all that. I'd like for you to read the same stories your dad's looking over right now, but first the brushing."

"You're the boss."

"Don't think too much of my corncob reference. Nobody feeds chopped corn anymore, but there used to be dried cobs laying around every barn in East Texas. You don't want any horse hair sticking up, much less dirt and debris, where the saddle sits or the cinch runs. Something like that will rub back and forth until it makes a sore place. At the very least, a horse man or woman will run a hand across the back and up under the belly before saddling. On a mule or work horse, you'd check where the collar sits and the harness lays, but that's a lesson for another day."

"So, you're really okay with Dad reading your stories?" Kimmy asked as they worked over the animal together. "I like having him around for a change."

"It's good for y'all to spend some time together. Besides, he used to look over almost everything. My attempts at creative writing ended shortly before the divorce."

"Yeah, about the time I came along."

"Why, Kimmy, don't say it like that. I wouldn't swap you for all the literary success in the world. Of course, there was no need for a trade-off. Had my writing career ever truly launched, I would've taken you and your dad along for the ride."

"Dad, too?"

"Well, yes, depending on the timing. As it was, I collected rejection letters from all the major New York houses and smaller publishers scattered across the country. Your birth is the most important event of my life, apart from eternal salvation, and it quite simply convinced me to make a change. Ever heard the expression fish or cut bait?"

"Um, no. Must be a Red Bog thing, but I see your point. What about Dad? He's still fishing?"

"Pshaw," Laura Beth snorted, "we could take that off in several directions. Plenty of fish in the sea and so forth, but your dad's photography always outclassed my writing."

"You two get along so well, even now. Was I the problem?"

"No, honey," and she stepped around the horse to clasp her daughter in a hug, "not in a million years! You know, I shouldn't have said that about *fish in the sea*. Didn't mean to imply that Bradley has been out there looking for someone else. He just never quit chasing his dream. Your dad will make every effort to step up when you need him, Kimmy. Didn't he come running to check on us the day after my accident?"

"Yeah, well," and her quiet sniffle took some bite out of the words. "Maybe I need him a little more often, not just in the unlikely event one of us gets hit by a car."

Laura Beth felt the words "me too" rise in her throat but fought them back down. She gave another tight squeeze and then stepped away long enough to pull herself together while grabbing a saddle and other necessary gear.

"Kimmy, I failed. I couldn't raise you as a little vagabond, but I couldn't find it in my heart to tie him down either. Ask Granddaddy and Alma and Nadine about poverty sometime. You ask them about scratchin' a living out of this Red Bog dirt. Of course, they had deep roots on the homeplace and drew strength from each other. Me, I just felt so alone."

"Mama, nobody's blaming—"

"My own weakness caused our trouble." Saddle in place, she tightened the cinch with one quick jerk rather than her usual gentle increments. Gopher, an old campaigner, only grunted his disapproval. "I just couldn't face the prospect of traveling from a hunting camp to a motocross event, one freelance job to another, with you on my hip. If I was going to be the only solid anchor in your life, I needed a tangible foothold. Given my knack for hospitality and organization, I latched on to that kind of thing and built a career.”

“Failure? Weakness? You’re literally the strongest person I know.”

“Not only weakness, baby girl, but a lack of faith.”

“That’s crazy! Everything I know about the Lord, I learned from you.”

“Thank you, baby. Please don’t misunderstand… I’m not questioning my relationship with God, just some of my choices. Your dad was sort of footloose at the time, but maybe I should have trusted him a little more. Trusted him, and trusted the Lord to bring us through it.”

“Look, Mama, I’m just a teenage kid. I don’t have any answers, but if you’re blaming yourself and Dad is blaming himself, surely there’s some middle ground somewhere. I mean… We’ve never exactly talked about it, but he’s not gonna blame you.”

“I’m very proud of you, Kimmy, and so is your dad. Right now, that’s all the middle ground we need.”

“No, Mama. No, it’s not. I think Dad is lonesome, and we both know you are.”

“Oh, baby girl, I’ve kept Bradley at arm’s length for fear of getting hurt again. Maybe hurting him, or even you, along the way. No more of that, I promise. You’ll have some kind of a family life from now on, but I’m afraid it’s too late to hope for anything more. Not your worry, anyhow. I’ve saddled this horse, and now you’re gonna ride him.”

Laura Beth watched as Kimmy walked old Gopher around the largest corral, offering some basic instructions. Sight of her daughter on horseback gradually eased the nervous tension. Bradley arrived to find her as cool, calm, and collected as ever. He loved reading her work again, and the intimate nature of those Pate family stories drew him back into a remembered closeness. He longed to walk over and slip an arm around Laura Beth's waist, to pick up right where they had left off all those years ago. Instead, he found an unobtrusive spot near the barn and started snapping away with his camera. Lacking any ability to undo the pain he had caused Laura Beth, he knew exactly how to capture Kimmy's first ride and the enjoyment so plainly visible on her mother's face.

Caught up in her riding, Kimmy remained unaware of his presence, but Laura Beth acknowledged him with a glance and a fleeting half smile. Gopher seemed quick and responsive despite his age, but the steady little horse also made allowances for his inexperienced rider. Once they moved through the basics, walk and trot and turn both ways and stop, Laura Beth signaled for a halt.

"What is it, Mama? Me and Gopher have a good thing going here."

"I know it, but you can't make circles in this pen forever. How about taking a little jaunt with me and your dad?"

Hearing the exchange, Bradley stowed his camera and drifted over to stand at her elbow.

"I'll saddle a couple of horses for us," he offered, "if you'll point them out."

"Catch the buckskin geldings, Woody and Buzz. They're a couple of Granddaddy's customer horses and can use the miles."

"Customer horses, huh? Not many men pushing eighty will take in outside stock to ride, but I didn't figure they got those names around here."

"Take Kimmy with you and teach her how to saddle one. I jumped straight to autopilot and did that part myself." Laura Beth watched the two of them stroll happily off together but called out to her daughter with a lighthearted reprimand as she stepped over to lay a hand on Gopher's sleek neck. "Horse don't come with a kickstand, you know. It won't do to just walk off and leave him."

"No worries," Kimmy answered, smiling back over her shoulder. "My mama's got things under control, just like always."

Long in the habit of masking constant stress, Laura Beth had grown used to certain physical reactions. Now, it took several seconds and a couple of ragged breaths to distinguish her joyful anticipation from run-of-the-mill anxiety. Gopher, with his calm almost lazy presence, helped to keep her grounded.

"You're bound to be a good'un," she murmured, breathing in the horsey aroma as she stroked his neck. "Horses come and go around here, but Granddaddy picked you for Aunt Nadine. Kimmy's starting out clueless… Gymnastics has taken a backseat to her artwork over the last couple of years, but she's still an agile little thing. Wise old rascal," she finally observed with a chuckle. "Gymnastics is a little outside the scope of your experience, but you're listening to every word I say. Be kind to my baby girl."

Father and daughter soon returned, both of them all smiles.

"Kimmy saddled your horse," he said, gesturing proudly at Buzz, "while I saddled mine."

Laura Beth inspected the saddling job, smiled warmly at her daughter, and stepped aboard. They rode through a pasture gate, heading in the general direction of Caney Branch and the little stretch of timbered bottomland. Influenced by her grandfather and other farm folk around Red Bog, Laura Beth viewed open ground as inherently more productive. Still, she understood the attraction of moving through the woods. Wooded trails, no matter how short, hid whatever waited up ahead and gave a rider the sense of going somewhere.

"I knew you'd look great on a horse, Mama," Kimmy blurted with her usual enthusiasm. "Grew up around them, and you're so graceful anyway. Dad's the one who surprises me a little."

Nudging his horse forward, Bradley rode up alongside her and answered with a wink.

"Don't be too surprised, kiddo. I'm the first generation, on Pop's side, born into city life. An early taste for outdoor adventure brought me into contact with horses, but I pretty much considered them nature's dirt bike. Something to get me from point A to point B…"

"You mean there's more to it?" Kimmy joked, a goofy expression giving her away.

"Well, it generally goes smoother if you make a little effort to connect with your horse. Helps keep things enjoyable, too. Your mother showed me some finer points of horsemanship more or less unintentionally. I copied her ways, because they got results, and asked a few questions. Even now, whenever I ride for work or for fun, I think of Laura Beth."

"Ah, 'tis sweet to be remembered." The lady in question mimicked a dreamy sigh but then allowed some humor to creep into her tone. "You're probably not the only man to equate his ex-wife with a horse."

"Stop picking on him, Mama. You know that's not the way he means it."

"Maybe not," Laura Beth tossed back over her shoulder, "but he set himself up for that one. Now, lean forward over your horse's neck, and watch these low-hanging limbs."

They rode single file for a short distance before the mix of pine and hardwood opened into a small clearing. Bradley urged his gelding up next to Buzz while Kimmy lingered just behind them in the edge of the woods.

"Thanks for letting me read, Laura Beth. I think it's some of the best stuff you've ever written."

"Really?" she asked, frowning momentarily as she reined to a stop. "Something that simple? Well, I suppose it does have a good deal of my heart in it."

"Exactly, and the simplicity is beautiful. I've missed you," he added, lowering his voice, "and I found something wonderful in those pages. The material deals with Missy, Big Jim, and others from their time. Not autobiographical at all… But you're in there, Laura Beth. You've been so distant for so long, and reading those stories, I felt a kind of homecoming."

Chapter Thirteen

Laura Beth zoned out completely for a moment, and the world stopped. Gradually, then, everything slipped back into focus. She heard a faint ringing sound in her ears and felt more than a little queasy. The fingers of her free hand had woven themselves tightly into the horse's black mane. Every muscle felt tensed to drive him forward in a gallop, but she knew the pain of running away all too well. Drawing in a deep breath, she shifted slightly in the saddle to loosen her body's instinctive grip. Love welled up inside her, strong and undeniable, but too many unspoken hurts lay between them. Kimmy came first, and Kimmy sat her horse right back there in the woods.

"Bradley, I… I'm sorry for your pain. It hasn't been easy for me, either, but there's not much we can do about it now."

She took a deep, shuddering breath and nudged her horse forward.

"Laura Beth, darling? Surely we can—"

Ducking her head for an instant, she knuckled away the hot tears and whirled her buckskin around to face him.

"Like I told you, I'm sorry. Now," she continued, reverting to a businesslike tone, "what do you think of my little project? Any constructive criticism? Praise makes me feel all warm and fuzzy, but it doesn't generate much improvement."

"Pick your stories apart? After the way I laughed and cried over them?" He reached out and touched her hand, clenched as it was over the saddle horn, before drawing reluctantly away. "There's not much I wouldn't do for you, Laura Beth. If criticism's what you need, I'll give it a shot."

"Thank you." Her voice shook slightly, but she tried for some normalcy as their daughter closed the gap. "We didn't bring Kimmy out here to sit around. Can't you ride and talk at the same time?"

"Well," he ventured as they moved off, "your family stories may be difficult to sell. They don't fit neatly into a single genre, and none of the people or locations involved are particularly well known. The thing is, not all art has to be marketable. You enjoy writing. Those stories will open up a bygone way of life for Kimmy, and your uncle probably has some grandchildren of his own by now."

"Not yet. Uncle James Allen is younger than Dad. Besides, we started early. Kimmy's the only great-grand at the moment."

Bradley shook his head, thoroughly confused by the last couple of hours. Laura Beth's open and honest writing style simulated access to the love of his life, but her stubborn independence stood out as a dose of reality. Heartache, disappointment, and maybe even a touch of anger all faded quickly. In their place, he felt a familiar and still powerful attraction along with an overwhelming tenderness toward the girl who had long ago captured his heart. Anxious to give her what she wanted and smooth things over for Kimmy, he swallowed the hurt and tried for a bit of humor.

"Don't give me that business about starting early, Laura Beth. You were as old when I married you at nineteen as you will be at ninety."

"Ouch," she shot back, wrinkling her nose at him. "That one hurt a little."

"Well, it wasn't supposed to. Mature, not old. You were— You *are* a very graceful and levelheaded young lady."

"Better," she decided with a nod, "but I wasn't quite mature enough to hold our little world together. Scarcely more than twenty when Kimmy came along and not quite twenty-three by the time things fell apart."

~July 1942~

Late for dinner, fourteen-year-old Jimbo Pate stripped the saddle and other gear from his stocky dappled gray mare. With most of the hard riding young men who edged him out in terms of experience and physical strength gone to war, Jimbo found plenty of cowboy work. And Sassy, handy as the pocket on a shirt, made a valuable partner. He never thought twice about turning her loose to roll and shade up alongside the house. The little mare was agile as a cat and smarter than a good many folks he knew. Just a word or even a noise of rebuke from one of the open windows, and she'd steer clear of Missy's yard flowers.

"Half past noon already, little girl," he murmured, and Sassy swiveled her ears attentively in full sympathy with his predicament. "If Missy don't scold me, Gert sure will."

A familiar green Ford clattered suddenly around the house. Jimbo still thought of the Model A as Uncle Cleve's shiny new roadster. Only, the car showed plenty of hard use now, and his father sat incongruously behind the wheel. Cleve drove a '39 model pickup these days and had swapped the roadster to Big Jim. The sight of his daddy in a car, showering the gas to it and steering wildly for all he was worth, always tickled Jimbo. His next thought, generally, was to hunt some kind of cover. Despite all his finesse with a driving horse, Big Jim handled the car more like a runaway freight train.

Unfazed by the racket, Sassy rolled the sweat from her back and then stood up to shake off the yard dust. Her movement caught Big Jim's eye, and he hauled the roadster around in a precarious about face. He managed to stop alongside the yard fence but stalled out his motor in the process.

By the Light of a Memory 207

"Blasted thing won't run about half the time," he grumbled. "I'd get more use out of a stringhalted horse!" Cigarette gone out, he scratched a match on the once glossy outer door panel and then glanced up at his son through the smoke. "Where you been? I needed you in the field this morning."

"Huntin' screwworm cattle, sir," Jimbo answered. "Didn't know you was shorthanded. I'd planned on ridin' with Hoyt tomorrow. Mr. Charlie Briggs is short some fat steers on that army contract."

"That's how come the grass got ahead of us to start with. Plenty of men gone into the service and others workin' defense jobs, but I reckon steers are about as scarce as farm help nowadays. Most folks are scared to cut their calves on account of the screwworms."

"Yes, sir. Likely as not, we'll gather some fat bull yearlings and make steers out of 'em a day or two before they ship. Everybody's crop must be goin' to grass. I heard some talk about it around the store."

"Yeah, and while you was layin' around the store, chasin' wormy cattle, and I don't know what all, your old daddy was followin' after a plow."

"Cotton's too far along to plow, ain't it?"

"Mighty near… Got hoe hands workin', too. Alma come out from town to help, and her brand-new husband leaves for basic training any day now. Missy won't trust just anybody to plow out a crop when it's that far along."

"No, sir, and you don't find many plow hands like good old Tobe anymore. Hard to believe he's been gone nearly two years."

"Me and that old man seen a right smart together. You're every bit as good with a plow but less apt to stay at home. So, I had to catch a mule this morning and go to work my own self."

The boss man schooled young driving horses, traded livestock, and assisted Missy with management tasks, but Jimbo could count on one hand the times he'd seen his father plow. A couple of those times had been short but instructive lessons for him.

"I'm sorry, Daddy. Didn't know things had got bad enough to call Alma out from town and all. I'll catch a mule after dinner."

"Never mind sorry… It's natural for a boy to branch out on his own some. But never mind dinner, too. Grab a biscuit and get on out to the field. I'm headed down to Concord to try and scare us up some more hoe hands."

Jimbo pictured old men, women, and kids piled into the roadster and perched upon its running boards. "They'll be plenty scared by the time they ride back to Red Bog," he conjectured silently, grinning as he vaulted over the yard fence to re-crank the Model A.

"Yessir," he ventured aloud. "Let's get this thing started again, and I'll head yonder."

Jimbo's upbringing left no room for laziness. While he never shied away from swinging a hoe, the boy felt a kind of pride in being set apart as a topnotch plow hand. And plow he did, until the daylight failed completely. The sooner they got ahead of the grass, the sooner he could return to horseback work.

As a newly graduated pharmacist, Alma's husband was more valuable up town than in the cotton field. Having already left work in preparation for his military service, though, he labored alongside her. "Alongside don't quite get it," Jimbo reasoned with a smile, "but Bud Evans is doin' all he can to keep up. Gonna raise his first set of blisters 'fore the good old U.S. Army even takes their turn at him."

"Tell you what," Big Jim drawled the next morning, pausing briefly to light a cigarette. "Charlie Briggs' beef contract is right valuable to him and might help the war effort, too. If you want to go along with Hoyt, I'll plow this morning. You can take it up again after dinner."

Missy's devoted Shep had succumbed to old age the previous fall. But two half-grown pups, dingy yellow in color and out of Hoyt Kimbel's line of cur dogs, trooped after Jimbo as he headed off without waiting around for breakfast. The young horseman never thought much about short rations or lack of rest. Gathering cattle on his good mare came with a set of built-in thrills. Farming, too, lost some of its dull routine when undertaken with real urgency and enlivened by the company of family and friends. Even at fourteen, though, adrenaline could only sustain a body so long.

"Ain't complainin' none, Sassy girl," Jimbo ventured as they finally neared the house once again, "but I'll be mighty glad to get my dinner this time. Even if we did leave old Hoyt a little shy of being done." Once again, he stood his saddle, cantle up, on the back porch and released the mare with a grateful slap on the neck. "You'll get a good bait of feed corn when I go to the barn for a mule."

He darted noisily into the kitchen but pulled up short. For the first time in Jimbo's young life, his elegant and almost imperturbable mother looked tired. Grease stains and a light dusting of flour coated her ruffled apron, and sweat trickled plainly down the near side of her neck as she tended several pans on the woodburning stove.

The boy realized in that moment that Missy was doing all the cooking from her awkward high-wheeled chair while Gertie Washington, now a sixty-eight-year-old widow woman, toiled in the field as hard and long as anyone else. Being stuck inside wore on Missy. Her every nerve strained to get out and work the crop. Then, too, preparing three big meals a day without help tested her body's limitations.

Sometimes afflicted with the tunnel vision common to young boys, Jimbo had also been taught from childhood to look after Missy. She usually glided through his life as a queenly presence, improving everything she touched and requiring very little looking after, but he knew his duty when he saw it. He washed, actually washed, without being told and took up kitchen work just long enough to lighten her load.

Ultimately, they defeated the grass. Plowed it out, hoed it out, and just plain stomped it out by force of will, finishing up late on a Thursday evening. Proud of their victory, Jimbo scraped dried sweat from his mule's shoulders and back with the same care he generally used on Sassy. Having educated his son and heir to the manly virtues, Big Jim no longer made much effort to conceal manly vices. The boy knew, or had better know, what was fit for Missy's ears and what would only upset her. He worked over the mule more or less unnoticed while the boss man visited with Bud Evans in the hallway of the barn.

"Everybody on the place is just about worked down, Evans. You pulled your weight, too. Rub some bacon rind on them blisters. They'll heal over and make a callous."

"Well, sir… They never taught us that in pharmacy school, but I do appreciate the advice."

"Anyhow, the womenfolk have their ways of bouncing back after this kind of a hard uphill pull, and we've got ours. There's a jug of white liquor waitin' up yonder in the loft. That'll do for my hands, and they've earned it. But with you headin' off to the big fight, the two of us ought to venture on over to Kilgore. That oilfield bunch works awful hard, and they know something about relaxation! Yes siree! They got a billiard hall over there with 'lectric lights in it and great big ceiling fans, too.”

“Those big fans sound fine and dandy,” Bud decided, mopping his brow. “Only, I don’t know the first thing about playing billiards.”

“Shoot fire, I don’t neither! Beer’s ice cold and sells legal to boot. If a man’s quiet and just a touch savvy, he can turn up a bottle of somethin’ stronger without half trying.”

“To tell the truth, sir, I’m not much of a drinker. Still, anything cold sounds good right about now. Do you think Alma will mind very much?”

“Not if you don’t tell her. She’s overdue for a nice, quiet evenin’ with Missy and Nadine, anyhow. Let’s you and me get washed up and go! We’ll take my old Model A, but you’d better drive.”

Missy fed them purple hull peas, vine ripe tomatoes, a pot of mixed greens, stewed potatoes, and hot water cornbread that night. She seasoned her peas and greens with plenty of salt pork, like always, but served no other meat. Not much need, she reflected, after everyone had put in a long, hot day in the field. Toward the end of the meal, she sent Nadine into the kitchen to fetch a special surprise.

“Long as I didn’t have to cook it,” came the half-jesting response, “I sure don’t mind toting it out to the table.”

Nadine balked a little at the notion of treating her older sister, the natural homemaker, like company, but she knew better than to disobey Missy. Alma was a guest of sorts. She and Bud had come out to help without any real obligation to do so. Her own beau, Floyd Webber, was already fighting in Europe, but that was no reason to begrudge them these last few days together. Especially if they chose to spend their time in the cotton field.

Finally, Missy swung her gaze around the table. Jimbo fought the urge to squirm as her questioning look settled on him.

"Son, did your daddy take Bud out to run the hounds?"

"No'm, I don't believe so."

She looked at him for a long, uncomfortable moment but eventually laid her napkin on the table.

"Well, if he's not gonna run 'em tonight, I reckon we will. I've been stuck in this house too long what with all of y'all tied up in the field."

"Yes, ma'am!" he agreed readily, glad to be off the hook. "I'll hitch Midnight, bring your buggy around, and untie some of the hounds."

The big black gelding from Jimbo's early childhood had recently turned up again. Sold at some point to old Dr. Brown, Midnight served the senior physician faithfully up until his death. Then, with automobiles already well established, young Dr. Brown simply gave the horse back to Missy. Vincent Brown, somewhere near Missy's age, would probably be called "young doctor" for the rest of his natural life. Big Jim never seemed to care much for the man but put up with him, these days, as the only country doctor left to serve Red Bog.

Before Jimbo could run for the barn or the shady spot that functioned as a dog yard, Nadine swept in with a pan of fresh berry cobbler and set it in the middle of the table.

"Goodness," Alma breathed, "that looks delicious! Please don't go chasing off after those hounds, Missy. Can't we just make some ice cream?"

"Last block of ice is near 'bout gone, but you're welcome to use what's left and see how far it goes. I'm better off listening to a good hound race. That music's sweeter than any dessert and easier on my figure, too."

"Oh, Missy… You needn't worry about such things. Besides, I want to visit with you."

Alma's pleasant bit of newlywed bloom had melted away over the past three days, leaving her fit, trim, and still quite pretty. Even so, Missy eyed the girl with a knowing smile.

"I don't know, honey… Let somebody tote you around every step for a day or so, and you'd start to think about it, too. Remember, I can't get out there and work in the cotton no matter how much I've learned to love this land."

"You're right, Missy. You're right as usual. Tell you what… Stay here and visit, let Jimbo turn the ice cream freezer, and we won't make you eat any cobbler."

"How very thoughtful of you," Missy said on a sigh and then turned her attention back to Jimbo. "Set them dogs loose, anyhow. Maybe they'll strike a fox right close to the house. One of the girls can wheel me out to the porch, and we'll listen from there."

Jimbo turned the foxhounds out and headed back, nothing more than ice cream on his mind, but Alma caught him at the edge of the yard.

"Where'd they go?" she hissed. "Tell me quick."

"Aw, Alma… You know about as well as I do."

"Aunt Alma to you," she corrected rather sharply, "and that's about what I thought. My poor Bud has no idea what he's gotten into."

"He'll be fine. Just don't say anything to Missy, okay? No call to worry her."

Most of the snap left Alma's tone, and her next words came out on a sigh.

"Jimbo, your mother is smarter than all of us. Don't you figure she knows?"

"Maybe so," he shot back. "But if she wanted us to talk about it, don't you figure she'd bring it up? Just take a breath and settle your nerves. Big Jim always comes home sooner or later. I reckon he'll bring Bud right along with him."

"I sure hope so," she answered softly, draping an arm across his shoulders to pull him in close as they started back up to the house.

Grown, married, and somewhat sophisticated, Alma still drew comfort from their easy, sibling-like bond. Jimbo might be just a boy… But he was a Pate boy, and that made all the difference.

Alma drew a rocker up next to Missy's wheelchair, Nadine settled on the steps, and Jimbo cranked the hand-turned freezer at one end of the porch. Taking his cue from Missy, the boy dismissed any tension in the air and enjoyed a fine summer evening.

"There's old Nancy," his mother declared in response to a bell-like hound voice floating back through the warm night air. "She'll get us up a race!"

Minutes later with a full chorus of ancient music swelling on the breeze, Alma ventured a soft whisper.

"I love you, Missy. But to be such a lady, you've got a wild streak runnin' wide and deep. That racket sends a shiver right up my spine."

"I love you, too, honey child," and Missy's whisper vibrated with intensity. "Don't worry none about that little shiver… That's how you know you're alive!"

Nadine snorted her amusement and then offered a quick bit of insight.

"Y'all are livin' out two different races. Missy's heart is in amongst her lead hounds, and you're runnin' with the fox."

Jimbo nearly choked at the startled look on Alma's face, but Missy winked without breaking her concentration.

"Takes all kinds, I reckon."

The hounds eventually ran out of hearing, and of course, they knew how to come home. When Missy requested a quick sponge bath from the girls, Jimbo turned in ahead of them. He slept like a rock, but one look at his mother the next morning told him something had gone terribly wrong overnight. Missy wore her good navy dress despite the summer heat. Then, too, her face looked dangerously pale and more than a hint of strain showed around the hazel green eyes.

"Bud already apologized, Missy, and I'm sorry we didn't wake you. Nadine and I tried to handle the news like adults and let you sleep."

"Y'all didn't handle anything. That's the whole trouble," she shot back at Alma. "Jimbo would've come for me."

"Maybe so," Nadine admitted regretfully, "but there was nothing much to be done in the night."

"A deal like that, in a strange town, could drag on for days and maybe even cause my Bud real trouble with the Army."

"Army's liable to chew him up and spit him out, anyhow, if I don't do it first. I don't know what he'll do over yonder where the bullets fly, but that's the last time he'll run off and leave my man in a bind."

"To be honest, Mrs. Pate, I had no idea what to do when they took

Big Jim and his car. I finally caught a ride into Henderson and then walked most of the night to get back here."

Missy's voice lost much of its edge, her answer sounding strangely flat and controlled.

"You'd best get out of my sight," she advised, "and do it in a hurry."

Jimbo, always a quick study, eased over to the wood box and picked out a nice-sized stick of stove wood.

"Mornin', Missy," he quipped, and even managed a grin as he stepped up alongside her.

Bud left, shaking his head in bewilderment, and the more or less one-sided conversation continued.

"You girls are my daughters. I'll never love you any less than my own boy, but I've never been more disappointed in my life. Now, here's what we'll do. Jimbo, you scat right along and find Cleve Pate. I want him over here with that pickup, and yesterday wouldn't be soon enough. Alma, trail your husband outta here if you figure he's worth keeping. Nadine, go roust out all hands and get the corn worked while I'm gone. Gert can rustle up a set of clean bedsheets, fry some pork chops for Mister Big Jim's dinner, and then take her ease."

Jimbo tore out for the barn and his waiting cowpony, and Gert spoke softly from an opposite corner of the room.

"Now, Missy... You know my brothers; they'd do just about anything for you, but I reckon the Havard boys put in a rough night of their own. Them corn patches are a long day's work with the whole bunch cold sober."

The boss lady flicked a marginally apologetic glance toward Gert and then honed in on the shellshocked girls once more.

"I'm just about out of sympathy for anybody's rough night. They can work that corn out clean as a whistle by dark, move plumb off this place, or line up on the wall of the barn and take a lickin'."

Nadine turned every bit as white as the boss lady. Alma, too, looked sick as she opened her mouth to speak.

"Please… God, no… This is 1942! You just can't do that."

"Not me," she answered icily, "Nadine, and then she'll come up to the house and take her own dose of it."

"I'm sorry, Missy, but that makes you sound almost unhinged. Why Nadine?"

"You're a married woman now, already out in the world. Nadine's still livin' here on the homeplace, and she's gotta learn what that kind of error in judgement can cost."

"What error? What unforgiveable crime have we done?"

"You knew about Big Jim's little misunderstanding and didn't tell me." She practically spat the words. "Your own brother, might as well say father, and y'all left him lay in jail all night! Called it an adult decision, at that, because *Missy needs her rest*. Now, do like I told you, and while you're at it, stay out of my way. I'm fixin' to root through the safe and gather up what little bit of cash money we've got on hand."

The sisters looked at one another for several long moments. And both girls flinched when, for the first time in their lives, Missy's office door slammed shut.

"I'm sorry you had to hear that kind of talk, Gert," Alma ventured uncertainly after a long and awkward silence. "I've never seen her throw such a fit, but I can't believe she'd act on any of those awful threats."

"Awful's the word, right enough, and you've got a powerful lot to learn about our Missy. I love that girl almost like she was one of my own, but she'll do every bit of what she said. A man like Big Jim, plenty stout and rough, he can afford to say something and then back off a tad. Folks are apt to call that mercy, not weakness. Sweet little thing like Missy, and her crippled… That tender heart will break, sure, and she'll cry into her pillow at night. But, 'less we get busy lifting that awful load from them pretty little shoulders, she's got it to do. Which in turn, my beauties, makes a tolerable grim outlook for Mama Havard's boys. Y'all just listen to old Gert, now. Ms. Alma, you change the bedclothes and cook up some pork chops. Ms. Nadine, take 'at soldier boy and hit the first corn patch. I'll handle them confounded little brothers of mine and roust us out a crew before you know it."

Chapter Fourteen

Sassy practically flew, partway over the road and sometimes across stretches of pastureland. Jimbo leaned in tight over her neck and blessed that big Texas heart. They reached Uncle Cleve's upper field just as he arrived with another pickup load of extra hoe hands.

"Somethin' a-fire on the homeplace, boy, or did you just take a notion to stretch that good little mare out and let 'er dig?"

"Wellsir, the sparks comin' off Missy are apt to burn something down sure enough if we don't get right back over there with your truck."

"Harold," Cleve barked, calling his sixteen-year-old son rather than one of the hands. "Cool this mare out, strip the gear, and then turn her loose to water and graze."

"Yes, sir…"

"Crawl on in here, Jimbo. Missy callin' for my shotgun, too, or just the truck?"

"Mainly the truck," Jimbo decided, hopping into the cab, and then set himself to shed a little light on the situation.

Once on the homeplace, Cleve ventured a halfhearted argument in the front yard.

"Now, Missy… I've handled this kind of thing before. It'll only shame him, you coming into a place like that."

"I'm the one ashamed, leavin' him over there so long. No offense, brother-in-law… But this particular deal fell into my lap, and I'll handle it. If you don't think that man of mine would raise old Ned to get to his Missy in a tight… Now, quit jawin' at me and let's move!"

While this little exchange took place, Jimbo vacated the cab of the truck, swinging himself up into the bed and more or less out of sight behind the high wooden stock rails. Unaware of his mother's ironclad deadline on the corn-patch chore, he gave in to youthful curiosity. Besides, with Missy bound for some kind of predicament and Big Jim there ahead of her, their only boy belonged squarely in the middle of it. Cleve settled his sister-in-law gently on the bench seat, and hoisted her special chair over the side without further argument. In fact, one wheel nearly clipped Jimbo's blond head.

Missy soon worked through the heightened stage of anger that bordered on physical tremors, but Cleve saw plenty of reason for his nephew's urgency. By the time they reached the constable's office in Kilgore, with its well-used holding cells, she seemed her usual charming self. Unloading the chair, Cleve caught sight of Jimbo and shook his head with a wordless scowl. Any talk of Missy waiting in the truck would have been pointless, so the younger Pate brother wheeled her in dutifully.

"How do, sir?" she inquired almost brightly of a self-important young deputy manning the outer desk. "I'm Mrs. James Pate of the Red Bog community, and this is my brother-in-law, Cleveland Pate. We understand y'all might have my husband here."

"Took six of us," the young officer grumped, "and I'm still none too sure this jaw of mine ain't broke, but yeah… We've got him locked up tight, and that's just where he'll stay for a while yet."

"I'm afraid you're mistaken."

"How's that?"

"For a start, buster… If Big Jim Pate ever set out to break your jaw, you'd be conversing with me by pencil and paper right now. There's one other little matter, too. I've come to take him home to Red Bog. Mind you, I didn't come to argue. I came to get him."

"Well, whoop-de-do. He ain't all that big, lady. But I'll admit he bites like an alligator and kicks like a bronc mule."

"Big Jim's easier to say than *Jim Pate the elder*, but I reckon he's got size enough. As for the biting and kicking… What was he supposed to do, with six of you brave lads piled on, lay down and quit?"

"If he had," came the rueful answer, "I just might turn him loose today."

"His dinner's waitin' at home, and we've got crops in the field. Of course, I'd say you know that… Unless maybe you grew up with your head stuck down one of these oilwells. Name the fine, and we'll strike out for home."

"No call lookin' down on oilpatch folk, lady. I've seen your kind before. Does Big Jim own the cotton gin or has your old daddy got it?"

Missy met the world squarely, without looking down on anyone, but the offhand guess at her background hit pretty close to home. Hair stood up on the back of Cleve Pate's neck as her voice struck a strangely soft and compliant tone.

"If you can't find it in your heart to release my husband today, sir, may I at least sign for his personal effects? A pocket watch, sharp Barlow knife, perhaps some cash, and a little Colt revolver chambered in .32-20."

"Well," he decided after a long moment of thought, "I reckon that'd be alright. Hard as your husband fought us, and him drunk as a lord if you'll forgive my sayin' so, he never went for that gun. There's some around here that might've pulled down on us. Anyhow... Here's his personals, just as you say. Sign right there, ma'am."

A hoarse but familiar voice called out unexpectedly. The speaker stood shrouded in shadow, and presumably behind bars, at the rear of the small building.

"Say, Donny boy... Did you take the trouble to shuck them shells outta my sidearm?"

"Naw, and I sure don't need no mean drunk tellin' me how to run this office."

"Far be it from me, Donny. Far be it from me. But if you'd like to keep your little desk job and still make it home this evening, don't you hand Missy Pate no loaded revolver and go on talkin' down your nose about holding me in here for a while yet."

"Better let him out, *Donny boy*. My big brother's standin' back there sober enough to save your pompous hide. I know pretty well how Missy thinks, too, but I kept my country mouth shut tight."

The jailer swallowed hard and then swallowed twice more. Reaching for his keys, he slid them across the desk with rapid and slightly jerky movements.

"Take him and cut a trail. That piece of a roll we took off him will cover the fine and then some. You'll find his rattletrap car parked out back." Cleve released his brother while Missy gathered the pistol and other belongings into her lap. Seconds later, as the threesome started out into bright summer sunlight, the young deputy spoke once more. "I'm beholden to you for the timely advice, Mister, but it wouldn't exactly hurt my feelings if you stayed clear of Kilgore for a spell."

"Take me around to the Model A," Missy requested gently. "I'll ride home with Big Jim."

"Pick her up, and put her in the car for me, Cleve. I smell like a swelled-up old possum three days drowned to death in a brewery."

"Yeah, I noticed."

"Damn the smell," Missy asserted, shocking them with the raw intensity of her feelings and a totally uncharacteristic choice of words. "Nobody else does that chore with my own and only man standin' by."

Big Jim lifted her from the chair, almost hesitant in his shame. Once situated in his arms, though, Missy kissed him soundly on the mouth. This action startled both men once again, but she claimed her exclusive right for all the world, or at least brother Cleve, to see. Reflex kicked in, and Jim clasped her petite form (lovely in its feminine softness) to his unyielding chest as he returned the fervent kiss.

"When y'all get that over and done, big brother, put Missy in the middle and then scrunch in next to the door. Jimbo's waitin' yonder in my pickup. Best let the boy drive y'all home."

"Jimbo?" and Big Jim nearly choked on the question. "Missy, I don't know what to— He's bound to be ashamed of me, and got every right."

Missy cut a glance at Cleve, eyes snapping, but spoke consolingly to her husband.

"I didn't aim to bring him, Jim. In fact, this is the first I've heard of it. But it'll take more than a little scuffle to make our boy duck his head."

"Don't look at me," Cleve demurred with a grin. "Missy was spittin' fire when we left the homeplace. I expect the little stowaway thought she might need him."

"Can't fault him for that," Big Jim said huskily.

"He showed a sight more grit than Bud Evans," Missy breathed, but with the situation under control, most of the venom had gone from her tone.

"Lack of grit won't never be Jimbo's trouble," Jim predicted and his voice went soft and tender as he reached into the car to trail a thumb down her cheek. "Bud Evans didn't have you for a mama."

Cleve loved his kinfolk but seldom missed a chance to lighten the moment.

"I picked my wife to water down that wild strain in the Pate blood, big brother. You're 'bout the only one who figured it might need some more fire to it."

With that, he turned on his heel and went to fetch Jimbo. When the boy arrived, Big Jim tousled his hair, squinting down through the smoke of a freshly lit cigarette.

"Slide under the wheel, son, and leave me to turn the motor over. Let's go home."

Jimbo drove capably but depended on Big Jim to point the way back to Red Bog. They traveled mostly in comfortable silence until Missy voiced some regret.

"I talked awful ugly to our girls this morning, Jim, and set a more or less impossible task for the hands."

"Can't imagine you was none too gentle with Evans, either," he surmised.

"I told him to git, and Jimbo picked up a stick of stove wood. But that don't bother me like the other."

After listening to a little more explanation, Jim squeezed her hand and spoke comfortingly.

"Well, Missy… I ain't exactly proud of my last ten-or-twelve-hours' work. Besides, you didn't set 'em no impossible task. You laid it out, so me and Jimbo will just have to get home and help see to it."

"I could've stayed home and gone to the field," Jimbo ventured uncertainly. "But, Missy, I didn't know about any deadline. You left home this morning huntin' trouble."

"No, son… I left going to meet it. There's a difference."

"Maybe so," Big Jim put in, "but the difference is almighty slim. You done right, boy, to trail after our Missy."

Big Jim choked down most of one pork chop and some coffee before heading to join the hands with Jimbo right behind him.

"I told Gert to rest," Missy called after them, voice sounding small and forlorn as she realized the morning's one act of kindness had probably come to naught.

"Surely you didn't expect her to do it," Big Jim tossed back, lightening her load with a rakish smile. "With me and Jimbo off the place, Tobe gone, and that kind of job hangin' over them… Gert took to the field."

Father and son moved along side by side, hoeing grass and weeds out of the corn crop. Big Jim had yet to shed his soiled town clothes or recover from the previous night, but he held the pace. Eventually, he found the energy for some hushed conversation as well. He gave Jimbo the details of his exit from the little auxiliary jail and then laid out the seriousness of the situation.

"Son, that deputy constable has got a wife and kids at home. Even after I told him, he don't know just how close they come to losin' their only means of support. Him laid up with doctor bills and no paycheck at best… That's if he came out of it without needin' the undertaker."

"Missy's not crazy," the boy objected. "She wouldn't want to cause any harm to those folks."

"Want to, no, but she'd have done it in a Dallas minute. Can't blame your mama for being who she is, Jimbo. I'm the one done wrong, but there's a lesson here for you, too. When you've got somebody in your life who's loyal to a fault, who'd do near 'bout anything for you… You just can't put them in those situations."

"No, sir."

Besides the all-important cotton, each tenant household raised a patch of field corn. A certain percentage of these vital commodities, one a cash crop and the other necessary for livestock feed, served as a kind of rent. The Pates raised their own cotton and corn, too, along with enough homegrown vegetables for everyone. Missy and the boss man held a final say on most critical decisions. In busy seasons, like this unseasonably wet summer, everybody on the place worked their crops together with little regard to individual ownership. At present, the whole bunch moved steadily through Tully Havard's struggling corn. Big Jim fought down Johnson grass, Dallas grass, and various weeds as well as his own nausea with a practiced and rhythmic chopping motion. Staying out ahead of the hands allowed a more or less private exchange of words with his son, but only fervent prayer afforded him the strength to continue this particular conversation.

"I drank before goin' to France, Jimbo, but no more than many a farm boy. Saw some things over yonder that ain't hardly fit to speak of and learned pretty quick how to get rip roarin' drunk. Liquor eased my nerves, alright, and then pride took a-hold. See, I've always figured I was man enough to whoop it up some and still handle whatever came my way. That foolishness ended today."

"You can handle just about anything, Daddy. That's what Missy says."

"Lord help us all… She believes it, too. I didn't show Mister Constable no fear, but I stood back there shakin' like a leaf. Desk jockey like that, with just a little bit of power, he's apt to get stubborn and prideful. She'd have shot him, if he pushed her to it. Shot him just as sure as you're born, Jimbo, and then where would we be."

"What about Uncle Cleve?"

"Pshaw, my little brother's too smart to buck Missy on a deal like that. And me locked up back there, helpless as the day I come into the world."

"That's a bad feelin', I reckon, but we got by."

"Got by on the grace of God… There's somethin' I can't tell Missy, son. Can't tell her in case I might fail. But soon as we get the grass out of this corn and these Havard boys out of a bind, me and you are goin' to see Papa Kimbel about two good swallows of peach brandy. Your first drink and my last."

Jimbo felt his throat go tight. Big Jim always talked plainly but had never entrusted him with a man-sized problem before today.

"Tell you what, Daddy… We'll make it my last one, too."

"That'll suit me just fine! 'At Cleve can crack all the jokes he wants to about Missy adding fire to the Pate line. What she added was a soft heart and a backbone of steel. Son, you show plenty of both."

~November 2007~

Laura Beth felt strangely conflicted in the wake of their unexpected family time on horseback. She loved having Kimmy in Red Bog and even relaxed her approach with Bradley. She soaked up the warmth of his presence but steadfastly avoided any discussion of their future. She wanted time to stand still. Wished she could hold them together in close proximity, almost as a family, without opening herself up to be hurt again, but the last few days of October slipped away with no real solution in sight.

Kimmy treated country life like a new adventure, surprising everyone, and her parents took a front row seat. They helped her fish, move cattle, and generally learn her way around the homeplace. Laura Beth kept George Kelly or some of her kinfolk around as an added buffer against painful conversations, but there was no real need. After that first effort, Bradley resolved to wait, enjoying her nearness and hoping for something more.

Jimbo and the aunts needed their time with Kimmy as well, so Laura Beth turned to the kitchen as a safe space. With or without Aunt Alma, she cooked and baked to fill the time between outings. Her writing project fell by the wayside until Bradley and George took a reluctant Kimmy out squirrel hunting.

"Watch that dog work, pumpkin," George said, tickled to find that one of Jimbo's young curs showed plenty of inclination to tree game, "and don't think too awful much about the squirrels. The good Lord made plenty to go around. Besides, it ain't like we're wastin' anything. If your mama don't cook 'em, Ms. Alma will."

Jimbo, Alma, Nadine, and Laura Beth ended up seated on the porch in a rare moment of daytime stillness.

"You done got tired of stories?" Nadine inquired gruffly. "Been a while since our last session."

"No, ma'am," Laura Beth answered with a chuckle. "I'm not tired of listening. In fact, I want Kimmy to join us soon. Reading my little keepsake articles is one thing, but hearing the memories in your own voices is another."

"That's mighty sweet and all," the old woman shot back, "but there's a few stories that ain't fit for tender ears, even if your granddaddy was just about her age when he lived through 'em."

"Steady, Nadine," Jimbo drawled mischievously, and the words came out as if meant to sooth a fractious mare. "Don't go tellin' everything you know."

"At least not until I grab the laptop," Laura Beth quipped, and her obvious anticipation made everyone smile.

Less of an instigator than Nadine, Alma could still follow her sister's line of thinking. She spoke with all her usual gentleness and backed it with the lifelong authority of an eldest sibling.

"Tell Laura Beth about your first and last taste of peach brandy, Jimbo."

"Yeah," Nadine seconded, "and be sure to tell how it came about."

"Well," the old gentleman began reluctantly. "Papa Kimbel, Missy's daddy, was never what you'd call a drinker."

"Bear in mind," Nadine added dryly, "nobody we knew could hold a light to Big Jim. Except maybe Tully Havard, and he seldom gathered up enough money at one time to make a decent try at it."

"Anyhow," Jimbo continued, scowling just a little at the comparison, "Papa Kimbel loved peaches. Right off the tree, baked in a cobbler, as filling for fried pies, or distilled into his homemade brandy. Men who sure ought to know said that stuff made just about the smoothest drink you could get in these parts during prohibition and for a good many years thereafter."

"Must've beat vanilla extract all to pieces," Nadine asserted with a conspiratorial wink.

Laura Beth typed busily, trying for something approaching the poise and nonchalance of a court reporter, but that little wink proved her undoing. She nearly choked on a snort, and once out, it unleashed a wave of spontaneous laughter.

"Would you hush and let him tell the story," Alma chided. "You'll have poor Laura Beth thinking you're some kind of expert on the taste of liquor."

"How do you know I'm not?" Nadine asked, purposefully goading her sister.

"Because I helped Missy raise you. If you'd ever… Why, she'd have thrashed us both within an inch of our lives!"

Shaped in large part by his parents' uncompromising view of the world, Jimbo also inherited enough country wit to chuckle at himself and even, respectfully, at them. Love for Big Jim and Missy didn't mean he wanted to deprive their great-granddaughter of a good story.

Her sudden tears, near the end of the tale, caught him completely off guard.

"Now, don't go cryin' on me. Big Jim made it home again, and Missy never even had to use that pistol."

Setting her laptop aside, Laura Beth stood to pace the length of the porch and back before speaking in a muffled, tear strained voice.

"I'm not crying over what nearly happened to the constable, although that's more than a little disturbing."

"Then, what, doodlebug?"

"I—" and Laura Beth pulled in a long, shuddering breath as she fought for control. "I'm crying because Missy never pushed Big Jim away. Never even scolded him after all the grief he'd caused."

"Scold him?" Nadine scoffed. "She scared the liver and lights out of him without so much as knowing she'd done it."

Laura Beth laughed a little through the tears but quickly shook her head.

"Missy's special blend of feminine grace and rawhide nerve is not my main focus at the moment," she almost whispered. "How— How do I let Kimmy read that story and then explain that I somehow thought it best to quit on her daddy, the only man I ever loved?"

When the usual blend of toughness and humor seemed inadequate, Nadine pushed stiffly to her feet and gathered Laura Beth into her arms.

"A love like they had takes two," she murmured into the soft blond hair. "Sure, our Missy was a jewel," and Nadine raised her voice slightly to garner support from the others, "but just look what Big Jim did for her. The man was an alcoholic, and so far as any of us knew, he never touched another drop. Well, except for that last taste of peach brandy with Jimbo and Papa Kimbel."

"Woman oughtn't be asked to hold a family together all by herself," Alma observed. "That's a pretty tall order, even for Missy Pate."

"Same holds true for a man," Jimbo added quickly. "Daddy was tough as nails, but he needed Missy like the air he breathed."

That said, he rose from his chair and offered Alma a helping hand. They eased over to join Nadine, and all three huddled close around Laura Beth.

"I built a safe little world for my Kimmy," she confided brokenly, "and that's exactly what I meant to accomplish. But why do I love Bradley so terribly much if it's all one sided?"

"I don't know that it is, child. I just don't know that it is."

"It's just got to be one sided, Aunt Alma. That, or we're both foolish beyond belief."

"Not necessarily, sometimes life gets in the way."

"Life is just life," Nadine deadpanned. "I wouldn't go rulin' out the *pair of fools* angle too quick."

This won a genuine smile from Laura Beth, albeit a little damp around the edges.

"We meant these old stories to take your mind off things, doodlebug, not set you up for some kind of comparison to my mother."

"Thank goodness," she answered, finally managing a light tone. "I'd fall a-way short."

Jimbo gazed into his granddaughter's eyes for a long moment, cleared his throat forcefully, and then spoke.

"Missy wouldn't think so, and I don't neither."

"Oh, Granddaddy," and she trailed off, struck by the gravity of his words.

"I told you how we got the grass out of that corn crop and about our little ceremony at Papa Kimbel's store, but I didn't tell you what we found waiting for us back at the house. Uncle Cleve and his bunch showed up with a freezer full of ice cream."

"Of course, we'd used up the last of our ice without laying in another block," Nadine said as if thinking aloud, "No way for them to know, but Cleve had a knack for things like that. Ice cream two nights in a row made a mighty rare treat in those days."

"The berries had just about played out, like they'll do," Alma recalled, "but Missy somehow acquired enough for another cobbler. My favorite, back then. She fussed over me and Bud a little extra that night and never once mentioned ordering him off the place. Her kind of apology came through clearer than words."

"Them Havard boys was grown men and past middle age," Nadine snorted. "They never got so much as a pat on the head by way of apology, and I didn't come out much better. 'Course Missy knew I was too thick-skinned to lose any sleep over a little taste of her temper." Then, as if imparting a secret to Laura Beth, "Alma takes after our mother's people with that sensitive streak. Now, me… I'm something like brother Jim, a Pate clean through, and Missy always read me like a book."

"You never were too sensitive or too subtle, neither," Jimbo recalled. "Anybody that couldn't read you was a payment or two behind on the attention bill."

Nadine joined the rest of them in a chuckle but turned her head attentively when a .22 rifle cracked in the distance.

"That's about the fifth or sixth shot since they left here this morning," she observed. It's a cinch they'll want fried squirrel for dinner."

"I'll do the cooking," Alma volunteered, "as long as somebody knows how to clean a squirrel without gettin' hair all over the meat. There's banana pudding, too, made fresh this morning."

"Reckon I can still peel the hide off one if it comes down to that," Jimbo admitted.

Laura Beth glanced from one face to another, searching for signs of humor. It hardly seemed possible that she and Kimmy might actually be confronted with a lunch of fried squirrels. Suddenly, though, Aunt Nadine saved the day.

"If they can't skin one the right way," she determined with a wave of her hand, "let 'em eat it hair and all. I got enough squirrel to last me a lifetime when we were growin' up. Now, a mess of fried quail is an altogether different matter. I do miss our bobwhites, in the fields and on the dinner table alike."

"Who's the prissy sister, now?" Jimbo teased yet again. "Me and Alma ain't backin' off from a mess of fresh squirrel, but there ought to be enough cold fish left for any delicate eaters in the bunch."

"Well, Granddaddy," Laura Beth admitted, "I'm afraid you'll just have to count me among the delicate eaters."

"That's alright," he said with a note of laughter in his voice. "I reckon my doodlebug can have just about whatever she wants. Here it is comin' on to noontime, and I ain't stirred out of the yard except to give them horses a bite of feed. Ordinarily, I'd go slap crazy settin' around, but your company acts just like a tonic."

Washing dishes after what she considered an odd but enjoyable luncheon, Laura Beth heard the dogs baying their perfunctory challenge to an unfamiliar pickup and stock trailer. Nadine, working beside her, glanced out the window and raised a hand to the base of her throat in an obvious gesture of concern.

"What's the matter, Aunt Nadine?"

"Not much telling," she admitted wryly. "Do you remember my grandson, Dalton?"

"Yes, ma'am," she replied, with a touch of humor in her tone, "but I can't say I remember him as a problem."

"He ain't, necessarily. But you'll learn soon enough how things work. Alma's kids and grandkids won't visit us unless they schedule it three weeks in advance, but my bunch ain't quite figured out that a telephone works two ways. If they venture plumb out here to the homeplace, you can just about bet on some kind of mischief doggin' their heels."

Chapter Fifteen

"Mischief? You must be exaggerating, Aunt Nadine. It can't be like that all the time."

"Exaggerating my foot, and with Dalton pullin' that trailer, I can make a pretty good guess at the particular brand of mischief. He's brought us a flashy colored bundle of horse hide and dynamite or, if we're lucky, some kind of orphaned critter. What's more, he didn't acquire no hot-blooded horse or baby animal on his own. There's a girl in back of it somewhere."

"Ohh, don't look now. But I see crutches and a long, tall redhead."

"I won't look, child. You just tell me the crutches are for the redhead."

"No, ma'am. Dalton's the one hopping."

"Naturally," Nadine said on a sigh, "and that pretty well rules out a baby animal. It takes quite a bit to embarrass me, Laura Beth, but if that boy wants his Uncle Jimbo to knock the edge off some bronc…"

"Granddaddy's just liable to do it, too, or at least try."

"Jimbo can probably get it done, but the main trouble is that Alma's apt to throw a shoe. She thinks Jimbo's too old for about half of what he does anyhow. We're all gettin' old," she finished with a shake of her head. "Why, ten or fifteen years ago, I would've topped most any bronc myself."

"Let's don't borrow trouble," Laura Beth murmured comfortingly. "Maybe he wants to sell a horse or just stopped by to say hello."

In reality, though, Nadine's prediction proved all too accurate. The bronc in question was a delicately made palomino mare with the disposition of a cornered wildcat. Everyone gathered around the stock trailer, and young Dalton Webber lost no time in telling his story.

"This little kitten struck out with a front foot and snapped my leg like a toothpick before I ever got her saddled," Dalton recalled with a shamefaced grin. "I'm out of commission for a little while, Uncle Jimbo. Sweet Abby like to have worried herself sick on the idea that this particular mare might be untrainable, but I come up with a handy solution. Told her the horse that could bluff you and Granny ain't been foaled yet."

"I'm not family here and may be speakin' outta turn." The words carried a certain amount of apology while sounding nonetheless dry and direct for it. "But, sonny boy, that little mare ain't bluffin' even a little bit. She's scared or spoiled, likely some of both."

"George Kelly," and Jimbo inclined his head briefly by way of introduction. "Pretty good fella, if a body can overlook his taste in friends. Then again, I guess you remember Bradley Chandler."

The fleeting trace of a smile softened this little jab at Bradley, and Dalton answered with a grin.

"Yes, sir… Even recognized Kimmy and her nearly grown up on us."

"Anyhow, I'd say George is right about the mare. Horse market's come down right sharply, and you could buy the young lady a gentle mount pretty cheap without givin' up much in the way of looks."

"Oh, but what about Tinker Bell?"

This wide-eyed question from the redheaded girl made Jimbo feel suddenly protective. His drawling answer, not meant to be coarse or insensitive, arose out of concern for her safety.

"Well, now… They've regulated the slaughter deal down to just about nothing, but I've got an old buddy that'll slip this firecracker onto one of the last truckloads."

"Sound advice," Dalton admitted, letting one crutch fall to the ground as he pulled his stunned girlfriend into a reassuring hug, "but Abby's kinda sentimental. Don't tell me the best rider in the family's done got scared?"

"I'll look the other way," Nadine drawled with a bemused half smile, "if you want to kick that other crutch out from under him, Jimbo."

Tenderhearted as usual, Alma put an end to their rough-edged humor.

"Oh, for pity's sake… If Dalton really thought such as that, he'd never say so out loud."

"Well, exceptin' the one-way truck ride, there's just a couple of options left. If Miss Abby is a paying customer, she can leave the mare here for me and doodlebug to gentle along real slow. If this is a kinfolk deal… I'll hook her to the wagon alongside that Bertha mule of mine, knock some of the edge off, and then put a good ride on her. In that case, y'all stay for supper and load Tinker Bell up when you leave."

"Thank you," Abby cried, her youthful face brightening with a sudden rush of hope.

"In other words," Dalton drawled, "somebody go catch that mule."

Seeing the good-natured humor flash in her granddaddy's eyes, Laura Beth sprang immediately into action.

"Come with me, Kimmy, and we'll go fetch old Bertha. You're

welcome, too, Abby, if you want to tag along."

"Bring up Gopher while you're at it," Jimbo called as all three girls trooped off together. "Old rascal's still one of our better using horses. A fair hand in the saddle might just help me keep 'em pointed straight."

"That all sounds fine, Mr. Pate," Bradley said, "but I'd never feel right about standing by to watch you put on a bronc ride."

"Y'all can tell me to dry up any time," George Kelly ventured. "Until then, I'll just speak my mind. Jimbo, you're the top rider in this bunch. Not much doubt about that. Bradley's youngest and stoutest, but I come out somewhere in the middle with more saddle time than him and fewer birthdays than you. Why not let me ride the little yella horse?"

"Not a thing left for you to prove," Nadine put in quietly, stepping up close beside him. "Think some about Laura Beth, too. Your doodlebug still figures you hung the moon, but she's a woman grown and enough like Missy to try that mare herself. Where she might stand back and watch George pull a harebrained stunt, she'd follow you right into the very same jackpot and never think twice."

Kimmy smiled somewhat shyly at the redhaired young woman accompanying them and received an awkward little wave in return. Though older, Abby seemed just as uncertain as the teenage girl and perhaps more so. Laura Beth, completely at ease and focused on the task at hand, ducked into the barn to grab a feed bucket and some halters. That done, she headed out toward the horse pasture.

"You'll probably get a wagon ride out of this, baby," she observed happily, "but I don't want you in there until Granddaddy figures it's safe."

"Okay, Mama," Kimmy agreed and then lowered her voice just a little, "but you can stop calling me baby in front of strangers anytime now."

Catching the exchange, Abby laughed softly and seemed to lose some of her shyness.

"You'll always be your mama's baby. I've got a fulltime job and my own apartment, but I'm still *sugar bear* to my folks. Know something else," she continued whimsically, "I don't mind it nearly as much these days."

"I guess you're right," Kimmy admitted, watching with quiet admiration as Laura Beth caught the little bay gelding, handed him off to Abby, and then haltered the mule. "Mama's been gone nearly a month, out here making up for lost time in Red Bog. I stayed back home in Houston but started to miss her after a while."

"I just assumed y'all lived around here. Laura Beth is awfully handy with the livestock."

"Mama did live here until she was twelve or thirteen. She came back every summer, for a while, but it's all new to me."

"This is kind of a new experience for me, too. I've been around some horses but never anything as pretty as my new palomino." Then, after a moment's hesitation, "Never anything quite as wild, either."

The white mule, though gentle and well suited to her job, tended to get a little pushy when handled from the ground. Laura Beth doubled the lead rope, neatly removing the slack, and then backed the mule out of her space with three quick jerks on the halter. After that, Bertha walked respectfully just behind her right shoulder. Glancing at the girls on her left, Laura Beth easily picked up the thread of their conversation.

"With horseback jaunts, fishing, squirrel hunting, and now a wagon ride," she cautioned her daughter, "you're liable to get the idea that country life is all play. Naturally, I want you to enjoy your time here on the homeplace, but it won't do for you to lose sight of all the work that goes into it. Why, in a month or less, we'll be feeding cattle every day."

"We, Mama?"

Laura Beth fell silent for a moment, caught off guard by the question and by her own assumption.

"Well, I… Granddaddy'll need… Somebody ought to help him. You'll be out for Thanksgiving and then Christmas before we know it. Things worked out well for us, but I can't imagine who planned your fall break right ahead of those others."

"So many factors go into planning a school calendar," Abby volunteered, "that nobody's ever completely happy with the end result. I'm working as a paraprofessional right now and plan to get my teaching certificate someday. Of course, my experience is with the smaller schools around here. I can't imagine the complex scheduling for one of those huge districts down around Houston."

"You're probably right, and like I said, it all worked out for us this time. I took you for a cowgirl," she continued, changing the subject with a smile. "You certainly dressed the part today."

"If I knew as much about horses as I do about clothes," Abby snorted, "poor Dalton might not have that cast on his leg."

"My cousin is a grown man," Laura Beth replied with a smiling shake of her head, "and I expect he inherited some of Aunt Nadine's hardheadedness. Don't go blaming yourself for his choices, but thanks for the honesty."

"Sure… No point pretending to be something I'm not."

"That being the case, you'd better stay out of the wagon until they call for Kimmy to ride."

"What about you?"

"I grew up on this kind of thing, and it's all come back over the last few weeks. Of course, we never used a wagon to wear the riding stock down. But I'd sometimes go along on a gentle horse and do my best to steady whatever bronc Granddaddy might be schooling that day. Guess I'll be in the thick of it one way or another, wherever I can do him the most good."

"Thanks for the warning. I'll just stick close to Kimmy."

George knew something about hitching up a wagon team from his long and varied experience as a backcountry hunter and guide. Bradley possessed enough horse sense and natural agility to keep hold of the thrashing mare without getting stomped. Jimbo turned away from the struggle long enough to harness and hitch his mule.

"Throw your saddle on Gopher," he told Laura Beth in passing. "Help us all you can out there, but don't take no wild chances. I've got old Bertha and hydraulic brakes all the way around. Any man that can't come out alright like that had ought to hunt up a rockin' chair."

She flashed him a grin and moved to obey as he darted back into the fray to doublecheck buckles and straps. Finally, the three men maneuvered their unwilling charge up close to the wagon tongue and hooked her alongside the mule. When Jimbo scrambled into the driver's seat without further instructions, George tossed a lively glance at the photographer.

"I'm goin' with him! Throw the gate back and then catch us on the way by if you take a notion."

Sure enough, Bradley stepped aboard as handily as any old-time railroad bum and found himself a seat. The golden mare plunged and reared and squealed, but none of it altered their course. With big Bertha hitched on the right and Laura Beth riding wing to the left, they managed something close to a straight line. After a couple of wide turns, Jimbo signaled his granddaughter to open a gate going out into the big pasture and leave them to it for a while.

"Ask Aunt Alma to give you a jug of water and whatever snacks y'all want," he called, jamming on the brakes for a little more conversation. "We'll circle back by the house directly, take on some passengers, and strike out down the road. And, doodlebug… You can tie Gopher in the barn lot and load up with us. He don't need the extra miles, but we may want him when it comes time to saddle this mare."

As the palomino settled down, their little chore turned into a nice outing. Kimmy scooted in close to Dad and claimed the next seat for Mama. Dalton clambered up onto the wagon, crutches and all, and rode alongside Abby.

"Thanks, Uncle Jimbo. Like I've been tellin' Abby… Slow and easy is the best way with a horse but sometimes a little bit of dust and hair needs to fly, just to get their attention, before the real training sets in."

"Ain't over yet," the old man cautioned. "Not unless Miss Abby figures on buyin' a wagon and a gentle horse to match this one. If it's all the same to y'all, George says he'll put the first ride on her."

"Me and Abby sure don't care, but it looks to me like you've gone soft in your old age."

"Do what?"

"Well… We might've wasted a good opportunity by using this mule and wagon first. I've seen the time you would've strapped some old junk saddle on and pushed at Laura Beth's ex-husband hard enough to make him crawl aboard."

"Couldn't hardly do him that-a-way in front of Kimmy," came the drawling answer, and Bradley whooped his amusement right along with the rest of them.

Abby sat across from Kimmy and, despite her natural shyness, whipped out a cellphone to capture the girl and both parents in a moment of shared laughter.

"Aww," she confided softly to Dalton, tilting the screen for him to see. "Turned out good."

They all enjoyed the leisurely trip, and Jimbo liked for the mare to stand occasionally as part of her education. During one of these stops, Bradley and George piled off the wagon, taking Kimmy with them to investigate an armadillo hole in the roadside bank and further her own education as to the local wildlife.

"Show Laura Beth that picture," Dalton prodded gently.

Abby shifted across the wagon, phone in hand, and perched there for a moment. The photo made Laura Beth catch her breath, but lifelong habit brought gratitude to the surface well ahead of other, more complex emotions.

"Oh, how wonderful. Thanks for taking that. I want to give you my number, but you'd better send it by email. I'm carrying a flip phone right now, and the picture might not come through quite as well."

"Okay… Just text me your email, and then I'll have both. I've really enjoyed meeting you, Laura Beth."

"She has that effect on people," Dalton teased. "Why, I've seen her hold court at more than one family reunion. Then, after a while, she got too highfalutin' to come home a-tall."

"You just hush up over there. I've learned my lesson once and for all. Coming back home keeps me sane. Besides, I owe Granddaddy and them more than an occasional visit. Why, I'll be around Red Bog so much that they're apt to run me off."

"I doubt that," he quipped on a short burst of laughter.

"Thanks for making me feel welcome," Abby almost whispered. "You're naturally so warm and bubbly, but it takes me a while to loosen up. Once I do, I usually put my foot in my mouth. Feel one of those moments coming on right now, but I've just got to tell you, Laura Beth… Y'all are a lovely family in spite of the divorce."

"I don't call that putting a foot in your mouth, but it sure puts a lump in my throat."

Nervous and quick, Abby pulled Laura Beth into a hug and then scrambled back to her seat.

"I'd like to know you better if we get the chance. You, and Kimmy, too."

"Come see us whenever it's handy," Laura Beth invited, "or make Dalton bring you to church sometime. The pastor's wife is a real sweetheart, and I think you'd like her."

"Look what you've started now," Dalton chided playfully. "Laura Beth may be as bad as Granny about wrangling me into church. Take the girl out of Red Bog, but you'll never get Red Bog out of the girl."

"I'd like to work the little mare some more," Jimbo observed, "but we'd best circle on back. That'll put ten miles on her, time we get home. Any further and dark's liable to catch us before George can make his ride."

Once back at the house, Laura Beth stepped from the wagon with a contented smile.

"That was fun, y'all, and probably the first real work Tinker Bell's ever done. I don't expect she'll put on much of a show now."

"Hope not," Abby confided, standing close beside her.

"I've seen lots of this kind of thing over the years, so I'll run to the house and give Aunt Alma a hand with supper. Aunt Nadine may want to come down and watch since she missed our little wagon trip."

"Dalton's granny scares me a little, but I'm willing to help in the kitchen if y'all need me."

"No, it's your horse. You stay here and watch. Kimmy will want to see the ride, too."

"Okay, if you say so."

"And don't worry about Aunt Nadine… Just try not to act so timid. Let her smell weakness, and she'll put you up a tree for sure." Laura Beth followed this statement with a wink and then softened her assessment just a bit. "She's goodhearted, though, when you come right down to it."

Supper consisted of homemade stew and fresh cornbread. After a slice of Alma's coconut pie, Dalton thanked Jimbo and the others once again for their help. Abby, still a bit awkward with Nadine, leaned in for a quick hug from Laura Beth.

"I emailed that picture from my phone," she remembered suddenly.

"Thanks bunches… I've got my laptop, but there's no internet connection. Here, let me see your phone. I'll text the picture to Bradley. We'll pass his phone around and look at it on that larger screen until I can check my email."

"Being a little younger," Dalton teased as Laura Beth glanced up from texting, "I never realized how much you'd picked up during those summers with Uncle Jimbo. Anyway, you were dead right about that mare. If I'd known she was gonna ride off that easy, I might've followed you on up to the kitchen."

A moment or two of quiet followed the usual round of goodbyes, and then George broke the silence.

"Let me and Kimmy see about the dishes, Laura Beth. The rest of y'all might as well take it easy for a while."

"Gee, thanks, buddy," Kimmy groaned, but a smile took the sting from her sarcasm.

"I don't need any hound-dog-chasing rambler meddlin' around in my kitchen," Alma teased gently. "You men go on in the front room and sit with Laura Beth for a minute. Won't be long until y'all head up to Jimbo's for the night. Kimmy might as well visit, too. I'll put her to work after breakfast in the morning."

Instead of adding her two cents, Nadine simply turned back to the table and started cleaning up while the rest of them drifted into the front room as directed.

"Good of you to ride that mare," Jimbo said as George settled into a rocker, "especially for a couple of strangers."

"Nothing to it. You put more work in than I did. Besides, I didn't necessarily ride her for them kids. The horse was there, and it needed to be done."

"Don't know if you've noticed," Bradley joked, "but Laura Beth's got old George wrapped around her little finger. I'm not sayin' he rode the horse to impress her, but him getting on instead of you probably eased her mind a little."

George's grin acknowledged the truth of the statement, but he waved the notion away at the same time.

"Makes very little difference who got on in the end," he concluded. "Old Bertha and that wagon took the starch plumb out of our yella bronc."

"Started all our riding stock that-a-way in my boyhood, but I'd got away from the wagon deal before Laura Beth ever came along."

"Easier like this," his granddaughter observed, "and I'd say Bertha sure earns her keep."

"Get your laptop, Laura Beth, and read us a story."

Bradley's suggestion caught her off guard, and Laura Beth barely suppressed the urge to bite her knuckle. Instead, she chewed her lower lip as her mind raced. He and Kimmy had already seen nearly everything she'd written, and thoughts of the latest story gave her pause. Big Jim's night in jail and Missy's absolute loyalty were not exactly the stuff of light conversation. How could she share that tale with this particular audience when she'd given Bradley his freedom, practically shoved it on him, over a superficial difference in their goals.

Jimbo caught the distress on her face and sat upright in his chair. Bradley saw it, too, and his reaction proved even swifter.

"Aw, never mind. I want to show y'all this picture."

"Yes," Laura Beth agreed, almost giddy in the moment of relief.

"With the three of us? I sent that to you from Abby's phone."

"I'm glad she took it. Never even thought to grab a camera or two."

"Just as well," George quipped. "Tinker Bell might've stamped all over 'em before we got her hooked to that wagon. Anyhow… It looks to me like you could miss a right smart, always lookin' at the world through a camera lens."

"When you offered to travel along," Bradley shot back, "I sure never knew I'd be gettin' me a life coach."

Despite this friendly jab, George's weathered features brightened considerably at sight of the little family photo. Jimbo looked at it for a long moment, and his eyes went uncharacteristically soft before snapping back to their usual alertness. He lifted the phone carefully from Bradley's hand and then beckoned for Kimmy.

"Tote this thing in yonder, little bit. I want Aunt Alma and Nadine to see that picture, but I'm apt to call Kansas City or some such place 'fore I get to the kitchen with it."

Struck by a sudden idea, Bradley got up and followed his daughter from the room. While Alma and Nadine oohed and aahed over the screen, he spoke quietly to Kimmy.

"Did you ever finish that sketch of your mother? The one you showed me and Vida back in Houston…"

"Sure, Dad. I finished the drawing our first morning at Red Bog, but she never knew it. Easier to capture her sitting on the porch and looking off down toward the barn lot once we got here. Don't know why I put the long dress on her, though. She mostly wears jeans around here unless it's Sunday or something."

"That's alright. She'll like it, dress and all. Then, too, your

Granddaddy Pate is apt to decide it's just about the finest piece of art ever made. Run and get it, but don't show them until I'm in there to watch. Might even grab a camera so I can capture the moment."

"Uh uh," Kimmy decided with a negative shake of her head, "better listen to your *life coach* on that one."

"Okay, the artist has spoken. Now, scoot."

Bradley pocketed his phone and then helped to finish up the dishes. That done, he ushered Alma and Nadine into the front room for a big reveal. With everyone looking on, Kimmy handed the sketchpad to her mother almost uncertainly.

"Oh," Laura Beth murmured, "you must have spent hours working on this, baby. The detail… I almost hate to admit it, but you made me look better than real life."

"Never," Kimmy demurred, enjoying the praise of her work nonetheless. "I started it back at the house. Missed you, I guess, and it was easy enough to picture you at Red Bog. Then, when Dad and George brought me up here to visit, I put the finishing touches on it. Glad you like it, Mama."

Laura Beth's eyes glistened with happy tears, but when she handed the drawing off to her grandfather, his reaction proved even stronger.

"Good Lord," he whispered after a moment of stunned silence. Then, in a slightly stronger voice, "Look at this, Aunt Alma, and tell me what you see."

Alma adjusted her glasses slightly and answered without hesitation.

"Same thing you do," she offered with a warm smile, "It could just as easy be a picture of Missy."

"Oh," Kimmy said, slightly deflated, "it's supposed to look like Mama."

"It does, child," Nadine decided, looking over her sister's shoulder. "The two of them could've passed for sisters, and the sketch is just vague enough to turn back time. You drew Laura Beth, and by the light of a memory, we've caught a glimpse of our Missy."

Chapter Sixteen

Kimmy's time off from school ended all too soon. Hating the thought of parting from her daughter as much or more than she dreaded the frantic pace and personal isolation of her former life, Laura Beth opted for a compromise.

"How about letting me take baby girl back to Houston and get her settled?" she proposed at the supper table on the final evening of Kimmy's visit. "I need to check on things at the office, too."

Picking up on the slight hesitation in her voice, Bradley and Jimbo tripped one another up in their efforts to comfort her. Grinning slightly in the wake of this conversational collision, Bradley fell silent and let the older man speak first.

"Sounds like a good idea to me, doodlebug, and there's no call for you to decide on anything permanent just yet."

"Your granddaddy's right," Bradley seconded. "Make this little trip, come on back, and take all the time you need. There's nothing on my agenda more important than being available for Kimmy."

"Thank y'all," and the words came on an unconscious but heartfelt sigh of relief. "It feels somehow irresponsible or at least overly indulgent, but I could definitely use the extra time in Red Bog."

"It feels good to know that I can finally do something for you, Laura Beth. If you'd ever asked me to— Well, if you'd ever asked for anything, I'd have tried awfully hard to make it happen."

"Day late and a dollar short," Nadine muttered, locking eyes with Jimbo across the table, but no one else paid her much mind.

Laura Beth sat there in silence for a long moment, very much aware of the others around the table.

"That's very kind, Bradley, and I don't exactly know what to—"

"Don't say anything," he advised gently. "The days you're giving me with Kimmy are the real gift. If you're up to driving, just take your car. Me and George will try to lend a hand around here. Let us know when you get ready, and I'll find a way down there to trade off with you."

"Oh, yes," Kimmy quipped. "Let's get the babysitting schedule all worked out. I don't really care who drives me down or who stays here. Just so long as I can finish out the semester, or maybe the year, say goodbye to my friends, and resign myself to high school among the pines."

"Kimmy, nobody said—"

"I'm joking, Mama. Well, kinda. Definitely joking when I said I didn't care about the *babysitting schedule.* I've missed you. Now, I'll miss Dad and then miss you again. But anybody can see you're happier here."

"My preferences shouldn't take you away from… Happiness has never been my first priority."

"Yeah, and maybe smacking into somebody's car was a blessing in disguise. You're blooming from the roots up, Mama. Whether anybody noticed or not, the bouquet was beginning to droop some, left unattended in that big-city vase."

"Alright," Nadine called, rapping her knuckles on the edge of the table. "If y'all make Laura Beth cry, Alma's bound to join in… I'd just as soon pass on the waterworks."

The wave of laughter that followed Nadine's characteristically blunt declaration gave Bradley a moment to gaze at his daughter with loving pride. Highly talented, Kimmy had inherited his knack for the visual arts. Now, for the first time, he suspected she might also share her mama's way with words. For a thirteen-year-old child to notice the return of Laura Beth's vibrant glow and then verbalize such complexities…

~ ~

Happy chatter eased Laura Beth's nerves on the long drive. Mother and daughter shared meaningful conversation about their time in Red Bog and touched occasionally on plans for the future.

"You know," Kimmy observed at one point, "I never realized before how much you and Dad still love each other."

"Of course we do, baby. How could we share you, a precious gift in both our lives, and not feel some appreciation for one another?"

"No, ma'am… That line won't cut it anymore. I watched the two of you in Red Bog, and we're talking l-o-v-e."

"Kimmy," Laura Beth chided, blushing a little in spite of herself. "Please don't set yourself up for disappointment. Your dad and I love… I mean, we did love one another very much, and when we broke apart, it left scars on both sides. Even if he could forgive me for pushing him away, I don't know if I could trust that restless nature of his for a second time."

"Well, that's depressing," and Kimmy brushed her hands together as if scrubbing something off. "Here's the deal… You survived city life more or less alone, and gave me a great childhood. You'll be much happier in Red Bog with Granddaddy Pate and the aunts around, but until you and Dad figure things out, there will always be something missing. For you, Mama, not for me. Even separately, y'all are great parents, so I'll be just fine."

Spotting a small gap in the Saturday traffic, Laura Beth whipped on her blinker and made an unplanned exit.

"After all that wisdom, baby girl, I need a dose of fresh air and something chocolate. If there's no specialty candy for sale in this outlet mall, we'll settle for a vending machine."

By mid-afternoon on Tuesday, Laura Beth cracked open yet another Dr Pepper and rummaged through her purse for the near-forgotten bottle of nerve pills.

"You okay?" Vida inquired with a raised eyebrow.

Though passionate in her zest for life, the younger woman seemed almost immune to daily stressors. She also possessed a rare knack for seeing through Laura Beth's outer layer of ladylike tranquility.

"Not really," Laura Beth admitted on a pitiful sigh, and then elaborated with a question of her own. "Remind me why I'm not interacting with customers this week? That's what drew me into this line of work in the first place."

"Sorry, boss. You're only here for a week, so Belinda and I need to keep some kind of system going. Besides, it wouldn't be fair to give a few customers personal attention from *the Elizabeth Chandler* and then subject others to a backup plan."

"Don't be silly. Y'all have done a good job here. Bradley, too."

"Yeah," Vida murmured appreciatively, "he's a real charmer. And don't you flash those eyes at me… I don't mean a lady's man in particular, but good with *all* the customers. Somebody's got to smooth things over with Belinda around. If you ask me, though, he's safely heartbroken, just the way you left him."

"Would you please hush," Laura Beth shot back and then changed the subject. "I hate taking those pills. Nothing wrong with medication if it's truly needed, but I was just fine back home. Not quite two days here, and I remember exactly why my doctor prescribed them. Like it or not, I'll probably need a little extra help getting to sleep tonight, too."

"Maybe not," Vida offered with a gentle smile. "I'll order some pizza and come over for a girls' night with you and Kimmy. Get your tummy nice and full, put the Dr Pepper down at a reasonable hour, and we're talking fast track to dreamland."

"You're a sweetheart, Vida, and that sounds like a plan."

"Anybody's a sweetheart compared to Belinda," she retorted, raising her voice so that it would carry, in good fun, to the outer office. "But this evening when I'm the caffeine police, you may have some other names for me."

"Vida, honey," and Laura Beth waggled her finger playfully, "over the course of our friendship, you've switched from cigarettes to a vape to nicotine gum… Scolding me for Dr Pepper seems just the teeniest bit hypocritical."

"Hey, I'm making progress. Sleep just fine, too, thank you very much."

True to her word, Vida showed up that evening right behind the pizza delivery. She even brought a liter of diet root beer to further the cause.

"No sugar and no caffeine," Laura Beth enumerated, ticking off the missing elements on her fingers. "Did they leave anything but the bubbles?"

"Water's always a good option," Vida countered smoothly.

"Don't be silly; I'll take the bubbles. Kimmy made plans with a friend tonight, but that went out the window once she heard you were coming.”

“Glad somebody still thinks I’m fun… A tablecloth, Laura Beth? You’re the boss and all, but I’m not having a girls’ night in your dining room.” That said, she flopped onto the couch beside Kimmy and opened a pizza box. “See if you can satisfy that southern belle hostess urge by gathering up some cups, ice, and paper napkins.”

In her rush to speak, Kimmy suppressed a snort of laughter.

“You *are* fun, Vida, and funny, too. But I’m really here to make sure my oh-so-perfect parent doesn’t hide her true feelings under a layer or two of polite conversation.”

“Spill it, quick,” Vida shot back with a grin, “while she’s still processing the idea of paper napkins.”

Always ladylike but too deeply influenced by her country upbringing to ever approach their highfaluting stereotype, Laura Beth mimicked a graceful pirouette and left the room with a smile.

“Seriously,” Kimmy confided, “I’ll try to be quiet so you and Mama can talk, but you need to quiz her good. Call me a hopeless romantic or a dumb kid, but I know what I saw.”

“What did you saw?” Vida teased gently.

“Sparks, real sparks, between her and Dad.”

“Cozy fireplace kind of sparks or ignited gasoline kind of sparks?”

“Nice, like a fireplace, and heating up just fine without even a hint of explosion!”

“Only two days back in school, young lady,” Laura Beth observed, gliding back into the conversation, “but you had better be discussing a science project."

Vida winked at the girl conspiratorially, and all three of them shared a good laugh. Making every effort to relax, Laura Beth enjoyed the pizza more than she cared to admit and did her best to answer their pointed questions with unguarded honesty. Much later, with Kimmy asleep on the opposite end of the couch, Vida glanced up from the faint glow of a computer screen and blinked away her misty-eyed reaction to one of the Red Bog tales.

"I don't read. Never have, and here you are making me question that basic life choice. This is really good stuff! Obviously, Scarlett O'Hara, there are cultural differences, but your descriptions of warmth and closeness sound a lot like my own extended family way down in rural Zacatecas."

"Scarlett?" Slightly off base, the comparison triggered a moment of contemplation, but Laura Beth shook it off with a playful toss of her honey-colored locks. "If you're going to tease me, get it right. Missy will do quite nicely."

The little performance not only made her point but won a grin from Vida.

"Well, I stand corrected."

"You know," Laura Beth ventured thoughtfully. "Kimmy is actually encouraging me to consider a permanent move back to Red Bog. I've always shied away from the thought of uprooting her, but she doesn't seem particularly concerned. Still, I'm afraid her attitude about moving comes from unrealistic hopes for me and Bradley. She not only saw my happiness on the homeplace but, with him there, experienced something close to the typical American family."

"First off, don't worry about *uprooting* Kimmy. She doesn't care about this house or the neighborhood. Not much, anyway. You're her home, Laura Beth. You're her family. You've always put her first, but Kimmy is mature and perceptive enough to choose for herself."

"What do you mean?"

"I've never even been to East Texas, but I know there's something in Red Bog that enhances your sparkle. Kimmy's choosing the happy and authentic version of Mama over the I-*will*-make-this-work version."

Laura Beth drew in a sharp breath, and for a moment, looked almost childlike in her uncertainty.

"Do you think— Have I shortchanged my daughter by trying to pour from an empty cup?"

"Well, that reaction is just about true to form. Mustn't cut yourself any slack. Kimmy keeps telling you she's fine, so believe her. The girl's only worried about one thing, apart from the usual teenage stuff, and that's her mama."

"If Kimmy's doing well, that's all that matters."

"Yeah, just keep on telling yourself that. But when you step out in front of the wrong car or drop dead from a heart attack, who's left to pick up the pieces?"

"Vida, that's not fair."

"Fair? That's the truth. I know you can't flounce immediately off to Red Bog and live happily ever after, but Kimmy's only asking you to think about it."

"Okay," Laura Beth answered slowly. "Let's think about it, but first I want a Dr Pepper."

"Nope, just concentrate. Red Bog... How can we get you and Kimmy back home to Red Bog? Belinda and I can manage for a while, but the business requires so much from you personally. Not the only way to run things... But that's your way, and it works. If y'all left permanently, you'd need to sell."

"Can we be perfectly honest here? I do not like change. I don't like thinking about it or talking about it. Even when a major shift looks like the best option. I hated change way back when my parents moved us out of Red Bog, and I still hate it."

"Pobrecita," Vida murmured, giving Laura Beth's hair a comforting stroke as she reverted momentarily to Spanish.

"I'll take all the sympathy I can get," the older girl admitted with a whimsical little smile, "but it's not solving anything."

Vida smiled back and then reduced the problem to dollars and cents.

"I've never had anything more than the basic necessities, Laura Beth, and money has never been your main focus. But we've both worked for some wealthy people over the years and seen the way they operate. Just say you managed to get a decent price for the business you've built. How would you invest that money? How could you make a living up there at home? What is it, exactly, that your grandfather does?"

"Granddaddy doesn't necessarily have to make a living these days, but farm folk and ranchers seldom ever retire. Maybe cut back just a little... Still, the notion of dying in the saddle wouldn't bother Jimbo Pate a-tall."

"Don't know if that's admirable or slightly insane, but getting back to you..."

"I don't own any land, Vida. My heart may belong to the homeplace, but I suppose Dad and Uncle James Allen will inherit it in the normal course of things.”

“After seeing your face light up when you talk about your grandfather and getting to know him a little in those stories, I can’t imagine that he’d deny you much of anything. If batting those expressive eyes of yours won’t change *the normal course of things…* Then, buy a few acres.”

“The average cow-calf operation is little more than a savings account nowadays. You’ve just about got to have some outside income.”

“So what?”

“So, I’m middle-aged and too soft to jump out there now and start ridin’ for the public like Granddaddy’s done all these years. Besides, the horse market is atrocious at the moment. Hard to collect decent monthly training fees on a seventy-five-dollar colt.”

“Would owning some of the family land give you a sense of security?”

“Well, my future’s ultimately in the Lord’s hands,” Laura Beth replied thoughtfully, “but I suppose it might. Over the course of five generations, my folks have poured themselves into that place and seen their effort come back in the form of blessings when they were caught in a bind. A little stand of timber to cut or some yearlings to sell or, once upon a time, a decent cotton crop… God provides those things, but we’ve watched Him work through the homeplace time and again.”

“Slow down,” Vida teased, masking the impact of her friend’s passionate answer. “I can’t tell if you’re trying to turn me into a good Baptist or just plant the love of Red Bog in my heart. Bradley likes it way out there in the sticks, huh? He might be an easier convert.”

"Leave Bradley out of this, please ma'am."

"Maybe I will, and maybe I won't. But asking him to build a life with you out in the country is a totally different proposition than asking him to sink roots through concrete. Don't turn your world upside down over a slim chance with Bradley… But why not increase the odds by doing what you want to do anyway?"

"And just what is it, Vida, that I want to do?"

"Sell the business, eventually, and go live in Red Bog. Being there to help your grandfather and those aunts will minimize one source of worry. But day-to-day farm life probably involves more physical labor than you're used to, so take my advice and find a desk job in some air-conditioned office. You can work during the week without going too far from home or the people you love. Except for me… I'd rather face Belinda any day than deal with a bunch of rednecks."

"Pshaw," and this drawling response to the little joke sounded an awful lot like Missy Pate. "Poor folks from Maine to Matamoros, especially those living close to the land, tend to have more in common than they think." The two friends enjoyed a moment of shared laughter before Laura Beth shifted back to her businesslike tone of voice. "I'd never make the kind of money at home that I'm taking in here."

"Money from the sale of your business… You wouldn't necessarily put it all into land. A cattle operation sounds risky enough. So, why put those extra funds into another venture that's equally uncertain? Rural America may not be the place for event planning or a bed and breakfast. Buy some stocks or bonds as a cushion, manage your land, maybe even write about the lifestyle, and then go to town and be somebody's topnotch secretary or administrative assistant."

"Our cost of living would be slightly lower, and when you consider the extra layer of investments and a little something from the homeplace now and then, it might actually work.”

“Well, I’m not dumb. A little crazy, sure, but not dumb. Would you like for me to prove it?”

“You’re plenty sharp, Vida. That was never in doubt. Besides, we’ve come further this evening in mapping out my future than I have over the last decade.”

“Thanks, but you misunderstood. I’m offering to prove just how crazy I am.”

“Okay, you’ve aroused my curiosity.”

“Here goes… I’m guessing the non-compete clause Belinda signed when she sold her firm has expired. Otherwise, she’d never have come back to work, not even to help you. The woman is mean, but she’s honest as can be. How would you feel about selling *Finishing Touches* to us? I’ll sign a contract to pay three-quarters of what you think the business is worth over time. That way, you can discount her half for a cash offer. Make sense?”

“Kind of,” Laura Beth admitted, “but I’m supposed to feel sleepy at the moment, not giddy with anticipation.”

“Take it easy. Belinda will have to chew me out at least two or three times before she comes around. You go to bed and rest, work your magic around here for a few more days, and then go on back to the farm. I’ll let you know when it’s time to make our move. Oh, and by the way, if you can sell outright to somebody else, do it. I’m not standing between you and a life in Red Bog.”

“What did I ever do, Vida, to deserve a friend like you?”

“Believe it or not, lady, you’re a pretty rare jewel in this world. A real-life princess who treats everybody fair and makes us all feel special at the same time. You stepped in as the buffer between me and Belinda before I learned to handle her. Somewhere along the way, I made it my goal to grow up one day and become Laura Beth Chandler."

The rest of the week played out more or less as predicted. Laura Beth continued working behind the scenes, but Vida's proposal with its suggestion of a definite goal added a touch of genuine excitement. She replaced her blackberry, determined not to let this new phone contribute to her anxiety with its buzzing demands, and even found time for a little after-school shopping with Kimmy.

"It looks like I'm going back to Red Bog to assess our options, baby. How do you feel about a few more weeks with just your dad and George here?"

"We'll be alright. I sure missed my mama during your first trip, but maybe the whole experience will remind me not to take you for granted."

"What a mature attitude. You're turning into a regular young lady."

"Maybe one day, but don't count your goofy teenager out just yet. I'll want to finish the school year here, and Dad's really stepped up. George… He's kind of like free entertainment and a bodyguard all rolled into one, but I can't quite picture the old rascal swapping Red Bog for another taste of city life."

Savoring the warmth of a tall gourmet coffee against the slight chill of an approaching Texas winter, Laura Beth reached across the outdoor table to clasp her daughter's hand.

"Your dad and I… Well, our situation is more uncertain than ever, but I'm so glad to see y'all getting closer. Bradley has always treated me with the utmost respect, and I would never do anything to come between the two of you. But I don't want your heart set on some fairytale ending."

Kimmy's sly grin caught Laura Beth momentarily off guard.

"Well, Mama, there's respect and then there's adoration."

"Oh, Kimmy, be serious."

"I am, serious as a traffic accident." Laura Beth opened her mouth to object once again, but Kimmy cut her off. "Okay, Mama. Okay, that was my last joke. I understand your warning and the reasons for it, but I'm old enough to survive even a major disappointment. Would you rather I never hoped at all?"

"No, baby, I guess not…"

"Don't beat yourself up," Kimmy quipped in response to the apologetic tone. "All good mothers hover, but according to Vida, the ones with southern belle tendencies are a little over the top."

"Is that so?" and the words came out on a snort of laughter. "Better get you moved out to Red Bog soon so you can see just how normal I am."

Bradley drove into Houston on Friday afternoon and found himself at loose ends. With Kimmy in school and Laura Beth at work, he decided on impulse to swing by his father's downtown headquarters. Several employees recognized him and offered knowing grins. A few even called out short greetings, but only the longtime secretary ventured to comment on his unexpected visit.

"It's been a long time, Bradley," she said, glancing up momentarily from her work, "but you still don't need an appointment. As it happens, you caught the old lion in his den."

Meeting this dubious encouragement with a smile, he stepped

around her desk and into the private office.

"Hello, Pop."

"I hear good things about you from Kimmy," Braxton Chandler grunted and then swiveled the desk chair around to face his son. "Looks like my granddaughter inherited her sainted mother's one and only blind spot."

"It's good to see you, too, old man."

Braxton gave the general impression of a bulldog, jaw in motion as he chewed on an unlit cigar.

"Ain't no charge for looking, just so you don't take too long about it."

"I stopped by to shake your hand, Pop. Shake your hand and say thank you. Think what you want to, but there's never been a day when I didn't have Laura Beth and Kimmy on my mind. No way I could've stood the miles between us without knowing beyond a shadow of a doubt that you'd watch over them."

"Don't you underestimate Laura Beth. That sweet girl… The one-of-a-kind lady you married and then ran out on… She never took so much as a thin dime off me."

"No, sir, but you were here just the same. See, I'm starting to wonder… I'm hoping there might be just the glimmer of a chance left for me and Laura Beth. Anyway, I wanted you to know."

Braxton pushed slowly to his feet and extended a work-roughened hand across the desk. They shook almost warmly, but the next words carried a decidedly uncompromising edge.

"Jimbo Pate's aging on up, and Billy… Well, he never was quite as tough as the old man. Hurt Laura Beth again, son, and I'll kick your worthless tail myself.”

Bradley bit back a smile and turned to leave, but he paused to gesture at a worn leather sofa.

“How about letting me crash here tonight? See… I’ll be staying at Laura Beth’s house, but she’s not leaving for Red Bog until tomorrow morning.”

“No,” Braxton answered gravely, weighing their long estrangement against his wife’s feelings in the matter. “I reckon you’d better come on home tonight.”

“May be late, Pop. I kind of planned on asking her out for supper.”

When Braxton chuckled, his rare laughter came slowly, and the eventual answer seemed just as unhurried.

“Do that, son, and do it with your hat in your hand. We’ll leave a light on for you.”

~ ~

“Kimmy talks and talks about missing me and then makes spur-of-the-moment plans with a school friend on my last night in town.” Laura Beth delivered this statement with a mock pout but eventually smiled her resignation and continued the late afternoon conversation with Bradley. “She said George wouldn’t leave Red Bog for another trip to Houston, and I guess he didn’t. Are you really staying with Pop and Gran tonight? I could always go to my folks if that’s easier.”

“No, this is your house. Besides, it took Pop so long to unbend that I can’t afford to turn him down.”

“That reminds me,” she said, reaching into her purse for the nondescript company phone. “Give this back to Pop. Thank him for me, and tell him I’ll see him soon.”

"Might just leave the thanks to you, Laura Beth. I'm sure he'd like a hug and kiss, but not from me. Now, about this evening, the old man's invitation didn't include supper. What does your schedule look like?"

"I don't have any real plans, not since our daughter abandoned me."

"Laura Beth, I— Please don't let me upset you. If friendship is all you need, I'll give that my best shot. The truth is, though, I'm still in love with you and always have been. Never should've left in the first place, but I'd sure like for us to try again.

"Bradley…" The familiar name caught in her throat, but she took a breath and forged ahead. "That's just about the craziest notion—"

Closing the distance between them with one long stride, he laid a finger gently against her lips.

"Miss Laura Beth Pate, will you please have supper with me this evening?"

"Supper?" and the word came on a soft murmur even as she pretended to miss the romantic implications. "I suppose we've both got to eat." Something in his eyes bypassed all her defenses, and Laura Beth dropped the act rather suddenly. "I love you, too, Bradley. But, the thing is, saying it out loud scares me plumb to death."

"Some things never change," he observed, clasping her hand with a gentle smile. "As your stress level climbs, that East Texas drawl gets slower and slower."

"I suppose," she admitted on a sigh. "If my words start to slide out like butter off hot cornbread, I'm either nearing the danger zone or in a state of complete and total relaxation."

"Wouldn't have you thinking I took anything for granted, Laura Beth, but I made a reservation at the old Brenner's Steakhouse. We're due over there in about an hour if... Will you go back with me and kind of relive our first sure-enough date?"

"I'll go," she decided and rose on tiptoe to kiss his cheek.

Laura Beth hurried off to change, leaving Bradley thunderstruck by the tenderness of her sudden gesture. All but floating from the room, she plucked a package of Kimmy's gum off the coffee table. An anxious feeling in the pit of her stomach contrasted with undeniable pangs of hunger, but the sweet taste and frantic chewing motion somehow eased both. She selected a dark blue dress with touches of lace detailing, long enough for this semiformal outing but not some floor-length ballgown that might hamper her gait. Finally, she swept her hair into a simple yet elegant updo and discarded the gum before rejoining Bradley.

He stood near the center of her living room, turned out sharply in pressed slacks with a sport coat and tie.

"How in the world, Laura Beth?" he asked, and the admiration in his soft, awestruck mummer came through loud and clear. "How can you possibly be even more beautiful today than the first time I laid eyes on you?"

Chapter Seventeen

~December 1943~

With Bud Evans serving in the U.S. Army Medical Corps and Floyd Webber island hopping in the Pacific, Alma and Nadine awaited each new radio bulletin with a kind of unspoken dread. Big Jim listened right along with them, smoking countless cigarettes and occasionally consulting a map of Europe as he recalled his own military service. Jimbo met his educational obligations, however reluctantly, and built up a cow herd while doing the work of a grown man on the farm.

Missy, like her son, seemed more or less untouched by the outside world. She prayed for American servicemen, sympathizing with her girls in their anxiety, but never lost sight of the seasonal patterns that anchored life in Red Bog. The days grew shorter as Christmas approached. Alma and Nadine often took turns with the milking, but Jimbo fed the mules, Missy's driving horse, and his own cowpony each morning before catching the bus at daybreak. Though he still missed riding Sassy back and forth, more than a year had passed since he left the rural eight-grade school at Red Bog for an unfamiliar high school in town.

"How 'bout running a stalk cutter for me tomorrow?" Missy asked one Friday evening as her son climbed the back porch steps in the fading light of dusk. "There's another rain coming on, and we ought to cut those cotton stalks so we can turn them under and start breakin' land soon as it's dry enough."

"Whatever you think best, Missy. But I had it in mind to go catch that brindle cow and big heifer calf I bought off Isom Wallace last week."

"I can ride a stalk cutter until you get back, son, if you'll hitch the team and heft me up to the seat."

"Uh huh…" Gertie Washington's loaded observation drifted from the kitchen and out through the screen door. "Mister Big Jim's apt to wear you both out for pullin' any such stunt. Got no business a-tall bouncin' over them old cotton rows behind a team of half-broke mules and without so much as a back on that seat."

"Some mighty big ears 'round here," Missy commented with a tolerant smile that only Jimbo could see. "Come to think of it, though, she's on the right track. Go ahead and move 'em cattle in the morning. Your daddy can start in cuttin' stalks."

"Better have the boss man stash a few Chesterfields somewhere around that radio," he observed mischievously. "Else, Nadine's in for an unpleasant morning, and she's apt to wear out a hole in your floor pacin' back and forth."

"*Aunt* Nadine," she corrected from force of habit before her gentle laughter escaped, "and I'm not supposed to know about her smoking. Besides, you're in no position to come tellin' tales on somebody else."

"Maybe not," he answered with a broad grin, "but at least I'm sharp enough to figure out that nobody on this place ever fools you for long."

Such honesty won him a loving, if somewhat exasperated, smile.

"I can't say I like it, for Nadine or for you either. The doctor stays after Big Jim to cut down, anyhow. Claims the cigarettes are makin' him short winded, but I expect there's worse habits you could pick up in this life. Just gather your stock in the morning and get on back as quick as you can."

"Daddy ain't likely to take much scolding from young Dr. Brown. Anyhow, me and the dogs oughta could drive that pair home in an hour or so, but if I have to rope and drag 'em out to the road one at a time, it may take a little longer.”

“Sure wish I was goin’ with you. I don’t mind this chair so very much, Jimbo. Been a fact of life for a long time. I can recall your daddy teasing me about how I never walked much in the first place. But wartime help is awful scarce, and not being able to lend a hand around here is enough to drive me crazy.”

“Aw, Missy… Somebody’s got to run things. I hear tell you helped gather plenty of cattle before…”

Her pretty face lit with enthusiasm and the intervening years fell away, taking with them any thought of physical limitations.

“Son, I can still feel the wind in my hair! We didn’t have to ride quite as hard after Hoyt got that first set of yella dogs, but there’s a reason I was his favorite cousin. He liked the free help.”

“Free, and better than any he could hire,” Jimbo tossed back. “Hoyt says you made some rides that flat turned his stomach to watch, and made ’em sidesaddle to boot. I’ve always wondered what happened, Missy. Did Laddie or some other horse come down on top of you?”

The question nearly stole Missy’s breath, but she played it off with only a momentary hesitation.

“Not my big red Laddie… That long, tall bundle of horsehide and heart never laid a foot wrong in his life. I declare, Jimbo, you’ve turned back the clock for me. Now, let me enjoy it for a spell. Besides… My limitations, such as they are, ain’t nothing for you to fret over.”

“Alright, Missy. Whatever you say. I just wondered is all. With school out next week, maybe you won’t feel so shorthanded around here. Got plenty of stove wood and kindling on hand for tomorrow?”

A few days later, young Dr. Brown, now in his middle forties, stopped by on one of his semi-regular but unscheduled visits.

"I declare, lady," he observed with a hint of bemusement, "you're a wonder. According to everything I've learned, in medical school and since then, you ought to show complications from living these fifteen years as an invalid. Lung trouble or back trouble or at least swollen ankles, but here you sit… Hardheaded, beautiful, and apparently untouched by such mundane ailments."

"Just because I can't get up and down on my own, Vincent, doesn't mean I sit around like a knot on a log."

"No, I reckon you don't… The more I see of life, Missy, the less I seem to understand. Little Betsy Wallace had twin girls before daylight this morning with never a minute's trouble."

"What a blessing! I figured 'twas an early morning call brought you out this-a-way. No wonder Isom needed to sell a cow or two."

Struck once again by the relentless positivity of her outlook, he met the radiant smile with a rather somber expression.

"The night your Jimbo was born still haunts me, and I can't explain what went wrong any more today than I could back then."

"The good Lord's got His reasons, and I'm prouder of that boy than just about anything else in my life. Why, I'd do it all over again and never even bat an eye. Made a fresh batch of syrup cookies this morning, if you're interested. We cooked off so much ribbon cane this past fall until last year's leavings are just in the way. Besides, I like to keep a little something sweet on hand with Christmas right around the corner."

"Just a few more days now," he answered with a genuine smile. "Them twins like to have made Betsy and Isom a sure-enough bundle of Christmas joy. Say, Missy… With sugar rationed on account of the war, my wife and plenty of other folks up town might like to have your recipe for those syrup cookies."

"No recipe to speak of, but I guess I might come close if I sat and thought about it."

"Syrup making and ribbon cane seem so commonplace to an East Texas country doctor that I looked right over it until you mentioned the cookies. Dad used to bring part of his pay home in those gallon cans. Altogether different from the maple syrup Mother bought, time to time, but he liked it."

"If you don't cook those cane squeezings down just right, you can end up with something that tastes like the mule stepped in it while he was turning the mill, but good syrup's hard to beat. I'll write down the cookie recipe as nearly as I can, and you tell 'em they can get all the syrup they want at Papa's store."

"That's the Kimbel head for business alright," he observed lightheartedly. "Perhaps the old gentleman's indestructible constitution is helping you fight off all the maladies you're supposed to have at this point. Crawford Kimbel looked like the prosperous middle-aged owner of a country store in my earliest memories, and that's pretty much what he looks like today."

"Prosperous might be stretching the point, but well-kept is a fairly apt description. Now, wheel me on into the kitchen. You'll find some fresh milk cooling in the icebox and cookies under a cloth on the sideboard."

He maneuvered the old-fashioned chair with ease, and before leaving her little office, Missy picked up a pen and piece of stationery. Moments later, she bit her lower lip in thought while working over the recipe card at one corner of her kitchen table.

"I guess you know about the cooperative they've started with one of those REA grants," Vincent Brown observed conversationally as he placed the pitcher of milk on its cooling tray, once again, beneath a suspended block of ice. "Electric lines are bound to reach Red Bog before too long."

"Yeah-boy," Big Jim drawled from the doorway, "and maybe one of these days we'll get us a halfway decent doctor."

"Now, Jim," the doctor replied without so much as turning his head. "Like I've said before, you can't blame me any more than I blame myself."

"Dog take it, Vincent, I know that. Still… Old habits are hard to break. Besides, I done it mainly to see the flash of temper in Missy's eyes. It ain't in her nature to scold me right out in the open, but she sets a high standard when it comes to company manners."

For the first time in years, the three of them chuckled together. Missy's came out with a gentle kind of warmth while the men's laughter sounded somewhat dry and brittle. Big Jim shook a cigarette from his pack and lit up, the action slow and deliberate, but Dr. Brown chose not to comment on it directly.

"I expect Missy sets a pretty high standard in general. My congratulations on livin' up to it."

"Well, she can be mighty forgiving, too. You ought to know that your own self. Go ahead and eat them cookies," he added with a flash of genuine humor, "but there ain't no need to camp here 'til dinnertime."

"Anybody that can't make a meal on homemade cookies and fresh milk ain't never run from one sickbed to the next without stopping to eat."

Missy shook her head in mild amazement as these longtime antagonists laughed again, the sound loosening up some as they gradually accepted the notion of shared amusement. Darkhaired and pretty, twenty-four-year-old Alma Pate Evans walked in on this little scene with a brown paper parcel under one arm and immediately froze in her tracks. After exchanging a meaningful look with Missy, she swept her lively glance over the room.

"Well, looks like old home week. Hope I'm not interrupting, Missy, but I picked up that vanilla extract and the other things you wanted so Snap can make his Christmas goodies."

"You're not disturbing us, child. Dr. Brown just dropped by to check up on my health. Way it looks, I'll live 'til I die." Then, shifting her attention briefly to the menfolk, "Gert can't hardly stand for Snap and Virgie to take over this kitchen once a year. They're apt to use up my ration of sugar along with Papa's and their own, too. Snap Havard may farm for a living, but it wouldn't be Christmas if he didn't get to ply his chosen trade just a little. I think half the enjoyment comes from puttin' Gert's nose out of joint. If he'd just let her help some, and maybe leave Virgie at home… But that's the way with little brothers, I reckon."

"Good hands are gettin' scarce," Big Jim added. "Snap ain't no Tobe Washington, but if a little storebought sweetenin' keeps the man happy, I say it's money well spent. Besides, we get a pretty good taste of his finished product right along with everybody else on the place."

"Old Gert," the doctor said on a heavy sigh. "She was in the room that night along with one scared little girl a-looking on from the doorway. I saw you before anybody else did, Alma. But I was too busy and, truth be told, too frazzled to do much about it. Gert's a midwife, you know, and her mother likewise, but she felt as helpless that night as I did."

"Well," Alma ventured, somewhat uncertain of this long-avoided topic, "I can't say the fright did me any permanent harm. When Missy raised her head off the pillow and started tellin' us what all to do, my world shifted back into place."

"At one point there," the doctor recalled, "I started to send for Dad, but Gert stopped me with some gentle advice. 'Old Doc couldn't do no more than what you're doing, even if he got here this very minute. Holler for help midway through, and it's apt to send Mister Big Jim into apoplexy. Our Missy is as strong as they come, but this kind of thing rests in Jesus' hands alone.'"

Jim dropped into a kitchen chair across from the doctor and ground his cigarette forcefully into the nearest ashtray.

"I set a lot of store by old Dr. Brown, and he told me himself that he couldn't have done anything different. I finally owned up to him, Vincent, that I put more of the blame on my own shoulders than on you. But I had to live with myself, see, so I'd let off a little steam once in a while by pawin' and snortin' at you."

"I'll swan," Missy drawled in a light but definite tone. "You two sure know how to damp down a fine morning. I'll not have any more talk of blame. Listening to all that, a body'd never know I came out of it with a fine, healthy son. Jimbo's brought us more joy than I could ever say. Why, he's out yonder right now breakin' land. With the war and all going on, I'd have to take the battery out of that radio and hide it to make this old place run without him."

The corners of Jim's eyes crinkled with a loving smile. Such veiled criticism seemed almost endearing, just so long as it came from his Missy.

"I know where our boy's at," he retorted mildly, pausing to light another cigarette. "Been runnin' the stalk cutter right ahead of him."

"Does Jimbo ever ask about what happened?" Dr. Brown inquired. "This is Red Bog, after all, where most everbody's business is common knowledge. If y'all haven't told him by now…"

"He asked about it just the other night," Missy admitted, "but I've always let him think there was some kind of mishap with a horse. Plenty of tales circulate as to my wild riding, and his mind just naturally went that-a-way. As a matter of fact, I'm not even sure what Nadine knows about all of that."

"I finally told her what happened," Alma admitted quietly, "and then warned her it might just break your heart if she ever said anything to Jimbo. Thought about tellin' her I'd beat her half to death, but the other was more effective and more believable, too, coming from me."

"Yes," Missy answered with a reluctant smile. "Nadine would've taken the prospect of a sisterly thrashing as more challenge than threat."

Despite her unique status in the combined roles of sister-in-law, eldest daughter, and close confidant, Alma tread lightly when giving unsought advice. She left her parcel on the sideboard and crossed the room to kneel down beside the wheelchair. Gazing up into a familiar pair of hazel green eyes, she laced her own fingers into a strong but delicate hand.

"You really ought to tell him, Missy, especially if he's asking questions. Jimbo's old enough, now, to understand the plain truth. Get it out in the open, and there won't be any deep, dark secret."

"You're right, child, and I know it. Still, I couldn't stand for him to up and take the fault on himself."

"That might be the first natural reaction," Alma answered quietly, her thumb stroking the back of Missy's hand, "but it won't last long.

We raised Jimbo right, and he's got too much sense to hang onto that kind of a fool notion."

"Jimbo's levelheaded and strong, but I'll not saddle him with—"

"Look at it this way, Missy. Do you consider yourself a burden on this family, or do you feel loved and needed and sometimes smile a little, wondering how we'd ever get along without you?"

"I see your point," she murmured, the little smile slipping into place. "That notion of being a burden crept in right at first, but y'all never gave me time to dwell on it."

~November 2007~

Bradley opened the passenger door for Laura Beth, watched her settle into place, and then stepped around to get behind the wheel.

"Thanks again for the use of your car," he said, backing out of the driveway. "I've got Aunt Alma's Buick all gassed up for your return trip in the morning."

"*Aunt* Alma?" Laura Beth inquired, comfortable enough to tease him just a little.

"Well, she's Kimmy's great-great whatever, and she did let me drive her car."

"A kind lady for sure," she conceded, thankful for the uncomplicated small talk.

"That Buick's not too trendy, but the big old thing rides good and drives good. I don't imagine you'll have any trouble with it."

Walking into the restaurant, Laura Beth felt strangely at home on his arm. An anxious prickle in the back of her mind warned against such unguarded contentment. She wanted to relax and enjoy the moment, but what if she grew accustomed to this feeling of rightness only to lose it, lose Bradley, all over again? Tenderness and admiration showed plainly in his unfaltering gaze, but this was not her awestruck beau or her fun-loving spouse. He looked like the same Bradley. His strong arm settled quite naturally at her waist. Even his scent seemed achingly familiar, but this man was her ex-husband, a comparative stranger who had been largely absent from her life over the last decade.

The unmistakable aroma of beef, perfectly cooked and seasoned, filled the stately old building. Even so, Laura Beth temporarily forgot hunger as she measured the huge risk of lowering her guard against the familiar heartache of playing it safe. Suddenly, Jimbo Pate's voice replaced the anxious chatter in her head. Laura Beth smiled slightly to herself as she recalled an oft-repeated phrase. "Ain't but one way to find out, doodlebug." She hadn't met anyone special (or really even tried) since the divorce, and yet here she sat on an honest-to-goodness date, once again, with the love of her life.

"So," and her voice shook ever so slightly even as she fought to steady it, "tell me a little about yourself."

"Laura Beth?" Momentary concern flickered in his eyes before a smile chased it away. "Oh, I get it. Like speed dating or something."

"Yeah, that was my attempt at a little joke. Only… I really do want to know. What's it like traveling the world as a successful photojournalist?"

"I've left a good chunk of the world untraveled. Photographed a couple of African safaris and one mounted fox hunt in the UK, but those were my only overseas trips. The American landscape is so rich in scenic vistas and wildlife that I've stayed busy on this side of the pond."

"I'd like to hear more, Bradley. I wouldn't trade the blessings of motherhood or even the emotional roller coaster of starting my own business for anything, but the day-to-day routine since we parted ways makes for pretty dull conversation. Stress, anxiety, success, rinse, and repeat."

"Sounds awful… You always seemed so confident and self-possessed. I never thought of you as a worrier."

"The girl you knew wasn't anxious, not really. What did I know, back then, about worry?"

"I should have been there, Laura Beth, to break up that pattern or at least go through it with you. Hard for me to understand such a burden. I've known moments of danger, plenty of them, but things generally happened so fast that I didn't have time to worry. My only lasting concern has been for you and Kimmy. Missed y'all something awful, but I knew Pop would never stand by and watch you struggle. Even when I tried to worry, it was difficult to imagine any problem my Laura Beth couldn't handle."

"Your confidence is flattering but more than a little infuriating, too, when I remember endless nights and a chronic lack of sleep. Still, there's no way you could've known. The more worry crept in, the harder I tried to come across as self-assured, capable, and ladylike."

The softspoken waiter placed a bread basket in the middle of the table before taking their orders and then returned briefly to top off Laura Beth's glass of Dr Pepper. Catching her glance toward the basket with its warm rolls and creamy butter, Bradley extended his hand across the table.

"I know you'd like a blessing before the meal, Laura Beth, but I'd better not pray out loud this evening. You can do it, or we'll just bow our heads and offer a silent thanks. Don't look so shocked," he continued, greeting the sudden concern in her eyes with a warm smile. "I'm still on speaking terms with the Lord above, but if I say what's really on my heart tonight, you'd probably try to answer my prayer instead of letting Him do it."

"Aww," she drawled, touched not only by the sweet sentiment but also by his forethought in avoiding undue pressure on her. "I suppose most every girl wants to be the answer to some gentleman's prayer, but when you come right up to it, the task is rather daunting."

"Downright impossible," he quipped. "Then again, I've seen you do the impossible a time or two."

She grasped his hand with a fleeting smile and bowed her head to pray.

"Dear Heavenly Father, thank You for Bradley and for the precious gift of our daughter. I ask that You'd bless this time we're spending together. Grant us the wisdom, moving forward, not to hurt one another or especially Kimmy with unrealistic expectations. At the same time, Lord, I ask that You'd help me not to be paralyzed with fear and call it caution. Bless our meal and those who work to prepare it. In Jesus' name…"

"Amen," Bradley echoed, not the least bit surprised by this open and seemingly effortless expression of her faith.

Laura Beth buttered her roll in one fluid and graceful motion.

"These are good," she noted, "but when it comes to bread, hardly anything measures up to Aunt Alma's homemade biscuits. Naturally, though, I'm starving."

Grabbing a roll for himself, Bradley laughed with her. Light conversation helped to ease his own well-concealed case of nerves. When the courteous and efficient waitstaff departed after serving their meal, he tried to focus on his own delicious steak. No one, especially a fastidious lady already a bit self-conscious about her appetite, wanted to be watched while eating, but Laura Beth's beauty drew his gaze like a magnet.

"You've changed, darling," he finally ventured. "The full effect took a while to register on me, but I can see it now."

"Getting older is pretty much inevitable," she quipped. "Still, you needn't remind me."

"Calendar years have nothing to do with it," he said, brushing aside her mild protest, "nothing negative anyway. Meant what I said earlier, about you being more beautiful than ever, but I never quite put my finger on the difference. That daily grind, the repetitive cycle you described… Instead of dimming your glow, it just enhanced all of your fine qualities. You're like some kind of precious metal, Laura Beth, refined by fire."

"Mercy sakes," she all but whispered, actual heat rising in her cheeks. "What am I supposed to say to that?"

"Nothing much," he assured her. "I just stated a simple fact. Like, maybe, 'The night air's a little cool this evening, Laura Beth,' or 'This is a good place to eat a steak.' You need only smile, nod, or murmur that soft little noise of agreement from the back of your throat and then move along."

"Ah," she deadpanned, "the globetrotting photographer prefers his women with a generous dose of ego. I suppose any jetsetter worth her salt would accept such a breathtaking compliment as offhandedly as some sparkling bauble."

"One woman, Laura Beth, and I'd *prefer* that she know her own worth or at least come close."

"All this time, I thought… You mean there's never been anyone else?"

Ice cubes rattled as he finished his water in a single gulp, and Laura Beth suddenly longed to crawl under the table. The question, having tumbled out in a rush of vulnerability that derailed her practiced banter, lay between them like some kind of unexploded bomb.

"Believe me, darling, I know exactly how you feel. Not a proud moment, but I went so far as to ask Kimmy if you'd been seeing anyone special."

"If you know how I'm feeling," she interrupted, voice strained with a kind of frustration that felt much safer than the raw heartbreak lingering just below the surface. "Then, don't drag this out any longer."

"The words that old Baptist preacher in Red Bog spoke over us sounded a lot more final to me than what we heard from a Harris County judge. Besides, the women among those so-called jetsetters shared a peculiar flaw; not a one of them was my Laura Beth."

"Oh, Bradley," and then a slow, mischievous smile displaced the look of absolute relief as she slid her plate gingerly toward the center of the table. "You keep tying my stomach in knots that-a-way, and I won't feel the slightest need to count calories."

"I never meant to ruin your appetite," he apologized, "but you can always take some steak back to the house. Let's sit and talk for a minute and then look at the dessert menu."

"At this point in life, my appetite needs very little encouragement." She breathed the words out on a sigh but finally offered a tentative smile. "Even so, I'm not particularly anxious to end our time together."

They sat in comfortable silence for a minute or two until Bradley's lively blue eyes telegraphed sudden amusement.

"If today's media and entertainment is any indication, the two of us must be an odd pair. It looks as though we've had more trouble mastering divorce than we ever did adjusting to married life. The last woman who even caught my eye was a fair-haired English girl. She was an honorary whipper-in to one of those prestigious old hunts before the ban.

"I caught some snippets of news coverage on the fox hunting ban, but you're talking over my head just a little. What in the cat hair is a whipper-in?"

"We'd probably describe her as an out rider," he answered with a chuckle. "She and others rode hard to help the huntsman manage his pack. From a distance, on horseback and chasing those hounds over uncertain ground, she made me think of you. Then, too, laughter gave her eyes something close to the same sparkle. I about broke my neck keeping up, but she provided some great action shots for the article. That afternoon, evening, and on into the night, we got pretty well acquainted."

"Wait, Bradley— I can't stand any of the details."

"Don't get ahead of me," he advised reassuringly. "Everything came to a screeching halt, at least on my end. The woman had a husband and two kids. We'd been divorced for more than a decade, Laura Beth, but I was more married than she was!"

Color rose in Laura Beth's cheeks, but she finally showed her amusement with a brief smile that disappeared before it could spill over into a giggle.

"Pretty?"

"Quite British in carriage and appearance," he recalled after a moment's thought. "Still, she favored you too much to be anything less than a beauty."

"Was she slender, the trim and athletic type?"

"Well, yes. I guess you'd have to say… She might have been in her mid-twenties at the time and fairly close to a certain image of you in my mind's eye. Where's this going, anyway, Laura Beth?"

"Doesn't it bother you that I've changed, Bradley? You needn't tell me again about *refinement by fire*. We've been over that. I'm talking about the extra weight and, well, aging. Kimmy's starting to look more like me than I do."

"My preferences seem to have changed right along with you. A real surprise, even to me, because your beauty stood out from the very beginning. It may sound like empty flattery, Laura Beth, but you really do get prettier with each passing day."

It took several moments for his words to soak in, and then a playful little smile danced around the corners of her mouth.

"Convenient to know," she teased. "Especially now, right before dessert." Then, her tone turned thoughtful. "Your little English beauty… There's not much to be said for her morals, but I sure can't fault her taste in men."

Chapter Eighteen

~December 1943~

Though swept yards had once been commonplace, the Pate house looked a bit drab from the outside due to a wintertime absence of flowers. Young Jimbo raked a booted toe over the bare ground before finally addressing his mother.

"Fact is, Missy, I don't feel much like celebratin' after what you told me just now. With Aunt Alma married and Nadine right on her heels and me nearly grown, there's no call to go out and cut a cedar, except maybe to get it off the fence line."

"Son…" A slight tremor in this customary form of address drew his gaze unwillingly back to her face. "I never lied to you, none of us did. We just kept back this little piece of truth until you'd grown up enough to handle it."

Highly uncomfortable topic notwithstanding, the words pulled him step by step back up on the porch to kneel alongside her.

"Yes, ma'am," he managed, squeezing Missy's hand in a reluctant but nonetheless heartfelt gesture of understanding. "Who all knows?"

"Most everybody of a certain age. This is Red Bog, for goodness sakes. Those tales about my reckless abandon on horseback are fairly accurate. Grown folks understood how anxious I was to keep things quiet, so they played up that particular local legend. Younger people, from Alma's age right on down, figured I took a bad tumble one day and never got up again."

"I guess a mother's love makes plenty of allowances, but how did Daddy, Alma, and Nadine ever keep from blaming me? Their lives changed overnight, right along with yours."

"You won our hearts from the very first day. Besides… I wasted no tears lookin' back and never gave them any time for such foolishness, either. You've added so much to our lives, Jimbo. Imagine if I'd actually been crippled by one of the wild chances I took. I'd be stuck in this chair thinking how I should've left one certain bunch-quitting cow to her own devices, or maybe let Hoyt stop her with a rifle. Watching you grow into a fine young man, though, there's not a single regret."

"Well'm, I'm tickled to hear you don't have no regrets up to this point. But it kinda puts the pressure on me goin' forward, don't it?"

Missy's smile lit his world like an early taste of summer sunshine, nonetheless radiant for the tears gathering in her eyes.

"You'll always be my boy, mine and your daddy's. But I'd a lot rather you please the good Lord than to try and live up to some silly, overblown notion of Missy and Big Jim Pate. Now, touch up the cuttin' edge on your axe and then go catch us a pair of mules."

"I'll do it, Missy," he agreed with a smiling shake of his head, "but I still say we don't need no tree in the house this year."

"Your Uncle Cleve has always been a favorite with Big Jim," she declared on a tolerant sigh.

"Much as anybody, I reckon. Only, he's a-runnin' way behind you in that department. What about Uncle Cleve, anyhow?"

"He wrote us a week or so ago about jobs for Big Jim and the girls. Defense work, alongside him and a few Red Bog neighbors, in the shipyard down yonder at Orange. The girls seem inclined to go, and I won't hear of them making the trip alone. Your daddy knows pretty well that me and you can run this place. I'd say Cleve's letter is pullin' at him a right smart."

"So," the boy muttered in a far-off tone, processing yet another piece of new and startling information. "This could be our last little bit of family time on the homeplace for a good while. Let's go pick us out a Christmas tree."

With the tree selected, placed, and decorated, days passed in a blur of seasonal joy. Alma and Nadine looked forward to a new chapter in their lives and told anyone who would listen that working to support the war effort just had to be better than the dreadful monotony of waiting for news. Even so, with the reality of separation looming, both girls hovered close around Jimbo and Missy.

Big Jim participated in the festivities, always ready with a grin or a whooping burst of laughter. In moments of silence, though, he brooded over three immovable facts. His deep sense of family duty stood like a wall against any notion of sending the girls a-way down to the coast alone, even with Cleve waiting for them at the other end. More troubling yet, his beloved wife would never turn her back on Red Bog or leave the homeplace unattended. And finally, while a good snort of whiskey might dull the keen edge of grief at leaving Missy behind, one drink would lead to several more, rendering him useless for days at a time.

Very nearly asleep on Christmas Eve, Missy felt her husband's encircling arms nestle her a bit tighter against him. The soft rumble of his familiar low tones, murmured directly into her ear, generated a pleasant rush of warmth. The words, however, caught her completely off guard.

"Reckon you could turn up a few new twenties in that old safe, Missy?"

The question, decidedly unromantic in itself, also seemed to cast doubt on her efficiency in managing their day-to-day finances.

Missy answered in a calm and reassuring tone, but hurt feelings quivered just beneath the surface.

"Why, Jim, I'd never let y'all leave home without some traveling money."

"Reckon not," he snorted and then redoubled her confusion by trailing kisses gently down her neck. "But I'm talkin' about new bills… Money that'll snap when a fella pulls it out of his overall bib. I figured we might as well give the hands somethin' extra for Christmas."

"We always do, but twenty dollars apiece?"

Slight misgivings fought against obvious delight in Missy's tone. She valued each family on the homeplace and wanted the best for them, but years of economic depression, uncertain weather, and low cotton prices had taught her to err on the side of caution.

"Just the Havard boys and Gert," he ventured, reluctantly shifting his attention from the heady satisfaction of her nearness back to the topic at hand. "Each household, so to speak. Most all of 'em are too old or too broke or some such thing to pick up and go to these defense jobs, but they've been with us a long time. Cleve thinks I can draw a dollar an hour pretty easy down yonder. The girls can keep what they earn. I'll send you enough money to make another crop, enough and then some."

"A whole dollar an hour? We've never hired much wage labor, but not so very long ago, a dollar a day was the going rate for general farm work."

"Times change, or so they tell me."

Big Jim punctuated his remark with a tender nuzzling of her neck, but Missy wasn't quite finished with their discussion. Though her bright smile went unseen in the darkness, such instant joy suggested the promise of some personal gift rather than a bit of Christmas bounty to share with others.

"Thank you, Jim. That money will make a real difference for them." She spoke these words on a sigh of pure delight and then allowed her mind to wander briefly toward the years ahead. "Some of the youngsters have done gone, and others are bound to follow, because there's nothin' to hold them here. Still, if we can take care of the old folks, they're apt to see you and me through the end of our farming. Jimbo won't need near as much help to run cattle."

"His cow chasin' bent come right down the Kimbel line through you. I say this old East Texas red land won't never see the end of cotton. Not unless it's farmed plumb out, and that ain't likely with readymade fertilizer on the market."

"You could be right, my love," she purred languidly and snuggled a little deeper into the familiar comfort of his embrace. "Anyhow, ain't likely we'll be around to fret over it."

"You've had more than your share of worry, Missy girl, but I'll tote the load from here on out. For however many years the good Lord sees fit to give me…"

The next morning, Alma received two new dresses. One handmade, with Missy's love poured into every little detail, and another from Papa Kimbel's store. Nadine got her own dress from Missy and, wonder of wonders, storebought slacks with a blouse to match. Despite their ages and Alma's status as a young wife, the girls oohed and aahed over the contents of their Christmas stockings as well. The relative success of last year's crop allowed Missy to give her Jim a new pocket watch along with the usual carton of cigarettes from Papa Kimbel.

"Daybreak, high noon, and sundown just won't cut it anymore, not with time sellin' for a dollar an hour down yonder."

Smiling broadly at Missy's unquenchable spirit, Big Jim produced a set of tiny brass bells for her driving harness. All the boss lady truly wanted was to keep her little family happy and healthy, but Alma presented a meticulously embroidered shawl. Nadine offered a box of chocolate-covered cherries, and Jimbo gave her a sack of crème drops. Missy expressed genuine gratitude but laughed in loving amusement because the dynamic duo each chose their own favorite candy as her gift.

Jimbo's stocking contained an assortment of small, edible goodies, but Nadine envied his bullwhip. The braided eight-foot lash with its perfectly balanced wooden handle replaced the one he'd worn out honing his skill.

With morning chores and a wonderful family breakfast behind them, he and Nadine drifted out into the front yard for a whip cracking contest. When Big Jim descended the front steps for a closer view of their doings, Nadine sidled up to him for a Christmas hug. When she plucked the cigarette from between his lips, Jim shot a warning glance toward the porch. Sure enough, Missy and Alma sat there visiting in plain sight.

"It's alright," she told him with a wink and flounced back toward Jimbo before purposefully calling for their attention. "Hey, y'all watch this little trick."

Sympathetic, for a change, Jimbo allowed her another puff or two before swinging the whip in its sudden cracking arc. Most of Nadine's cigarette promptly disappeared, cut neatly from between her lips.

"Both of 'em crazy as all get out," Alma huffed under her breath, but Missy smiled brightly at the display of nerve and precision.

"Wanna try your hand, Missy?" Nadine called lightheartedly.

"On the cigarette end?"

"No, ma'am, with the whip. I'll stand for you."

"Lordy, no! I'd never get the right angle from this chair. Likely cut you to the bone, and my heart couldn't stand it. I've still got nerve enough to hold a steady target, but if I hit one of you children…"

The hands came by to exchange Christmas greetings, Gert first and then all four of her brothers in a group. With everybody assembled, Big Jim peeled off five crisp twenty-dollar bills. The Havard brothers whooped and hollered, cutting up with the boss man, but each one quieted long enough to step away from the bunch and wish their Missy a Merry Christmas. When they drifted back to individual family gatherings and other pursuits, Gert lingered behind.

"I heard old Mr. Kimbel say somethin' about you and Miss Alma and Miss Nadine going off. You done been to war one time, Mister Jim, and them girls got no business—"

"Don't fret, Gert. We're just goin' down south to work in the shipyards. It'll help the war effort and make us a little money."

"You're apt to need some money," she ventured, patting her apron pocket with a brief smile, "if you keep givin' it away. But what's gonna happen 'round here in the meantime. There's stock to feed and a crop to put in and them confounded brothers of mine to look after."

"Nothin' to it… Missy and Jimbo will take care of the homeplace, but you've got to take care of them. She's my dearest treasure, Gert, and that boy is the light of our lives."

"Yessir, I know all that."

"Listen, Gert. You're gettin' older, and I know it 'cause I am, too. Don't you take too much on yourself and break down. Where'd Missy be then? If you get to needin' some help, holler at Virgie or one of my married sisters."

"Beg pardon, Mister Jim… But Virgie Havard and your two oldest sisters is 'bout the bossiest three women in the county. Me and Missy do just fine without no extra instructions. Have for years, and I expect we'll go right on that-a-way."

"String 'em along if you have to, Gert," he advised with a grin. "String 'em along, and put up with a helping hand if it's needed. Bear in mind, though, you don't take orders from nobody but our Missy."

As Big Jim strode away, seventy-year-old Gertie Washington squared her shoulders for the task ahead. A faint smile crossed her face as she recalled the kindhearted young lady who had ridden so boldly into their lives a little over twenty years earlier. Chair or no chair, Missy would run the operation with that same courage and grace. Meanwhile, somebody had to look after the boss lady. With Tobe gone, their children grown, and very little desire for a whole day off, Gert headed for the kitchen to doublecheck the preparations for Christmas dinner.

"Reckon I ought to put out some salt," Jimbo finally admitted, draping the whip loosely over one shoulder as he grinned at Nadine. "You comin' along?"

"Don't aim to bounce all over that wagon if I can help it, but I'll saddle a horse and drift through the pastures with you."

"I thought so," the boy shot back with a wink.

He might allow Aunt Alma a tearful hug before they left, but things were different with Nadine. Neither one of them needed to speak of their deep bond or of the uncertain future. They simply hitched a team, saddled a colt, swiped a pack of cigarettes, and headed to check cows one more time.

Jimbo dispensed salt blocks, each one at just the right distance from water or the pens and sometimes strategically placed to kill a pesky tangle of briar vines. Big Jim waited at the barn for their return. He gave Nadine's braid a playful yank and then stepped over to help Jimbo strip harness from the mules.

"Missy tells me that little cow herd of yours is the right way forward, son, but I just can't see it."

"Aw, Daddy, we've always kept a few cows. I aim to work this old place for a living, just like you've done, but if I can do it with a lariat rope instead of a turning plow, the swap won't hurt my feelings none."

 "Tell you the truth, it's the near future that's weighin' on my mind. You've already taken on a man's part around here, and I've no doubt you're up to the task. But to go off and leave Missy…"

"I'm old enough now to see that you two have something pretty special. She wouldn't hear of sending the girls off alone, and you know it. Taking her along might be an option, but I just can't feature her sittin' in some apartment, starin' at the wall, and waitin' for y'all to get off work. I'm too young to tag after Alma and Nadine and got very little inclination to pick up and leave here, anyhow. So, the way you've got it figured looks like our only real shot."

"Son, I just—"

"If you can stand to leave the homeplace, Missy can stand pining for you a while. Me and Gert won't just see to her and do as we're told, we'll keep her occupied, too, as best we can."

Later, with the family gathered for an extra special noon meal, Big Jim caught Missy's gaze and held it across the table. Their tender look lasted so long that Alma dabbed tears from her own eyes. Even Nadine and Jimbo, not always the most astute in such matters, picked up on it. Finally, Jim bowed his head and began a Christmas blessing. He began with heartfelt thanks for his Savior's birth and progressed naturally to the death, burial, and resurrection. Knowing Daddy as a man of few words, Jimbo figured his brief mention of the food would just about wrap things up, but the elder Pate forged ahead.

"Lord, You've held this family in the hollow of Your hand through so many of life's storms. We ain't never turned tail, but Your grace is the only reason we're still here. Shelter us, now, as we scatter for a while. And draw us back together in Your appointed season. Dear Lord, there's not a thing in this world hid from You, and You know I'm no bigger than the little end of nothin' without Missy. I just ask that You'd help her see it, too. Let her find comfort in that until You bring the rest of us home again."

The prayer ended with a familiar petition in Jesus' name, and Jimbo gulped half a glass of water to clear the unexpected lump from his throat. Missy, at her end of the table, laughed softly to keep from crying.

"Quite a prayer, my love."

"Under normal circumstances, right here with you, I've got more than I could ask for or ever deserve," Jim declared dryly. "So, a short word of thanks is prayer enough. Standin' at the base of a hill and lookin' up on a hard climb, though, a man with any sense will tuck pride in his pocket and holler for help."

~November 2007~

Laura Beth used the drive back to Red Bog as a time of prayer and reflection. Mounting uncertainty in so many facets of life contrasted jarringly with the neat and orderly existence she had cultivated over the years. As the city skyline grew smaller in her rearview mirror, though, a perfectly chilled Dr Pepper, four-part gospel harmony from the tape deck, and a hint of Aunt Alma's perfume lingering in the old Buick eased her nerves more effectively than any doctor's prescription.

"I'm home," she called, maneuvering through the kitchen door that afternoon with suitcase in hand.

The lighthearted declaration rolled off her tongue without a second thought. Once spoken, however, the words rang with an undeniable note of truth.

"This kitchen ain't safe today, Laura Beth," Nadine quipped almost immediately. "We're expectin' Vesper Denton for supper. The man eats like a horse, and Alma encourages it. Don't stop now, or she'll put you to work."

"Oh, I don't mind. Hospitality's a big part of what I do. Stopped in town, Aunt Alma, and topped off your gas tank."

"You didn't have to do that, child," Alma put in, glancing up from her developing cake batter, "but it sure is good to see you. About the biggest help you could give me right now is to take your Aunt Nadine off somewhere and get her out of my hair. Untamed and naturally opposed to any kind of housework, she's also just fussy enough to balk at ridin' the bench seat of a pickup in amongst three tobacco-spitting, dog-swapping men. Caught between a rock and a hard place that-a-way, she'll entertain herself by aggravating me."

"Never knew Granddaddy to chew tobacco."

By the Light of a Memory 298

"No… But George dips 'at snuff, and Vesper's been known to smoke now and again. Sounded good when I said it, anyhow. Will you babysit Nadine, or not?"

"Yes, ma'am. I'm up to it if she is, just let me change clothes."

"Thank you, Laura Beth," the sisters said almost in unison.

"Slip into a pair of jeans and grab Jimbo's old brush jacket," Nadine continued. "Vesper's a good twenty years behind me and can't raise his foot high enough to stick it in a stirrup. Much less swing a leg over the saddle, but I'll bet the other two are fit to be tied when they realize we got to hear them Beagles run from horseback while they bumped along in the truck."

"Vesper may be full of hot air and a little taken with the pleasures of the table," Alma noted sagely, "but he'll always find the time to drop by and visit. Been a good business partner to your Uncle James Allen, too, Laura Beth. No doubt as to who does most of the work, but Vesper bankrolled the boy years ago when he decided to quit cowboyin' and strike out in a different direction."

Laura Beth laughed softly to herself as she changed clothes. A girl couldn't transition from a fancy dinner date one evening to a mid-afternoon horseback jaunt alongside her eighty-six-year-old aunt the next day without feeling especially blessed. Life might be a tangle of loose ends at the moment, but she felt a surge of gratitude amid the chaos. For the first time in a long while, she didn't examine the fit of her jeans with a critical eye or worry about some number on the tag. They were just work clothes, offering comfort, maneuverability, and some degree of protection. This might not be an English foxhunt, but the hounds were running, and Nadine was chomping at the bit.

"Man who owns the buckskin geldings picked them up right after you and Kimmy left," Nadine observed as she strolled into the barn lot with Laura Beth on her heels. "Take that little baldfaced sorrel, or I'll ride him if you'd rather have old Gopher."

"No, ma'am… Kind of you to let Kimmy borrow your horse so she'll have something steady, but I'll not take him for my own use. Anything I should know about the sorrel?"

"Kid's pony, Jimbo says, and kind of barn sour. Don't seem to be any real meanness in him, though."

Sure enough, the little horse accepted Laura Beth's firm but gentle riding style with a philosophical sigh. She rode in silence for a while, getting the feel of this new mount, but eventually struck up a conversation.

"I'm thinking of selling my business, Aunt Nadine. Had a kind of tentative offer while I was down there."

"Well, now," the old lady drawled, "I thought you liked your work."

"Can't like it too much," Laura Beth answered with a chuckle. "I've been up here for most of a month. Oh, I enjoy using my organizational skills and creative touch to make people happy, but the deadlines and constant pressure… Besides, I'm tired of living so far from home."

Nadine let the statement hang in the air for a minute and seemed to study her niece as they rode along. Finally, she reined to a stop.

"We never talked much about stress when I was growin' up, Laura Beth. Didn't know what it was, I reckon. But hard times and struggles are forever a part of life, no matter where a body might live. Missy and Big Jim had to feed and clothe us three kids and keep this old place together through the Depression. Now, money's not so very tight, but the three of us are older than Methuselah. We'd be fools not to consider our health and what the future may hold. Whenever I step up on a horse, I wonder if it might be the last time. My soul rests securely in Jesus' hands, but the thought of getting sick or frail…"

Nadine nudged her horse back into motion without another word, and Laura Beth followed for several strides before venturing an answer.

"As I understand it, though, Missy handled her predicament with real grace and dignity."

"That's right. Watchin' her left me and Alma and Jimbo without any kind of excuse. Ain't lookin' for pity. We'll handle whatever comes along. Still, you ought to know that worries and cares are a fact of life. Keepin' your mind fixed on the good Lord is the only real answer, no matter where you live. I don't mean to talk down like you was some starry-eyed little girl. Just want it laid out there plain before you make any big changes."

This time, Laura Beth drew rein. A smile played softly at the corners of her mouth while she gazed steadily at her aunt.

"Wouldn't expect anything less from you, Aunt Nadine. Sure, there's a little girl in me who wants to run back to a simpler time and the happiest place I've ever known. And yet… I'm not blinded by nostalgia. We both know my relationship with the Lord is more important than any rural route address, but I feel somehow closer to Him out here. Even if it amounts to trading one set of problems for another, I think Red Bog is where I'm meant to be."

"Good to hear," Nadine tossed back with a grin as she started forward once again. "I'd sure hate for Jimbo to know I talked you out of any such notion."

When Laura Beth's younger ears picked up the distant clammer of six Beagles in a hot race, she caught Nadine's attention with a wide smile and tilted her head to indicate direction. Nadine listened for a moment and then took off in a long trot. She moved right along, without so much as a glance over her shoulder, but finally stopped on a gentle rise that offered good listening.

"Never heard hounds run before," Laura Beth realized, eyes shining with delight as her breath came a bit short from the hurried ride. "I guess the sound of Granddaddy's cur dogs baying a bunch of cattle is about the closest I've come."

"This here's a touch closer to Big Jim's foxhounds. But the rabbit runs a smaller circle, and you don't have to ride near as hard. Vesper's little Beagles make some big music for their size. I'll give 'em that." When the race fell briefly silent, Nadine expanded on her earlier statement. "Nobody around here rode after foxhounds until Missy done it. They'd build a fire somewhere inside the circle and listen. Naturally, me and Jimbo had to try it from horseback. Missy was settin' at the fire by then, but I rode that old Laddie horse of hers. He'd point them ears and line out behind the hounds of his own accord. Instead of pining over what she'd lost, Missy encouraged my happy chatter at the end of every good race. She wanted to hear all about how Laddie sailed over Caney Branch or nearly took my head off on a low hanging limb or caught and passed Jimbo's horse after he'd cut across on us."

"What a way to grow up," Laura Beth murmured, taking it all in even as she listened intently for the current race to reopen.

"Coming right at us," Nadine advised quietly when the Beagle voices reached them once again.

A couple of hours and several short races later, everybody gathered happily around the supper table.

"Them Beagle dogs been chasin' around here for years, Laura Beth," Alma recalled teasingly, "and I've yet to fry the first piece of rabbit."

"We're out for the race, Ms. Alma, just like your brother and all those old-time fox hunters. A dead fox won't run again tomorrow, and the same holds true for a rabbit."

Vesper Denton's quick defense of his Beagles was loud and jovial, if not strictly necessary. Uninitiated as she was, even Laura Beth saw the difference between a good hound race and a meat hunt.

"Matter of fact," George put in, "Vesper figures the bobcats are thinning out too many rabbits. One of them cat hounds I left out yonder with Quint is gettin' some age on her. I told Vesper he could have the dog if he'd pay to ship her in, and he took me up on the deal. Says he ain't much for walking in to a tree, but me or Jimbo either one can take old Bess and eliminate some bobcats."

"I've been worried we'd wake up one morning to find you gone," Laura Beth ventured with a smile. "Now, you're puttin' down a regular set of roots."

"I don't know about all that," George hedged with a grin of his own, "but the occasional paycheck won't hurt none. Vesper's done fooled around and hired me to give your Uncle James Allen some dependable help in the log woods."

"Well, how about that," Laura Beth drawled, eyes sparkling with obvious delight. Rising on impulse, she rounded the table gracefully and stunned him with a quick hug. "You're just like home folks, George, and I'd hate to see you go."

Surprised, but not to the point of losing his manners, the taciturn woodsman scrambled to his feet and placed a hand tentatively on her arm.

By the Light of a Memory 303

"I've been known to cut and drift without much notice, little lady. But I'm kinda partial to Red Bog and you, too. Mark it down as a promise… I aim to stay put long enough to see how things turn out for you and Kimmy, and unless the Lord calls me away in my sleep, I'll not leave without sayin' goodbye."

Chapter Nineteen

Despite the distance between them, Bradley's eager but gentle pursuit of Laura Beth added a touch of excitement to the comfortable rhythm of her days. A beautiful fall bouquet and perfectly crafted latte, delivered by a teenage kid who grinned in relief at finding such an obscure destination before the coffee cooled, stood out as a recent heartfelt gesture.

"Good grief," she stammered over the phone, her surprise giving way to laughter. "How much did that delivery cost? These flowers are just lovely! Thank you, Bradley."

"Red Bog is a long haul from almost anywhere," he quipped, chuckling right back at her. "I called the nearest florist, and her nephew charged so much that I insisted he pick up your coffee, too. Don't let Aunt Nadine laugh you and that fancy drink right out of the kitchen."

Her new cellphone streamlined communication, and with Belinda placing a strict limit on work-related queries, its buzzing usually signaled a thoughtful midday text or late evening call from Bradley. Deprived of George's entertaining shenanigans, he and Kimmy took a more active interest in Laura Beth's ongoing collection of family stories. The blackberry allowed her to share new vignettes, if only by texting pictures of her computer screen. Father and daughter often spent their evenings discussing the tales, fitting them like puzzle pieces with Bradley's photographs of Red Bog or a freshly inspired sketch from Kimmy. Though tempted to share these efforts immediately, they opted for the pleasure of seeing her reaction in person.

Laura Beth allowed the creative process to flow while her trio of storytellers, pleased and amused by such obvious passion, supplied plenty of material. They recalled a difficult period of separation during the war years, Nadine's post-war marriage to Floyd Webber, the loss of Papa Kimbel, and the joyous arrival of Alma's oldest daughter. As her fingers flitted across the keyboard, recording their words, Laura Beth envisioned Missy overseeing it all with unshakable faith, ladylike poise, and the comforting protection of Big Jim's love.

Humming a soft gospel melody in the predawn darkness, Laura Beth gathered the time-worn quilt close around her as she sat up to greet the day. November in East Texas might bring a bone-chilling dampness or, a day or so later, the balmy warmth of Indian summer. Distant thunder and the insistent patter of rain promised a muddy mess when feeding cattle with Granddaddy, but her radiant smile had little to do with the weather. Gradually, and without conscious effort, she began to sing.

"There's sunshine in my soul today, more glorious and bright than glows in any earthly sky, for Jesus is my light!"

Though she was mud spattered and wet to the skin, Laura Beth's spirits remained high at noontime. The cows had plenty of hay along with a daily ration of cubes, and she hoped for a long afternoon visit around the fireplace. Nadine looked the girl over from head to toe and then passed her a cup of hot coffee.

"You'd probably rather have a soda, Laura Beth, but that can wait 'til your teeth quit chattering. Ordinarily, I'd balk at givin' up my place on the morning feed run. Days like today, though, old age ain't so bad."

Laura Beth wrinkled her nose slightly at the bold flavor, but something about her own weary contentment and Nadine's well-meaning gesture made her reluctant to ask for cream and sugar. She drank the coffee just like Granddaddy took his, strong and black. She stood close beside him, both of them enjoying the warmth of

Alma's kitchen while making a conscious effort not to brush against anything and leave behind unwelcome traces of mud.

"Got a call from Patsy this morning," Aunt Alma volunteered, mentioning her eldest daughter. "Their church has moved on to some other kind of music, you know, but Patsy likes the old songs. She plays her piano at home, and Gordon sings along every once in a while. But I guess it's not quite the same. She wanted to know if we'd come over there after supper and sing a little bit."

"Let me handle supper. Then, I'll clean up the kitchen and do a little writing. Nobody's batted an eye at my extended visit, but I'll not follow y'all around like some kind of shadow."

"Pshaw," Alma replied gently. "You do what you want to, child, but Patsy's counting on you. Even asked me to round up a few more singers. If y'all want to go," she added with a cursory glance at Nadine and Jimbo.

"Might as well," Nadine quipped, and that decided it for them all.

Laura Beth's polite hesitation melted away in the warm glow of belonging. She was back home where most invitations remained general, promising a hardy welcome to kinfolks and friends alike.

"Good," Alma agreed with a nod. "Y'all get cleaned up and rest a little while I call around. Thought about checking with Brother Zack and Cindy. Patsy said not to fix anything because she had a bunch of sweets left over from her Bunco night, but I doubt she'll turn down my bread pudding."

"If y'all think it's alright," Laura Beth ventured, "I'll call Abby to see if she and Dalton want to meet us over there, too."

Nadine snorted in surprise but couldn't hold back a smile at the mention of Dalton's name. Her hardworking children and grandchildren showed a considerable touch of Floyd Webber's restless nature along with her own resilience and dry wit. Webber cousins generally brought fireworks or ATVs or maybe an illicit cooler to family gatherings. They came readily to mind when facing down trouble or tarping your roof but not necessarily when planning a quiet Tuesday evening around the piano.

"The boy probably ain't sang a lick since I bounced him on my knee, but he oughta could tote songbooks and help eat up some of them sweets. That little Abby is softspoken and polite which is more than I can say for most of his girlfriends. Go ahead and call 'em. I know you wanted her to meet Cindy, anyhow."

A warm bath and dry clothes felt good, and by the time Laura Beth finished an afterschool phone call with Kimmy, the smell of Alma's bread pudding wafted deliciously through the house.

"I hate to go over there emptyhanded, Aunt Alma. Won't you let me make us a couple of buttermilk pies?"

Alma smiled warmly and glanced at the kitchen clock before answering.

"It ain't hardly necessary, child. But we've got plenty of time yet, and I'd feel the same way. If you want to make the pies, we'll leave one here and carry the other. That daughter of mine's apt to fuss, but it won't mean anything."

Laura Beth drove the Buick due to fading daylight while Aunt Alma sat beside her and offered occasional directions. Nadine and Jimbo put their heads together in the back seat, and sporadic bursts of laughter echoed through the car.

"They always been like that?"

"Their whole lives… Missy knew how to rein 'em in, if need be, but ordinarily she just enjoyed the show."

Patsy's home seemed larger than average but not too showy or imposing.

"Gordon is some kind of doctor, right?" Laura Beth asked as she pulled into the spacious drive.

"Practiced family medicine here in town for years," Alma confirmed, "but he's only working part time now."

A grandmother herself at this point, Patsy looked like a younger and slightly heavier version of Alma. She bustled around with the same nurturing demeanor and genuine desire to make everyone feel right at home. She welcomed Jimbo and Nadine with her usual warmth but showered Laura Beth with a bit of extra attention.

"Sugar, you like to've scared us to death with that terrible accident. Mother had me and Gordon packing an overnight bag, but when Jimbo finally talked to you, he advised us to hold off."

"Well, I surely appreciate all the prayers and concern. It's good to see you!"

"Good to have you here, Laura Beth. We prayed for you, alright, and I tried to reassure Mother that Houston had plenty of doctors. Still, she thinks Gordon is simply the best. I've lived up here in town all my life, but Red Bog stands as a kind of nerve center for the family. Those three on the homeplace are too independent to call for much help. When they finally holler, you just ask where's the problem and what can we do."

"I know what you mean," Laura Beth said with a chuckle, deftly assisting Patsy as they arranged a wide variety of desserts.

Gordon conducted himself with quiet assurance but showed

considerable respect for Jimbo as he asked the older man about the recent movements of wild game and whitetail deer in particular.

"I've seen deer stirrin' around, but there's a pretty good ac'rn crop this year. Puttin' out corn won't do nothing but tempt somebody's old cows across the fence. You recollect Nadine's husband?"

"Yes, sir, I spent a little time around Uncle Floyd in his later years."

"Old Floyd was just about the cagiest man in the woods I ever saw," Jimbo ventured with a fond chuckle. "He was still tryin' to farm some when the state brought them critters back in here. Always claimed there were two seasons for deer, salt and pepper!"

"Never did much still hunting," Nadine added. "Tree stands and such would've left him a settin' target for the game warden. Floyd liked to slip through the woods and shoot his deer on the jump. Then, too, he could spool down the truck window and stick a rifle out in less time than it takes me to tell it."

"We don't farm anymore except for a little piece of a garden," Jimbo explained. "Seldom ever hunted as hard as Floyd, and I ain't near as mad at them deer as I used to be."

Dalton Webber showed up with a walking boot in place of his crutches and the usual haphazard grin. Lacking any exposure to gospel music, Abby took up a songbook and watched Laura Beth for her cues.

"Sit here at the piano, Mother," and Patsy's words were as much request as invitation. "These folks didn't come to hear me play."

"Well, now," Alma chided gently. "We don't know that. Did you ask 'em?"

"I know why I'm here," Dalton whispered to Laura Beth, leaning in close to her ear.

"Dessert?" she guessed with a twinkle in her eye.

"Not far wrong, but I'm really here 'cause you took it in your head to call Abby. What's the idea?" he wanted to know, "draggin' me up town to some quiet little indoor gathering and right before Thanksgiving, too. I reckon they'll hold that deal on the homeplace, and we can at least get outside."

"Thanksgiving couldn't be anywhere else but Red Bog," she tossed back. "Still, I'm sorry to know you find us all so boring."

"I wouldn't go that far with it," and his grin said more than the words. "Granny and Uncle Jimbo can be awful entertainin' under the right circumstances, but they'll try hard not to embarrass Aunt Alma up here."

Listening with half an ear to Patsy's gentle coaxing of her mother, Laura Beth flashed him a tolerant smile.

"I can play for myself any old time, but you know how I love your style."

"You're sweet to ask me, sugar," Alma relented. "I'll play for a little while, anyhow."

"Y'all know how it works," Patsy said to the group at large. "When you get a song picked out, just call for it. How 'bout *Living by Faith*, Mother?"

When Aunt Alma gave the page number, Laura Beth flipped through her songbook with familiar ease, but she hadn't quite finished with Dalton.

"Abby likes to be around your family even if you don't," she teased. "What, is my company not amusing enough for you?"

"Don't worry," he drawled as Aunt Alma set the tempo with a rousing and unmistakable introduction. "There'll be plenty of amusement the first time I get a chance to pitch a firecracker up under your saddle horse."

This last little jab startled Abby to the point of dropping her hymnal. For Laura Beth, though, the first joyful snatches of song bubbled forth on a barely suppressed wave of laughter.

"I care not today what tomorrow may bring, if shadow or sunshine or rain. The Lord I know ruleth o'er everything and all of my worry is vain!"

When someone eventually suggested *In the Sweet By and By*, Abby leaned confidentially toward Laura Beth.

"I know this one!"

Laura Beth tried not to look at Dalton as laughter threatened again, but she offered the girl a warm and encouraging smile. Taking note of Abby's interest, Dalton put his voice to good use on that particular song.

"Say," he observed afterward, "our little corner sounded better than average. If Laura Beth didn't act so prim and proper all the time, I'd take you girls out to a karaoke night."

"I just might go," his cousin retorted, "if you'll let us sing something out of the hymnbook."

"You wouldn't, either. Can't say I blame you; it just ain't your scene." Before the next song got underway, he turned mischievously to Abby. "I hear tell Laura Beth's been dating her husband again. Now, that's probably her idea of life on the wild side."

The next song proved unfamiliar to Abby, but once started, Dalton sang along without a second thought.

"If you don't act a little nicer to Laura Beth," his girlfriend said during the next brief lull, "I'm afraid she might not want us around anymore. She's been nothing but sweet to me, so you'd better straighten up already."

"Aw, she don't pay me no attention."

"Not much," Laura Beth responded, "but I do wonder a little as to just where you get your information."

"Didn't hear it from Granny. I'll tell you that much. The old girl's plenty tightlipped and more protective of you than any of her own grandkids. She figures us Webbers are mean enough, on average, to look out for ourselves. It's the sweet ones that worry her some."

Abby's eyes widened slightly at this little speech, but Laura Beth placed a comforting hand on her shoulder.

"There's different kinds of meanness, hon, and all the Webbers I know are good folks. With the right woman alongside him, this old boy might even amount to something one day."

"Aunt Alma may not be quite as tough as Granny or Uncle Jimbo," Dalton ventured sometime later around a delicious mouthful of pie, "but she sure can cook and play that piano!"

"Her musical talent never ceases to amaze me," Laura Beth said with a smile. "Still, I wouldn't sell Aunt Alma short when it comes to inner strength. Anybody who's nearly ninety years old and still going…"

"What about her cooking?"

"Simply wonderful, but that's my buttermilk pie you're eating."

Arching one eyebrow, Dalton indicated the remnant of crust left on his plate and gave a satisfied sigh. In spite of several animated conversations around the room, his thoughts continued on the original track.

"Aunt Alma will try to get out of playing just about every time. Could be modesty, or maybe the arthritis really bothers her that much. Either way… Nobody else can make a piano talk quite like she does, and when it comes right down to it, she'll play as long as there's somebody willin' to sing."

"People who label any kind of older music as dull certainly never heard your aunt play for one of these lively family sing-alongs," Abby declared.

"That's a fact, and Laura Beth's got a point, too. Nobody knows just how tough Alma might be. She never got too many chances to prove it."

"What do you mean?"

"Oh, you wouldn't understand. My dear cousin, though, ought to catch the drift. Granny and Uncle Jimbo hover around her pretty close. Before that, it was Big Jim and the old she-wolf herself. Family stories kinda run together on me, Laura Beth. Did she have a name, apart from *Yes'm*?"

These remarks, although meant in good fun, shot Laura Beth to her feet like a suddenly uncoiled spring.

"W-wolf?" she sputtered. "Why, you and I might never have seen the light of day without her. Missy Pate loved those two little motherless girls, claimed them as her own, kept them safe, and pointed them to Jesus. Loved Big Jim enough to pull him back from the brink of destruction more than once… Just about ruined herself bringing a son into the world and went right on loving the whole bunch. You can lose that grin, Dalton Webber, or I'll wipe it off for you!"

Dalton patted gently at one of the hands white-knuckling an edge of the tabletop. His gaze darted around the large kitchen, but no one seemed to have noticed this momentary outburst. Though frozen in shock, Abby read pride and faint amusement in the glance that flicked her way. Finally, he faced Laura Beth with absolute calm, echoing the tone he had heard Uncle Jimbo use on startled horses and even a time or two on Granny Webber.

"Easy, girl. E-e-easy… I won't forget that name again. And if your husband don't stick this time, he's nine kinds of a fool. Between the homemade buttermilk pie and that streak of lightnin' in your blood, I'd say you're a mighty rare combination."

Trembling almost imperceptibly as the adrenaline drained away, Laura Beth sank down into her chair once again with a weary smile.

"I'm sorry," she sighed, and a long look conveyed the apology first to Dalton and then to his slightly shaken girlfriend. "It's just that I've been collecting some of our family tales. Bygone days and the people who lived through them feel very real to me at the moment and somehow very close."

"You ain't done nothin' wrong," Dalton tossed back. "I knew you'd been asking Granny and them some questions. Guess that's why my mind reached way back to bits and pieces I'd heard about Missy. See, I've been haulin' fuel and runnin' after parts for your Uncle James Allen while this leg knits back together. No, Laura Beth, don't you apologize. Granny might've slapped my face for that she-wolf crack, and I'd never have said it in front of Jimbo Pate."

"No wonder you knew about my date with Bradley and even the little story project. Uncle James Allen hears from my dad and

Granddaddy, too. I'm just curious about one thing. With you on hand to fuel up all their equipment, what's left for Vesper Denton to do?"

"Ab-so-lutely nothing!"

 "Well," she answered with a fond chuckle, "that's just about the way he likes it."

Dalton grinned back at her and then leaned earnestly across the table, signaling a change of subject.

"James Allen don't say much, and you know that. Patsy's goodhearted but just a touch put out because she, oldest daughter of the oldest daughter, may never convince Aunt Alma to leave Red Bog again. Then, there's my dad and the rest of the Webbers, all walkin' pretty soft around Granny. The whole bunch gets along, more or less, and I hear 'em talk. You're making a difference out there on the homeplace, Laura Beth. They all know it, too. Even if nobody's come right out and said thank you."

"I'm glad to do whatever I can, Dalton, but the blessings go both ways. That bunch out on the homeplace has made all the difference in the world for me. I was so very lonely. Worn down and frazzled until I didn't know if I was coming or going…"

Startled by the unexpected depth of their conversation, Dalton masked the rough edges of emotion in his voice with a dry chuckle.

"Yeah, or when not to cross the street."

"Dalton!" Abby cried sharply, but he waved away her objection.

"You may see an elegant lady coming up on middle age, but I'm still looking at one of my favorite girl cousins. True enough, Laura Beth is a few years ahead of us. She's raised a daughter and carved out a life for herself in the big city, but none of that means she can't take a little teasing. Don't waste your breath takin' up for Jimbo Pate's granddaughter. She can look after herself pretty well."

"You're sweet to take my side, Abby, but I'm afraid he's right. I spanked Dalton for chunkin' rocks at the chickens when I was about sixteen and he was four or five years old. Strange as it may seem, the experience left him enamored with me. Then, over the years, I became the number one victim for his endless supply of practical jokes."

"Ain't so strange, really. I'd been whipped lots of times but never by anybody quite so pretty. Besides, she outran Granny and saved me from a sure-enough dose of wrath. Uncle Jimbo paid out good money for those layin' hens. Besides, the old lady generally showed more concern for animals than for knot-headed kids."

"Abby's already a tad leery of Aunt Nadine, and you're not helping."

"You bet she's leery… I try not to date anybody dumber than me."

"You're awful," Laura Beth teased but granted him a fond smile before turning her attention back to Abby. "Come with me, sugar. I want you to try some of Aunt Alma's bread pudding and spend a few minutes getting to know our pastor's wife before the singin' starts up again. Dalton can shoot the breeze with Granddaddy or go torment somebody else for a few minutes."

"What about Mrs. Webber? I feel like I should—"

"Oh, Abby… Don't look so grim. We'll work you up to Aunt Nadine in stages."

Cindy used her fear of riding as an icebreaker, laughing at herself without a second thought to put the younger girl at ease. Gaining some confidence, Abby reported on her progress with Tinker Bell, the palomino bronc. Laura Beth listened, sipping contentedly at her Dr Pepper until they abandoned the subject of horses and started to quiz her on the renewed romance with Bradley.

"I don't know," she admitted hesitantly in response to their eager questions. "I've always loved him, but I just don't know. Kimmy's definitely in favor of us dating. Bless her sweet heart. Our daughter wants us to try, even at the risk of failure, but I keep wondering if my little girl can stand that kind of disappointment. I'm still her mother, and I have to protect…"

Abby felt for her friend but trusted the pastor's wife, obviously kind and perceptive, to offer sound advice.

"She'll be disappointed if it doesn't work out," Cindy declared gently, "but how will she feel if you never try? How will you feel? Not to mention Bradley."

"We've never spent much time together, Laura Beth," Abby ventured shyly. "But, from where I'm sitting, there's no way you deserved to be left alone with a baby girl to love and bring up and provide for all on your own. That's a pretty serious mark against Bradley. Still, if I turned that cousin of yours loose on the wide world for ten years… Well, there's no way he'd come back begging for a second chance."

"Nobody can make these decisions for you," Cindy added. "Like Miss Alma said before, the main thing we can do is pray. And, honey, we've got that covered."

"I'm praying, too, but not for the Lord to wrap my relationship with Bradley in the neat and orderly package I always wanted. I'm just asking Him to guide me and give me the strength to follow one step at a time. I'm also asking for His loving care over everyone involved. I tried to protect my own heart by walling Bradley out, and any fool could see what a mess that made.”

“Taking responsibility is quite noble, but don’t bury yourself in regret. There are certainly legitimate reasons for divorce, Laura Beth. As children of God, we’re commanded to extend love and forgiveness. Sometimes, however unfortunate it might be, we must do so from a safe distance. Just know, this time, that you and Bradley won’t be trying to make the marriage work in a vacuum. Yes, there’s Kimmy to consider, but you’ll also have a strong community around you.”

After another hour and a half of gospel songs around the piano, Jimbo stood and cleared his throat.

“I’ve sure enjoyed it, y’all, but feedin’ time comes around pretty early.”

Nadine and Laura Beth took the lead in tidying things up while Patsy listened to her mother play one last melody. Finally, they exchanged goodbyes all around along with promises to do this again soon.

Despite the prospect of an early morning, Laura Beth put in her familiar request for another story session. With the four of them settled in the front room at home, Jimbo stirred up the fireplace coals and added a stick or two of wood.

“I think we left off in the summer of 1950, Granddaddy, just about the time you left home to serve in Korea.”

“That’s right, doodlebug, but don’t go thinkin’ the country jumped straight from World War II into Korea. Missy had this place and Uncle Cleve’s land to watch over, besides runnin’ the store, until those defense jobs played out in the middle 40s. ’Course I was her number one farmhand. Liked working a good pair of mules as much as anybody, but I don’t think we would’ve made it if I hadn’t talked her into lettin' me use Uncle Cleve's tractor."

"We made pretty good money down there in Orange," Nadine admitted, "but none of us liked being crowded up amongst so many other folks. What with the hurry and the noise and Big Jim lonesome for his Missy… I doubt if any of us got a good, deep breath until we made it back to Red Bog."

"Mechanized farmin' didn't hit us overnight, either," Jimbo continued. "I'd break ground with that poppin' Johnny, and then me and the Havard boys would come along to plant and fertilize and cultivate with mules like we'd always done. I tended my cowherd and sparked around with a few of the local girls in spite of it all. Time freed up some when Daddy and them come home, but most of my datin' prospects latched on to somebody headed for Houston or Dallas. If a man wanted a dollar an hour back then, he had to go somewhere and get it. Big Jim and Missy never set out to tie me down at home, but I guess the old place kinda got in my blood. If I spent an hour workin' up a horse trade or a cow deal and talked the other fella down twenty dollars, I called that makin' twenty dollars an hour. But mighty few marryin' age girls will go along with that kind of arithmetic."

"I'd say you did alright for yourself," Laura Beth assured him, laughing even as her fingers walked over the keyboard. "Speaking of girls, though, when did Grandmother come into the picture?"

"Well, it's kinda funny. I came home in December of 1952 to find her livin' in the house with Missy and Big Jim."

"Really? And you'd never seen her before?"

"Not even once… Melba was raised up down around Nacogdoches, but we considered that a long ways from here."

"Like Jimbo said," Alma put in, "it seemed like everybody was on the move in those days. Black folks, white folks, or whoever, and they all had a mind to leave the farm. Some of Gert's grown children took her off to Dallas for a while, and it kind of left us in a bind."

"I was overseas by that time," Jimbo recalled, "and Missy flat set her mind against bringin' in an outside caregiver. Gert was one thing. A fact of life, really. But Missy Pate never considered herself an invalid and sure never took too many orders. Aunt Alma and Nadine did all they could, but they were married and raisin' babies. Nadine got Papa Kimbel's house, just up the road in Red Bog proper, and Alma made her home in Henderson."

"Missy gave me and Floyd the store to run," Nadine explained, "but I remember times when Big Jim would bring her down there to *check up on things* just to keep from leaving her in the house alone."

"Daddy was a sure-enough horseman, but he never favored the saddle too much. Even so, I set him up with a nice little gaited mare before leavin' for the army. Hoyt Kimbel was too busy and gettin' too old to ride through all of my cattle and then his own."

"Wait a minute, Granddaddy. I never meant to pass over your military service. How about telling us some stories from that time?"

"Ain't very many of those stories that I care to recall, doodlebug. Done what needed doing, and by God's grace, I got back to Red Bog in one piece. I reckon most farm boys had a little advantage, and I'd spent some time trailin' after Floyd Webber. Anyhow, they put me to leadin' patrols because I could slip along quiet like through the woods and undergrowth and generally hit whatever I drew a bead on with that government-issue carbine. One story, or a piece of one, and then I'd just as soon get back to talkin' about my sweet Melba."

"Yes, sir. Whatever you feel like sharing…"

"One day, out on reconnaissance, we found a starvin' pup near this burned-out piece of a farmstead. Well… Missy or Big Jim or nobody I thought much of would've left him there. I could've knocked him in the head and stayed within army regulations, but I just scooped him up into my shirt. Grew into a middlin' sized dingy brown dog, and we took to callin' him Trooper. At less than a year old, that rascal could wind a bunch of partisan guerrillas or a lone sniper before I picked up on any kind of danger. Friendly South Korean troops all around us, mind you, and he never turned a hair at them. I saved his life once, but he returned the favor time and again."

"You've always been a dog man, Granddaddy, but Trooper sounds downright amazing. If his instincts helped to keep you safe, I mean. How'd he do it, anyway? That 38th parallel is just a line on the map. Was it by scent, maybe something unique in the diet of North Korean soldiers?"

"Trooper used his nose, alright. Lookin' back, though, I almost want to say he could smell a man's ill intent. Don't know much about body chemistry or all these modern terms, but I've seen it in wild game. You let a varmint go to slippin' around in a life-or-death situation, and his scent will change. Me and Nadine picked that up years ago by watchin' Daddy's hounds whenever they had to put in the work and really grub out a trail."

Laura Beth wondered how Trooper might have finished his career but withheld that particular question out of respect for her grandfather.

"Melba left nursing school just one semester shy of graduation to care for her sick daddy," Alma volunteered, steering them back toward the subject of Jimbo's courtship and marriage. "Then, the old man died and the last bit of her tuition money went to final expenses. Poor girl was more orphaned than me and Nadine ever thought about being. Only, she happened to be near enough grown before losing her last parent. My Bud owned a part interest in the pharmacy by then, and they generally used high school kids to run the soda fountain. Anyhow, Melba ended up in Henderson with an old friend of her mother's. That friend brought her in looking for a job, and Bud just couldn't turn her away. He put the high schoolers to sweeping up for a day or two and let Melba run the soda fountain while the rest of us went to work on Missy's good heart."

"Later that same week," Nadine recalled, "Bud and Alma brought her out to our store at Red Bog for a kind of informal interview. I remember meeting Melba for the first time, and I remember just what Floyd said after studyin' the situation for about two minutes. 'Let's take her on out to the homeplace, y'all, but don't nobody even whisper the word nurse around Missy. Long as she's just offerin' this young lady a place to live, we might get by with it.'"

"War changes most men considerably. Reckon I wasn't no different. By courtin' Miss Melba, though, I came right on back to myself. Lived up at Red Bog with Nadine and Floyd for a while, just to keep down talk, but bein' off the homeplace didn't set too good. 'At Floyd would get into something, work to beat the band for a little stretch of time, sell out to the first passerby, go off a'hunting, and come back home lookin' for the next hot deal. When he bought him a sawmill, I seen my chance. Me, Big Jim, and Tully Havard cut the logs and snaked 'em out behind a pair of mules. Floyd turned out the lumber, and Melba picked a spot for our little home. 'Cross the road yonder, but within sight of this house."

"Melba and Missy needed one another," Nadine offered sagely. "By the time Jimbo came home again, that girl was a part of our family."

"The whole bunch fell in love with your grandmother before I did, but I fell the hardest."

"Y'all married in '53, right?" she prompted with a fond smile. "And Dad came along just over a year later?"

"Yes'm, that next fall. We named Billy Boy after Melba's late father, and your Uncle James Allen didn't get here until 1960."

"One more Jim Pate," Laura Beth observed with a smile.

"That's right, and the boss man was able to enjoy his namesake just a little before he really got down sick. Daddy's breathing hadn't been good for a while, but he kept right on going. Even took a hand in building my house. Doubt there'd be a wall left standin' without him and Floyd. Me and Hoyt and old Tully wouldn't have made a decent carpenter if you rolled all three of us into one."

Chapter Twenty

~May 1961~

At fifty-seven, a few strands of silver glinted among the rich amber blond of Missy's hair. Hazel green eyes contained the same vibrant spark Jim Pate had admired on their first evening together. Even in her new wheelchair, a fold-up convenience on car rides to the county seat, such timeless beauty looked out of place within the cold, sterile confines of a hospital.

"Your husband could go today. Then again… He might linger for a week, but there's nothing more we can do for him."

The strange doctor conveyed an appropriate amount of impersonal regret as he looked down into Missy's face. She took in a deep breath and glanced momentarily back through a half-open door to where Jimbo sat with his Uncle Cleve by the bedside. Then, she closed off the sickroom and angled her wheelchair back around to speak.

"Thank you, doctor. If my Jim is nearing the end, I'll take him on home to Red Bog, but I'd like to speak to young Dr. Brown first."

Something very near a frown crossed the physician's face before his impassive professionalism returned.

"I'm sorry, ma'am, but Dr. Brown is no longer affiliated with our organization."

"Vincent Brown helped build this hospital," Missy objected automatically.

"Maybe so, but he doesn't see patients here anymore. In case you haven't noticed, he isn't young anymore, either. As for the question at hand, you cannot move the patient at this stage. He couldn't survive the trip, and we won't sign off on such a thing."

Missy went stock still for a moment as hot words rose in her throat, but she finally dismissed the uncooperative stranger with one quick shake of her head. Her gaze darted up the hallway toward a small waiting area and the lanky woodsman holding up a near corner.

"You, Floyd," she called in a tone more suited to a wide-open cotton field than the ominous quiet of a hospital. "Go get Vincent Brown and fetch him back here."

Floyd Webber glanced over at his wife and then back toward Missy. Rather than ask where to start looking or why Vincent Brown was wanted, he simply pushed off the wall and took the task in hand.

Another deep breath, a moment to compose herself, and she wheeled back into the hospital room. To her surprise, Big Jim's eyes fluttered open, and he greeted her with a weak grin.

"Didn't get much from that doctor's muttering, but when you closed the door and then hollered out to Floyd, I started puttin' things together."

"Gettin' plumb nosey in your old age," and the soft-spoken words passed for teasing despite a slight tremor in her voice.

"Wish I could call back them years of drinkin' and the pain it caused. Some of these newfangled notions on cigarettes might be right, too, but none of that nor even the gradual effects of hard work could take me before my time. The night I walked into the bedroom to find you near about bled out but plumb tickled over our brand-new baby boy… Well, I reckon the good Lord knew it all along. But I figured out once and for all that I just couldn't bury you. Hate to leave you, Missy girl, but that's the way it's got to be. Not much point asking you to look after Jimbo and the girls. You'll go right on doin' that, anyhow."

Clasping his outstretched hand, Missy blinked back tears.

"Go if you have to, Jim, but not just yet. We'll be alright, I reckon, but how about comin' home with me first?" Then, repeating a phrase from their past in soft and heartfelt tones meant for his ears alone, "Hold me close, love, and I can face anything."

By the time Floyd returned with young Dr. Brown, Jim Pate had drifted once again into a state somewhere between sleep and unconsciousness.

"It wouldn't surprise Big Jim to know that I've failed you again, Missy. Medically speaking, there's nothing else to be done."

"Nobody expects you to alter God's timetable, Vincent, whether I like the schedule or not. What do you think of my chances? Getting him home one more time?"

"For anybody but you and Big Jim, almost no chance at all. You've got a nurse and a pharmacist in the immediate family. As your physician, my advice is to go on home and try to rest while one of them sits with him through the final hours."

Bud Evans cleared his throat from a corner of the small room and stepped up a little closer to the bed.

"That's probably for the best, Missy. I ran out on Big Jim once, but I'll not do it again."

"I know you'd stick this time, Bud," she said and held his gaze for a long moment, "but there's no way I can go off and leave him."

"As your friend, Missy… And maybe Big Jim's, too," Dr. Brown finished without acknowledgement of the brief interruption, "I'm willin' to play this thing out just as you think best."

She nodded, his loyalty fetching up a weary smile, and then turned her attention to Jimbo.

"What about it, son?"

"You ain't missed Floyd yet? I just sent him after Milo Jackson's ambulance."

"The hospital won't technically release him in this condition, but they can't stop us. If we load you into the ambulance with Jim, close enough to hold his hand and talk some, I don't think he'd dare die this side of Red Bog."

Jimbo smiled grimly at the doctor's words and then locked eyes once again with his mother.

"Me and Uncle Cleve will get ahead of y'all. That'll give me a minute with Melba and the boys. We'll have fresh sheets on the bed by the time you get home."

"No, son. Let Bud and Alma do that. If they give us any trouble about takin' him out of here, I want you on hand."

"I'll stay around, too," Cleve added dryly. "Me and Vincent may be gettin' old, but if need be, we'll load y'all while Jimbo and Floyd mop up whoever's standin' in the way."

"I never did count you out of it. We've been in some tight spots before this one. Besides, anybody tough enough to trail after Big Jim couldn't have no quit in 'em."

"You ought to know, Missy. Yes'm, you sure ought to know."

The ride home passed in a blur. Missy prayed inwardly and recounted memories out loud while young Dr. Brown checked and rechecked Big Jim's vital signs, regulating the oxygen accordingly. With the calm assurance of a longtime family matriarch, in her element once again, Missy supervised Big Jim's transfer to his own bed and then gave the children and in-laws a few moments alone with him. Out on the wide back porch, she turned once again to her brother-in-law.

"Slip down to the dog yard, Cleve, and cut them hounds loose. Just might be old Rambler and them can strike us a daytime fox somewhere close."

"Untie all of 'em? Dogs ain't likely to jump no fox in the middle of the afternoon, but they'll hunt the livelong night. Some of Jim's hounds are worth a little money nowadays…"

"Let me worry about that. You just cut 'em loose, every last one."

The weight of impending loss seemed to slip from Cleve's shoulders as he grinned down at her.

"After all these years, Missy, you'd think I'd know better than to argue. We'll do it your way."

Rolling back into the bedroom, she cleared her throat, a subdued but definite signal. In a few words, she made her wishes known to Jimbo and the girls. They laid her carefully in bed beside Big Jim and filed out along with their spouses.

"Wait a minute, Melba," she called gently. "Give us James Allen."

"Alright, Missy, if you're sure."

Despite her limited mobility, Missy inched closer to Big Jim until she lay nestled in his arms with the baby between them. Her silent tears finally stopped when the hound music floated to them through an open window.

"They did find one," she murmured with a satisfied half smile. "Now, let's see if they can jump it to run."

As the race heated up, Big Jim stirred and opened his eyes.

"Raise James Allen up a little so he can hear old Maude run…"

Missy fought back fresh tears as the words told her the extent of Big Jim's drifting through time. He was well aware of her presence and their youngest grandson but also listening for a long-gone hound.

"Yes, my love," she finally managed.

Missy watched the beloved eyes close, saw his lips form a smile, and wondered if he would ever speak again. She cooed softly to the baby and chuckled when a particularly hot stretch of the race brought Cleve Pate's familiar whoop from somewhere outside.

"Just listen at 'em run… Them cotton pickin' hounds don't lack much bein' as hardheaded as Missy!"

Finally, Jimbo reentered the room with Melba, Alma, and Nadine following close behind. They sat around the bed in silence until Big Jim burst out with a sudden announcement. Eyes still closed, he sounded surprisingly strong.

"Hoyt Kimbel's out yonder callin' for you again. I ain't got nothin' against old Hoyt, but it looks like he could hire some help to ride after wild cattle with him. Times, you and that big red gelding make my blood run cold. I know you love it, Missy girl, and I reckon you've got to go. Just be careful, you hear?"

Jimbo drew in a sharp breath, let it out slowly, and then ventured an opinion.

"Daddy can't leave you, Missy. He can't turn loose, not with you and James Allen right alongside him."

One long sob wracked Missy's body, but she steadied herself before answering.

"Melba can take the baby, but I'll stay with him a little longer."

Nobody questioned her decision out loud, and Jimbo closed the door softly as they left. Fading daylight made little to no impression on Missy. When the door finally opened again, Gertie Washington, who the last they'd heard was still up in Dallas, called to her softly out of another time.

"Mister Hoyt's stompin' and snortin' all over the front yard, Missy. Claims them dogs of his are bayed up on some cattle and he's just got to have you. I sent Tobe to fetch Laddie around by the door."

"They call you all the way home just to get me out of here?" Missy asked without turning her head.

"No'm, but I'm here… And, hard as it is, we'd best let him go now."

~November 2007~

"I've been gone from Red Bog a long time," and Bill Pate smiled fondly at his daughter from the kitchen doorway. "But I can't say I remember us having cornbread for breakfast."

"No, Dad," Laura Beth teased right back, placing another pan on the ageless enamel worktop to cool, "and you're not fixin' to take up the habit. Aunt Alma will need every bit of this when we start in to make Gert's famous chicken and dressin' tomorrow. I'm so glad you and Mom will be with us on Thanksgiving. Sleep alright?"

"So-so," he answered, pouring himself a cup of coffee. "Kimmy all but insisted we come, and I understand Bradley's parents are driving up early on Thursday. Speaking of a good night's sleep, you look very chipper this morning. Every hair in place, and Aunt Nadine would call that a go-to-town outfit."

"Got started pretty early," she offered by way of explanation, "and

By the Light of a Memory 331

it's been too wet for George to work in the log woods. With him and Bradley on hand to help feed, I just decided to dress up a little."

"From the time you were a little girl, Laura Beth, you had very definite ideas as to your appearance. Never vain… Perhaps meticulous is the word. Still, I can't help but wonder if the extra effort this morning has something to do with Bradley."

"Not much," she answered breezily. "Seldom ever wore this denim skirt before coming back to Red Bog, but Aunt Alma added a ruffle onto the hem for an extra bit of detail. Her work is always pretty, so I decided to get it out and swish it around some. If Bradley happens to notice, that's his business."

"Fair enough," her dad decided with a glint of humor in his eyes. "Things seem to be going well for you two. I wouldn't mind having a little talk with Bradley, but I'm sure your granddaddy's already done it. You're a grown woman, Laura Beth, and wise beyond your years. Still, just know I'm available whenever you need me."

"I know, Dad, and I appreciate it. You and Mom see the world a little differently than I do, but I'll always be your little girl." Having mixed up another pan of cornbread while they talked, she slipped it deftly into the oven before glancing up at him once more. "Anyhow, Granddaddy and them trooped up the hill from his house better than an hour ago. We all sat down to breakfast and then scattered to different chores."

"All?" he questioned.

"Aunt Alma, Aunt Nadine, the menfolk, and me. I can feed you and Mom and Kimmy in shifts or all at once, however it works out. Aunt Alma fixed a plenty of her biscuits."

"Not quite seven o'clock," he observed with a grin, "and here I am, late for breakfast. Part of me still can't believe you'd want to move back into all this, but your happiness is plain to see.”

“Yes, sir   ! I’ve still got some details to work out, but this is where I belong.”

“My hardheaded daddy has never stopped loving us. But he’s never really forgiven us for taking his doodlebug out of Red Bog, either. Can you, Laura Beth? After all, your mom and I made what we thought was the best decision.”

“There’s nothing to forgive, Dad. Maybe my life has taken some unexpected turns. But… Meeting Bradley, sweet Kimmy’s birth, my career, all those things are products of the time I spent in Houston. People live happy and fulfilling lives in all kinds of places. How were you and Mom supposed to know that you’d been saddled with an incurably nostalgic daughter and her deep set of roots.”

“As much as I love Daddy and the aunts, I didn’t want them to fill your head with some obligation to be another Missy Pate. I thought of you as my daughter and a highly unique individual. No doubt you are, but they were right as usual. You show an abundance of my grandmother’s grace and resilience. Even amid your personal stress and anxiety, everyone else described you as oddly soothing.”

“Dad, I just can’t see—”

“Maybe not, but that’s exactly how you calmed all those bridezillas and other demanding customers. Now, without forethought or consideration, I’ve come to you with my guilt and doubts. Just like me and James Allen used to go to Missy with our scraped knees and childish heartaches, and sure enough, you’ve made it all better.”

Blinking away the unexpected threat of tears, Laura Beth stepped over to place a quick kiss on his cheek.

“That’s very sweet of you, Dad, and if our little talk helped, I’m glad. The more time I spend here on the homeplace, the more settled I feel in my own heart and mind." Then, with a mischievous gleam in her eyes, "Hope I don't start puttin' folks right off to sleep."

"Never," he decided instantly. "There's a difference between calming and dull. I'm not sure what that difference is, but you and Missy got it in spades! Don't see myself ever moving back here, much less your mom, but we'll visit regularly once you and Kimmy are settled. I should've visited Daddy and them all along, but you know how it is."

"Now," she assured him quietly, "we can all make up for lost time. Kimmy and I will try to visit y'all, too. Depending on what kind of job and how much flexibility I end up with here, I might even do some fill-in type work for Vida and them."

"So, that deal is actually going through? I never really thought you'd sell your name, even if they came up with the money."

"Belinda can't use the name of her old firm after selling out. *Finishing Touches by Elizabeth Chandler* is just an idea in people's minds, Dad, and Vida's perfectly capable of upholding the image I developed. Besides… In my heart, I've always been Laura Beth."

"See there," he mused, chuckling at her explanation. "I knew good and well that Jimbo Pate's darling granddaughter would never sell her name at any price, but I didn't quite follow your peculiar thread of logic to its inevitable Red Bog end. Will the money be there when it's needed?"

"Yes, sir. Belinda gave me her part up front, and Vida will pay on a bimonthly schedule. The contract is on file with my attorney, all legal and proper, but more than that, Vida is a good friend. I know that girl, Dad, and she'll make good. In the meantime, how about taking a little wagon ride with me and Bradley and Kimmy?"

"Wagon— Thank you, but no. That sounds like a nice family outing for the three of you. Daddy going along to drive?"

"No, sir. Somebody wanted this nice little pair of black mules tuned up for parade season. Blackjack and Coaly don't give no trouble, really. Driving them will just be an added enjoyment, for me or Bradley either one."

"Well," he said, adjusting to the idea with a quick shake of his head. "Your mom and I never set out to raise a muleskinner, but Missy would be proud."

Later that morning, Laura Beth threw on a blue jean jacket over the green blouse and headed down to the barn lot with her basket of oatmeal cookies and a jug of drinking water.

"Can I saddle Gopher instead of riding with y'all in the wagon?" Kimmy wanted to know. "Dad said to ask you first."

"Almost like taking a ride by yourself," she mused, liking the idea. "Only thing is, we'll take the mules and wagon out on these county roads. You stay behind us and watch for traffic."

"Thanks, Mama! May want to ride up alongside the wagon for a cookie, but I'll pick my spot and wait for you to give me the all clear."

"Well, you made her day," Bradley commented as their daughter ran off to catch the old horse. "George helped me hitch up the team, but you're welcome to look them over if you'd like."

"I don't know much more about it than you do," she admitted. "Granddaddy focused on the cow business during my girlhood years. Tractors replaced the mule, and with Missy gone, we had no call for a driving horse. I'll walk around the team, though, and give you one more set of eyes."

Finished with her brief inspection, Laura Beth accepted Bradley's courteous support as she started up into the wagon. Pleased to feel her hand resting in his, Bradley scarcely noticed the moment of hesitation until she stepped back out onto the ground.

"What's the matter?"

"One of us had better look at Gopher," she answered. "I don't want that saddle rolling with Kimmy."

"Just like a mother hen, but I guess you're entitled in this case. Get up there and take your driving lines. I'll see about Kimmy and then get the gate."

"Step up, Coaly. Get ahead, Blackjack," Laura Beth sang out eventually. She put her team through the gate, pulled up far enough for Kimmy to ride out, and stopped them. "Granddaddy says those Christmas parades are an awful lot of hurry up and wait, so they might as well get used to it."

Bradley watched her drive for a few minutes, throwing occasional glances back at their daughter, and finally started a conversation.

"You've been calling it a *little project,* but transposing all those stories from the spoken word into a readable collection was quite the undertaking. It's high-quality work that your whole extended family can be proud of. I know I am."

"Well, that's very kind… But you and Kimmy enhanced things on the visual side. Our child never ceases to amaze me, and I still can't believe y'all kept the surprise quiet for so long."

"Wanted to show you in person," he explained briefly.

"With Kimmy's drawings, a few old photographs from Aunt Nadine's collection, and your more recent shots of life on the homeplace, the stories almost come to life."

"The pictures don't hurt, but when your unique writing style encountered a vibrant impression of Missy Pate in the minds of those three old-time storytellers, something wonderful happened. I told you once that it might be difficult to find a market for those family stories. But looking at them now, I can see an outstanding coffee table book."

Laura Beth felt a sudden catch in her throat. Rather than scramble immediately for the right words, she focused several moments' attention on the mules. The measured sound of their hoofbeats on blacktop provided a counterpoint to the rising tide of her excitement, and occasional patches of late fall color glinted in the sunlight.

"Oh, Bradley, do you think it might actually publish? I'd love to see all our material come together in a single well-executed project, but personal satisfaction won't really justify the printing expense."

"Hard to make any promises, darling. Most of my publishing contacts specialize in visual art. Maybe add a line here and there to place Red Bog in the broader context of American history. The Spanish flu, the Prohibition era, the Great Depression, and so on… I think you'd find some very real interest out there. Sales probably won't be anything spectacular, but the work is good enough to pay for itself. Kimmy and anyone else who wants one should end up with a nice keepsake, and it might provide a bit of name exposure if you decide to follow up with a more traditional novel."

"It's all so exciting," she gushed in spite of her best efforts to avoid premature celebration, "but the greatest thrill is knowing you and Kimmy helped to shape the finished product. All three of us working together, not to mention a real family Thanksgiving! Speaking of work, though, how have you managed to split your time between here and Houston for so long?"

"Picked up a couple of one-day shoots while Kimmy was in school, things I might not have bothered with ordinarily, but they allowed me to stay close and focus mostly on her. I'm booked for a cross-country ski race during the first part of her Christmas break. She can spend that time here with you unless the two of y'all want to come along."

"I love you, Bradley Chandler, but the only way I'm moving around in deep snow is with a big fleece-lined jacket and one tough booger of a saddle horse. I'd probably avoid it even then without a mighty compelling reason."

"What about a dog sled?" he offered jokingly.

"Not unless it comes with a driver and I can sit bundled up on the sled," she answered more or less automatically.

"Sounds like you're not totally against travelling with me," he ventured with a smile. "I'll snag us something warmer and maybe a little closer to home, just as soon as the opportunity arises."

"Kimmy will need to chaperon," she teased, "unless you know something I don't."

"I love every bit of you, Laura Beth, even those unbending Red Bog ethics. Having Kimmy as our chaperon is a nice gesture, but I expect most folks would consider it awfully late."

They laughed warmly together until Bradley found himself watching her with rapt attention.

"How'd you get to be so pretty?"

Honest but lighthearted, his question dated back to their brief years of marriage and maybe even the engagement. In those days, she had answered only with a smiling sigh or perhaps a quick kiss on the cheek. Now, for the first time, she managed a verbal response.

"Clean livin' and good country air," I suppose.

"No, ma'am… I saw you fresh out of a big-city hospital just over a month ago, and you took my breath away then, too."

Laura Beth's heart gave an involuntary flutter, but she managed a drawling comeback nonetheless.

"Well, then… Shall we credit Missy Pate's good genes or just say you're easily impressed?"

He sat there in stunned silence for a moment and then smiled at her adoringly. One hand reached out slowly, almost questioningly, to brush a lock of hair from her face.

"After reading those stories, I'm willing to give Missy some credit and, of course, our marvelous Creator. I've been all around this world, Laura Beth, and never found anyone like you."

With a driving line in each hand, Laura Beth leaned over and dropped a spontaneous kiss on his cheek.

"Guess that's what you've been after all along… Come to think of it, though, I could use your advice on the question of Missy."

"What about her?"

"So far, I just can't bring myself to ask direct questions about her passing. It sounds silly, Bradley, but hearing them recount her loss of Big Jim nearly broke my heart. I know Granddaddy and the aunts are strong enough to share details about her death, but I wonder if I'm strong enough to watch them relive it."

"Laura Beth, darling…" Then, after a brief stretch of silence, "Have I mentioned how much I love you? As far as advice goes, I say end the project at Big Jim's passing. Leave Missy on the porch, shellin' purple hull peas with Gert. Then again, she might let Billy Boy and James Allen convince her to take them for a nice little buggy ride."

"I like it. Yes, I like that idea quite a lot. I may take down the details of her passing one day, just to have them. But Missy's long gone to her heavenly reward, and there's very little point in subjecting readers to my unexplainable sense of personal loss."

"Why not put together a little afterword? Maybe a few pictures of us with Kimmy or even some from the gathering tomorrow? Life on the homeplace nowadays, so to speak."

"That sounds workable, Bradley. And I'm awfully glad to hear that you consider yourself a part of *life on the homeplace nowadays*."

"With Mr. Pate and the aunts around, I figured maybe you could tolerate my traveling for work. Let's not forget good old George, either. There ain't a whole lot he wouldn't do for you. And I know how he feels, Laura Beth, because if you say so, I'll hunt up some other way to make a living."

"No, Bradley," she answered softly, and one lone tear rolled down the cheek nearest to him. "You go right ahead and do the work you've always loved. Granddaddy's already given me a gentle kind of talking to, trying to prepare me for a time when he and the aunts won't be here any longer. Still, I don't think I'd ever feel so all alone in Red Bog. Besides, my faith is growing a little stronger each day. I'm learning how to truly trust the Lord, Bradley, and I might as well trust you to come home to us."

"They swore up and down that no flatlander could find his way off that Wyoming mountaintop at night," he recalled, sharing what seemed at first like a random bit of information. "I think George trailed along just to watch the show."

Laura Beth shuddered a little to think of the risk, but one side of her mouth finally quirked upward in a smile.

"They just didn't know that Jimbo Pate's granddaughter taught you how to ride."

"Picked our way as best I could and followed what little advice George offered. In the tough spots, though, I'd give that old mule her head and goose her real good. If the shortest distance was straight down, then so be it. Of course, I felt some fatherly concern for Kimmy, but the truth is our folks would care for her as well as anybody could. I ran straight home to you, Laura Beth, and from now on, it won't take an emergency phone call to get me started."

Chapter Twenty-One

Laura Beth greeted his declaration with a deep, shuddering breath. A mile or so further on, she pulled Blackjack and Coaly off to the right where a forgotten homesite, marked only by its leaning stone chimney, made for a scenic stop.

"Best let 'em blow a little," she murmured in reference to the mules.

Caught up in the joy of her own ride, Kimmy took one look at her parents, snagged a couple of oatmeal cookies, and went back to stand beside old Gopher. Laura Beth's feelings seemed too immense, even for her considerable talent with words. Finally, she shifted over into Bradley's lap, resting her head against his chest, and allowed him to hold her for several precious moments.

"I'm so sorry, darling. Never should have—"

Laura Beth stopped the apology she no longer needed to hear by laying a single finger lightly against his lips. Then, however reluctantly, she moved back to her own seat.

"On the subject of coming home," she ventured after some time, "Granddaddy wants to meet with me and both of his boys this evening. I expect Aunt Alma and Aunt Nadine might sit in on it, too. Despite Vida's little joke about batting my eyes, I'm not out to take advantage of anyone. Land values have changed, even in Red Bog."

"Sure, but you sold a thriving business, and there won't be any shortage of buyers for your house. How do things stand with the homeplace?"

"Years and years ago, after Big Jim's parents died, the Pate land split six ways. At least on paper… Over time, Big Jim bought out Cleve, Eva, and Annette. He made the deals, anyhow. Missy, and her uncanny instinct for managing the vagaries of an East Texas cotton crop, kept most of his mule tradin' profits on hand to buy the land whenever it came up for sale."

"So, that gave Big Jim four shares while his two youngest sisters held one each?"

"Only, he and Missy had raised them like daughters. When she passed away in 1972, Missy left the house and two shares to Granddaddy along with most of Papa Kimbel's holdings. Nadine already had the old gentleman's home and store, so Aunt Alma got the gin site in Red Bog and all of Missy's livestock."

"Which Mr. Pate bought back?"

"The livestock, yes. Missy's horses and some few cattle, but Aunt Alma kept her double lot where the cotton gin used to sit. And of course, both girls got an additional share of the homeplace."

"Only a true Red Bog native could follow all that, but if my head's spinning in the right direction… We're left with three equal shares held by Jimbo, Alma, and Nadine."

"Very good," she agreed, teasing him with her impression of an enthusiastic kindergarten teacher. "Dad and Uncle James Allen don't have a whole lot of sentimental attachment to the homeplace, but in all fairness, they should eventually get something. This evening, we'll try to sort out who's willing to part with what and how much of it I can afford. James Allen already holds title on those scattered tracts of Kimbel land, so that ought to work in my favor."

"If you need any money or—"

"No, Bradley. This urge to make a life on the homeplace is all mine. I hope you'll play a major part in that life, but you needn't finance it."

Smiling, he shook his head once again at her trademark independence and then waved their daughter back over to the wagon.

"We didn't mean to run you off, kiddo."

"Ran myself off," Kimmy explained with a shrug. "From the look on Mama's face, I figured you were in for a flood of tears or, just maybe, the kind of kiss you'd never forget."

"We managed to avoid both," Laura Beth admitted, sending Bradley an almost apologetic smile, "but covered a lot of ground in our discussion. How about another cookie?"

"Sure, thanks. They're awfully good, and I fed one of mine to Gopher."

"I guess he liked it, too," Laura Beth ventured, one hand reaching up to rub gingerly at her temple. "I should've brought along a Dr Pepper. Don't seem to be drinking quite so many of them lately, and I guess it slipped my mind."

"Try a cookie and some water," Kimmy suggested with a quirky grin. "Maybe you can trick that headache."

Chuckling along with them, Bradley reached immediately to pour a cup of drinking water and slide the cookie basket in her direction.

"Sleeping better and all, I might not require quite as much caffeine and sugar, but it will definitely be a gradual adjustment. Gopher knows how to follow the wagon on a loose lead," she finally told her daughter. "Why don't you sit up here with us and help me drive this team?"

Not completely reunited just yet, the little family felt an undeniable bond as they jounced homeward behind the matched pair of mules.

It rained on and off all the next day. While Laura Beth and Kimmy helped with ongoing preparations in the house, Bradley accompanied Jimbo Pate on his morning feed run.

"A cowman don't get rained out," the old rancher observed wryly. "He just gets rained on."

"It warms my heart to know that our Kimmy will have both sets of grandparents here tomorrow," Laura Beth confided to Bradley after a quiet supper. "We ought to take some pictures, but there's no reason for you to hide behind a camera all day. Why not let me get some shots of you and Kimmy with your folks?"

"I realize we're technically back in the dating stage right now, Laura Beth, and I'm thankful to have come that far… But I'd like some photos with all of us together. If you're willing, I'll line George up to take them. Anybody who can knock a squirrel off a limb at thirty paces should surely be able to handle a Nikon."

"Sounds reasonable to me," she answered with a smile.

"How'd the little conference come out last night?"

"About the homeplace, you mean? Better than I had any right to expect. Uncle James Allen is satisfied with the Kimbel land Granddaddy has already deeded to him. Dad just laughed and reminded me that I'm his only child. So, that pretty well takes care of our part. Aunt Nadine is willing to sell me hers as soon as we can get the paperwork done."

"Goes without saying that Mr. Pate and the aunts will be thrilled to have you around on a more permanent basis."

"Yes," she admitted with a fond smile. "Kimmy and I can live quite comfortably with Aunt Alma and Aunt Nadine for now. If our circumstances were to change, Granddaddy's more than willing to move up here and make his house available."

"Circumstances?" he asked on a faintly teasing note.

"That's the way Granddaddy put it. Meantime… It's probably good for Alma and Nadine to have someone on hand, and I hope Kimmy will be as happy here as I am."

"Me, too," he answered sincerely. "What does Aunt Alma say about her share?"

"I expect she's got her reasons for wanting to hold on at the moment, and nobody could ask for a sweeter partner. Living here and taking an active interest in the homeplace, I might get a chance to buy her part at some time in the future."

Thanksgiving morning dawned clear and cold, and soon enough, the old Pate house turned into a hive of bustling activity with last-minute goodness pouring out of the kitchen and early arrivals adding their voices to the happy clamor. Patsy dived right in, working alongside her mother, Nadine, and Laura Beth. Somehow, the four ladies managed to avoid tripping over one another until the roar of a particularly loud engine drew Laura Beth's glance to the window.

"Some of your bunch, Aunt Nadine," she volunteered with a faint but perceptive smile. "Best go on out and say hello."

As she passed by, the old lady took a playful swat at Laura Beth.

"Go on out and say hello," she mimicked. "I'm goin' out yonder and jerk a knot in somebody's tail for winding up 'at motor. No call for that much unnecessary racket around livestock. And just so you know, I can read that little grin of yours like a book."

Minutes later, Abby ducked into the kitchen and made her way to Laura Beth's side.

"Mrs. Webber said I'd find you in here. Even smiled at me, but she's still out there chewin' on Dalton and them."

"Was that y'all with the loud muffler?"

"One of his younger cousins, I think, but we kind of got caught in the crossfire. Dalton did, anyway."

"Too many cooks in the kitchen," Laura Beth confided softly. "I've done just about all I can for now. Patsy and Aunt Alma will like it better if we get out of the way. Did y'all bring your mare?"

The last question came as they paused in the washroom just off the back porch in search of a marginally quiet place to visit.

"No, but we probably should have. Don't know that I've ever seen desserts arranged on a washer and drier before, and there's so many of them."

"Takes a good many to feed this bunch, and I thought the big tablecloth was a nice touch. Let's go out front and look for my in-law— Bradley's folks. They're supposed to be here. I'd like for you to meet my parents, too."

People, most of them kinfolk in one way or another, spilled off both porches of the old house. Laura Beth whispered a prayer of gratitude for the bright sunshine, and noted with a smile that some of her Webber cousins had built a small but warming outdoor fire. Younger participants seldom thought about it, but Pate family get-togethers followed a bygone pattern of East Texas farm life with the largest meal (Thanksgiving dinner, in this case) served at noon. Having sent James Allen out to ring the little-used dinner bell, Granddaddy offered their traditional blessing from the front steps.

In no hurry to fix her own plate, Laura Beth glided naturally around the gathering, making sure everyone felt at ease. The first round of dressing disappeared almost immediately, so she brought in a fresh pan from the kitchen and placed it carefully in the center of the table.

"I need to talk to you." Vesper Denton spoke the words without preamble, glancing up briefly from his second helping. "Besides, you flit around here about like Ms. Alma and Ms. Nadine. Probably ain't had a bite since breakfast. Fix your plate, and then you can borrow George's chair. He'd just as soon hold up a wall, anyhow."

"Be right back," she answered with a smile and then sent a quizzical glance over her shoulder to Abby who had followed her around as silent as a shadow and as helpful as an extra pair of hands. "No telling how long this might take," she confided softly. "You might as well go and find Dalton."

"Both daughters invited me over for Thanksgiving," Vesper commented when she finally settled down across the table from him, "but it's kinda hard to choose one over the other. Nobody makes dressin' quite like Ms. Alma, and I sure don't want to lose my status as an honorary Pate."

"I wouldn't say too much to your daughters about the dressing, but we're glad to have you any old time. You wanted to talk to me?"

"Yes'm... Buddy of mine owns a truckin' company just on the other side of Henderson. They run all over the country, I guess, but his yard and main office are right there on the edge of town. I heard you was movin' back to the homeplace for good. And, well, the long and short of it is... I've got you an interview set up Monday mornin' if you're willing to go."

"Well, sir... That's very kind, but I hadn't gotten around to thinking much about work."

"Pardon me, Laura Beth, if it seems awful sudden. Mama Gail broke her hip, you see, and they've got to get somebody in there before the place falls down around 'em."

"Bless her heart… Your friend's mother?"

"Not his mother, but she's worked there nearly sixty years and got 'em all pretty well spoiled. They'd like to hire somebody who can take a turn at the front desk, fix up a pot of peas with hot water cornbread, and still get the payroll done on time. If you're comfortable turning on a computer without callin' over somebody from the dispatch side of things, they'll be plumb impressed."

"Reckon I could manage that," she ventured, "but the job sounds kind of temporary. What about Mama Gail?"

"Gail looks after all them drivers and the dispatchers, too, but she's run off three different payroll clerks they brought in for training. You've got too much Pate in you to spook easy, but more than that, you've got a mighty fetching personality. Get in there and train yourself, visit her out at the rehab with regular updates, and maybe when the time comes, you can sweet talk her into retiring."

"The chore nobody else wants?"

"Don't fret, Laura Beth. You're up to it. Pay's not too shiny, after what you've been making, but it comes with pretty good insurance. Nothing like the burden of running your own business, either. You can worry 'bout the cow market if you want to, but all them trucks will be somebody else's headache."

"Thank you, Vesper," she said with a whimsical little smile. I'll go in for the interview and see how things play out from there."

"No thanks necessary," he drawled with a broad grin. "I eat dinner in there two or three times a week. Besides, they're good folks. Jimbo wouldn't much cotton to the notion of you working just anywhere."

Wrapping up the conversation, Laura Beth finished her meal and headed off to find Kimmy. This put her on hand a short while later when Bradley started asking questions about Red Bog's general store.

"Why, sure," Nadine snorted. "I still own the store building. Papa Kimbel's house didn't sit empty long before one of my daughters moved her family in there. They've been after me to do something with the store, but seeing as how the roof don't leak, I reckon it'll stand right where it's at. Floyd told it around that me and Missy run a goin' out of business sale for ten years. I loved that man dearly, but if he'd ever buckled down to one thing the way I did with that store, there ain't no tellin' what all he might've got done."

"Does it still look like a general store? Inside, I mean?"

"It had better," she shot back. "Me and Jimbo caught some of the kids pilin' their junk in there a time or two, but they piled it right back out again. The thing is… When I closed up for the last time, I just took the money out of the cash register and locked the front door behind me. 'Course, we got the foodstuffs out before they spoiled. Ate everything up or give it away, don't you know. But there's harness and plow parts and nails and I don't know what all gatherin' dust right where I left 'em. Maybe even a box of King Edward cigars, if that strikes your fancy."

"No, thank you, ma'am. I don't want anything in particular, but I sure would like to take a few more pictures. Already got some shots from the outside, and Laura Beth will probably enjoy looking around, too."

"She's been in there, but not since we started telling her all about Missy. Just let me get the key… Bring some of the others along, if you want. Maybe it'll keep 'em from ridin' the hair off every horse on the place."

"Now," Laura Beth chimed in, "there's an idea. If I can talk George into helping me hitch the team, we'll load the wagon and drive up there."

George proved willing, and Jimbo took an interest as well. Cousins filled the wagon and then the back of a pickup for one more *trip to the store*.

"Mercy," Nadine huffed as the front door swung inward, "Good thing Alma didn't come. Look at the dust!"

Dust notwithstanding, the old store struck Laura Beth as a kind of time capsule. She noted blind bridles, collars, and trace chains hanging from one wall as well as various hand tools on another. Beyond all of that… A high-wheeled chair, indistinguishable from its mate at home and seemingly ready for Missy's use behind the long counter, aroused an unexpected pang of loss.

Chapter Twenty-Two

~April 2008~

Laura Beth enjoyed catching glimpses of the four photographs on her desk but angled them slightly outward for display to customers and coworkers alike. The oldest was a black and white shot of Missy on the front porch of Papa Kimbel's store. Another captured Jimbo, Alma, and Nadine in late middle age. The third showed Kimmy's bubbling enthusiasm, her own soft smile, and Bradley's trademark grin. Efficiency came in handy, but genuine charm secured her relatively new place at the heart of this longstanding company. Naturally, the fourth picture stood as a tribute to her legendary predecessor, Mama Gail. The sudden chime of Kimmy's incoming text message drew her eyes momentarily away from the desktop with its ever-present spreadsheets.

"Not catching a ride to your office today. Aunt Alma and Nadine will pick me up instead."

"Please don't ask them to come all the way into town. Won't you need a snack after school? One of the drivers smoked some ribs last night. I fixed beans and potato salad to go with them. There's a little of that broccoli and white queso you like, too. By the way, why are you texting me before the final bell?"

"Texting in study hall doesn't count. Everybody's at Patsy's house, anyway. I'm going over there to help them finish up spring flower arrangements. Are you coming to Patsy's or meeting us out at the cemetery? FYI... What you just described is not a snack, but I doubt Patsy will let me starve. Love you, Mom."

"Love you, too, baby. I'll call when I leave the office to find out where to meet y'all."

A couple of hours later, Laura Beth shut down her computer and exchanged pleasantries with the newly arrived nighttime dispatcher. Before she could leave her desk, though, the cellphone rang in her hand.

"How's my darling?" Bradley inquired through faint static.

"Been a good day," she answered lightly, "but the sound of your voice makes it even better. I'm just leaving the office to meet Kimmy and them out at the cemetery."

"I promised you forever and meant it," he said on a passing chuckle, "but don't you think it's a little early to be setting out our double headstone?"

"Quit your teasing, Bradley. It's time for spring flowers on Missy's grave and the rest of them, too. You ought to know that."

"Speaking of Missy, I bought you a little present."

"Bradley, you know I don't need any—"

"Aunt Alma sold me her share of the Pate land. Evidently, that's been on her mind all along. She wanted me to have a stake in our home, but I told her I'd rather give it to you. Wherever you are, Laura Beth, that's home to me."

"Oh, Bradley, I sure do love you! You're right, of course. It takes more than good East Texas dirt to make a home, but I've learned so much on that old place. The notion of making a life there with you and Kimmy seems almost dreamlike."

"Listen, darling… I'm at the trailhead now and will probably lose cellphone service. I remember when you thought publishing a book seemed pretty farfetched, but that first shipment is apt to beat me back to Red Bog. Just keep on dreaming, my darling. I like the way they're turning out."

Soon enough, Laura Beth pulled off the highway south of Red Bog to park between Alma's Buick and Patsy's Suburban. Her sleek little sedan seemed slightly out of step with life in the country, but she kept postponing the headache and expense of a new vehicle.

Kimmy jogged brightly up to meet her, slowing the customary sprint in an instinctive gesture of respect brought on by the orderly ranks of headstones. They hugged and then walked back more sedately to join the older women. Laura Beth enjoyed Kimmy's chatter, but the names on certain markers triggered enough stories to drown out the noise of traffic. Eva, Annette, Cleve… Near the center of the row, an unadorned slab of marble stood over the final resting place of Missy and Big Jim Pate.

"What do you think of the flowers, Mama?" Kimmy inquired almost hesitantly.

"They're lovely," Laura Beth murmured in answer, trailing one hand across the ageless stone.

"Kimmy suggested most of these arrangements," Patsy volunteered. "Mother and I did the prep while she was in school today, but your girl finished each one to her satisfaction."

"She's really got an eye for this kind of thing," Alma added fondly.

"Ain't taking nothin' away from Kimmy's hard work," Nadine hedged. "The whole family can be proud of these arrangements, but if y'all clutter up my grave with silk flowers… Well, I never did much believe in haints. But pick something growin' wild or leave my marker alone."

Laura Beth wrapped one arm around Nadine's slight form as they moved on down the row. The springlike but artificial splashes of color stopped abruptly at Bud Evans' grave. A mix of tiny natural blooms and wild greenery adorned Floyd Webber's plain granite marker.

"You'd just better plan on outliving me," Alma declared, voice gentle even in her teasing. "I'll not tromp through the sticker burrs and chiggers just to suit your fancy any more than I'd let your marker stand bare."

Nadine's answering scowl shifted reluctantly into a smile as she raked loose grass away from the monument's base with a worn boot toe.

"Three game wardens, two retired and one still on active duty, showed up at the funeral visitation," she recalled wryly. "Just to verify the rumor of Floyd's passing. Milo Jackson stood by a-wringin' his hands in fear I'd talk rough to them boys or set Jimbo loose on 'em. But they was members of the community, more or less."

"Something tells me there's a little more to this story," Laura Beth speculated with a mischievous half smile. "Go ahead and finish the tale, and I'll see to it you're not bothered with any silk flowers in years to come."

"I greeted them boys just like anybody else, but the youngest one couldn't quite leave well enough alone. He just had to speculate on why anybody who raised so much beef needed to put a year-round dent in the local whitetail population. Old Milo like to broke a sweat, but I extended a polite invitation for all three of them to stop by and eat with us after the funeral. When they'd gone, Milo finally mumbled something about how well I'd handled it all."

Laura Beth turned an angelic smile on her aunt, but the languid drawl of her next statement carried a hint of mischief.

By the Light of a Memory 355

"I suppose you told Mr. Jackson something about raisin' beef to pay for overpriced funerals and eatin' wild venison on general principle."

"Now, that's the Missy Pate in you," Nadine asserted warmly, "and just about what I would've told him if I'd thought of it in time. Needed Jimbo close that evening, but Milo was still moppin' his brow when I looked down there on the front row and caught sight of my older brother. Cleve got around on a walker by then, but he still had a good dose of vinegar left in him. 'You'll find a light behind the seat of Floyd's pickup. Take James Allen and get started. I want plenty of fresh backstrap on hand tomorrow!' None of us ever hunted much after that, but my Floyd sure got the last word."

Laura Beth laughed until the tears came and then pulled Aunt Nadine into a fond embrace with Alma, Patsy, and Kimmy gathered close around them. Moments later, she dabbed at her eyes with a handkerchief and patted her hair back into place.

"What about Uncle Cleve's children?" she inquired suddenly. "Eva and Annette had families, too, didn't they? Maybe we ought to put together some kind of reunion."

The notion seemed to take them by surprise, but Alma finally pieced together an answer.

"The three of us, Missy and Big Jim's little brood, so to speak, have all stayed close. Most people in today's world would consider that quite an accomplishment. Those older siblings, older than us and younger than Big Jim, raised families, alright. But you see who's puttin' out the flowers."

"Cleve put together a good-sized place of his own," Nadine recalled. "Right up the road from home, too, but they sold it before we scarcely got him buried. None of them are bad people, you understand, just up and gone. Alma's got them all on a Christmas card list somewhere, and they might even take some interest in your book when it finally hits the shelves."

"I'll say one thing about Eva and Annette," Alma put in softly. "Despite all them years of peckin' away at Missy, they looked on her death as the end of an era. Their families are pretty well scattered, too."

"Let's don't blame anybody for not putting out flowers," Laura Beth ventured playfully. "I notice Granddaddy didn't come along this time."

"He's busy on the homeplace," Nadine offered in automatic defense. "Huntin' for a baby calf when we left, and I'll bet he's been down to the road half a dozen times to check for your shipment."

"Well, Aunt Nadine… If they've got any Pate in 'em to speak of, they're probably busy somewhere. How is being busy on the homeplace any different?"

Nadine only snorted in reply, but Kimmy burst out with a stream of excited chatter.

"Shipment? Granddaddy Pate's looking for packages? You don't mean our books?"

"Sure," Laura Beth asserted lightheartedly. "The first batch is set to arrive any day now."

"*Any day* can't come soon enough," Kimmy shot back. "It feels like waiting for Christmas or something."

"I love springtime," Patsy chimed in, "but it's almost hot out here in the evening sun. I'll follow y'all back up to the homeplace, Laura Beth. Could be the books came today. In any case… Mother and I have a little surprise for you.”

“It’s been a day for surprises,” Laura Beth quipped, and Alma read the meaning behind her dazzling smile.

“You’ve talked to Bradley, I reckon. The boy claimed that last deed would make you a perfect wedding present, but I never figured he’d keep quiet about it long.”

“Means a lot to me, Aunt Alma, and I sure hope you’re happy with the deal.”

“I’m happy, child. What’s more, Missy and Big Jim would be plumb tickled.”

Driving up to the house with her windows down, Laura Beth detected a familiar racket from the dog yard. A fenced enclosure these days, it held cow dogs instead of hounds but occupied the same shaded area behind their family home.

“Must be feeding time,” she mused at first.

In the next breath, though, she noticed George’s red-speckled cat hound trailing behind Jimbo as he paced back and forth across the porch. Keenly aware of his nervous energy, old Bess had stirred up the pen full of cur dogs with her anxious whining.

“We got books,” Jimbo called and trotted down the steps to meet Laura Beth at her car.

“I know good and well that Bradley is somewhere along the Appalachian Trail without even a hint of cellphone service,” she muttered, fingers trembling as she placed the unsuccessful call, “but I’ve got to try at least once.”

“He’ll be home soon enough,” Nadine decided, sizing up the situation dryly. “Can’t have much of a wedding without no groom, but Bradley ain't exactly needed for this little operation. We all know Jimbo's got a pocket knife, and I aim to look at one of them books!"

They gravitated automatically to Missy's kitchen. One box waited in the center of the table while the others sat half-forgotten in a corner. The sharp blade of Jimbo's Case knife flashed, and eager hands scooped out the first copy of *Snapshots in Time* by Laura Beth Chandler. Already satisfied as to the content, Kimmy, Laura Beth, and the three storytellers focused most of their attention on the physical book. But Patsy saw more than a display worthy cover, durable pages, and crisply printed text. Tears shimmered in her eyes as she revisited one well-loved family story after another.

"Oh, Laura Beth," she gushed, pulling the younger woman into a hug. "It's simply wonderful! And these amazing sketches, Kimmy… Your Dad's photography makes a nice contribution, too."

"Laura Beth did us all proud with this book," Nadine finally asserted, "and whether I like it or not, today must be our day for sentimental tears. You'd best go on out to the car, Patsy, and bring in that dress."

"Dress?" Laura Beth wondered aloud, but nobody answered until Patsy returned with the garment in question.

A delicate shade of eggshell blue and lovely in its simplicity, the garment caught Laura Beth's gaze and held it.

"Mother called me the other day," Patsy explained, "more or less in a tizzy because your wedding is less than two weeks away and you've yet to pick out a dress. Anyhow, this is the only thing I asked for when Missy died. Kept it in a cedar chest all these years and haven't tried to wear it."

"Patsy, I could never take—"

"Swap me a book and we'll call it even. You've given us a glimpse into the world that shaped Mother. She enjoyed reliving childhood days, and without you, nobody could've gotten more than a story or two out of Jimbo or Nadine. Anyhow, Mother made this dress for Missy to wear on her twenty-fifth wedding anniversary. For whatever reason, sentimentality or a scarcity of material during the war, she cut up an outdated sidesaddle frock and made it over into this dress."

"Not just any old frock," Alma stated quietly. "It's made from the springtime riding habit Missy wore on that very first evening she spent with Big Jim. Sidesaddle riding called for a good deal of excess length, and that left plenty of material to make Missy a nice dress. The color is beautiful, even today, and I can still see her smiling up at me from the chair. 'I love the dress, child. Could be my imagination, but it still carries just a hint of horses and campfire smoke.'"

After expressing her heartfelt thanks, Laura Beth hurried right off to change. Even Nadine shed a tear or two, remembering their Missy and days gone by.

"You favor her so much," Patsy finally murmured, "and I knew the dress would look wonderful on you. Suits you very well as it is, but Mother and I can make an adjustment or two so as to keep busy between now and wedding time."

"Wedding time," Laura Beth echoed, blinking away tears once again. "Bradley and I are getting remarried, alright, and I'd love to wear Missy's dress. But there won't be any elaborate ceremony, not the way you and Aunt Alma think of a wedding. I've seen those from every angle and even had my big day as a bride. Now, all I want is a life with Bradley. We'll exchange the necessary vows right out yonder on the porch. Our very few guests, if blessed with a fine spring day, can watch from shady spots around the yard. If it rains, we'll just have to make do in the front room."

"The basic vision is fine, Mom," Kimmy assured her, "and we'll pull it off. But don't set your heart on a small crowd, not with so many Pate family connections and everyone from your office. This may not be the last surprise, but you'll like them all. So, trust us, and go with the flow."

The intervening time passed quickly, but Laura Beth's newly developed calm extended even to her upcoming wedding. The mid-April day turned out pleasant with a cool breeze and plenty of bright sunshine. The first of its surprises came when Granddaddy suggested she get ready down at his house.

"Walking the aisle is surely a time-honored custom," she quipped with a loving smile, "but tromping all the way back up that hill right before my wedding is an entirely different matter."

"You leave that to me and old George. Now, scoot, so I can fetch Bradley up here from the barn lot."

"Having dated the man twice, married him once already, and raised his daughter… I don't see how letting him catch a glimpse of me before this second wedding could make much difference, but I'll play along."

Aunt Alma and Aunt Nadine helped her dress, but Kimmy and Abby would serve as her attendants while George and Dalton stood up with Bradley. The girls left by car with her aunts. But when Granddaddy led her to his front door, George waited there with a horse and buggy. Not just any old rig, but Missy's buggy with a recent coat of red paint on the wheels and its black umbrella top laid back.

"Found this hanging up between the trusses in your Uncle James Allen's shop, little lady. We shined it up some and thought you might like to use it today. You and Jimbo give me just a minute to get back up yonder alongside the luckiest fool I ever run across and then come ahead."

"Bradley can't be too foolish, now, can he?" she murmured, placing a fond kiss on George's weathered cheek. "After all, he manages to keep both of us hangin' around. Is that Aunt Nadine's Gopher? I didn't know he'd pull a buggy."

"Gopher didn't know it, either, until right lately," Jimbo snorted, assisting her gently up into the seat. "I'm awful proud of you, doodlebug. Accident, nervous exhaustion, or whatever it was you went through, you've come out the other side stronger than ever. And while most people would've had all they could do pickin' up the pieces, you managed to set the Pate legacy down in a book. If Missy was here, she'd look right back at you with them same pretty eyes, then tell you to lean on the Lord and hold your head up high."

As they neared the old Pate house, Laura Beth gazed out over a yard full of guests, noticing her parents as well as Mr. and Mrs. Chandler. Among those waiting on the high front porch, she spotted gray-haired Brother Rufus Hays. In the next moment, though, she locked eyes with Bradley. Tending toward self-criticism in terms of weight gain or other physical changes, she caught a momentary glimpse of her own breathtaking beauty reflected in his loving gaze. Everything in the background seemed to fade away as he descended the steps, exchanged a word or two with Granddaddy, and lifted her effortlessly from the buggy.

"O give thanks unto the God of heaven, for His mercy endureth forever," Brother Hays intoned a few moments later. "Laura Beth asked me to read that from Psalm 136:6 because she and Bradley are thankful for the second chance God has extended today. I first saw this home nearly forty years ago when the late Missy Pate and her remarkable circle of kinfolk welcomed me as the new pastor of Red

Bog Missionary Baptist Church. I was young and completely inexperienced, but Missy took me in as one of hers from the very first day."

About half way through the ceremony, George's perceptive ear caught a familiar and exhilarating sound on the breeze. One look at the constrained laughter shining in Kimmy's eyes told him she heard it, too.

"Your mama didn't think she needed any wedding music," he recalled, their arrangement on the porch allowing for this quiet exchange, "but with old Bess runnin' a bobcat, I reckon she'll get some, anyhow."

"Judging by the glow on Mama's face… If she hears anything at all, it just might pass for one of Big Jim's foxhounds on a hot track."

"Yeah," he whispered back as the ceremony drew to a close, "but I hope old Bess don't fall treed right on the edge of the yard. She's comin' this way, now."

Jimbo heard the approaching race, broken at intervals when the bobcat took a tree only to jump out and run again. Dalton heard it, too, but everyone held their places, maintaining the dignity of the occasion even as the actual ceremony ended. Most assumed Laura Beth and Bradley were too wrapped up in the special meaning of their day to take much notice, but Bill Pate caught a flash of Missy in his daughter's eyes and reverted momentarily to boyhood. Heart pounding with joy and exuberance, Laura Beth gave her dad a quick wink and tilted her head almost imperceptibly in the direction of the dog yard.

Even as she and Bradley swept down the steps and into the buggy, five or six of Jimbo's cow dogs streaked off to put an end to the bobcat chase. Unfortunately, one of them ran right under Gopher.

The old horse reared immediately onto his hind legs, and Laura Beth attempted to steady him by way of her voice and the driving lines.

"Whoa, son. Whoa-op… Keep still, now."

Without a second thought, the formidable Belinda Radcliff took command of the situation.

"Laura Beth has planned some breathtaking finales in her day, but this one may take the grand prize. Join us inside for cake and punch, or remain outdoors for a closeup view of life on the land."

Nadine stood frozen for a moment, unsure how she felt about this Houstonite and onetime yankee making pronouncements. Upon reflection, though, the words made good sense, and she stepped quickly out of the doorway.

"There's a gate, y'all… Sort yourselves."

"Stay with it, doodlebug," Jimbo called across the yard. "He'll level out directly."

"Stay with it?" and Bradley's repetition tickled close to her ear as his arm tightened around her waist to ensure added stability. "Tell me something, gorgeous. Is that a reference to Nadine's trusty steed or some kind of Red Bog twist on marital advice?"

"Take it whichever way you like, my love," and her East Texas drawl sounded completely untroubled, even as she fought to regain control of the startled horse. "From here on out, I don't aim to quit on either one of you."

Acknowledgments

Ms. Delorese Quackenbush saw something in this story from its earliest days and never gave up on the process of helping me bring it into print. Having Ms. Sandy (a dear and trusted friend) as my primary beta reader gives each new story an all-important vote of confidence, and I'm also deeply grateful to her husband, Brother David Gatlin, for all he does as my pastor. Daddy and Momma, Kenneth and Rhonda Keeling, are entitled to more gratitude than I can accurately express. I am continually thankful for my church family at Friendship Missionary Baptist in the Jumbo Community and, most of all, for Jesus Christ as my Lord and Savior.

Author's Note: I wrote this novel as a tribute to the people and culture of rural East Texas. However, it remains a work of fiction. Any resemblance to actual persons or events is purely coincidental. My aunts (Donna Simmons Howeth and Linda Keeling Sledge) read the manuscript and offered valuable suggestions as did Karen Mobbs, Kevin Plaster, and Nell Ann Untiedt at the Mount Enterprise branch of the Rusk County Library, but all errors are my own.

About the Author

Blessed with a fulfilling life despite (and in some ways because of) the physical limitations of cerebral palsy, Jake Keeling teaches U.S. and Texas history as an adjunct instructor at East Texas Baptist University in Marshall. His father and several trusted riding buddies go to great lengths in supporting his love of horses and mules. Involvement with the family cattle operation continues a six-generation connection to the land. Deeply humbled by the opportunity, he continues to serve his church family as a deacon.

Jumbo Exchange and Communications
8515 State Hwy. 315
Long Branch, TX 75669
903.658.0128
jumboexchangeandcommunications@gmail.com
or
visit our Facebook page